Philip Gwynne Jones was born in Swansea and grew up in South Wales. He spent twenty years in the IT industry before realising he was congenitally unsuited to it, and now works as a writer and translator.

Philip lives in Venice with his wife, Caroline, and a modestly friendly cat called Mimì. He enjoys cooking, classical music and horror films. He also listens to far too much Italian Progressive Rock.

Also by Philip Gwynne Jones

The Venetian Sanctuary

Philip Gwynne Jones

CONSTABLE

CONSTABLE

First published in hardback in Great Britain in 2024 by Constable

This paperback edition published in Great Britain in 2025 by Constable

A CIP catalogue record for this book is available from the British Library.

ISBN: 978-1-40871-538-3

Typeset in Adobe Garamond by Initial Typesetting Services, Edinburgh
Printed and bound in Great Britain by Clays Ltd, Elcograf S.p.A.

Papers used by Constable are from well-managed forests
and other responsible sources.

MIX
Paper | Supporting
responsible forestry
FSC® C104740

Constable
An imprint of
Little, Brown Book Group
Carmelite House
50 Victoria Embankment
London EC4Y 0DZ

The authorised representative
in the EEA is
Hachette Ireland
8 Castlecourt Centre
Dublin 15, D15 XTP3, Ireland
(email: info@hbgi.ie).

An Hachette UK Company
www.hachette.co.uk

www.littlebrown.co.uk

In memory of Brian Arthur Jones, 1939–2023

Thanks, Dad. The boys of the Old Kings Arms will always have a pint waiting for you.

'Remember that when you leave this earth, you can take with you nothing that you have received – only what you have given.'

St Francis of Assisi

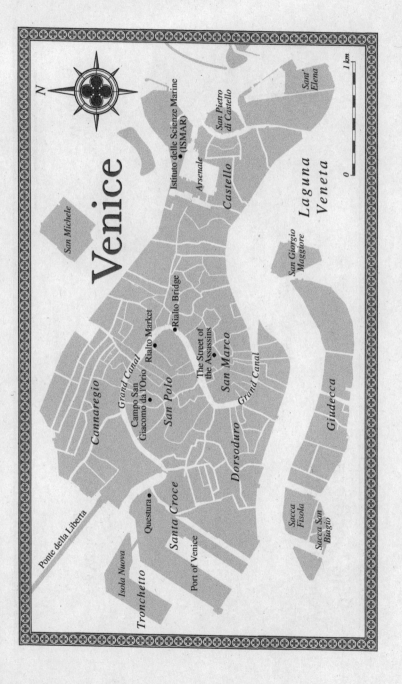

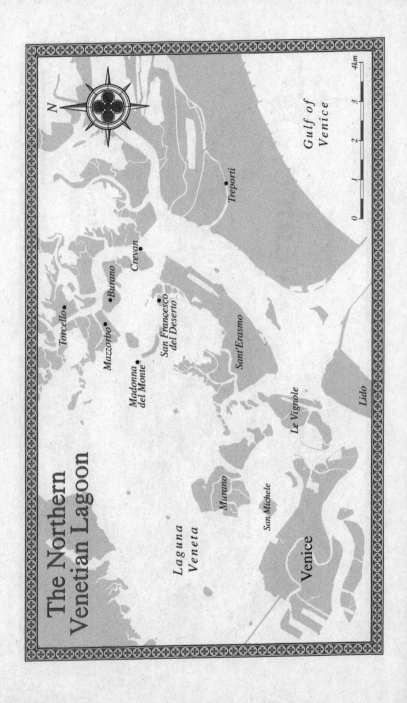

The Northern
Venetian Lagoon

N

Torcello

Burano

Crevan

Mazzorbo

San Francesco
del Deserto

Madonna
del Monte

Sant'Erasmo

Treporti

*Laguna
Veneta*

Murano

Le Vignole

San Michele

Lido

Venice

*Gulf of
Venice*

0   1   2   3   4km

Prologue

Francis of Assisi passed this way, some eight hundred years ago, they say. Barely forty, recently returned from the Holy Land, and wearied by his attempts to stop yet another bloody war in the cradle of Christianity; he took himself to a tiny island in the Venetian lagoon, sat himself down, and talked to anyone who would listen.

Napoleon's armies also passed by, six hundred years later. The Little Corporal, however, was not inclined to listen to anyone, least of all the acolytes of a long-dead saint scratching out a living in the middle of a swamp. He had no time for holy men or monasteries and so, for the first time since an outbreak of malaria in the sixteenth century, the island of San Francesco del Deserto was abandoned once again.

Not for long, however. When the Austrians took possession of La Serenissima, they decided they could find a use for the ancient stone buildings. Meditation and prayer were no longer the order of the day. The storage of gunpowder, however, very much was. Swords might once have been turned into ploughshares, but the occupying forces were more than a little keen on turning them back again.

Yet the wheel continued to turn, and in 1858 the island

was returned to the Patriarchate of Venice, and monastic life resumed. Just five brothers now remain, seeking God in the silence of a tiny island a few hundred metres from one of the busiest cities on earth.

But even monks must move with the times, and eight-hundred-year-old monasteries need more than prayer to sustain them, and so the island opened itself to visitors eager to escape from the crowd of tourists on the nearby island of Burano; and to pilgrims on retreat, eager to shake the dust from their feet in search of enlightenment.

In search of understanding. Of life. And of death.

Chapter 1

It was so blue.

That's what I remember the most, when I think back on it now. It was so blue.

Sometimes, when I needed to get out from under Federica's feet, or if Gramsci had become more than usually insufferable, I would fill out the papers explaining exactly why I was leaving my place of residence, and where I was going; and would head off to the Rialto Market to buy fish.

I would make my way downstairs, and look over to Gabriele's bookshop. It was closed, of course. Books, unlike fish, were deemed non-essential. Then I would look in the windows of the Magical Brazilians in the hope that something, anything might have changed. Some sign of normality returning. And then I would start to fret about Eduardo. I hoped he was doing okay.

I walked onwards past the empty shops that lined the Calle della Mandola, and over the bridge past Daniele Manin, who gazed down impassively upon his deserted city. There might even be people there, actual people. Perhaps bored-looking cops who may or may not ask to check your papers, but more likely shoppers, each of them with a *carrello* in order to demonstrate that they were abroad for a good reason; or simply those on a *passeggiata* with the best-exercised dogs in the city on a lead. Occasionally I might even see someone I knew and we would perform the awkward dance of the casual acquaintance as we wondered whether to bump elbows or merely to nod and smile behind our masks. Difficult in a country where a hug and a kiss would be the normal way of greeting somebody you'd seen only ten minutes previously.

I turned into Campo San Luca, where the Black Jack bar advertised a jazz festival that would never take place. Marchini Time, a fine *pasticceria* in a city not short on fine *pasticcerias*, was closed up. The Bar I Didn't Go To looked sad and empty and, for a moment, I wished I could just stop by for a coffee. Even if I would be overcharged.

I stood in the middle of the *campo*, and slowly turned around, seeing nothing but closed-up shops that the government had decreed non-essential. Then I saw two cops enter the square and I scurried off in the direction of Rialto, eager to look as if I were a man going about his permitted business, and not just wandering aimlessly.

On, then past the Teatro Goldoni. Would it, I wondered, ever open its doors again? On down the narrow Calle Bembo, where I pressed myself into the wall in order to distance myself from an elderly *signora* as best I could. And then I emerged on to the Riva del Carbon and, in spite of myself, I smiled.

It was so blue. So blue, and so quiet.

The *vaporetto* service had been cut in half, there being no tourists to ferry around, and precious few locals on essential business to make use of them. Few transport boats plied their trade on the Grand Canal these days, because what was there to transport? And woe betide anyone who risked taking a private boat out along the canals or into the lagoon without good reason. Drones, and the occasional helicopter, made sure we stayed at home. Occasional news stories surfaced about local *ragazzi* taking a boat out late at night, to drink beer and smoke and flirt and do all the sorts of young things that daft young people are supposed to be getting up to late at night. And Federica and I, whilst disapproving, would also feel a little pang of jealousy. It had, after all, been quite some time since we'd been invited to that sort of thing.

So the waters of Venice lay as still and undisturbed as they had done in over one thousand years, perfectly reflecting a sky unmarked by vapour trails; and where the only sound was that of birdsong.

That's what I remember the most. It was so silent. And so blue.

A banner with the crudely inked words *No Mafia, Venezia è Sacra* had hung from the windows of one of the apartments overlooking the Rialto Bridge for as long as I could remember. Now it had been joined by another, a rainbow flag with the words *Tutto andrà bene* scrawled across it.

Tutto andrà bene. Everything will be all right. And as I crossed an empty Rialto Bridge and made my way to a near-silent market, I thought that – in spite of everything – perhaps it just might.

On March 8th, 2020 Venice was finally returned to the Venetians, and silence fell upon the city.

Federica had spotted the way the wind was blowing long before I did, and moved her mother in before we locked down. There was little I could say. In my heart of hearts, I knew she was right. Marta was in good health, and fiercely independent. But she also lived in Chioggia; a place we were unlikely to be visiting any time soon.

Marta was against the idea from the start. It was ridiculous, she added, as well as being impractical. Moving in with a newly-married couple and their unfriendly cat, she told us, was the last thing she should be doing. Besides, she told us, she had friends back in Chioggia who'd look after her.

So we explained that we weren't quite as newly-married as all that and that it would only be for a couple of months, and that – even though she was quite right about the cat – the flat was spacious enough for the four of us. Which is how Fede and I came to spend the period between early March and mid-May sleeping on the sofa and in danger of developing permanent cricks in our backs.

I grew a beard for about a week until Fede, probably correctly, made me shave it off. We may or may not be facing the apocalypse, she told me, but that was no reason to descend into barbarism.

I worried about Sergio and Lorenzo. I hoped they were being sensible and not organising clandestine meetings in the Communist Bar. I fretted about Eduardo and the ultimate fate of the Magical Brazilians. He ran a cocktail-making masterclass every Friday night on Zoom, but it wasn't quite the same. Similarly, Dario and I would meet up for virtual drinks once a week, when we would have given almost anything to be sat outside Toni's in Mestre, chilled to the bone and choking on traffic fumes.

Work was never a problem. All of a sudden, I was hit with

a rush of emergency notices and documents to be translated. Similarly, consular work had never been so busy and the day was typically filled by fending off requests from those desperate expats who had suddenly realised the place they called home really wasn't, and wanted to get back to a country where – if things, perhaps, seemed even more chaotic – they could at least speak the language. And my response to them was the same every time: nobody, but nobody, is travelling anywhere. This, like it or not, is where you live now. I was more diplomatic than that, of course. Or at least I hope I was.

Ambassador Maxwell gathered all the consuls together every Monday afternoon, in order to tell us – as best he knew it – the most up to date news. He even organised the occasional quiz night, in the hope of keeping our spirits up. I don't think any of us particularly enjoyed it but he, like everyone else, was trying his best and so that was enough.

Across town in Dorsoduro, Father Michael Rayner held online services from his kitchen every Sunday morning, and distributed virtual communion to the faithful. Michael, I knew, was on his own and so I worried about him the more. Then I realised I had no idea about the domestic arrangements of Sergio, Lorenzo, Eduardo – so many of my friends. When this was all over, I told myself, I'd take more of an interest. Perhaps everybody would do the same? We'd become kinder, less self-obsessed people; and after having been apart for so long we'd find better ways of being together.

Slowly, but surely, the figures began to turn. Every night, at 18.00, we would check the latest online figures and see the curve flattening ever so slightly.

Slowly, but surely, Italy climbed its mountain. And relentlessly, inexorably, Italy buried its dead.

And then the day came. The day for haircuts and for coffee with friends, and of the simple pleasures of a spritz with the sun upon your face. All the things we used to call 'normal'.

We knew it couldn't last forever, of course. We wondered just how much of this 'new normal' we might be allowed, and for how long.

In my case, it lasted about a week.

Chapter 2

'So how are things out there?'

Fede smiled. 'I love the way you say that. It makes it sound like I've been testing the atmosphere on an alien planet, instead of going out to the shops.'

'Seriously, though. What's it like out there?' I yawned and stretched. Last night had been stormy and I'd slept badly. 'And what's the weather like?'

'Gorgeous. And the streets are full of Italians.'

'I don't understand.'

'The streets are full of Italians. And that's it. Not a French, German or Russian voice to be heard.'

'Brits? Americans?'

'A few. You probably know them. But otherwise,' she put the shopping bag down on the table, 'all Italians. More *Veneziano* being spoken on the street than I've ever heard before.'

'Still nobody travelling, I guess? Despite them lifting the restrictions.'

'Not a sign of it. I suppose if you live in the Veneto and there's no chance of getting away to Croatia for the summer, then why not head to Venice? Face it, it's never going to look better than it does now. So it's busy, yes, but manageable. It's kind of nice.' She looked around. 'How's your cat?'

'Our cat, I think you'll find.'

'Okay then, our cat. Where's he got to? And that question is not to be misinterpreted as me missing him.'

I raised my eyes to the top of the bookcase. 'The usual place.'

'He's still there?'

'In his strange kitty brain, he thinks it's cooler up there. Hence, the top of the bookcase is his equivalent of going to the mountains for the summer. Oh, and I think he's worked out that when we can't stand the heat any more and turn on the air conditioning, he'll be in the direct line of the blast.' I grinned. 'See, I told you he was a smart cat.'

Fede yawned and stretched. 'It's starting to get hot. Maybe I'll join him up there. So, what's for lunch? Is that bread still viable?'

'Maybe for *panzanella* or *pappa al pomodoro*. Or hitting people.'

'The Brazilians then?'

'I think it has to be. Ed needs the money.'

'So we can tell ourselves it's for a socially positive reason.' She checked her watch. 'It's still quite early. But we can call it brunch.'

'Breakfast spritz?'

'Absolutely.'

'Okay, then. Is it a jackets day?'

She shook her head. 'That moment has passed, *caro*. Shirt sleeves only until September.'

'Oh hell.' I looked up at Gramsci. 'I don't suppose you could fit three of us up there, could you?'

Gramsci miaowed, and spread himself flatter, as if to suggest that this was not an option.

'Okay. Well then, lunch it is.' I reached for my jacket on the back of the door, only for Fede to take it from me and replace it. She shook her head. 'The moment's passed, remember?'

Ed smiled at me. 'Good to see you again, Nathan.'

'Good to be here, Ed. It still feels like a novelty, just being able to go downstairs and have a drink.'

'You weren't here yesterday, though.'

'That was a mistake. I promise. I'll never leave you alone again.'

He grinned. 'What are you having?'

I looked over at Federica. 'What are we having?'

'Spritz Bitter? Too early in the day for a Negroni without very good reason, I think.'

'Two spritzes then, Ed. And some random things on sticks.'

Eduardo looked pained. 'Look, do you have any idea how much time and effort and, well, love goes into making *cicchetti*? And then you reduce them to "random things on sticks"?'

'Sorry. In that case can I have a small octopus on a stick. Some *olive ascolane* on a stick. And some fried calamari rings on a—'

'On a stick, yes, I get it.' He turned to Federica. 'Fede?' he asked, with hope in his eyes.

'*Baccala mantecato*, a couple of *sarde fritte* and perhaps one half-egg with truffle?'

'Coming right up.' He turned to me. 'You see? That's how you do it.'

'Sorry.'

'So how has your morning been?' said Fede, as Ed made his way back inside.

'Same as it has been for much of the past four or five months. A mixture of boredom and fire-fighting. Mainly people asking if it's possible for them to come back. And I tell them that, yes, if they can find a way of getting here. And then some of them ask if it's safe to come back and, well, that's a different question altogether.'

'So what do you tell them?'

'I tell them it's as safe as anywhere. And it's up to them what they do with that.' I yawned and stretched. 'I'll never complain about bloody lawnmower manuals again, I tell you.'

'Well, when you do, I guess that'll be a sign that things really are back to normal. I called *mamma* earlier. She sends her love.'

'How's she doing?'

'Settling into her home again. She sounds happy to be back.' She took my hand. 'It was kind of you, you know? Letting her stay.'

I shrugged. 'We were the lucky ones, really, weren't we? The worst thing that happened to us was having to spend ten weeks on a sofa bed. So many people had it so much worse.' I nodded over at Gabriele's bookshop, and then back at the Brazilians. 'Haven't got to look far.'

Ed arrived with our drinks and snacks. 'There we go. A plate of lovingly designed and prepared *cicchetti* for Federica. And for you,' he glared, 'we have some things on sticks.'

'I'm sure they're lovely, Ed. Thank you.'

'Don't tell me I've missed eating?'

It was a voice I hadn't heard in over three months, and I smiled up at the familiar moustachioed figure.

'Vanni!'

'The very same.'

I got to my feet and made to shake hands. And then I made to hug him. And in the end we settled for a bump of the elbows.

'I thought I'd find you here,' he said.

'Of course. We're helping rebuild the economy, one spritz at a time.'

'It's your patriotic duty, Nathan.' He smiled and nodded at Federica. '*Dottoressa*.' Then he turned to Ed. '*Signor* Eduardo, isn't it?'

Ed nodded, suspicion in his eyes.

Vanni, I noticed, was eyeing up the space between the tables, as if trying to determine that they were suitably distanced.

'Everything in order?' said Ed, with a note of challenge in his voice.

Vanni nodded. 'Absolutely. You've done a very good job indeed. If all the bar and restaurant owners in town were such good citizens my job would be very much easier.'

Ed smiled, but the suspicion did not leave his eyes.

'You do know,' Vanni continued, 'that under the emergency regulations your *plateatico* might be expanded by a further fifty per cent for the duration of the emergency?'

'I know.' Ed shrugged. 'But where would it go? Another fifty per cent,' he gestured across the street, 'and people are practically sitting in Gabriele's bookshop.'

Vanni nodded. 'I appreciate it's difficult. All we can hope is that it's not for too much longer.'

Ed turned and walked back inside, muttering under his breath.

'Did I say something wrong?' said Vanni.

'He's had three cops around since reopening. Each of them measuring the distance between tables. He's pissed off.'

'We're all pissed off, Nathan. We're just trying to do the best we can. Anyway, I'm glad to see you.'

'Do you not think, Vanni, that it might just be easier to phone me?'

He shrugged. 'Well, Nathan, am I likely to find you anywhere else?'

'That's a little harsh. But not entirely inaccurate.'

'Besides, if I meet you here it's an excuse to have lunch.' He checked his watch. 'Or breakfast, or brunch, or whatever we're calling it.' He sat down, patted his stomach, and smiled. 'So, what's good?'

'All of it.'

'Okay. Thank you, Nathan. Narrows it down.'

'Things on sticks are even better.'

'Narrows it down even further.'

Fede groaned. 'We're not going to start that again, are we?'

'Sorry,' I said.

Vanni changed the subject. 'And so, what might you be working on at the moment, *dottoressa*?'

'Still at the church of San Polo. Or better to say I'm back there. Working on the ceiling wasn't classed as essential work. Surprisingly so, given that being on a platform ten metres up is as good a form of social distancing as I can imagine. But I'm back there now. At least for the time being.'

'And how about you, Nathan?'

'Oh, I'm fine. Consular work is keeping me busy. I even got some translation work the other day that wasn't pandemic related. That was a change, at least.'

'Consular work.' He nodded, and smiled. 'That's why I'm here, Nathan.'

'Someone in trouble?'

He shook his head. 'Not any more.'

'Oh shit. Come on then, tell me all about it.'

'A Mr Domenico Vicari.'

I frowned. 'That sounds more like one of your lot.'

'You'd think so, wouldn't you. But no. British passport. Apparently more commonly known as Dominic Vicari.'

'And what's happened?'

'Poor man was staying on San Francesco del Deserto. On a retreat, as I understand they call it.'

'With the Franciscans?' said Fede.

'Quite so, *dottoressa*.'

She frowned. 'He chose one hell of a time to go on a pilgrimage. It can't have been easy to get there.'

A thought struck me. 'Italian name. Pilgrimage. Was he ill?'

Vanni shook his head. 'Not as far as we know. No, complete accident it seems. Fell from the *campanile* last night.'

I winced. 'Ouch.'

'And so some of our men have been round but – *pffft* – it's a monastery, Nathan. It's a monastery on an island. It must have been an accident.'

'I guess so. So, what exactly can I do for you? I mean, sure, it's nice to sit down and have a drink and things on sticks,' Fede winced, 'after all this time, but couldn't you just scan all the relevant stuff and email it to me?'

'Well, I could, but Fra Vincenzo – he's kind of the main

man there – is an old friend of mine. We haven't seen each other in quite some time. That's down to the nature of his job, I suppose. I thought perhaps I could allow myself some time to head out there and have a chat with him.'

'You have a friend who's a monk?'

'Strictly speaking, he's a friar. And, what, you think I only have police friends?'

'I hadn't thought about it. It's just that Vanni and Vincenzo, the crime-fighting monk sounds like the set-up for a TV series.'

'I'd watch that,' said Fede, munching on a sardine.

'Me too. But why do you need me along?'

'You'll be needing to contact relatives, I assume? In which case I imagine it will be helpful for you to know about how he spent his last days.'

'I guess so. It helps a bit when you've got some proper information to give them. Sure, I'll come along.'

'You'll get him back by early evening, won't you, Vanni?' said Fede.

'Of course, *dottoressa*. Do you have plans?'

'No, I just need him to sparkle. Tonight's the big one – pizza and beer with friends, for the first time since February.'

'Ah, *pizza e birra*. How much would we have given for a simple night out with friends, and pizza and beer over the past few months?' He beamed at us both. 'Excellent, Nathan. Marco will be along with a boat in about twenty minutes. Which gives me plenty of time for an octopus. On a stick.'

Chapter 3

'Marco, just take it easy around here, eh? We don't want to damage the crabs.'

Marco turned and nodded, a MS cigarette dangling from his lips, and throttled back.

'Crabs?' I said.

Vanni gestured vaguely in the direction of the island.

'I don't see anything?'

'What, you think I'm imagining crabs now? Take a closer look. Just beneath the surface.'

Marco throttled back even more taking us gently in towards the jetty on the island of San Francesco del Deserto. I looked over the side of the police launch, shielding my eyes against the light that sparkled and danced on the surface of the lagoon. Then I jerked my head back in shock, as something beneath the surface formed itself into a grotesque shape. Encrusted with barnacles, spindly-legged and furnished with fearsome claws; they were undoubtedly crabs, but not the sort ever likely to find themselves on a platter of *cicchetti* or a plate of *fritto misto*.

Vanni laughed and patted me on the back.

'What the hell are they?'

'Crabs, Nathan.'

'Not like any I've ever seen. I don't fancy my chances of getting one of those in a pot.'

'I don't imagine there's much good eating on them anyway, Nathan. No, these are art.' He shook his head, but smiled. 'Or, at least, that's what they tell me.'

'Oh. It's a Biennale thing?'

He nodded. 'From last year.'

'It's still there?'

'Supposed to be removed back in January, they tell me. Only thing is, that was just before the virus hit us. And it seems removal of giant steel and glass crabs didn't meet the criteria for "essential work".'

'So they're just going to stay there?'

He shrugged. 'For now. The artist has offered to make them a gift to the city. The Brothers would rather they weren't accepted. Anyway, for the moment, there they stay.'

'As a hazard to shipping?'

'Pretty much. You've got to take a bit of care when piloting in, isn't that so, Marco?'

Marco nodded behind his aviator shades. 'Take the wrong route and – *kerrunch* – one less glass crab in the world.'

'And I guess nobody wants that?'

'Couldn't give a crap. Just don't want the engine fouled up.' He flicked his cigarette over the side of the boat and into the lagoon, drawing a reproving hiss from Vanni.

Marco shrugged. 'Sorry.'

Vanni just shook his head.

'So tell me again about Mr Vicari,' I said.

'I don't think I've got much more to tell, Nathan. He is

– was – one of your lot, as I said. The Brothers found him dead this morning in the courtyard. I hope you don't mind coming along?'

'Not at all. This is the furthest I've been out of my house since the end of January.'

'I don't think it'll take much of your time. Accidental death, as I said. So just form-filling.'

Marco piloted in, then leaped onto the jetty and tied up the boat. Vanni jumped ashore, and then Marco stretched his hand down for me. Vanni, as both a Venetian and, more importantly, his boss, could be trusted around boats. Me, as a middle-aged *straniero*, less so. I felt slightly patronised, but took his hand anyway.

'Thank you.' I looked back out at the lagoon, and sighed. 'It's a lovely day.'

And it was. One of those glorious early summer mornings, in those days before the sun becomes unbearably hot and the sky oppressively blue. The pretty, multicoloured houses of Burano shone in the distance, awaiting the tourists who – this year, at least – would be coming only from Italy and not from further abroad.

Denuded of tourists during the early months of the pandemic, visitors were slowly creeping back, but the difficulties of long-distance travel meant that, for the first time in decades, the majority of accents heard in the *calli* were Italian ones. In the early summer sun, Venice was cautiously returning to life. Restaurants, bars and shops were reopening, people were attempting to have a good time and the city felt manageably busy. Even walking through Piazza San Marco was now more of a pleasure than a contact sport.

Vanni clapped me on the back. '*Un soldino per i tuoi pensieri*, Nathan?'

I grinned. 'They're not worth that much. It's just that this,' I spread my arms wide, 'all feels so good, you know? Being outdoors. Wide-open spaces around us. The sun on our faces.'

He smiled back at me. 'I know. But for how long?'

'Don't spoil it.'

'I'm a cop. They pay me to have dark thoughts. Come on, we've got work to do.'

I turned to follow him, and then stopped, shaking my head. Then I turned back, scanning the lagoon in search of giant crabs.

'Something wrong?'

'I don't get it. What's the point of an installation that you can't even see unless your boat is practically on top of it?'

'You can, so I believe. But only during *acqua bassa*, when the lagoon's at its lowest level. They're supposed to, you know, emerge.' He mimed, as best he could, a crab in the act of emerging.

'Right. Like in *Attack of the Crab Monsters*?'

'What?'

'It's a Roger Corman film.'

'I don't know it. Is it any good?'

I scratched my head. 'As good as a film called *Attack of the Crab Monsters* is ever going to be, I suppose.'

He shook his head. 'I knew it was a good idea to call you, Nathan. At least, I thought, I'd be sure to learn something.' He turned back to the pilot. 'Marco, just stay here with the boat. We'll be as quick as we can.'

Marco adjusted his shades, which I assumed was an acknowledgement, and sparked up another cigarette.

'And don't smoke too many of those. They're not good for you.' Quitting smoking barely six months ago had turned Vanni into something of a zealot.

He led me past the giant wooden cross at the end of the jetty and along a gravel path bordered on one side by a row of cypress trees.

The entrance to the monastery was a simple structure in marble and terracotta brickwork. A statue of St Francis was set into the wall beneath the lunette window, clutching a Bible and a cross to his chest and gazing towards heaven. Above the heavy wooden entrance door the Franciscan motto of *Pax et Bonum*, though heavily weathered, could still be deciphered.

He raised the heavy iron ring fixed to the door, but it swung open before he could knock. In the entrance stood a tall, thin man clad in a dark brown habit, a cincture with three knots tied at his waist.

'Fra Vincenzo?'

'Commisario Girotto?'

The tall man looked stern for a moment, but then the lines around his eyes crinkled – just like Dario's, I thought – and the two men exchanged hugs and kisses.

'Enzo, *carissimo.*'

'Vanni, *mio caro.* I'm so glad you're here.'

'Enzo, this is Mr Nathan Sutherland. He's the British Consul in Venice—'

'Honorary Consul,' I interrupted.

'—the British *Honorary* Consul in Venice. I thought he should be here.'

Fra Vincenzo smiled, and spread his arms wide in greeting. 'Thank you for coming, Mr Sutherland.'

I found myself trapped, once again, in the eternal British dilemma. Italians, I knew, would happily exchange a hug and a kiss with someone they once met whilst waiting to buy fish. For Brits, however, this degree of familiarity was something to be restricted only to one's closest acquaintances and, even then, only at times of special celebration.

Fra Vincenzo spotted my awkwardness, and smoothly turned the incoming hug into a handshake. 'Thank you both for coming out here.' He looked at Vanni. 'It's been a long time.'

'Too long, Vincenzo. I'm sorry.'

'Don't be. These things happen. But let's not leave it so long in future.'

'Enzo and I were at school together,' Vanni explained. 'I've known him pretty much all my life. From the first day of *scuola elementare*, anyway. And then one day I went off to study history at Ca'Foscari and Enzo told me he was going to the seminary.'

'You studied history? I never knew.'

'What, you thought because I'm a cop I did a degree in crime-fighting or something?'

'Well. Yes.'

He shook his head, whilst Fra Vincenzo laughed. 'It was a close call. We were both terribly in love with the same girl. There was going to be a dance on Friday night, and I'd screwed up my courage to ask her out. And then I found that Vanni had asked her the day before. And she'd said yes.'

Vanni, I noticed, was blushing. Just ever so slightly. 'Well, it wasn't deliberate. I just thought that if I asked and she said no, that would still leave me Friday to try and find someone else.'

Fra Vincenzo patted his arm. 'Anyway, by that stage I thought I might as well give anything a go and so I asked if she might change her mind.' He raised his eyes, briefly, heavenwards. 'That, I suspect, wasn't a very good or Christian thing to do. Fortunately, however, she declined. Otherwise our personal histories might have been very different.'

'You mean, you might be in the police force and Vanni might be living the monastic life somewhere?'

'Can you really see me as a monk, Nathan?'

'Oh, you'd look great in a cassock, Vanni.'

'I keep having to repeat this, Vanni. Technically I'm a friar not a monk.' I must have looked confused. 'Would you like me to explain the difference?'

'Er, maybe not now.'

We all laughed, and then Vincenzo's expression changed, remembering why we were all here.

'I think you should come with me, now.'

Chapter 4

'This is where Gregorio found him,' said Vincenzo.

The midday sun shone down on the cloister as the smell of fresh-cut grass on a summer's day filled the air. A small *vera da pozzo* in pink Verona marble stood at the centre. There was no sound, save the buzzing of insects, which reminded me that I should have applied mosquito repellent before coming out.

'He was lying here. There was nothing to be done, nothing to be done at all, poor fellow.'

I looked around the cloister, and then back at the spot where Vincenzo was pointing. I frowned.

'Something wrong, Nathan?' asked Vanni.

'Nothing. I was kind of expecting a chalk outline, that's all.'

Vanni rolled his eyes. 'What do you think this is, Nathan, *CSI Burano*?'

'Sorry.'

Vanni harrumphed and turned to Vincenzo. 'So, tell us what happened.' Then he smiled. 'I'm sorry, I know you've been asked this already. But for my benefit, and for Mr Sutherland's of course, could you go through it once more.'

'There's nothing really to add, Vanni. Fra Gregorio found him here, as I said.' He looked upwards to the *campanile*, casting a long shadow across the cloister. 'He must have fallen from up there. He,' Vincenzo paused, weighing his words, 'I imagine he would have hit the roof of the refectory on the way down, and then slid off into the cloister.'

Vanni and I both winced.

'There was nothing to be done, as I said. We did move the body – I'm sorry, I know we shouldn't have done that – but Gregorio attempted the kiss of life, chest compressions, everything. It was far too late though. I suspect from that height he would have died instantly.'

'What was he doing up there?'

'He would go up there every night, in the small hours. To look at the stars, he said.'

'He was some kind of amateur astronomer?'

'I don't think so. I think he simply enjoyed the peace and the stillness. I can understand that.'

'Was he trying to "find himself"? That sort of thing?'

'Everyone who comes here is looking for something. Christ, in many cases. We can help with that. Perhaps a feature for a glossy magazine. We can even help with that as well. And sometimes, I think, they're running away from something. And that's rather more difficult for us to deal with.'

Vanni looked upwards at the *campanile*, shielding his eyes against the sun. 'So. Are we going up then?'

'Do we need to?'

'Nathan, the man fell from up there. I think I need to have a look around, no?'

'Right. Yes, of course. But you don't actually need me to

be there, do you?'

Vanni looked at Vincenzo. And then they both looked at me.

'Stricty speaking, no.'

'Oh good.'

'However, as a good and diligent Honorary Consul you might, perhaps, wish to see the spot where your unfortunate compatriot met his end.'

'Strictly speaking, Vanni, that was here.' I pointed at the ground.

Vincenzo winced.

'Too soon?'

He nodded.

I threw up my hands. 'Right, right. I'll go up. Why not?'

'Heights still a bit of an issue for you then, Nathan?'

'You can tell?'

'It's a lovely view. Just try opening your eyes. Just a little. One at a time. Ah, there we go.'

Vanni was right. No, it was better than lovely. It was spectacular. Ahead of me lay the picture-perfect houses of Burano, and the *campanile* of Santa Maria Assunta on Torcello. To my right, the golden sands of Cavallino-Treporti. Behind me, the agricultural island of Sant'Erasmo. And then to my left, sandbanks stretched away to the crumbling remains of what might once have been a monastery. Try as I might, I couldn't recall the name. Another deserted island abandoned by the Austrians, I assumed.

It was one hell of a view and, in spite of myself, I smiled. Vincenzo patted me on the back. I would have reciprocated but I wasn't ready to remove my hands from the railing. Not quite yet.

'So, where would he have been?' said Vanni.

Vincenzo patted one of the ledges. 'Here, I imagine. Looking up at the stars. And then, for whatever reason, he overbalanced.'

He sat himself down, and leaned back, just a little, as if to illustrate just how easy it would have been to topple over by accident. He kept one hand firmly on one of the pillars, yet I was gripped with terror and clamped my eyes shut.

I heard Vanni sighing, and forced them open again. He was looking over the side, and I made myself follow his gaze. In truth, the *campanile* was not *quite* as high as all that. But it would have been high enough. I looked down, and saw the roof that would have broken his fall halfway down, before the final drop to the courtyard.

The view started to spin around me, and I stepped back, breathing deeply and pressing myself against the wall.

Vincenzo looked at me with pity in his eyes.

'I think we can go down now,' he said.

'Thank you, Enzo. I think that's all for now.'

'Thank you for coming out, Vanni.' He nodded at me. 'And thank you, Mr Sutherland, as well. Is there anything more that I can do?'

Vanni shook his head. 'I'll be in touch, Enzo. It depends on what the autopsy results are but,' he shrugged, 'let's be honest, it just looks like a tragic accident. Nathan here,' he patted me on the back, 'will have the unenviable task of contacting Mr Vicari's next of kin. Once we've identified them that is. That's why we have such a special relationship with the consular service. Saves us doing all the shit jobs.' Vincenzo winced at the mild profanity. 'Sorry. Anyway, is there anything else you need, Nathan?'

'I don't think so. Oh, hang on, could we maybe take a look at his room?'

Vincenzo nodded. 'I don't see why not? Vanni?'

'I guess so. Is it important, Nathan?'

'Not important, *per se*. It's just it's nice to be able to give relatives a little bit of background. After the shock, it's one of the first things they ask. *Where was he? What was he doing?* That sort of thing.'

'Okay then. Lead the way, Enzo.' Then he turned back to me and wagged a finger. 'But don't go touching anything.'

I smiled. 'Just in case?'

'Just, as you say, in case.'

Chapter 5

A heartless Jesus looked down at us from the bare walls of Dominic Vicari's cell.

I'd once told Father Michael Rayner that I found the whole 'Sacred Heart' iconography a little disturbing, and so, with great patience and over a Negroni, he'd explained exactly what it meant in symbolising the boundless compassion of the Redeemer towards all mankind. I'd nodded and said, yes, I understood all that. But I couldn't help finding it all just a little creepy. At which point Father Michael had sighed and ordered more Negronis.

It was one of the few points of decoration in the simple, bare cell. Jesus, his head surrounded by the crown of thorns and pierced by the spear, looked down on us with grace and benevolence in his eyes. Albeit holding forth his heart. Which was on fire.

Fra Vincenzo smiled at me. 'I hope you approve Mr Sutherland?'

I smiled back. 'It's – simple.'

'Of course. If it wasn't, it would be a Holiday Inn. No wi-fi, no television. We ask our guests not to bring laptops or tablets.'

'But how do you manage?'

'We have a landline. We have a single – rather old – computer. We do need to keep in touch with the outside world, after all.' He chuckled, the corners of his eyes crinkling. 'The outside world sounds so far away, doesn't it? Whereas we're really only talking about ten minutes across the lagoon. So, no, we're not completely cut off from modernity. But our guests rarely stay longer than a weekend and so we ask them to rid themselves of all their toys before they settle into the life of retreat. It can only get in the way, otherwise, given the timescales.'

'So they're basically cut off?'

He chuckled, again. 'Hardly. You make it sound very dramatic. If they need to send a message or call someone, then of course they can use their telephone. My point is rather that if someone comes here in search of Christ, or simply in search of tranquillity and reflection, then modern technology can only get in the way. Ridding themselves of it makes it easier for them. And then when they return to the world beyond the island, perhaps they'll have learned there are ways to tune out the relentless noise of the world.'

Vanni nodded. 'Is that the only reason?'

Vincenzo sighed. 'There was also an – incident – a couple of years ago.'

'Incident?'

'A journalist. Now, we have no objection to them *per se*, but this particular one was – I believe the expression is *live blogging* his experience here.'

'Not in a good way?' I said.

'"*Come and look at the friars still trying to live in the mediaeval period.*" That sort of thing. And that was unkind. If somebody wants to write an article like that about us, then that's their decision. I don't imagine it's the sort of thing any of us here would ever see. We have a library, but it's rather light on lifestyle magazines. But I'd rather they'd just waited until they left before sitting down to write it. After all, it's quite conceivable we might have challenged their preconceptions, had they given us a chance.'

'Do you think that's what Mr Vicari was doing? Challenging his preconceptions?'

Vincenzo shrugged. 'It's not our place to judge why people may come to stay with us. Mr Vicari only said that he'd like to have some time to simply wander around the island, and to get his thoughts in order. In return all we asked of him – as we ask of all our guests – is that they dine with us and attend worship.' He paused and smiled. 'Four times a day.'

'Four meals a day?'

'I think you know that's not what I mean, Mr Sutherland. Four acts of worship. Early morning, midday, afternoon and after dinner.'

I whistled. 'Wow. That can't have left much time for anything else.'

'It's not quite as arduous as all that. In Francis's time, prayers would have been about five hours.'

'Blimey.'

'That's communal prayers. Private worship would probably have been about the same.' He smiled. 'So as you can see, we're terribly relaxed these days. Dear old Francis would probably think us the most ungodly slackers.'

'Prayers, meals and stargazing. That was it?'

'That was it. Oh, and there were the chickens. He seemed

rather fond of them.'

Vanni looked at me. 'So, is there anything you need, Nathan?'

'I don't think so. There might be things to be sent back to his family. What did your boys find?'

'Not very much. Mr Vicari seems to have been travelling light. Clothes, mobile phone – smashed on impact, sadly. A pair of binoculars, also smashed. For stargazing, I imagine. Airport novel in the drawer. Not much more than that.'

'Uh-huh.' I nodded at Vanni. 'In that case, I think that's all we need for the moment.' I turned to go and then heard something clunk and roll away under my feet. 'What's that?'

I dropped to my knees, and saw something glimmer under the bed. 'Hang on a moment.' I reached out and pulled out a bottle.

Vanni looked at me. 'What have you found?'

I held the bottle up. '*Pride of the Glens*. What the hell's that?'

'Whisky?'

'Not one I've ever heard of.' I peered at the label. 'Apart from the name, it's all in Italian.' I looked at Vincenzo. 'You ever heard of this?'

He gave a little cough. 'I think you might be asking the wrong person, Mr Sutherland.'

'Oh yes. Sorry.'

'However,' he smiled, 'the wrong person might possibly say that this is a budget brand of supermarket whisky best described as "cooking alcohol".'

I looked at the level remaining in the bottle. Perhaps an inch at best. 'Blimey,' I said, 'he must have been doing a lot of cooking.'

'There are no rules against alcohol here. Mr Vicari was quite at liberty to bring this in if he so desired.'

I looked again at the bottle. One litre. Precious little remaining. 'How long was Mr Vicari here, remind me?'

'Just the four nights.'

Four nights. Perhaps a quarter litre of cheapo whisky every night. Plus whatever was served up at dinner.

'Are you a whisky drinker, Nathan?' said Vanni.

I shook my head. 'Always took more out of me than I took out of it. As a wise man almost said.' I tapped the bottle. 'Four nights. Nearly a quarter bottle a night.'

Vincenzo looked at me. 'What are you trying to say, Mr Sutherland?'

'Nothing at all. It's just that after a quarter bottle of whisky, getting up in the small hours of the morning to climb a bell tower and look at the stars would come a very distant second to a pint of water and the prospect of a long lie-in.'

He smiled. 'And that's something I really wouldn't know anything about. Well, now. The others will already be at lunch. Perhaps you'd like to join us? Or do you need to get back?'

'Vincenzo, I don't think there's anything more that we can do for the moment. So yes, lunch would be good. What say you, Nathan?'

'Nathan says lunch is always good.' I looked at Vanni and grinned, as I remembered the *cicchetti*. 'And lunch after brunch is even better, right, Vanni? That's very kind of you, Fra Vincenzo.'

'It'll be simple, I'm afraid.'

'Because of your beliefs, of course?'

'No, it's just our new chef isn't very good. She's trying hard, bless her but she's not really a natural.' He paused. 'Perhaps it would be better if we ate in my rooms instead of the refectory. It's been a distressing day for everyone. The presence of the police is upsetting for the others. Fra Raffaele is very old, for example.'

Vanni nodded.

Vincenzo led us across the courtyard, and to a heavy oak door. He paused for a moment, noticing that it was ajar slightly, and knocked gently.

'*Avanti.*'

He turned to us, a quizzical look in his eyes, and pushed the door open.

The room, like Vicari's cell, was plain, and bare of decoration save for the obligatory metal crucifix and a simple icon of St Francis. A heavy wooden table, with four chairs around it, stood on top of a plain, slightly worn, rug. Italian rap music blared out from a small radio on the windowsill, more than a little incongruous given the surroundings.

Vincenzo sighed, walked over, and clicked it off. 'Maria, what have I said about music while you're working?' He put his hands to his temples. 'Earphones, please!'

The young woman with a duster in one hand and a can of polish in the other sighed even more theatrically. 'You don't pay me enough to afford decent headphones, Fra Vincenzo.'

'That's not so, Maria. Anyway,' he ran a finger across the back of a chair and frowned at the layer of dust it revealed, 'take a little more care and we might even think about paying you a bit more.'

'Was that Jax?' I said.

Maria frowned. 'Who?'

'Oh sorry. Perhaps I'm wrong. I was on holiday last year and his music was everywhere at the beach. I thought his name was Jax.'

'It's J-Ax – "Jay Axe" – not Jax.'

'Ah. My mistake.' Never again try to be cool and down with the kids, Nathan.

'Anyway, Maria, I think you can take a break from cleaning for the time being. Could my friends and I perhaps take lunch here instead of in the refectory. Just for today.'

'Of course, Fra Vincenzo.' She paused. '*Insalata caprese*?'

Vincenzo winced, ever so slightly. 'Again?'

Maria smiled, and for a moment there was genuine warmth in it. 'It's my speciality, Fra Vincenzo. And think of the good it's doing you.'

She nodded at Vanni and me, then tucked the duster and polish into her tunic, picked up the radio, and left.

Fresh tomatoes and mozzarella. As much basil as you can be bothered to tear up and the best olive oil you can spare. It's as simple as that. It's as difficult as that.

Maria put three plates on the table and returned with a heavy stone jug and three tumblers.

'Thank you, Maria,' said Vincenzo.

She smiled and nodded. 'Anything else, Fra Vincenzo?'

'I don't think so. Just look after the others in the refectory, and then I think you could probably go home for the afternoon.'

'But you need me back this evening?'

'Of course. Our lives may be simple, but even we can't manage on an empty stomach in the evening. Francis might have been made of sterner stuff, I admit.'

'Fra Vincenzo, by the time a boat comes out to pick me up it'll be time to come back again.'

'Oh.' He frowned. 'Well, feel free to take yourself off to some other part of the island. Enjoy the sunshine. We've got books you can borrow if you get bored with Mr Jax on the radio.'

She rolled her eyes. 'God, this is better than Disneyland.'

'And what have we said about casual blasphemy?'

She sighed. 'Okay, okay. I'm sorry. Is it okay if I go and sit under a tree and think beautiful thoughts?'

'That'd be perfect. We'll see you later, Maria.'

'Never mind the headphones, I think the least you could do is hire me a boat, you know?'

'We'll think about it. If the dusting improves, and, perhaps, just a little variation in the cuisine.'

She sighed, spun on her heel, and stalked out, her sandals flapping angrily against the stone floor.

'So now you've met Maria,' said Vincenzo. I nodded. 'And I know what you're thinking.'

'That she doesn't exactly look like a Bride of Christ?'

'Not exactly. I know her father. She's had a bit of trouble at school. And outside.' He mouthed the word 'drugs'. 'So she's working here during the summer. He hopes that will help straighten her out a bit.'

'Well, I've heard of being grounded, but being exiled to a monastery is taking it a bit far.'

'Oh, she's not living here. That would be a little, well, inappropriate to say the least. We do let her go home in the evenings.'

'And it's working out?'

'I think so. Oh, it might seem as if I'm being a terrible ogre, but it's really not so bad here.'

He stood up and bowed his head, making the sign of the cross over the bowls of food.

Benedici, Signore, noi e questi tuoi doni,
che stiamo per ricevere dalla tua generosità.
Per Cristo nostro Signore.

'Amen,' said Vanni.

He stared at me.

'Amen,' I added.

Vincenzo took a forkful of his *insalata caprese* and smiled. 'And despite what I said about the lack of variety, she really is very good at this.'

'It's the very thing on a hot day,' I said. 'Especially with a nice crisp glass of white wine on the side.' I reached for the jug and poured myself what turned out to be a lukewarm glass of water.

He caught the disappointment in my eyes. 'I'm sorry, we don't have any wine.'

'I understand. Because of your beliefs, of course?'

'No. It's just that Maria wasn't able to get to the shops today.'

'Oh.' I sipped at my water, wishing that Fra Vincenzo's employer could have been with us.

'What are you thinking, Nathan?' said Vanni, as Vincenzo escorted us back to the boat.

'I'm thinking Mr Vicari had terrible taste in whisky, but nothing more than that. What are you thinking?'

'The same as you. I think we might have got lucky this

time, Nathan. We'll need to wait on the final report. But I think this is just as it looks. Unfortunate tourist just has one drink too many and,' he frowned, 'something bad happens. Not so lucky for him, of course.'

'No. But better for his relatives. Simple accidents are better than – other things. It does make breaking the news just a little easier.' I sighed. 'Which reminds me, I need to get back and have a conversation with the next of kin. I'll need their details from his passport.'

'Sure. I'll send them to you as soon as I get back to the *Questura*.' Then a grin slowly spread across this face. 'And do you know, Nathan, that's given me an idea.'

'Yes?'

'Yes. I think maybe I'll be needing to have a difficult conversation with you at some point.'

I frowned and reached over to tap his forehead. 'What's going on in there, Vanni?'

'Oh, just an idea, Nathan. But rather than spoil your journey back I'll tell you about it later.' He shook hands with Vincenzo. 'It's been good to see you again.'

'It has. Let's try not to leave it too long next time.'

'Agreed.'

'When do they next let you off the island?'

'Vanni, this isn't Alcatraz. I'm free to come and go as I please. But I'll be over in the *centro storico* in a couple of days. And then heading further afield. A pilgrimage to Assisi, and perhaps further beyond that.'

'You're going on tour?' I said.

'You might say that. But sadly, we have no T-shirts.'

Marco was seated in the back of the police launch, his

hands clasped behind his head and his eyes hidden behind shades.

'You ready, boss?'

'We are.' Vanni turned to hug Vincenzo. 'We'll have time to meet later in the week, yes?'

'I hope so.' Vincenzo turned to me, spread his arms wide, and, once again, turned it into a handshake. 'Mr Sutherland.'

'Fra Vincenzo.'

'I'm sorry your visit here was for distressing reasons. Do come back and visit us, any time.'

'I will.'

Marco revved the engine, just ever so slightly, as if to encourage us to get on board. He cast off, and spun the boat round, preparing to take us back past Burano, through the lagoon and back to the *centro storico*.

'Keep an eye out for the crabs,' Vanni called to him.

Marco nodded, and adjusted his shades. Then he reached into his breast pocket for his cigarettes. He clicked at his lighter, swearing softly as it failed to light. Taking his hands from the wheel, he cupped his hands around the flame as he puffed away at the cigarette in his mouth.

'*Gesù.*' The lighter clattered to the deck as Marco wrenched the wheel to the right, sending me tumbling from my seat.

'Marco, *che cazzo*?'

Marco idled the engine, and bent over the wheel, breathing deeply. 'Shit, that was close.'

I got to my feet, brushing myself down. 'Ouch.'

Vanni grabbed Marco by the shoulder. 'Stupid bastard, I warned you about smoking on the boat.' He turned back to me. 'You okay, Nathan?'

'I'm fine. Probably a few bruises.'

'*Cazzo*,' Vanni swore again. 'You nearly took the life of the Honorary Consul there. That could have caused a diplomatic incident. All because you couldn't wait to get back to the *Questura* to have a smoke.'

'Sorry.' Vanni raised an eyebrow. 'Sorry, *sir*.' He jabbed a finger towards the water. 'I saw someone down there.'

'What?'

'A diver. Not just someone swimming, I mean. An actual diver.'

Vanni raised a hand to shield his eyes, and scanned the lagoon. 'Can't see anything. No diving buoy as far as I can see.'

'Sir, if I'd seen one I'd have taken it slower. Whoever's down there isn't using one.'

'You're sure it was a diver. Not, I don't know, a dolphin or something?'

'Definitely a diver, sir.' Marco took a deep breath and wiped the sweat from his brow. 'Look, people are being silly bastards ever since things got back to normal. Fed up being told what to do, maybe. Or just that someone goes diving and forgets their SMB, and thinks, you know, that it's probably safe enough round here.' He shook his head. 'Silly bastards, as I said.'

'Where do you think they came from?'

Marco shielded his eyes to scan the lagoon, and then shrugged. 'Maybe Sant'Erasmo? Do you want me to take a better look.'

Vanni shook his head. 'Not worth it. Let's just get back, eh?'

Marco bent to pick up his lighter, and looked at his boss with a quizzical expression.

Vanni sighed. 'Oh for Christ's sake, go on then. Just light it before we get going this time. I'll feel better knowing you've got at least one hand on the wheel.'

Marco nodded, and lit up.

'And keep an eye out for crabs, as I said.'

'You know,' I said, 'I wonder what he'd have made of them. The crabs, that is.'

'Who?'

'St Francis, of course.'

'Oh I imagine he'd have talked to them. Like he did to everything else.'

'I wonder what they'd have to say.'

Vanni rubbed his chin, and then turned and looked back at the monastery island, receding behind us. 'I wonder too, Nathan. I might be interested in listening, as well.'

Chapter 6

'So how did you find life with the Brothers, *caro mio*?'

'It was – well, it was all right. But I don't think it's for me. It seems to consist mainly of disappointing lunches, and high towers. Oh, and lots of praying, of course. But Fra Vincenzo seems like a nice man.'

'Is that it, then? Vanni doesn't want anything else from you?'

'I don't think so. I just need to be the bearer of bad news. As usual.'

She gave me a hug and a kiss. 'I'm sorry. Never gets better, does it?' I shook my head. 'But we'll be out tonight with Dario and everybody. That'll cheer you up, yes?'

'Oh, it will.'

There came a little *m'yeep* from above our heads as Gramsci, still installed atop the bookshelves, rolled over in his sleep.

'How do you think he does that?' said Fede.

'Sleep anywhere, you mean?'

'No, that's not so impressive. I can manage that. I meant, what stops him falling off the edge when he turns over?'

'I imagine it's some sort of primal instinct. If he fell off, he'd look embarrassed and we'd point and laugh at him. And, for a cat, that would be unbearable. Ergo, over the millennia, they've evolved a way of not falling off things.'

'I suppose so. Oh, I envy him. It's getting hotter out there and it's only going to get worse. I don't suppose there's any chance of us getting away on holiday this year?'

I shrugged. 'I don't know. Funds are a bit thin on the ground. I did get a new contract for translating toaster manuals. That'll help.'

'Oh well done, *caro*.'

'Except I'm not sure the money will get us much further than your mum's house in Chioggia.'

Her face fell. 'Oh.'

I kissed her forehead. 'Still, you never know. Something might turn up. And now I guess I really ought to try calling Mr Vicari's relatives.'

I counted the seconds as I let the phone ring and ring. As I had on the previous four occasions, I stopped at sixty elephants. Then I hung up.

I swore, a little louder than I'd intended, and thumped the table making Fede start and Gramsci throw a paw over his head.

'No luck?'

'Nothing at all.' I shook my head. 'I bloody hate it when this happens. Every time I call I have to brace myself once more, to screw myself up into delivering bad news. Every. Single. Time.'

Fede slipped behind me, and kissed the top of my head. 'I'm sorry, *caro*. I know it must be horrible.'

I rubbed my forehead. 'Okay, I think I'm just going to have to let this go for the day. I'll call again as early as possible tomorrow.'

'Who's the next of kin?'

'A woman called Catrin Vicari. His mother.' I shook my head. 'In other words, the worst of all possible worlds.'

'Isn't there anybody else you can call?'

I shook my head. 'No. I think there was once, though.'

'What do you mean?'

I clicked away and brought up the scan of Vicari's passport that Vanni had sent to me. 'See here? There was a name there once. But it's been crossed out.' I yawned, and made to close the laptop. 'Father, I suppose, presumably deceased.'

Fede leaned over my shoulder, and stopped me. 'Let me see.'

I shrugged. 'Sure.'

She adjusted her glasses. 'It's not just crossed out though, is it?'

She was right. Whatever the name and contact details had been, every word had been obscured with a thick scribble of black ink.

'Does that mean anything? Guy just updated his passport, and removed Dad – or whoever it was.'

'Yes, but wouldn't you just stick a line through the whole thing? This looks like he's intentionally tried to remove every trace of it.'

I smiled, hugged her, and closed the laptop lid. 'Wanted to do a proper job, that's all. Now then, I think we can squeeze in a quick Negroni downstairs before we have to sparkle over pizza.'

'Are you in a particularly sparkly mood, *caro*?'

'Sparkly? Oh, I'm positively glittering.' She smiled back at me, but glanced down at the laptop. 'And don't worry about that.'

She smiled again. She was right. It was something to worry about, tomorrow.

Chapter 7

'Hey, Nat! How you doing, buddy?'

I grinned. 'I'm doing fine, Dario. You know, you look different in real life.'

'How so?'

'Well, bigger for one thing.'

This was true. Zoom calls had never been quite capable of containing Dario.

'You're looking good, Nat.' He smiled at Fede. 'And your wife is even lovelier in real life.'

Fede frowned.

'Too much?'

'Trying way too hard, Dario.' Then she gave up trying to look cross. 'But very kind.' She held her arms out. 'Are we doing hugs?'

Dario Costa had waited over four months to hug someone who wasn't part of his immediate family, and was not going to pass up an opportunity now. 'It's good to see you, Federica. Hell, it's even good to see your reprobate husband.'

'"Reprobate"? What did you do during lockdown, Dario? Eat the dictionary?'

'Cheeky bastard.'

There came a cough from Valentina who, far too late, had put her hands over their little daughter's ears. 'Dario, we've talked about this. How long did it take to stop her saying it last time?'

'Sorry, *cara mia*.'

There came a cough from behind us. '*Signor* Costa, I believe we've seen each other in the *campo*. I'm Giacomo Maturi. *Zio* Giacomo to Federica and Nathan.' He extended his hand.

'Dario. My wife, Vally.' Then he smiled, as he always did when talking about his daughter. 'And our little girl, Emily.'

Zio Giacomo, I knew, was always just a little wary of small children, regarding them as an otherworldly species beyond his understanding. Nevertheless he smiled down at her, and went so far as to give a little wave.

Emily flushed, and hid herself behind her mother. *Zio* Giacomo looked a little disappointed. Oh well. He'd tried.

Dario picked up the menu. 'So, what's it to be?' He pretended to do a quick headcount, pointing at me, Fede, Vally, Emily and Giacomo. 'Pizza, pizza, pizza, pizza, pizza and pizza?'

'Pizza!' shouted Emily, briefly emerging from behind her mother and clapping her hands together.

'Pizza it is, I guess,' I said.

Fede held the menu out in front of her and adjusted her glasses. 'I suppose the monkfish might be nice?'

We stared at her.

'Joking. Pizza is good.'

Vally smiled. 'That's the spirit. Imagine, three months of lockdown, with nothing but Dario's pizza on Friday night.'

'Friday night? Oh, that was Nathan's pizza night as well.'

'I think it's a man thing. Like barbecuing, you know? It's something which they think they ought to be able to do. How was Nathan's?'

'It was,' she searched for the right words, 'very welcome. At the time.'

'Look,' I said. 'It's not easy to do in a domestic oven. It's always going to be a compromise.'

'He tried to persuade me that we needed a pizza oven,' said Fede.

Dario brightened. 'I've always wanted one of those.'

'I kept telling him that I was fine with the oven. The well-ventilated and, ideally, outdoor space in which to use it might have been more of a problem.'

'I still think I could have stacked it up on breeze blocks and it would have been perfectly safe,' I said.

'Yes, "It looked perfectly safe" would look just wonderful etched onto a tombstone, *caro mio*.' She gave me a little peck on the cheek. 'But it was very welcome at the time as I said. It's just—'

'You're glad we don't have to do that any more?'

'Exactly. Come on,' she gestured around her, 'normal people doing normal stuff. It's just nice, isn't it.'

Vally nodded. 'Normal stuff. I just wonder how long we might have.' She covered Emily's ears again, the little girl squealing and pretending to be outraged. 'She's been asking when we might see *nonno* and *nonna* again. I've told her it might be a little while yet. Maybe towards the end of summer, we'll drive up to Trieste and see them. If things seem safe.'

The waiter arrived and took our orders for six pizza

Margheritas. Boring, perhaps, but the simplest really are the best.

'And to drink?'

'Coca-Cola for the *bella signorina*.' Emily clapped her hands together again. 'And five beers.'

I coughed. 'Erm, any chance of getting maybe half a litre of red wine with mine?'

There was, as I had expected, silence around the table.

Dario shook his head, 'What have I explained to you, *vecio*?'

'The whole *pizza/birra* thing? Yes, I get it. Which is to say, I don't get it.'

'It's just pizza, Nat. It's nothing fancy. It goes with beer.'

'I just like mine with red wine. It doesn't even have to be a decent one. In fact, the rougher the better.'

The waiter's face fell.

'I just don't get you Brits,' Dario continued. 'Red wine with pizza. I mean, why?'

Everyone around the table laughed, as did the waiter who hastily turned it into a cough when he caught the expression on my face.

I sighed. 'Look, there are three reasons. One, I am out eating and drinking with Italians. Now, don't get me wrong, I love your country and its people. Firmly on board with all that. But what I don't get is your ability to make a small bottle of beer last the time needed for the pizza to arrive, to be eaten, the entirety of the small talk afterwards and even, in some cases, the coffee. I'm from the cold north. We don't do things like that.

'The second thing is that, to your average Brit, pizza is just a bit foreign. A bit exotic. Which means it demands something a little bit classier, a little bit away from the norm, such as wine.

'The third reason is – okay, let me ask you a question. What would you drink with, oh let's say, *pasta alla sorrentina*?'

Dario shrugged. 'I dunno. Probably a red wine though.'

I pointed a fork at him. 'Ah-hah!'

He pointed his knife back at me. 'What do you mean *Ah-hah*?'

'What's in a *pasta alla sorrentina*, Dario?'

He scratched his head. 'It varies, I suppose.'

'Yes, but the classic version. What's in that?'

'Tomato. Mozzarella. Maybe some basil.'

'Anything else?'

He shrugged. 'Well. Pasta.'

'Well done. Pasta. There's a clue in the name. So, what's that made from?'

Fede rolled her eyes, knowing what was coming. 'He wants you to say flour, Dario.'

'Okay. Flour.'

I grinned. 'Ah-hah! So, there we have it. Flour, tomato, basil and mozzarella. In other words, the same as pizza. And yet red wine is seen as an act of cultural blasphemy with one, and yet not with the other. So why is that?'

Federica looked first at Emily, and then at Valentina. 'You won't let her grow up to be like this. Will you?'

I turned to the waiter. 'And so, I think we'll be needing one Coca-Cola and then—'

'Beer,' said Dario.

'Beer,' said Valentina.

'Beer,' said Federica.

'I think perhaps red wine might be nice,' said Giacomo.

There was silence around the table for a moment. I continued. 'He gets it. You see, *zio* Giacomo gets it. So, as I was saying, one Coca-Cola, three beers and *zio* Giacomo and I – *we* – would like a half litre of the house red.'

'Why don't we make that a litre, Nathan? Just to be on the safe side.'

'What an excellent idea.'

The waiter scribbled away at his pad. 'I'll see if I can find you something suitably rough, sir,' he said.

Emily snored gently on Vally's arm as we looked out upon Campo San Giacomo dell'Orio. The waiter collected the last of our plates, as Dario and Vally smiled and nodded at almost everyone who passed.

'Do you really know all these people?' said Giacomo.

'Almost everyone,' said Vally. 'It just seems so long since we last saw them. And not because of lockdowns or staying at home or anything like that. It just seems like we're seeing our friends around so much more than we used to.'

Giacomo nodded. 'Fewer people in the streets. Fewer people visiting. And so it follows that the people in the streets that we meet are our friends. Or, at least, our neighbours.'

Federica smiled. 'The streets are full of Italians.'

'Exactly, dear Federica. The streets are full of Italians. We are no longer the Anonymous Venetians. The lagoon is cleaner, the skies are clearer, the streets are emptier. One can even get a seat on the *vaporetti*.' He paused. 'And so, if perhaps only for a few months, we have what we've always wanted. Venice has returned to the Venetians.' He paused. 'I wonder how we feel about that?'

Vally smiled, as she stroked her daughter's hair. 'I like it. It feels like it's really home again.'

Dario nodded. 'Me too. I remember yesterday, just walking through the streets, smiling and nodding at everyone. People I know, everywhere. It's just nice.'

'Nathan?'

I sipped at the remains of my red wine. *Zio* Giacomo was in a mood to talk, it seemed, and so I wondered if we should split another half litre. On the other hand, Dario and Vally would be wanting to get Emily home. 'It feels – well – normal,' I said.

'That's the way I feel,' said Fede. 'It feels normal. We have the right number of visitors for the size of the city. It feels manageable. Going to work doesn't feel like being in a fight any more. The other day I even walked through Piazza San Marco and enjoyed it.'

'Trouble is,' said Dario, 'just look around. There are bars here that haven't reopened and maybe never will again.'

'I know what you mean,' I said. 'I worry about Ed and the Brazilians.'

'Oh, my boy, I'm sure you're doing all you can to help,' said Giacomo.

'I am. But there are only so many hours in a day.'

He shook his head. 'You see, we've shaken off the incubus of mass tourism. But we don't know what's going to come next. I wonder if perhaps we're only inventing new nightmares for ourselves.'

Much as I liked *zio* Giacomo, I was starting to realise

why Dario and Vally were unlikely ever to call upon him for babysitting duties.

Federica patted his arm and mouthed the words 'He's always like this' to Dario and Vally. 'You couldn't just enjoy the moment for what it's worth, *zio* Giacomo?'

'Oh, I suppose I am, Federica. It's just one can't help but worry. That's all. Let's change the subject. How does it feel being back at work, my boy?'

'Well, I never really left it. But at least I can go for a proper stroll around if it starts getting on top of me.'

'I don't imagine there can be a lot of consular business at the moment.'

'Not so much. There was, in the early days of course. And then it calmed down. But I did get called out to San Francesco del Deserto today.'

'How lovely. But what on earth took you out there? Her Majesty's Government aren't thinking about opening an embassy, are they?'

I shook my head. 'It was all a bit sad, actually. There was a British man, on retreat there. Fell from the *campanile* some time after midnight.'

'Poor fellow.' He smiled. 'I'm sorry, this was supposed to be my attempt at lightening the conversation. It doesn't really seem to have worked out that way. But how on earth did he manage to do that?'

'Nobody's quite sure. It's possible he'd had a bit to drink. But he used to like going up there in order to look at the stars. And then, I don't know, perhaps he was just sitting on the ledge and overbalanced for a moment and—' I shook my head.

Zio Giacomo frowned. 'Well, that's a damn silly thing to do.'

'I don't know. As I said, he might have drunk a little bit too much.'

'No, not that. Stargazing. It was a cloudy night. Stormy. He wouldn't have been able to see anything.'

I put down my wine glass. 'Do you know,' I said, 'you're absolutely right.'

'So, what was he doing up there, I wonder?'

'I don't know, *zio* Giacomo. I really don't know.'

That, I thought, was something to run past Vanni.

Chapter 8

Dick Barton's fish and chip shop, Mam always said, was the best in Swansea. Which, of course, meant it was the best in Wales and, by extension, in the world.

Dad would tut, and make his opinions on British food – just in case we had forgotten – well known to us.

Joe's ice cream, Mam always said, was the best in Swansea. Which, of course, meant it was the best in Wales and, by extension, in the world.

Dad would shake his head and remind us again that British people knew absolutely nothing about gelato. At which point Mam would remind him that Joe had actually been Italian, as he well knew. And Dad would go off on one, about how it might have been okay back in 1922, but they'd obviously been in Britain way too long now.

Swansea Bay, Mam always said, was the most beautiful in all of South Wales which meant, by extension, that ... look, you've got the idea by now.

Dad would say that it was a toxic swamp, not fit to hold a candle to anywhere on the Amalfi coast.

They stayed married, somehow, for twenty-something years; until one day Dad came home, packed a case and was gone.

I never saw him again.

It's Friday afternoon, school has finished, I've got some money in my pocket, and the weekend is stretching out before me. Maybe there'll be football tomorrow with Dad. I hope not. All he seems to do these days is complain about how rubbish the Swans are and how rubbish Wales are and how football is so much better in Italy. He goes on about it so much that everyone sitting around us is starting to get pissed off.

'Tell you what, Gianni, if it's so much better over there why don't you go home, eh?'

'Yeah? Well, just maybe I will.'

'No you won't, mun. All talk and trousers, that's what you are.'

'You just watch me.'

He feels me stiffen beside him and turns to look down at me. 'Joking, boy, that's all.' But there's no humour in his eyes.

But now it's Friday, and maybe Dad won't want to go tomorrow, or maybe I can just say I'm not feeling good and sag off. And he'll complain and say he's wasted money on tickets, but then Danny'll go. He always does.

I stop off at Dick Barton's on the way home. I'm not supposed to be going to the chippy by myself, Mam says Dick Barton's is only for a special treat, but still ... I've got some pocket money and so in I go, and come out with a bag of chips drowned in salt and vinegar with a wooden fork sticking out of the top, and I stand on the corner of the street and tuck in.

Dad'll talk about proper Neapolitan pizza, and things called pasta alla genovese *and* sfogliatelle *and other things I've never even heard of. But I don't care. I've got a bag of chips from Dick Barton's and the smell of the salt and vinegar is stinging the back* of my nose, but in a good way, and the first out of the packet sears my tongue and is as fine and crispy as you'll find anywhere. And I look out at Swansea bay, beyond the line of the trees, and think maybe this is as good a view as anywhere in Wales. Which means, of course, the world.

'Oi!'

The shout doesn't really register, as the chips still have my full attention.

'Oi! Vicar!'

Oh shit.

The West Cross Boys do not like me. To be fair, they don't seem to like anyone. But they especially don't like me. Because my name is 'Dominic' which is, apparently, 'posh' and there is no greater crime to the West Cross Boys than that of being posh; and my surname is 'Vicari' which is funny and foreign and sounds a bit like 'Vicar'.

I've tried explaining that there have been Italians in this part of Wales for over fifty years, but you don't do explaining to the West Cross Boys. Posh is what I am. The Vicar is what I am.

'Oi, Vicar! Talking to you. You being ignorant, or what?'

'Sorry.'

'Why, what you done?'

'Nothing.'

'Hasn't done nothing, he says, boys.' I don't even know his name, but the others seem to be hanging on his every word. 'Those chips good?'

I nod.

'Going to share them around, then?'

I know what's coming, and sigh, inwardly. Oh well, the first ones were nice.

'Sharing's important, teacher says. Isn't that right, boys?'

There's a general chorus of yeahs and nodding of heads. A couple of them are laughing already.

I hold out the bag of chips, and he throws up his hands in mock amazement, turning to his friends.

'The Vicar's sharing his chips, boys!' He turns back to me. 'Good boy. Mam will be proud of you.'

He stares at me, and I hold out the bag of chips. He doesn't move, just keeps staring at me. And then he lunges forward, snatching the bag from me, in the hope that I'll flinch or at least try and stop him and give him an excuse – as if he needs one – to hit me.

He crams a few into his mouth. 'Good, these,' he says between mouthfuls. 'But sharing's good, isn't it? Come on, boys.' He passes round the bag, and the others fall upon it.

And then, just as I'm going to give up and start walking home, he holds a hand up and stops them. 'What did I say about sharing? These are the Vicar's, remember? Give 'em back.'

There are a few scraps remaining at the bottom. Still, this is better than I'd expected. He holds the bag out to me, and I reach for it. He pulls it back out of reach, waving a finger. 'Uh-uh. What do we say?'

Of course. It was never going to be so easy. Some sort of tribute will need to be paid first. I'm tired now, and no longer want the poxy chips, but I force a smile onto my face. 'Please,' I say.

'"Please". That's it. That's the magic word. Being polite's important, isn't it, Vicar?'

'It is,' I say.

'Here you are, then.' He holds the bag out to me and then, just I reach for it, he drops it and the few remaining chips spill out across the pavement.

'Shit.' He puts his hand to his mouth. 'Sorry, Vicar, that was my fault.'

I shake my head. 'No problem.'

'Seriously? Still friends then, Vicar?'

I nod.

'Tell you what, though. What if I buy us another bag, eh? Would that be all right?'

I nod once more.

'Okay, then. Just give us a minute.' He pats his pockets, theatrically. 'Shit, but I don't have no money on me.' He smiles. 'But tell you what, why don't you go and buy us another bag, and I'll pay you back next week?'

I'm tired now. I just want to go home. But, it seems, the usual tiresome game will have to be played out yet again.

'I don't have any money,' I say.

'No money?'

'No. Spent it all.'

'All of it? Every penny you spent in the chipper?'

I nod.

He turns back to his mates. 'He's got no money, boys.' There's a chorus of awwwwws before he turns back to me. 'Jump up and down, eh?'

I'm about to protest, but he puts a finger to his lips. 'Jump up and down,' he repeats.

And so, I jump up and down on the spot, and everybody in the gang is laughing. Then he turns to them once more. 'Shut up,' he says, without raising his voice.

They fall silent, and he turns back to me. 'I'm sorry,' he says. 'Rude, they are. Ignorant, they are.' He smiles. 'Don't stop jumping though.'

So, I carry on jumping, and he cups a hand to his ear. 'Did you hear that, Vicar? Coz I think I can hear something there.' He smiles. 'Empty your pockets, eh?'

I've had enough now and turn around to walk away. Except that one of his mates is there blocking me off. I turn back the other way but there's another one in front of me. I move to the left, and he moves to the right. And then vice-versa.

I empty my pockets, and there's maybe a quid in change there. More than enough for a bag of chips at any rate.

'Vicar, it's a miracle! You had some money all along! Now, why don't you hand that over and I'll go and buy us all some chips.'

I sigh. Looks like I'm broke for the weekend. Dad will shout when he thinks I've spent all my pocket money. At best I might just avoid taking a kicking here, but I wouldn't bet on it.

'The fuck you want?'

The voice comes from behind me. Danny's voice.

He's shot up in the last year. He's now almost as big as me, and the hours he spends in the gym have filled him out as well. But the West Cross Boys don't see that. All they see is a boy they know to be just thirteen years old sticking up for his big brother and that, right now, is the funniest thing on earth.

'Bloody hell, boys, it's the Miniature Vicar. What are we going to do?' He crosses himself and puts his hands together in prayer. There are caws of laughter, and cries of Nooooo, it's the Mini Vicar.

He walks towards Danny, palms outstretched. 'Hey, it's okay Mini Vic. Your big brother here's just about to buy us all chips.'

Danny shakes his head. 'No. He's not.'

'Tell you what. You wait out here, eh? And maybe we'll give you some chips. Have a sit down in the meantime.'

And he moves to push Danny in the chest, but Danny's too fast for him and steps to his right. He bends his knees just slightly, and his fist flashes out, two lightning-fast jabs catching my tormentor in the face. Then he pivots on one leg, and a straight cross catches him for a third time.

He drops to the pavement, blood streaming from his nose.

One of his mates rushes forward, but Danny catches him straight in the face, and then doubles him over with a blow to the stomach.

He's breathing heavily now. One of the West Cross Boys looks as if he's about to have a go, but then thinks better of it.

'You leave us the fuck alone, you understand?'

Then Mr Dick Barton, who is not actually called Dick Barton, comes out of his shop, shouting at us. 'Bugger off you little bastards or I'll call the police.'

We run off towards home, the West Cross Boys in another direction.

Later that evening, in our bedroom, Danny stretches his hand across and pokes me in the shoulder.

'You okay, Dom?'

'Yeah, I'm fine.' Except, of course, I'm now the guy who's had to be saved from bullying by his little brother. But apart from that, I'm fine.

'We look after each other, don't we, Dom? That's what we do, isn't it?'

I do my best to keep my voice steady. 'That's what we do.'

'Always?'

'Yeah, Danny. Always.'

Chapter 9

Catrin Vicari, resident in Swansea. Dominic's mother. And the only name I had to go on.

I picked up my mobile, feeling its weight, toying with it as I passed it from one hand to another. Then I took a deep breath and punched in the number.

I counted ten rings and then hung up. It seemed as if she was never going to answer. I looked again at the scan Vanni had sent me. Vicari's passport was seven years old. Plenty of time for people to have moved, for numbers to have changed. Whoever thinks of changing a contact number in a passport anyway? I'd give it one more go. And then I'd think about what else I could do. In a minute, anyway.

Gramsci shuffled around on top of the bookcase, and miaowed down at me, simultaneously calling for breakfast and chiding me for my cowardice.

'I'll give her five minutes, okay? I'll try again in a bit.'

He miaowed again, and yawned, stretching himself to his full height. Then he turned and padded his way to the end of the shelf, the better to stare down at me.

I sighed. We had, I thought, been unusually good flatmates in allowing him to spend the summer months on top of the bookcase, and had gone to every length to make it comfortable for him. Admittedly some of these procedures had been for our own protection, such as the removal of vases from the upper shelves. The trouble was, once he'd installed himself up there, he found it very difficult to get down. Reaching up to give him a hand was, for obvious reasons, out of the question, and so he needed to be encouraged down by the strategic placing of cushions upon the floor and the shaking of a box of kitty biscuits.

Fede emerged, yawning, from the bedroom in time to see him plummeting earthwards and bouncing off a beanbag.

'You don't think you're spoiling that cat, do you?' she said.

'Not at all. I think between us we've worked out a path towards peaceful coexistence.'

Gramsci scrabbled at my trouser leg, attempting to claw himself towards the box of biscuits.

I sighed. 'Okay. One of us needs breakfast. Cup of coffee for me. Cup of tea for you?'

'That'd be nice.'

'So, what have you got planned for today?'

'I've got the day off. Some more scaffolding needs to go up at San Polo and I'm not the best person to help with that. So, I'm meeting *mamma* for lunch. Why don't you come along?'

'I'd love to. Depends if I can sort out consular stuff first though. And that might take a while.'

'Oh. Still trying to get hold of his mother?'

I nodded. 'She's not answering the phone. I'm trying to find excuses not to call back.'

'I can imagine.' She gave me a hug. 'But come on. It needs to be done. I'll even make your coffee if you like.' A plaintive *m'yeep* came from around her ankles. 'And feed your cat as well.'

This time I counted nineteen rings, with the intention of hanging up on the twentieth. Then the receiver crackled.

'Hello?' A male voice.

'Good morning. Could I speak to Mrs Catrin Vicari, please?'

'Erm. Hang on a moment, yeah?'

The sound became muffled, as if he'd covered the mouthpiece with his hand, but I could still make out the words.

'There's someone 'ere wants to speak to Mrs Vicari.'

'Well, that's going to be difficult, isn't it?'

'What should I do?'

'Chrissakes, just ask who's calling.'

The line cleared again. 'Who's calling, please?'

'My name's Nathan Sutherland. I'm the Honorary British Consul in Venice.'

A pause. 'You what?'

'I'm the Honorary Consul in Venice.' A pause again. 'Italy. You know, gondolas and stuff?'

'Yeah, I know what Venice is. I think you've got the wrong number.'

'Is that Mrs Catrin Vicari's address? 17 Fairwood Road, West Cross, Swansea?'

'That's it.'

'Look, can I just ask, are you a relative or a close friend? Something like that?'

'Mate, I work for Bergson House Clearance. That's why I'm here.'

'She's moving house?'

He covered the mouthpiece again. 'He's asking if she's moving house?'

'Tell him the bloody truth, *mun*, or you'll be on that bloody phone all day.'

Again, the line cleared. 'Look, I'm sorry to tell you bad news and all, but Mrs Vicari died a couple of months back now.'

'What?'

'The virus, you know?'

'I'm so sorry. Look, do you happen to know if there are any other relatives I can contact? It is rather important.'

'I could give you her son's mobile number, if that'll help. It's him who wanted the house cleared. Think he's selling up.'

I rubbed my forehead. 'Is that a Mr Dominic Vicari by any chance?'

'Hang on a minute.' He covered the mouthpiece again. 'He wants to know if it's a Dominic Vicari we're working for.'

'Yes it is. Now get off that bloody phone and come give us a hand.'

The line cleared. 'Sorry 'bout that. Yes, Dominic Vicari.'

'Okay. Things are getting complicated. That's why I was trying to get hold of Mrs Vicari. I'm afraid her son has died.'

'Died?'

'I'm afraid so.'

'What's that got to do with Venice? It was Venice, you said?'

'He died in Venice. I'm the Honorary Consul in Venice. That's why I was trying to contact his mother.'

'I see.' Another pause. 'Does this mean we're not getting paid?'

'Fat Cat, we've got a problem.'

Gramsci, having hauled himself back up to his position of surveillance, rolled over, turning away from me, confident in my ability to sort it – whatever it may be – out.

'Is that it? That's all the help I'm getting? A yawn?'

'I'm still here as well, you know, Nathan,' said Fede.

'Oh yes. Sorry, I was forgetting.'

'I mean, it's up to you. If you think your wife could be of more use than your cat, then I'll do what I can.'

'Sorry. It's just he's useful to bounce ideas off.'

'Does he ever bounce anything useful back?'

'Balls, occasionally. If he's feeling especially helpful.'

'So, come on then. What's the problem?'

'Dominic Vicari – the guy found on San Francesco – has no next of kin, his mother having pre-deceased him a couple of months ago.'

'Uh-huh. So what does that mean for you?'

'It gets complicated. Can't send the guy home if there's nowhere to send him to. Or, more importantly, someone to pay for him. Which means trying to find out if he had insurance.'

'And if he didn't?'

I shrugged. 'Then Italy will take care of him. Which usually means a common grave.'

'But that's horrible.'

'Is it?'

'Yes. That poor man, dying out here all alone and then

just being forgotten about as if he'd never existed. You can't let that happen.'

'I can't?'

'No, you absolutely can't. Maybe it's the virus, maybe it was the three months of being housebound, but this feels important. You need to sort this.'

'Sure. I'll do my best.'

'Well done *caro*.' She bent to kiss my cheek. 'I'm off to see *mamma*. I'll give her your love.'

'Do that.'

'Good luck!'

She was right, of course. So many months had passed. So much death, so many tears. And nothing that I, or anyone else it seemed, could do about it. But I could do something now. I could get Dominic Vicari home.

Chapter 10

Dad comes home from work, and starts packing. He's not drunk, because he's never drunk. He's not shouting, but then he rarely shouts. Maybe he's angry, though. It's difficult to tell.

Mam isn't upset. She just looks tired. As if this has been brewing for ages now, and she's had enough of trying to talk him out of it and just wants it to be done.

There's something about the way he's packing, though. It's an old leather suitcase with the initials GMV stencilled in two places, where the straps buckle. Gian Maria Vicari, Dad told us they stood for. His father. The suitcase is resting on the bed and me, Danny and Mam are watching from the door. I think he wants us to watch.

In it all goes. Shirts and sweaters, trousers, socks and pants. One of his suits (Dad is not the sort of person to have just one suit). A couple of ties (Dad would not feel dressed without them). A picture of the four of us on holiday, outside a caravan in Tenby. A copy of the Italian Bible. Dad's never been a reader. Neither has he been much of a churchgoer. But a copy of the Bible, in Italian, is perhaps the sort of thing he needs to travel with. Or needs to be seen to travel with. It's an indication, he's saying to us, of just how seriously he's taking this.

Grandpa Gian Maria has died. Dad got the news from a cousin, just over a month ago. And now he's going over there to put his affairs in order, he says. He might stay for a while, see how he likes it.

So he's getting a bus to Heathrow Airport from where a flight will take him back home to Naples. After which, he says, he'll be in touch.

I wonder how he'll find it. It will be strange for him, I think, not having the food to complain about. Or the weather. Or the football. Or the beaches. Or …

He clicks the suitcase shut, breaking in on my thoughts, and pulls the straps tight.

'That's it,' he says, and hauls it off the bed, testing its weight.

He kisses Mam on the cheek, and gives her a quick hug, but the contact is broken before she can return it. Then he gives us a mock salute.

'All right, ragazzi. *Look after* mamma *for me, eh? Give me a bit of time to get settled back over there, and then maybe you should come out for a bit. Even longer if you want.'*

He shakes my hand, and pats me on the back. 'Take care, Domenico.' Then he hugs Danny. 'Daniele. Arriverderci, ragazzo mio.' *Danny has always been Daniele to him, but I don't remember him ever using my proper name before.*

And then he's gone. Mam sighs, just a little. Then she changes the sheets on the bed, and folds away his remaining clothes into an empty suitcase.

'Stick that on top of the wardrobe, would you, there's a good lad?'

I nod, but Danny gets there first. 'Let me, Dom.'

Of course. Danny is bigger than me now. Bigger and stronger.

Only sensible to let him do it.

We get fish and chips from Dick Barton's that evening, and eat them in silence, sitting around the television. There's nobody to complain about the food this time. And that feels strange.

Chapter 11

'Please come home, Danny.'

'Heartbreaking Plea from Estranged Brother', *Swansea Evening Post*, 22nd November 2019

> *A West Cross man has made an emotional plea for his long-lost brother to return home.*
>
> *Dominic Vicari, forty-six, has not seen his younger brother Danny in over five years. Now, with their mother gravely ill, Dominic wants to put the past behind them.*
>
> *'Danny, I don't know if there's any chance you'll read this. But it might just be that there's somebody out there who might know where you are, or at least how to get in touch with you.*
>
> *'Mam is very frail now, and she wants to see you so much. Please, Danny, I know we've had our differences, but let's put them behind us. We said we'd always look after each other. Now I need you to look after Mam, just one last time.*
>
> *'We both love you, Danny. Please come home.'*
>
> *At the time of their last contact, Danny Vicari was*

recorded as living and working in Italy. Anyone with information as to his whereabouts is encouraged to contact his brother via the Evening Post, *in confidence.*

***

I tapped the screen of my laptop, and nodded. Catrin Vicari. Dominic Vicari. With names like that, the article hadn't been difficult to find.

I got to my feet and yawned and stretched. Dominic Vicari, it seemed reasonable to assume, had come to Italy to find his estranged brother in order to mend fences and tell him that their mother had died. It didn't explain why he'd thought he'd find him in a monastery in a middle of a swamp.

This, I thought, was a problem best tackled with a coffee. Or even with a spritz. I looked at my watch. Was it too early for that? My stomach rumbled, and I realised I'd skipped breakfast. Downstairs to the Brazilians, then? But then I'd run the risk of Federica arriving back to find me in the bar, and the unspoken assumption that I'd gone there five minutes after she'd left the flat. Which would be unfair.

I sighed. Middle age had well and truly arrived and, with it, the need to over-analyse everything. Back to the problem at hand.

Dominic Vicari had reached out to his brother via a local newspaper, despite knowing that he was, in all probability, over one thousand miles away. But there was, I knew, an Italian population of reasonable size in South Wales. It was a long shot but not impossible that someone might have had information on Danny's whereabouts.

Where might he have gone next? I picked up the phone. Perhaps the British Consulate General in Milan might be able to help. I sat through a couple of minutes of *The Four Seasons* before a familiar voice answered.

'Consulate General.'

'Helen? Is that you?'

There was a pause for a couple of seconds, and then she laughed. 'Nathan. Hello stranger. Lovely to hear from you. How're things in Venice?'

'Almost disturbingly normal. At least for now. But I've got a bit of a problem. I'm trying to trace a relative of a British citizen who died here the other day.'

'Oh dear. Was it the virus?'

'Bit more complicated than that. He fell from a bell tower. In a monastery. On an island.'

'What?'

'I said it was complicated. Anyway, I'm trying to find contact details for the only relative. I think he might be in Italy, and it's possible his brother was here looking for him. I get the impression there'd been some sort of family feud, and he was trying to put it right. So, I wondered if he might have been in touch with you?'

'Maybe so. Do you have a name?'

'Okay, the name of the missing guy is Vicari. Danny Vicari, or possibly Daniele. Welsh-Italian.'

'Let's have a look.' I heard her tapping away. 'Okay, yes, we had a contact from a Dominic Vicari in Swansea early last December.'

'That's him. The guy in Venice, I mean. Was there any follow-up?'

'Not really. We have no records of either a Danny or Daniele Vicari. The most likely answer is that he's registered here with an Italian passport and as such we'd have no records of his presence in the country. We did put a call-out on the web page for anybody with information to come forward.'

'Nothing?'

'Nothing at all. Hardly surprising though. Two months later and nobody was travelling and all we were talking about was COVID.'

'Okay. Thanks Helen. It helps to narrow things down.'

I hung up. This wasn't getting any easier.

Fede lay on the sofa, her feet in my lap, sipping away at her Spritz Nathan.

'So how's your mum?' I said.

'Pretty good. Got a bit weepy at one point, but I'm putting that down to being an Italian mother instead of anything more sinister. Still a bit nervous on public transport, but I guess that's only to be expected. So, how's your day been?'

I shook my head. 'Frustrating. I've been trying to track down relatives and failing.'

'What does that mean?'

'Bureaucratic nightmare, unless it turns out he's left both a will and a large pile of cash to get him back to the UK. Or he'll end up in a common grave but I don't really like the idea of that, and I'm not ready to give up yet. I think he's got a brother somewhere in Italy, but the Consulate weren't able to help.'

'Do you think he tried *Chi l'ha visto*?'

'Do you think he'd even know about that?'

'Worth a go, surely.'

I snapped my fingers. 'You know, that's not a bad idea.

Let's have a look.' I shifted her feet, drawing an irate *oi* from her as the sudden movement caused her to spill her drink.

Chi l'ha visto, a TV programme dedicated to tracking down missing persons, had been running on RAI for over thirty years. More importantly, for my purposes, they also had a website with an archive of current and closed cases.

I flipped open the laptop and tapped away. 'Here we go. Let's see what they've got on Danny Vicari.' I waited a few seconds, and then shook my head. 'Nothing. But he might actually be a Daniele.' I tried once more. 'No. Nothing.'

'Okay. Then just search on the surname.'

'There might be dozens of them.'

'It's worth a try.'

'Okay.' I blanked out the first name. 'Just the one. Vittoria Vicari. Described as "businesswoman". Last resident in Palermo, disappeared March 2019, aged 70. Wrong name, wrong gender, wrong age. I suppose she could be a relative but how many Vicaris are there in Italy? Thousands? Any other ideas?'

'Just try a general "Missing in Italy" search. There might be other sites beyond *Chi l'ha visto*.'

I tapped away, trying different variations on Danny's first name.

'Here we go.' Fede tapped the screen. 'Facebook group. *Missing in Italy*.'

I clicked on the link, and read.

Hello everyone, my name is Dominic (Domenico) Vicari, Welsh-Italian living in Swansea. I'm trying to contact my brother Daniele (usually known as Danny). Please contact me if you have any information as to his whereabouts. It's important family business.

'Any responses?'

'Lots. Mainly from well-meaning people wishing him well. But there's one that might be of interest.' I turned the screen so that she could get a better look. *Ciao, Domenico, I think I've got some information on Daniele for you. Don't want to discuss it on a public forum for obvious reasons. Please message me and we can talk a bit more.*

'Who's that from?'

'Some guy calling himself *Deep Dive*.'

'What sort of name is that?'

I shrugged. 'Search me.'

'Where's he based?'

'Profile just says *Italy*. But if we click on the link, we should find – ah, shit.'

'What?'

'His page has been deleted.'

'Any way of finding out more?'

I swivelled the chair to face her. 'You know much about hacking Facebook?'

'No.'

'Neither do I. So, I think we're stuck for the time being. But there's something not quite right here. Something I'll need to speak to Vanni about.'

Chapter 12

Packing again. Not Dad's big old leather suitcase, though. Danny's more practical than that and is stuffing most of what he owns into an enormous rucksack. I look at the size of it and wonder how on earth he's going to move it, but Danny picks it up by a strap and smiles and nods. Then he clips on his Sony Walkman and hangs the headphones around his neck.

'Music for the journey?'

'Not exactly.'

'What is it? Maiden, Motörhead?'

He shakes his head, and smiles. 'Teach yourself Italian. I've forgotten so much since Dad left. Figured it'd be good to know.'

'Wow. You really are taking this seriously, aren't you?'

'Got to, Dom. It's a chance for me, you know? What is there for me round here? Nothing, that's what.'

Danny was hoping there might be a career for him in boxing. He's probably better than ninety-nine per cent of the people out there. The trouble is, that still leaves an awkward one per cent who are better than he is.

'What are you going to do, Danny?'

'Dad says he can find me something. Management, he says.'

I laugh, and instantly realise I've done the wrong thing. His expression darkens. 'What you laughing at, Dom?'

'Nothing. It's, well, I never saw you as the management type, that's all.'

'What sort of type do you see me as, Dom?'

He steps towards me, and, for a moment, I'm afraid. 'Come on, Danny don't be daft, mun. *All I meant is that I don't see you as sitting behind a big desk all day long. Let's not fight, eh? Not today.'*

His face is still flushed red, but then he breaks into a big grin. 'Yeah. That's not really me, is it?'

'Come on then you daft bugger. Give your big brother a hug, eh?'

I'll never get used to how strong he is, as he almost squeezes the life out of me. Then he kisses me on both cheeks, which freaks me out for a moment, and then I remember he's just trying to be Italian.

'You could come over, eh? You and Mam, maybe Gran as well.' He pauses. 'Maybe you could stay? Maybe Dad could find you something as well?'

'Maybe, Danny. Just got to finish university first, that's all.'

'Bloody hell, Dom, are you ever going to finish school?'

'University, Danny.' I draw the word out to its maximum length. 'That's what it's called, remember?'

He shrugs and smiles. 'Still sounds like school to me. Anyway, I'd better be off. Bus to catch.' He pauses. 'Shame Mam's not here.'

I sigh. 'She's at Gran's. She, well, she's a bit upset you know.'

He looks surprised, as if the thought of Mam not being one hundred per cent thrilled at her youngest boy moving a thousand miles away to be with her estranged husband had not occurred to him. 'Is she? Oh. Right.' He looks down at his rucksack. 'Really need to be going, I guess.'

'Gonna give your big brother another hug?'

'Course I bloody am. Come here, eh?' He squeezes the breath out of me. 'And if there's any trouble with the West Cross Boys, you give me a call, yeah?'

I smile. The West Cross Boys haven't been a gang for years, now. The rumours are that one of them is in borstal or youth custody or whatever they call it now, and that one of them is dead from drugs. All that remains of them is some faded graffiti.

'Good luck, Danny.'

'Cheers bro'. I'll be in touch, yeah?'

He hoists the rucksack onto his back, looking around the room one last time. Then he notices the photo by the bedside table. Joe Calzaghe. Former super-middleweight champion of the world. Danny's hero.

'Bloody hell. I nearly forgot that. Gotta take Joe with me for luck.' He grins and looks at the poster of Debbie Harry on the wall. 'I'll leave you to look after her.'

He drops the photo into his rucksack, zips it up, and makes his way downstairs. From the window I see him walk across the street, and then break into a run as he sees the bus arriving. I give him a wave but I don't think he sees me.

I go downstairs and make a cup of tea. The house suddenly seems so much bigger, and so much quieter. Just me and Mam now.

'Goodbye, Danny,' I whisper.

Chapter 13

Vanni sat on one of the stone benches that were sited at regular intervals along the stretch of the Zattere that ran between San Basilio and San Trovaso, and took an experimental lick of his ice cream.

'What have you got there, Nathan?'

'Vanilla and pistacchio.'

'Good?'

'Very. What's yours?'

'Coffee. With extra coffee.'

'Isn't that a bit, you know, boring?'

He shook his head and took another scoop from the tub with his little plastic spoon. 'Not at all. Barbara thinks I'm drinking too much coffee. So I tell her that a *gelato* doesn't count.' He closed his eyes and smiled with pure pleasure. 'I suppose this is breakfast. When I was a small boy I would have dreamed about *gelato* for breakfast.'

I looked out upon the Giudecca Canal and over to the island beyond, and wondered if Sergio and Lorenzo would be playing *scopa* once more in the Communist Bar. Perhaps I should go over there and see, once I'd finished with whatever business Vanni had with me. Then I shook my head. Neither of them were young. It was too soon. Too risky.

Water traffic was creeping back. The *vaporetto* service had halved in frequency but occasional private boats could now be seen and the surface of the canal was not quite as mirror-like as it had been just a few weeks previously. The *Grande Navi* however, the great cruise ships, had gone, perhaps forever. Few people would miss them.

Vanni scraped the last of his ice cream from the tub and sighed with happiness.

'It's a lovely day, Nathan.'

'It is.' I looked at him, sitting on the other end of the bench. 'Do we have to sit like this? It makes me feel like we're in a 1960s spy film and you're going to pass me a microfilm hidden in a newspaper or something.'

'Nothing so dramatic, Nathan. It's just to encourage good behaviour, that's all.' He nodded as a couple passed us by, holding spritzes from the nearby *chioschetto*. They made to sit down together on the nearest bench and then looked over at us, and moved apart, taking their places at opposite ends.

Vanni smiled at me. 'See? It's all about encouraging little changes, that's all.'

'So, erm, why are we meeting here?'

'Because it's a sunny day, and I couldn't think of a better place to come and eat ice cream with my old friend than here. And,' he smiled, 'there are things I don't want to talk about at the *Questura*. Neither do I want to talk about them in a busy coffee bar near Piazzale Roma.'

'You could have phoned, you know?'

'I could. But then we wouldn't be having ice cream, would

we?' It was a fair point. He looked up at the skies. 'Lovely, isn't it? What do you see up there, Nathan?'

I followed his gaze. 'Um. The sky?'

Vanni clapped, slowly. 'Very good, Nathan, very good. I'll make a detective of you yet.' He smiled. 'Anything else?'

'Lots of blue. That's all there is. Not a cloud to be seen. Just a perfectly clear blue sky.'

'Which means?'

'I don't know. It's just so clear that's all. Not even any vapour trails.' I looked across at him. 'Oh.'

'Exactly. No vapour trails. There are hardly any flights leaving from Marco Polo at the moment.' He paused for emphasis. 'And vanishingly few to the United Kingdom.'

'So how did Mr Vicari get here?'

'A very good question. Most likely he managed to get a flight to Rome and travelled up from there. And there aren't many flights going there either. He must have really wanted to come here.'

'I think it was family business. His mother died recently. He was trying to get in touch with his brother.'

'Oh right. So you've found a relative? Well done.'

'I'm not sure about *found*. He has – or had – a brother called Daniele Vicari, last heard of in Italy.'

'Daniele, eh?' He took a photograph from his pocket. 'Something else we found in Vicari's cell. Do you recognise this guy?'

I reached over to take it from him. It showed a man in a dark suit, his fists clenched like a boxer's. There was a dedication and signature scrawled across it. *To Danny. Keep strong. Cheers, Joe.*

I shook my head. 'Sorry Vanni. No idea.'

'What about the signature?'

'Can't really make it out. Just looks like *J C something* to me. Not sure that narrows it down very much.' I passed it back to him. 'Trouble is,' I continued, 'if Daniele was ever here, he must have been registered with his Italian passport. The Consulate General has no record of him.'

'I see. Anything else you can give me. *Codice Fiscale*, something like that.'

'Not a thing. Just the name.'

'Hmm. That makes things difficult, doesn't it?'

'It does. I don't know where to go with this one, Vanni, but I want to get this guy home. It feels important. So, what have you found?'

'Perhaps nothing. Preliminary results from the coroner indicate that the level of alcohol in his bloodstream was just about 0.5 milligrams per millilitre.'

'What does that mean?'

'He was pretty much on the drink-drive limit. Slightly more than a glass of wine. Regular glass of spirits.'

'Would that be enough for him to lose his balance and fall? If he was, I don't know, sitting on the ledge or leaning over?'

'Possibly. It's not enough to be falling-down drunk, but perhaps if he was dizzy from looking up. But there was something else we noticed, from his clothes.'

'Oh yes?'

'Apart from the sweat and, well, the blood of course, they were soaked in booze. Far more than you'd expect given the levels in his bloodstream.'

'So what are you thinking?'

'Nathan, the powers that be,' he cast his eyes heaven-wards, 'are very happy to consider this as an accidental death. Everybody's tired after the last six months. All we want to do in the summer is make sure everybody's having a good time, within the parameters of not doing anything stupid. And, of course, all everybody wants is to show Venice is open for business, and it's a safe place to go.

'Remember last year? The *acqua granda*? The two cruise ship accidents? All Venice wants now is a nice, quiet summer. What it doesn't want is …' His voice trailed off.

'A murder?' I finished for him.

He winced but nodded. 'And there's more than that. Vincenzo's an old friend of mine, remember? This year is the eight-hundredth anniversary of the establishment of the monastery on San Francesco del Deserto. There'll be public events, the mayor is going to want to hold a reception for him. It's going to be high profile.'

'So I imagine the last thing you want is a "Murder at the Monastery" thing going on in the background?'

'Exactly. Better for everybody if it was just left where it was. An unfortunate accident and a warning against the perils of alcohol.' He shook his head. 'And I can't do that, Nathan.'

'No?'

'No. Too many things don't add up. I don't see why some-body would go to all the trouble – right now, of all times – to travel across Europe to look at the stars. And I know some people have problems with alcohol, but that usually extends to drinking it, not wearing it.'

'So where does that leave you?'

'It leaves me with my hands tied. But I want to look into this further.' He leaned over towards me, smiling now. 'I want *you* to look into this further.'

'Me? You're joking?'

'Not at all.'

'I mean, wouldn't it make more sense to have a, you know, *officer of the actual law* doing this?'

'It would. But, as I said, that's not going to happen. If I put a cop on that island, we'll go full "Murder at the Monastery" within hours. If you're there, there'll be none of that.'

'But why me?'

'Because you're involved. Given this is the death of a British citizen. And the sooner this is sorted out the sooner he can be sent home.'

I sighed. 'What do you want me to do, Vanni?'

'Just spend a couple of days on the island. That's all. Talk to people. Have a look around. Then tell me what you think. And if you tell me that everything seems fine, it was just a tragic accident, then I'll wipe my hands of the whole thing, I promise.'

'Spend a couple of days there? How do you mean?'

'Why, on retreat, of course, Nathan. Why else would you be there?'

'Hang on a minute, you want me to be an Undercover Monk?'

'Strictly speaking, you'd be a friar. But remember, you're only on retreat. You're not taking Holy Orders.'

I shook my head. 'Vanni, this is nuts. I've been locked up with my cat for three months and now you want me to go and closet myself away with a group of monks—'

'Friars'

'—friars, on an island. For how long?'

'I understand the typical retreat is only for couple of days. You could make it longer if you wanted. Let's say three nights?'

'If I wanted? Vanni, how do you think Federica's going to react when I come home and say "*Ciao, cara*, now don't get cross but three months of enforced living together has made me decide to try monastic life"?'

Vanni grinned. 'I've thought about that. Did you know Barbara's family has a property near Cortina?'

'No.'

'It's just that we probably won't be making use of it this year. And so, it would be nice if we had people to stay there for a bit. Just to keep an eye on the place. Especially in August. You know, when it's punishingly hot in Venice but blissfully cool in the mountains?'

I widened my eyes. 'Oh.'

'What I'm saying is that we'd be grateful if you were able to go and look after it for us.'

'You're making it sound like a remake of *The Shining*, Vanni.'

'Come on, Nathan. August in the mountains. Where else would you be? Sitting on the beach, complaining about getting prickly heat and worrying about not being able to get a seat on the *vaporetto* back to town.'

I rubbed my chin. He had a point. Then a thought struck me. 'What about Gramsci? Can I take him with me?'

'What?' He laughed. 'Not a chance.'

'Come on. He'll be good.'

'He will not be good, Nathan. He will be very, very bad. I've seen the state of your furniture, remember? You can stick him in a cattery.'

'I'm not doing that. The last time he was in Kitty Prison he didn't speak to me for about a month. He still gets flashbacks. It's like he was in some feline version of a stockade in Viet Nam or something.' I got to my feet. 'I'm sorry, Vanni, but I'm going to have to say no.'

I turned and made my way along the *fondamenta*, counting all the while under my breath. *Five-four-three-two—*'

'Nathan!'

Bingo!

I turned around.

'All right. I'll do it. You can take your damn cat.' He jabbed a finger at me. 'But you'd better come up with something useful.'

Chapter 14

'I have to say, *cara mia*, you're taking this rather better than I expected.'

She shrugged. 'Well, it seems like quite a good deal. You disappear and pretend to be a monk—'

'Friar'

'—friar for a couple of days, and in exchange we get Barbara and Vanni's house in the mountains for a month. In August.'

'Well, yes. Absolutely.' Vanni, as far as I could remember, had not actually told me exactly how long we could borrow it for but that, I was pretty sure, could be sorted out later.

'And a heated infinity pool, overlooking the mountains. It sounds wonderful.'

Again, there were certain particulars – such as the existence of said view and, indeed, said pool – that I hadn't been able to nail Vanni down on. But that was an issue for tomorrow's Nathan.

'There's only one problem, as far as I can see. Aren't people going to know who you are?'

'Ah, Vanni had thought of that. Fra Vincenzo's going to be away for about a week. He's going on a pilgrimage to Assisi.

He's the only one I've met. Well, apart from Maria, the Young Offender.'

'And what are you going to say to her?'

'What I'll say to everybody. I'm just exploring my spirituality.'

'Okay, I'm convinced. Now, is there anything particular you need to pack? You know, tunic, scapular, cowl? Things you won't be able to pick up along the way.'

'I was rather hoping that civvies would be the order of the day.' I chuckled. '*Order* of the day.'

'Yes. I see what you did there. On the subject in hand, I've been doing a little research myself.'

'Oh yes?'

'Vicari. The surname. There are about two thousand of them in Italy. And about two hundred of them in the Veneto. But, get this, just fourteen of them in Venice.'

'But that's brilliant. That's a manageable number.' I gave her a kiss. 'Well done. Perhaps I won't need to be a monk at all?'

'Trouble is – I checked the telephone book – there's no one called Daniele Vicari.'

'Oh. Maybe he's only got a *cellulare*?'

'Could be.'

'Which immediately makes it more difficult again. Oh well, a cloistered life for me it seems.' I yawned. 'Well now, there's packing to be done for tomorrow. But before I embark on my new ascetic lifestyle I think we should fit in lunch at the Brazilians. It might be my last Negroni for a while.'

'Hey, Ed,' I said. 'I was meaning to ask you something.'

Eduardo paused in the act of clearing away the detritus from the adjacent table, prior to spraying it down with disinfectant. 'Nat?'

'Have you had many Brits coming along here? Since things properly opened up again, I mean.'

He shrugged. 'Sure.'

'But what I mean is, actual tourists. Not people who live here. Visitors.'

He scratched his head. 'Difficult to tell, Nat. Normally everything's just a blur at this time of year, you know? But this year there aren't so many, that's for sure. Then again, there aren't so many people in general. Nothing like what it usually is.'

'There are enough though. Right?'

He shrugged, and then smiled as best he could. 'They'll have to be.'

I took my phone out and brought up Vicari's photo from Vanni's passport scan. 'Do you remember this guy?'

He stared at the screen, and then shook his head. 'Maybe so. But it's so difficult to say.'

'He'd probably have had a Welsh accent.'

'What's that like?'

I closed my eyes, and tried to draw on my years in Aberystwyth as I recited the first stanza of 'Do not go gentle into that good night'.

I opened my eyes again. Fede smiled and gave me a little clap.

Eduardo nodded in approval. 'That's really good, Nat.'

'Why, thank you.'

'The poem I mean. Not sure about the accent. Don't think I've ever heard anyone sound like that before.'

'Hmph. Oh well. Worth a go.'

Fede patted me on the knee. 'Did you know my husband's abandoning me to become a monk, Ed?'

He barely raised an eyebrow, as if this were the sort of thing that Nathan could be relied on to do from time to time. 'Is that so?'

'Just for a couple of days. To see if I like it.'

'Oh, right.' He paused. 'Are you going to have to stop drinking?'

'I'm not sure. I think that might be a deal-breaker though.'

'Ah well. Best of luck. We'll miss you.'

'I'll miss you too, Ed.'

He turned to go, and then bent to whisper in Fede's ear. 'He is just kidding, right?'

'I think so,' she said. 'If not, don't worry. I'll still be here.'

'Thanks, Fede. You two are all that's standing between me and bankruptcy right now.'

My life as a monk began with a late morning coffee, sitting outside a bar on Fondamenta Nove, and enjoying the gentle morning sun as I looked over to the cypress-covered cemetery island of San Michele. It wouldn't be long now, perhaps only a matter of weeks, until the heat would be enough to drive me indoors, wishing I could join Gramsci underneath the air-conditioning unit; but, for now, this was perhaps the best time of the year.

The smell of cigarettes and coffee, the sight of delivery barges going about their business and the chatter of a few excited tourists. Venice was slowly coming back to life.

I finished my coffee, slid a few coins across to the *barista*, and made my way to the *vaporetto* pontoon, noting where the edges of the *fondamenta* had been stained black with ink: seagulls, having had free run of the city for almost three months, had made the most of the opportunity to feast undisturbed on cuttlefish.

Vanni had apologised for not arranging a police launch this time. It seemed fair enough. I was now, after all, an Undercover Monk and would have to fall back on my own resources. However, ACTV – the public transport service – were finding it increasingly difficult to cope with the increased passenger numbers as the city returned to life. In the face of numerous protests by those left behind on the pontoon, the *marinaio* slammed the gate shut and the boat pulled away. Shouts and abuse followed him, as he shook his head and made his way into the cabin. I caught a glimpse of his face. Masked and gloved as he was, I could still see the stress in his eyes.

As I'd expected, most of the passengers got off at Murano. On a hot day the lure of the glass foundries and souvenir shopping won out over the prospect of the longer journey out to the more distant islands. I sat on the back seat, outside, and tried and failed to read my newspaper until I decided just to settle back and watch the islands of the lagoon pass by. Ancient Torcello, where the *campanile* of Santa Maria Assunta stood guard over the few remaining inhabitants. Mazzorbo, with its orchards and vineyards and a restaurant that would forever be beyond my means. And finally, Burano, impossibly pretty and, for the time being at least, free of the crowds that usually choked it throughout the summer months.

It was midday by now and, in spite of the breeze, I could feel my jacket beginning to stick to me. A gentleman, I had explained to Federica, did not head off on pilgrimage in shirt sleeves. Ahead of me lay – two, three? – days in the company of monks and perhaps very little wine. But just a short walk away lay *al Gatto Nero* with its prospects of plates of thinly-sliced raw fish drizzled with lemon and oil, followed by piles of crispy sardines and a half a litre of house white.

The only problem was that *al Gatto Nero* was also one of Fede's favourite restaurants. More than that, it was somewhere we hadn't been since her birthday of two years previously.

Would this, therefore, be something I could do in good conscience?

No.

Was I going to do it anyway?

Well, now. If I only had a plate of sardines, that would – at least in theory – be little different from going to a *bacaro* and eating them standing at the bar, with a spritz. And it was lunchtime, and she really wouldn't expect me to go without lunch and so …

My feet seemed to have made the decision for me, as I found myself staring at the menu outside the restaurant. Well, that was it. It was probably destiny or something. I sat down.

I made a play of pretending to read the menu but knew what I was going to have. I gave it a quick flick through and nodded at things that I wasn't going to eat but thought Fede and I should probably come back for, and then closed it again.

The waiter smiled. 'You've decided already, sir?'

'I have. The sardines, please?'

He nodded. 'Anything else?'

I thought about suggesting extra sardines but that would, perhaps, be a step too far. 'That'll be all,' I said.

'And to drink?'

'A half-litre of the house white.'

There was a second of awkward silence. 'I'm sorry, sir, but we don't have a house wine.'

'Ah.' Slightly more awkward, then. An actual bottle, or half-bottle, would immediately push things from 'lunch' into 'proper meal' territory. Still, I was here now.

'No problems. Perhaps a half bottle of the second cheapest white then?'

He grinned, pleased, perhaps, to find someone who took their sardines seriously.

'Coffee?'

'That'd be lovely, thanks.'

'*Digestivo*? Perhaps a *limoncello*?'

'I think a *grappa* would be nice.'

'Then a *grappa* it shall be, sir.'

He took my plate away, now covered in little more than cleanly skeletonised sardines, picked clean as perfectly as in a *Tom and Jerry* cartoon.

I sat back in my chair, and sighed with the simple pleasure of one who has eaten well on a sunny day. My eyes wandered along the canal, lined with boats, along the *fondamenta* with its rainbow of houses, and to the church of San Martino Vescovo with its crazily leaning tower. It was, I was told, perfectly safe, a programme of stabilisation having taken place in the late sixties. Nevertheless, it did appear to lean quite a lot and, I thought, if I were ever to move to Burano I would take care to rent a house situated on the non-leaning side.

The waiter arrived with my coffee. I inhaled its aroma and

sighed once more. A couple of days of exploring my spiritual side lay before me. That, I thought, should be more than sufficient to satisfy myself and Vanni that there was nothing untoward about Dominic Vicari's death. Perhaps, I thought, I could even break up the days by coming over here for lunch?

My phone trilled and I pulled it out of my jacket.

Ah. Federica.

'*Ciao, cara!*'

'*Ciao, tesoro*. How are things'

'Oh fine. Just fine. Miss you already, of course.'

'Oh, that's very sweet.' She paused, just for a second. 'How were the sardines?'

I nearly dropped my coffee cup. 'You what?'

'Sardines. How were they?'

I was, I thought, incapable of bluffing my way out of this, and looked around just in case there was a previously unknown public webcam that had betrayed me.

'Erm, they were very nice, thanks. Splendid, even. But how—'

'Oh, I knew you'd have over an hour to kill on Burano before your boat and I was pretty sure that you'd be more than likely to spend it in the *Gatto Nero* than walking around the lace museum.'

'Am I that obvious?'

'I'm afraid you are, *tesoro*.'

'Erm, sorry. Have I done a bad thing?'

'Not if you promise to take me there once you get back.'

'I'll do that. Promise. Tell you what, why don't you come out? Once my investigations have concluded.'

'I'll do that. Well, in the meantime enjoy the retreat.'

'I will.'

'Oh, and enjoy your *grappa*. But only have the one.'

I looked down at my glass, shaking my head. 'I will. Love you.'

'Love you too.'

I picked up my glass and downed it one. What would I do, I wondered, if my wife ever decided to use her powers for evil?

Chapter 15

Me and Mam sit in the front row of the crematorium in West Cross, and listen to the lay minister say some nice words about a woman she never met. Then she motions me forward, and I fumble my eulogy from my pocket, and spread it out as flat as I can make it on the lectern. One sheet slips, and flutters to the floor. I stammer out an apology as best I can, and bend to pick it up. Sorry, sorry, *I repeat. Every face stares back at me, smiling encouragement, wanting me to get this right.*

I say all that I can think of to say about Gran, whilst Mam dabs at her eyes, but in the back of my head, all the time, is the thought that now I'm going to be stuck here forever.

Because everybody has left her. Dad, Danny, and now her mam. I'm all she's got left. Which means the bright lights of London are never going to be more than a dream. I'll be in West Cross now until she dies.

I'm about to sit down when, from outside, comes the rumble of a car engine. The full-throated reverberation that only comes with something properly expensive or in need of a replacement exhaust.

And here he is. The golden boy. Literally so, now, as his thinning hair has been dyed blond and gelled within an inch of its life. He looks tanned and fit, and the suit he's wearing sure as hell did not come from Debenhams.

'*Danny?*'

'*I'm sorry,*' *he whispers.* '*Took me longer than I thought.*' *He shakes my hand, and then goes to hug our mam, who collapses into his arms and sobs and sobs and sobs.*

'Can I get you another?' I say.

Danny drains his glass, and shakes his head. 'Better not. Driving, you know.'

Driving, he most certainly is. The Alfa Romeo Giulietta sitting outside in the car park of the Coach and Horses has probably increased the value of the pub by about fifty per cent.

'Lovely car,' I say.

He looks a little embarrassed. 'Bit flash for a funeral, maybe. But Alfas are lovely cars. Well, they are when they're working, that is.'

'Come on, Danny. Have another drink, you can leave the car here overnight. It'll be perfectly safe.' I'm not at all sure about that.

'Can't, I'm afraid. I've got a flight tomorrow morning and the car's got to be back at Heathrow by tonight. I'm staying at the airport hotel. It's a bit of a dump, to be honest, but it's handy if you need to get up early.'

'Danny, you're going back tonight?' I'm unable to keep the surprise and the hurt out of my voice.

He looks at his watch. Smart, but not flashy. Like the suit. Like the car. 'Afraid so, Dom. But not for another half hour or so, mind.'

'Can't you stay overnight? I can make up a bed for myself on the sofa. Or we'll make you up something in our old room. Like *old times, eh?' There's desperation in my voice now.*

'Love to, Dom. But I've got an early flight, see.'

'Stay just a few days. Please, Danny. Look at her.'

Mam is over at the bar talking with neighbours. It's her mam's funeral, but her eyes are sparkling, and she's smiling as she's chatting away, and she can hardly take her eyes off Danny because her little boy is home again and she's proud fit to burst.

'Wish I could do that, bro'. But I've got to get back. Work, you see. Dad's pretty much retired now so I'm kind of running the business.'

I look at him again. The sun tan. The surfer hair. Back in the day we used to laugh at kids like that. Surfies, we called them. But as well as that there's the watch, and the suit, and the car and, for all I know, his socks. He's done well for himself. Very well. And I start to wonder.

'What sort of business is it, Danny?'

He shrugs. 'Just management, you know.'

'Yeah, but what sort of management?'

'Business management.'

'Danny, you've never done any sort of management in your life. Business or otherwise. Before you left home I had to help you organise your sock drawer.' I try to keep my voice light but can't quite conceal the bitterness.

He notices. There's just a little Guinness left at the bottom of his glass and so he swirls it around and takes an age, waiting for it to dribble into his mouth, before he answers.

'You jealous, bro?'

And I am. Hell, I am. Because I want that watch, and I want that suit, and I want that car and, yes, I want his bloody socks as well.

'I'm not jealous, no. I'm glad you're doing well. But I'm just wondering what it is you're actually doing. That's all. Just exactly what are you doing, Danny?'

He sighs, theatrically, and puts his now properly empty pint on the table. 'Ah, so that's it, is it?'

'What is?'

'Little brother's working in Italy, so must be something dodgy going on. That's it, isn't it?'

'No, I just—'

He waves a finger at me. 'No. I know exactly what this is. Couldn't possibly be that your little brother has actually made a success of himself, could it? No, it has to be something crooked. Because unlike sensible big brother Dom, Danny boy never got to university. Which means he doesn't deserve nice things.'

I reach over and grab his arm. For a moment I think he's going to shake it off. Or maybe even something worse. But he just sits there, looking across the table at me. 'I dropped out, Danny. I dropped out of uni. I just didn't have it in me.'

'Oh.' He looks down at the table. 'I didn't know.'

'I wrote to you, Danny. Actual letters, you know?'

'Sorry,' he mutters. 'I've been bad with family stuff. I'll try better, okay.'

'S'okay.'

'So what are you doing now, Dom?'

'I'm a private investigator.'

If he had any beer left he'd have sprayed it across the table. 'You what?'

'A private investigator.'

'You mean like who's that bloke? That actor you had a poster of on your wall.'

'Humphrey Bogart.'

'That's him. Remember, I had Debbie Harry on mine.'

'And because we were in the same room, whenever we woke up I'd find myself looking at Debbie Harry. And you'd be looking at Humphrey Bogart.'

'Yeah, well that was all sorts of confusing to say the least. I think you got the better deal.'

We laugh, and for a moment that easy friendship is back again, and I wish I could bottle that moment up.

'So what's it like, then? Being a PI?' He attempts an American drawl, which doesn't fit his Welsh-Italian accent, and we both laugh again.

'Well, it's not like the movies.'

'What sort of stuff do you do?'

'It's not glamorous. Lot of the time it's "Is my wife cheating on me?" or "I think my husband's playing away". Tracking down debtors. Missing people – that's not always the horrible stuff, mind you, sometimes it's just people trying to find family members they've lost touch with. Things like that.'

'Wow. Does it ever get, you know, a bit physical?'

I nod. 'Been in a couple of fights. Angry husband in two cases. And once someone who didn't want to be found. Which was natural, really, given he owed twenty thousand quid.' I smile, and flex my knuckles. 'But I'm better at looking after myself these days.'

'Wow.' He smiles. 'My big brother's a private eye.'

'And my little brother's a businessman. In some sort of business.' The expression on his face changes, and I shake my head. 'No, no. Not going to start all that again. But just tell me Danny, are you okay? Really, I mean.'

'I'm well okay, Dom.'

'Then that's all I'll ask.'

His phone plings and he swipes away the message that's appeared on the screen. 'Nothing important,' he says.

He switches the display off, but not quite quickly enough. There's an image of a young woman on his home screen. He catches the expression in my eyes.

'Who's that?'

He laughs, a little nervously. 'That's my better half. At least that's what she tells me.'

'You're not …?'

'Married. Bloody hell, no. It's not like that. I think she'll break my heart one day to be honest.'

We both laugh.

'Danny, why didn't you tell us?'

'I was kind of keeping it as a surprise. For when you come over, you know?'

'Who is she?'

'Daughter of Dad's business partner.'

'Let me have a look.' He turns the screen towards me. 'She's very pretty.'

'She is. And she's lovely. Most of the time. Can be a nightmare at others, mind. And, like I said, I think she'll break my heart one day.' He leans over towards me. 'But don't tell Mam. Not yet. You know what she's like, next thing is she'll be going out and ordering flowers and buying a hat, the whole works. Wait until you come and stay.' He checks his watch. 'Okay. And now I've got to be going. I'll just have a quick word with Mam.'

'Can't you stay, Danny? Just one night?'

He shakes his head. 'Can't, sorry. But I'll drop you a line, *okay? Soon as I get back. And then maybe the two of you can come over, for a proper break.'*

'That'd be nice. Thanks, Danny. Take care.'

'You too, bro'.'

He hugs me, and then goes over to Mam, holding court with her friends. He whispers something to her, and I see her almost collapse inwardly, as if she's physically shrunk in size. He hugs her, and she clings to him, not wanting to let him go.

And then he's gone, and the Alfa roars into life and he's away back down the M4 to Heathrow, and a flight to somewhere in Italy to do a job that he doesn't want to talk about.

Mam is now sobbing, less for Gran and more for Danny, and the gaggle of neighbours are trying to help, and there's a chorus of there theres *and* such a shame *from them all.*

'Come on, Mam,' I say. 'Good to see Danny again, wasn't it? And he says he's going to write when he gets back and maybe we can both go over there on holiday. I look out of the window, where the rain is pattering down. 'Bit of sunshine for a change, eh? And maybe I'll finally get to see if Swansea Bay really is better than the Bay of Naples, or if you've just been bullshitting me all these years.'

She stiffens, but then the tears stop and she smiles. 'Dominic Vicari, what have I told you about swearing?'

'Sorry, Mam.'

'And in front of my friends, and all.'

'Sorry.'

It's done the trick, at least for now, as she smiles and chatters away again. But I'm not convinced there's ever going to be a trip to Italy for us.

Chapter 16

On another day, I might have stopped to enjoy an ice cream in the early afternoon sun but I had, I thought, pushed Fede's goodwill to the limit. That was something that could wait for the journey back. And so I made my way over the Ponte Corte Novello, briefly pausing at the halfway point in order to stare upwards at the tower of San Martino Vescovo, and trying to reassure myself that, in the time needed for me to have lunch, it hadn't leaned over just a little further.

I walked down the *fondamenta* towards the furthest point of the island with its view out across the lagoon to where San Francesco del Deserto – identifiable by its wall of cypress trees and the jutting bell tower – lay in the distance.

In normal times, the jetty would be crowded with hundreds of tourists on day excursions to look at the pretty houses, and perhaps buy some lace for those back home. It hadn't always been that way. When I had first arrived in the city Burano had seemed a little oasis away from the hustle and bustle of the *centro storico* in the summer months and, on the rare occasions I'd had to come out, lonely and almost isolated in the winter. And now, for a few months at least, it had been returned to the locals again.

I shielded my eyes and gazed across the lagoon to the island, and then along the quayside in search of a friendly boatman to take me there.

'Hey, sir.' The voice came from a middle-aged man, bare-chested, curly haired and bronzed with the sun, stretched out on the prow of a boat as he smoked away with one hand and texted with the other. 'Hey, mister. You need a lift? Punta Sabbioni, Treporti? Anywhere. Murano, you go and buy some glass maybe? I've got a friend there, he'll do you a good deal. No rubbish for the tourists, no Chinese glass, just the good stuff.' His patter was well-rehearsed, machine-gun like, but with an edge of desperation.

'Thanks. How about San Francesco?'

He shook his head. 'You don't want to go there. Murano is better. Or maybe you like fishing? I can arrange that for you as well if you like. Have you bought any lace? You need to buy some lace to take home. My mother makes it. Good Buranese lace, not Chinese. I promise.'

'That's kind, but I really need to get to San Francesco.'

'You don't need to go to San Francesco. Monasteries and monks, all that stuff. That's not your thing, I can tell.'

I smiled back at him. 'Well, I can't believe I'm saying this but, at the moment, monasteries and monks are very much my thing.'

'Okay. I'll do you a good deal. First, we go and see my mother and her lace. And then I'll take you to San Francesco. Deal?' He held out his hand.

I looked into his eyes and saw the desperation of a man who had hardly worked in months. And for a moment I thought, why not? I'd go and see his mum and I'd buy some overpriced lace for Federica to admire and Gramsci to destroy. And then I'd go to San Francesco having been modestly ripped off but having done a good thing.

'Hey mister.' The voice came from further down the quay. 'I can take you out to San Francesco.'

'You can? Straight there, I mean.'

He nodded. 'Sure. Come on, jump in.'

I looked back at the curly-haired man. 'Sorry.'

He waved his hands. 'No. Wait a minute, wait a minute.' He turned to the other. 'I was there first. He's my fare.'

'You want to take him to buy lace and some shit, and then take him out to the island. What you going to charge him? One hundred? Two hundred? After you've sold him some lace, maybe?'

'He's my fare, you shit. And I work this route every day.'

'He's not your fare. And how are you going to get paid for this? In cash, yes? You going to give him a receipt, yeah? You know, for the tax people?'

I held up my hands. 'Look. Look. Both of you. I don't want anyone to get into a fight about this. But all I want to do is go out to the island. I'm, well, I suppose you'd say I'm on a pilgrimage. And so I don't need to go fishing or look at some lace.' I shook my head. 'I'm sorry. I really am.'

For a terrible moment, I thought I saw his eyes filling with tears. Then he spat upon the ground. '*Cazzo*,' he swore, and stalked away.

The other boatman shrugged. 'Still want to go to San Francesco?'

'I do.'

A smile broke across his face. 'Then hop on, my friend.

Hop on.' He stretched out a hand to help me on board, and started the engine. He wore a white baseball cap, turned back to front, in order to keep the sun off what I assumed was his bald head. He had a salt and pepper beard, and like the other boatman, was bronzed in a way that suggested much of his time was spent outdoors.

'You from London?'

'San Marco,' I replied.

'No, seriously.'

'I'm being serious. That's where I live.'

'Ah, I'm sorry. Didn't mean to be rude.'

'No problems. Everybody says that.'

'Must have been difficult for you. These past few months. Not being able to travel.'

'It's been, well, okay,' I said.

'I mean, you've still got family there, right?'

'I've got an ex-wife.'

'They're the best ones.' His expression darkened. 'Sorry, my friend. I shouldn't have said that. Just me being silly. Hell, I've never even been married.'

'Don't worry about it.'

'I was in London. Just once.'

'You have a good time?'

He shook his head. 'Too many people. I mean, people say there's too many people in Venice and there are. But London's got *way* too many people. And besides, I missed all this.' He swept his arm in a half-circle, illustrating the expanse of the lagoon.

'Yeah. I can imagine.'

'It's still quiet, you know? Compared to normal, that is.

Sometimes I can just lie on that boat all day, waiting for someone, anyone to turn up. But that's okay.' He laughed. 'Just about, anyway.'

'Listen – sorry, I don't know your name—'

'Bepi. Bepi Dei Rossi. Good *Buranese* name.'

'Buranese?' I tried not to sound surprised. 'Sorry, I couldn't place your accent.'

He looked cross for a moment and I cursed myself for having committed the cardinal sin of accusing a Venetian of sounding insufficiently Venetian. Then he smiled. 'Moved around a lot, I have. Working with *stranieri* on yachts all over the world. That's taken the edge off it.' He tapped his chest. 'Good money it was too. Better than here. But this is home. *Bepi la barca*, that's what I am. You need a boat out anywhere, you just call Bepi the Boat. Remind me to give you a card.'

'Do you get that a lot?' I nodded back in the direction of Burano. 'You know. What just happened back there.'

He sighed and shook his head. 'It's not his fault. It's not anyone's fault. Nobody with a tourist boat has been able to work for months. And now we can, but there aren't enough of them. And so, everyone's just on edge, you understand?'

'I do. Must be tough.' He nodded. It was time to get down to business. 'Bepi, this might be a long shot, but do you remember taking any other Brits out to the island in the last couple of weeks?'

He shook his head. 'Hardly any *stranieri* at the moment. If I'd met another Brit, I'd have remembered.'

'You'd have remembered this one. You probably know about him. The one who fell from the *campanile.*'

He whistled. 'Him?'

'That's right. Do you think any of the other boatmen might know about him?'

He removed his baseball cap and scratched his head. 'It's possible. Any reason you're interested? Are you an undercover cop, or with Interpol or something?'

'No. I'm the British Honorary Consul.'

He whistled. 'That sounds almost as good.'

'It's all glamour, Bepi, it really is.'

'So, what's your interest in this guy?'

'I'm the consul. I'm in charge of getting him home to his loved ones.'

'And there's a problem with that?'

'I can't find any relatives. That's the problem. I think he was over here in Italy looking for a long-lost brother.'

Bepi frowned. 'And, what, his brother's a monk or something?'

'I don't know. I'm just trying to a find a link. Any link as to where he might be. So, as I said, if you get the chance to ask any of the other boatmen who might have picked him up – well, I'd appreciate it.'

He grinned. 'Does this mean I'm working for the British government now? Like a kind of 007?'

'I guess it does, Bepi. Oh, mind the crabs.'

'*Vafancul*.' Bepi swore under his breath. 'I keep forgetting about those things. One day I'll write my boat off, I swear.' He throttled back as we approached the jetty, tied up the boat, and gave me a hand up.

'You got a business card or anything, my friend?'

'Sure.'

'*Nathan Sutherland, Honorary British Consul*.' He whistled.

'So you really are working for Her Majesty.'

'I suppose I am, Bepi.'

He tucked the card into his back pocket. 'Okay. I'll ask around. Can't promise anything, but I'll do what I can.' Then he frowned. 'Hey, nobody's going to shoot me or anything, are they? I don't want to be found floating face down in the lagoon or anything tomorrow morning.'

'I think it's unlikely, Bepi.' I tapped my nose. 'But in the service of Her Majesty, one needs to be prepared for everything.'

'I'll be careful.' He grinned. 'This is so cool, though. Here, take one of my cards. You need a lift, you call Bepi the Boat.'

'I will, Bepi. After all, we're partners now.' I took the card, one of those cheap ones that look like they've been printed from a machine in a service station. He gave me a fist bump, and both of us looked a little awkward at the physical contact. 'I'll see you around, yeah?'

I turned to make my way towards the monastery, when a little cough came from behind me. Bepi was standing in the boat, palm outstretched.

'Hey, my friend. Even 007 needs to pay the rent you know?'

I grinned, and reached for my wallet.

Chapter 17

COVID took Mam before the cancer did.

I don't know whether I should feel grateful for that or not. Thinking about it makes me guilty, and so I try not to think about it.

I hear the rustle of envelopes dropping through the letter box. Bills, bills, more bills. There's a limit to what a private investigator can do online and the business, day by day, week by week, is slowly going to crap.

I lay the envelopes out on the kitchen table, lining them up in order of how threatening they look. There are a couple for Mam, which means I'll have to write some difficult replies later today. But there have been a lot of these, and I have something of a pattern to follow by now.

Still nothing from Danny.

I've written to him at every address I could think of. The appeal in the Evening Post came to nothing. The consulate say they can do nothing. So, what kind of private eye am I?

Ah, Danny. You don't know what it's been like the past six months. Since Mam's diagnosis, I don't think a day has gone by without your name being mentioned. You've been ever-present despite not actually being here.

And it's pissed me off.

Every day, it's been, 'Any news from Danny? Do you think he's all right? Are you sure you wrote to the right address?' And, of course, and this never, ever bloody stops, 'I just want to see him one last time, you know?'

Oh, don't I just know it by now? Part of me wants to scream, 'I'm here Mam. I've always been here. I never ran off to Italy to do some dodgy job with my dad. I stayed here, with my crappy little job, to take care of you. So once, just once, could we hear just a bit less about bloody Danny and maybe a little more about good old Dom, and what a great son he's been.'

Of course, I say none of that. I smile, and I say I'll keep trying. 'He'll be here, Mam. Just you wait and see.'

But, of course, he isn't. And then, one day, Mam is taken away to hospital and I look at her for one last time and she looks old, and frail and confused. And worse, there's a look of terror in her eyes. Because she's read the papers, and she's afraid of dying alone.

I tell her that's not going to happen. Danny will be back, I tell her. Travel is a bit difficult, but you know my little brother, he'll always find a way. And I'll be there, as often as I can be. You won't be alone. Anyway, you'll probably be back home in a few days.

None of these things, of course, are true. I know it. And I fear she does as well.

The radio is playing terrible 1990s pop music, but even that seems more bearable than the silence. I fiddle with the dial, spinning it this way and that until I find something I vaguely recognise.

I tear open one of the envelopes addressed to mam.

'Dear Catrin,

I'm sorry to hear you've been so unwell, and that it's taken me so long to write.'

I read on. It's the usual thing. Thoughts and prayers. And then, the final gut punch.

'I know you miss your lovely boy and do hope he'll be home soon, and that that will be a comfort to you.'

Well, now.

I read the letter again. Nope, only one lovely boy is mentioned and it sure as hell ain't me.

The radio must be tuned to a classics station, 1970s or something like that, because this is a song I know.

'Carry On Wayward Son'.

I walk over to the radio, and stare down at it. And then I scream, sweeping it from the table and sending it smashing to the floor.

Silence. Deadly, terribly silence.

And I start to laugh. Just a little chuckle at first, and then howls that become great choking sobs. I slump into a chair, gasping for air.

Panic attack.

I haven't had one of these since I was a kid.

You know what to do, Dom.

I put my head between my knees, and clamp my eyes shut. I count to five. I breathe in, slowly, deeply. And out. And repeat. Until my head clears. Until the bad stuff goes away.

I make my way, a little unsteadily, upstairs to my bedroom. My picture of Humphrey Bogart is still on the wall. So is Danny's poster of Debbie Harry.

Bogie, I think, would have known what to do. But I'm no

Philip Marlowe or Sam Spade. I'm the guy you call if you think your husband is shagging someone else. I hang around hotels and bars, sitting for hours in my car, waiting to take that photo that you really, really don't want to see. Because doing my job properly involves you paying me for ruining your life. That's the way it works.

But this once, maybe just this once, I can get to be Bogart.

It's too late for you now, Mam. But I swear to you, I am going to find Danny.

Chapter 18

I'd never spent the night in a cell before but this, it seemed, was going to be part of the rich tapestry of new experiences.

The room looked similar to Dominic Vicari's. A crucifix hung on the bare, whitewashed walls, with an icon of St Francis on the bedside table. Otherwise the only furniture was a small wardrobe and a single bed.

Fra Vincenzo smiled at me. 'A simple room, but comfortable enough I hope?'

'It'll be fine,' I said. 'I've stayed in worse hotels.'

'I can at least guarantee that it will be quiet. You're our only resident in this wing of the monastery. Now, I'm afraid there's no air conditioning. If you do find it unbearably hot, we can probably find you a fan. Oh, and did you remember to bring mosquito repellent?'

I slapped my forehead. 'Stupid of me. I forgot.'

'Don't worry. Again, I'm sure we can find you some. Given the time of the year, all the greenery and our proximity to the lagoon – well, I'm afraid they are rather prominent and can stir even the best of us to the most ungodly thoughts. I wonder what dear old Francis made of them when he first arrived?'

'Perhaps he just told them to stop?'

He laughed. 'Perhaps so. Now, I'm afraid there's no television, of course.'

'That might do me good.'

'We do have plenty of reading material, however. Nearly all of it of a religious nature, but I think we have a copy of *The Da Vinci Code* which Fra Ezekiel bought at the airport the last time he returned from the Philippines. Have you read it?'

'I'm afraid not.'

'Well, you'd be welcome to borrow it. Although I'd better warn you that Ezekiel marked it up. There are quite a lot of scribblings of *No!* and *Wouldn't happen!* throughout. I think he took it all a bit too seriously.'

'Well, I'll keep that in mind. But I'm only here for a few days, I doubt I'll have time to get bored.'

'I'm sure you won't. I'm sorry I won't be here from tomorrow morning, Mr Sutherland. It would have been good to talk more. You seem to have a most interesting career.'

'Well, I'm not so sure about that. But, who knows, perhaps I'll still be here when you get back?'

'Perhaps you'll like the experience so much you'll decide to stay? We could always find space for you.'

I smiled. 'That would lead to an awkward conversation with my wife.'

'I can imagine.' He looked at his watch. 'Well, I'll give you time to settle in. There'll be prayers at six o'clock, followed by dinner.' He smiled again. 'We do have those guests who ask if they can go straight to dinner. I have to tell them that prayers are non-negotiable.'

'Ah. I did wonder.'

'It would, after all, seem strange to come on retreat and not take part. If silence and contemplation is all that's needed, well, one could do that quite comfortably at home simply by turning the television off. No?'

'I understand. Well, I think I'll just unpack and then see you at six.'

'Excellent. I wish you a very comfortable and very profitable stay, Mr Sutherland.'

'Oh, just one thing.'

'Yes.'

I mimed the action of locking and unlocking a door. 'I don't seem to have a key.'

He smiled. 'Nobody does. The cells are all unlocked.'

'What?'

'Important to build trust, I feel.'

'Yes, but what if somebody wants to, you know, *steal* stuff?'

'Mr Sutherland, if one wishes to commit a robbery I suspect there are easier ways than getting a boat out to a remote island in the lagoon and pretending to be on a pilgrimage. Just waiting for unsuspecting tourists with open handbags on a crowded *vaporetto* pontoon would be easier, surely?'

'Fair point. But don't you have valuable works of art? Things like that?'

'Oh, we have the usual collection of old vestments and altar cloths, and some books that might be of interest to a specialist collector. But there are no great Bellinis or Titians on our walls, waiting for an unscrupulous visitor.'

'Well, I'm glad to hear that. If you see what I mean.'

He smiled and patted me on the shoulder. 'I'll see you at

Evening Prayer then, Mr Sutherland. Oh, one more thing. If I could just have your ID card?'

This was a common request in Italian hotels, and monasteries, I supposed, were also in the hospitality industry. I handed it over.

'Thank you. Maria will take the details and give it back to you later, at dinner.'

I unpacked my clothes, and folded them away. Then I photographed my room, and sent it to Fede with a caption: 'My cell. Home for the next few days xx'

There was but one window in the room, looking out into the cloister. The cloister where Dominic Vicari had died. I looked up at the *campanile*, trying to reconstruct the events of that night. How long would it have taken to fall? Would he have been aware of it? Leaning over just a little too far, a moment of imbalance and then – I shuddered, and turned away from the window.

It was time for prayers.

Chapter 19

Light streamed in from the high windows in the chapel of San Francesco, dust motes dancing in the beams, and illuminating the two points of decoration in the bare, brick-lined space: a simple, silver cross above the altar, on which rested an icon of the Virgin Mary.

The chapel was blessedly cool, and smelled of incense, beeswax and a thousand years of prayer. At the grander churches of Venice – at St Mark's, at the Frari, at the Pietà – the sounds of the madding crowds outside never ceased to permeate the ancient stone. But here the silence was almost tangible.

I took a seat in one of the rear pews, and closed my eyes, breathing deeply. I might, perhaps, once have had the words for prayer in me. I didn't know if I had them any longer. But I was, at least, prepared to give them a go.

'You're very keen, getting here so early.' The voice came from behind, making me start and drawing a blasphemous *Jesus* from me.

The speaker was a man in early middle-age, wiry and tanned, with a shaven head. He gave a little smile. 'I'd watch the cursing if I were you. Some of the brothers get very cross at that sort of thing.'

'No offence meant. It was just a bit of a shock, that's all.'

'Well, I apologise if I startled you.'

I got to my feet. 'Sorry, have I taken your seat?'

He looked at me, and then at the rows of empty pews. 'No. I'm sure we'll all manage to squeeze in somehow.'

'It's my first day. I didn't want to be late.' I extended my hand, and then remembered that we weren't quite back to that sort of thing just yet. 'My name's Nathan. Nathan Sutherland.'

'Carlo Lucarini.' He gave a little bow of his head. '*Piacere.*'

'And what brings you here, *signor* Lucarini?'

He shrugged. 'Long story.'

'We're on retreat. Time's one thing we've got a lot of.'

He nodded. 'After prayers, maybe.' He made a little chatterbox motion with his right hand. 'I was told off for talking last night. I don't want to get in trouble again. Here we go.'

Five friars processed into the chapel. Fra Vincenzo, I recognised. Behind him came an older man with a greying beard. Then came a younger pair, possibly from South East Asia? I couldn't be completely sure. And, finally, a much older man, hobbling up the aisle with some difficulty.

A man in a light, crumpled summer suit slipped in behind them. He crossed himself, then nodded at Lucarini and gave me a quizzical look. He genuflected, awkwardly, then took a pew to himself on the opposite side of the chapel, and bent his head in prayer.

'One of our other pilgrims,' whispered Lucarini. 'Very keen on exploring his spiritual side. Well, certain types of spirits anyway.'

The other man's eyes snapped open, and he turned to glare at us, having evidently overheard.

Lucarini smiled, and put a finger to his lips. 'I believe it's time to begin.'

Fra Vincenzo spread his arms open in welcome.

O Dio, vieni a salvarmi
Signore, vieni presto in mio aiuto
Gloria al Padre e al Figlio
e allo Spirito Santo.
Come era nel principio, e ora e sempre
nei secoli dei secoli.

I stumbled over the words as best I could, dredging them up from memory, as Fra Vincenzo and his band of brothers repeated, once again, the words that had been worn smooth by time long before St Francis had arrived on this tiny island, eight hundred years ago. I saw a movement out of the corner of my eye, and looked over to see the man on the opposite pew bent over, his knuckles white as he clenched them together, praying fervently. I had no idea of his reasons for being here but, evidently, they were serious.

Lucarini caught my eye and smiled.

'Faith is a wonderful thing,' he whispered.

Chapter 20

Lucarini smoked away, quietly and steadily, in front of the entrance to the monastery. I went over to join him. The cigarette smoke would, I hoped, do something to keep the mosquitoes away.

He offered me the packet. I shook my head. 'Love to. But I've given up.'

He nodded. 'Well done. Don't worry, I won't tempt you again.'

'*Get thee behind me, Satan?*' I said.

'If you like. I suppose we're in the right place for that. So, what do you think of it so far?' He inclined his head back towards the monastery.

'I'm thinking it's not how I'd usually spend a Saturday night.'

He nodded. 'I can imagine.' He paused. 'Is that all, though?'

'I don't understand?'

'I mean have you found anything yet?'

I tried, and failed, to read the expression on his face. 'I'm afraid I'm still not following you.'

'You're on retreat. Which means, I imagine, that you're looking for something.' He smiled. 'That's what I meant.'

'Oh, I see.' I shook my head. 'I don't know. At least, I don't think so.'

'Well, you've only been here a couple of hours. Give it a few days, a few weeks and those twenty-first-century sharp edges will start to wear down.' He dragged on the cigarette. 'At least, that's what I'm hoping.'

'A few weeks? I was hoping to be back home by Tuesday.'

'As soon as that? You've come a very long way for a very short visit.'

I shrugged. 'It's not so bad. Not much more than an hour from San Marco.'

'Coming to Venice in the middle of a pandemic though. That must have taken some doing.'

'Ah, now I understand. No, it's not like that. I live in Venice.'

'Really? Full time?'

'Yes.'

'I'm impressed. So many of your countrymen seem to treat Italy as a home away from home. Somewhere for the weekend. No offence.'

I knew exactly what he meant, but felt annoyed anyway.

'So, what is it that you do?' he continued.

'I'm a—' I paused. The Honorary Consul thing would lead me into areas I didn't wish to go. Not yet. 'I'm a translator,' I continued.

'A translator?'

'Yes. Italian to English, mainly.'

'And what do you translate?'

'Anything that comes along. Academic work. The occasional novel or film script.'

'Oh.' He nodded. 'Anything I might have seen?'

I shook my head. 'Nothing that ever got made.'

'Pity.'

'But if you've got a lawnmower or a microwave oven,' I tapped my chest, 'those English bits in the manual? All mine.'

He seemed less impressed than I'd hoped.

I looked at the sun, now low in the lagoon, sending the shadows of the cypress trees spilling across the lawn in front of us. 'Lovely, isn't it?'

He nodded and drew on his cigarette. 'It is.'

'You said it was a bit of a long story. About why you're here.'

'It is,' he repeated. 'But the short version is that I just felt the need to get away. Given the events of the past few months. I suppose many of us feel the same.' He dropped the stub of his cigarette to the gravel and ground it underfoot. 'Maria will clear it away later.' He caught the look in my eye and shrugged. 'It's part of her job.' He took out another and gave the packet a shake. 'I've left myself a bit low. Looks like I'll be needing to get the boat to Burano tomorrow.'

'I guess they haven't got a vending machine here?'

He shook his head. 'No. And I don't know if any of the brothers smoke. Even if they did, there's something in my upbringing which would stop me trying to beg cigarettes from a friar.'

'I haven't really met the brothers yet. What are they like?'

'Well, now. The main man is Fra Vincenzo, but I assume you know about him already.' I nodded. 'The older one with the beard is Fra Gregorio. I understand he'll be in charge whilst Vincenzo is on pilgrimage in Assisi, making sure we don't have too many late night parties, and keeping our minds on godly things.'

'A bit stern then?'

'Not known for his sense of humour, put it that way. I'm told he's very wise.'

'Oh yes? Or is it just that anybody in a habit with a beard is going to give off a touch of the Obi-Wan Kenobis?'

Lucarini smiled, and whooshed his cigarette through the air as he made a lightsaber sound. Fragments of ash glowed briefly in the air before falling to earth, as smoke wafted into my face. I tried not to inhale too deeply.

'The old one – the very old one – is Fra Raffaele. Now you might think he's been here since Francis himself was a boy, but in reality it's only been about five years. This'll be his last monastery, he's told me. Several times.'

'And what does he do?'

'He's too frail now to help out much in the gardens. And his English isn't very good, so they don't let him guide visitors around. He's writing a book on the history of the island. I don't think anyone's expecting it to be a best-seller, or anything, but he's very enthusiastic about it. Oh, and he's cataloguing the treasury. You'd better watch it, he's very keen to talk about that and before you know it, whoosh, that's half your day gone.'

'And do they have anything of interest?'

He scratched his head. 'I can't really remember. It all seems a bit specialist. Should have paid more attention, I suppose. Oh, and to finish off the friars, you'll have noticed the two younger ones. Ezekiel and Jeremiah. They're from the Philippines.'

'Blimey. What brought them over here?'

'Missionary work, they call it. They work with visiting school parties and the like. Their English is probably the best of all of them. They're brothers, I understand. In both senses.'

'I'm sorry?'

'They're brothers. And also brothers. It's a little joke.'

'Oh.'

'And that just leaves our other pilgrim friend. Bruno Pagan, his name is. Businessman from somewhere in the Veneto. He's a strange one. Keeps himself to himself. Never got much more than a grunt and a nod out of him.'

As if on cue, Bruno appeared and scowled at us. 'Dinner in five minutes,' he said, before turning his back on us and making his way inside.

Lucarini smiled. 'You see what I mean?'

'I do. But I suppose we're not necessarily here for conversation.' He nodded. 'I suppose,' I said, trying to keep my voice as light and casual as possible, 'that you'd have been here when the accident happened?'

'Mr Vicari?'

'Yes.'

'Must have been upsetting.'

'It was. But I didn't see anything. They'd covered him up long before I got there.'

'You never thought about going home afterwards?'

'Why? Nothing to be done now.'

'What was he like?'

He tapped a cigarette three times on the packet, and lit up again. By now I'd had enough of enjoying my old vice by proxy and stepped back, just a little. He saw the expression in my eyes, but merely smiled. 'Are you quite sure you're a translator and not a,' he paused, 'a *journalist*?'

'Just interested, that's all.'

'Well, I understand he was here for a bit of personal reflection. He joined us for prayers and for meals – all non-negotiable, as you know – but he wasn't here for long enough for us to get to know him.'

'You never really spoke to him?'

He smiled. 'No, Mr *Translator*. I never really spoke to him. There is no gossip to share, I'm afraid, beyond the fact I think he enjoyed a drink a little too much. But then, I know it's not uncommon among the British. Again, no offence meant.'

'You saw him drunk then?'

'A little unsteady on his feet, let's put it that way. That's what happened, I imagine. He took himself up to the top of the *campanile* in the early hours of the morning, and leaned out just a little bit too much in order to get a better view of that perfect sunrise. And then,' he dropped his cigarette to the ground, '*pfffft*.' He clapped his hands. 'And with that, I think we should go in for dinner. Wouldn't do to keep the brothers waiting, would it?'

Chapter 21

The refectory was stark, almost minimalist, all dark wood and white stone, and there was no escaping the fact that it had been designed for more than eight people.

Fra Vincenzo saw the expression on my face and smiled. 'I know what you're thinking. The atmosphere is a little chilly in here, isn't it?'

'Well, it's quite big, you'd have to say. Considering our number.'

'It was redesigned in the last century. There would have been more of us here then. And more pilgrims. The trouble with a space this size nowadays is that everything seems amplified, somehow. Footsteps, the clatter of knives and forks upon the table, semi-whispered conversations. It all serves to emphasise how few of us there are. But there are compensations.' He smiled, and gestured towards the painting of *The Last Supper* that hung upon the opposite wall. 'It's not by anybody particularly notable. Although perhaps Fra Raffaele might correct me on that. But neither is it without merit. It serves to remind us why we're all here. About the importance of breaking bread together in the presence of Christ. And do you know, there's one tiny detail that always makes me smile. Can you see it?'

I scanned the painting as best I could. It was dark with age, and Federica would undoubtedly have said that a basic restoration and removal of the original varnish would have done wonders for it. But try as I might, I was unable to find anything that might have brought a smile to my face.

Vincenzo smiled at me again. 'Look at the figure leaning on the breast of the Saviour. The Beloved Disciple.'

'Oh yes. It's John, isn't it?'

Vincenzo nodded. 'Most likely.'

'Leaning on the shoulder of Christ. It's kind of a motif in Last Suppers.'

'It is indeed. But what else do you see?'

I strained my eyes again. 'Well, it's a very sleepy Beloved Disciple in this one. He looks fast asleep.'

Vincenzo patted me on the back. 'That's right. But not quite the whole story. What do you see on the table in front of John?'

I looked yet again, and then laughed. Directly in front of the Disciple Whom Jesus Loved lay a wine goblet, lying on its side.

'Oh, I see. So he's not just tired. He's—'

'He's perhaps been enjoying the Saviour's hospitality a little too much. Yes.'

'I can't believe the artist got away with that. I'd have thought he'd have been, I don't know, burned at the stake or something.'

'We're the Franciscans. We don't really do that sort of thing. And certainly not by the seventeenth century, which is when the painting dates from. I think the artist was attempting one of two things here.'

'Which are?'

'Remember that Jesus gives his mother into the care of the Beloved Disciple. Perhaps the artist is trying to say that Jesus is aware of John's all too human frailty, but, nevertheless, is aware of all that is good, of what is best in him. As He does in all of us.'

'Uh-huh. And the other?'

Vincenzo grinned. 'The other possibility is, as we would say today, that the artist was massively trolling us.' We both laughed. 'Ah, here's Maria.' He got to his feet, and held his hands up for silence. 'Mr Sutherland, perhaps you'd like to say grace.'

Every face in the refectory turned to look at me. I looked back at Vincenzo, but he merely gave me an encouraging little smile. I pushed my chair back, the scraping of wood against stone breaking the silence, and opened my mouth to speak.

'Erm.'

There was an awkward silence. Fra Gregorio stroked his beard. Bruno Pagan reached for the jug in front of him, only for Lucarini to move it out of his reach. Vincenzo smiled encouragement again.

'Erm.'

Something more than 'Erm', I thought, was desperately needed.

'Erm. It's been difficult these past few months. For everyone. We've taken so much for granted for so long. We forgot about so much that was important. And so, whatever we believe, I think we can just give thanks for the simple pleasure of being able to sit down and eat together. I think I can say a very hearty Amen to that.'

I sat down, shaking, my cheeks burning. Vincenzo reached over and squeezed my hand.

'I knew you could do it,' he said.

Dinner was spaghetti with *sugo di pomodoro crudo*, a simple, fresh pasta sauce made with tomatoes from Sant'Erasmo. Meals on the island, I had come to understand, were likely to be tomato based. Maria, it seemed, regarded anything with a tomato in as a signature dish.

There was also a modest amount of white wine. Fra Vincenzo must have noticed the disappointment in my eyes, and he chuckled softly as he refilled my glass from his own.

'Better?'

'Much. I've only been here half a day and, I have to say, I'm getting fully on board with this whole "Christian Charity" thing.'

He laughed again. 'I think perhaps a week here and we'll be measuring you for a cassock. Now then, I think we have perhaps thirty minutes before night prayer. Shall we take a stroll around the grounds?'

'That'd be nice. Thank you.'

Lucarini and Pagan both looked at us as we walked from the refectory. Pagan reached over to take the wine jug from his companion, and topped his own glass up generously. Annoyance momentarily flashed across Lucarini's face. Pagan caught his expression, but merely shrugged.

Vincenzo and I walked out into the warmth of the evening. We stopped in the shadow of the cypress trees and looked across the lagoon to Burano, its gaily coloured houses and its crazily leaning *campanile*. The only sounds were of the lapping of the waves, and the distant buzz of an outboard motor.

'Lovely, isn't it?'

'It is. It must be strange living here as you do, but, yes, there's something so beautiful about it at the same time.'

'We're very lucky, I feel. Many of us – Franciscans, I mean – are doing tough jobs in inner cities. Sometimes even in war zones. And we – the five of us – have this beautiful island to call home. It still seems extraordinary to me, even after all these years.'

'Do you think you'll stay here?'

'I don't know. It isn't necessarily up to me. Sometimes the Minister General will decide we need to be moved on. Or sometimes, perhaps,' and here he cast his eyes heavenwards, '*He'll* make it known to us. You understand?'

'I'm not sure I do. Does it really work like that?'

He nodded. 'Oh yes. Absolutely. Now, I'm not asking you to believe that. All I'm asking you to do is believe that I believe it. And so, as to your question, I'm not sure how long I'll be here. This is our eight hundredth anniversary and so, when that's all over, I wonder if the powers that be will decide I should move elsewhere. Or if perhaps I'll decide that for myself.'

'What would you like to do?'

He spread his arms wide, indicating the splendour of the lagoon and the islands before us in the early moonlight. 'Oh, it would be difficult to leave. So difficult. But if it happens, then it would be God's will.' I nodded, noncommittally. 'And, again, I'm just asking you to believe that I'm sincere in that.'

'What about the others? The other friars, I mean.'

'I don't think Ezekiel and Jeremiah will be with us for

long. They're still relatively young. At some point, someone is going to think their ministry is best pursued somewhere more urban. Raffaele will be with us until the end of his days, I suspect. And Gregorio has barely been with us for a month, so he'll be here for some time to come, I imagine.'

'Only a month?'

'He was supposed to join us back in February. Travel restrictions made that impossible.'

'I see.'

He smiled at me. 'So, Mr Sutherland. It seems our little community made a big impression on you the other day.'

'Oh, it did.'

'So much so that you returned to us just a couple of days later.' He paused. 'Why are you here?'

The directness of his question caught me by surprise. 'Well, I suppose the usual reasons.'

'Finding yourself, building a relationship with God, a desire to find simplicity and sense and patterns in the face of a complex and chaotic world?'

'Well. Yes.'

He chuckled and patted me on the back. 'Oh, I've heard that so many times.' Then he turned to face me, and stared directly into my eyes. 'But be honest with me. Why are you *really* here?'

I could, I suppose, have tried to bluff it out. But there was something in his expression that told me that a lie would disappoint him. Wouldn't it just be simpler to tell him the truth?

I decided to be honest. 'Because there's something that doesn't seem right to me about the death of Dominic Vicari.'

He smiled. I had, it seemed, passed some kind of test.

'Well, of course. Vanni told me to expect you and told me why you'd be here.'

'*Vanni*? How long have you known?'

'He telephoned me about five minutes after you had an ice cream together.'

'The son of a—'

Vincenzo waved a finger. 'No swearing and no casual blasphemy please, Mr Sutherland. It's just his sense of humour. I think he quite liked the idea of you turning up and pretending to be a stranger in search of enlightenment.'

I opened my mouth to swear, saw the look in his eyes, and closed it again.

'So, the question is,' he continued, 'what are we going to do about it?'

'We?'

'Well by *we* I mean *you*. The others, apart from Maria, don't know who you are. I don't think it's such a terrible sin if I keep it from them, at least for the time being. And I'll be safely away to Assisi before you rise in the morning, so then it'll all be down to you.'

'Then you also think there isn't something right about this?'

'I don't know. I had thought it was just a tragic accident. It almost certainly is. But if it isn't, then we have to put it right.'

'And so who better to investigate than the British Honorary Consul?'

He smiled. 'Vanni tells me you have, shall we say, *form* for that sort of thing.'

'Blimey. Is there anything he didn't tell you about me?'

'He also said you have a charming wife and a horrible cat. I think that was about it.'

'Well, I guess those are the most important bits. But anyway, let's crack on. It's getting late, and we've got night prayer coming up.' I frowned. 'And that's a sentence I never thought I'd say. But if I'm losing you tomorrow, I need to find out as much as I can now. What else can you tell me about Dominic Vicari?'

'Oh, I could tell he wasn't a pilgrim. After all these years, one can just tell. At the same time, I was sure he wasn't a journalist or a writer. Again, after all these years, I can spot those at a distance. But there was something about him, though. I could tell he was a man who carried sadness with him.'

'Did he mention his brother? A man called Daniele Vicari?'

Vincenzo shook his head.

I sighed. 'Pity. So, what do you think he was doing here?'

'There was something strange he said. When he arrived. It slipped my mind the other day, but there was something about the way he said it. Almost as if it were some kind of private joke.'

He paused, and looked back at the monastery.

'He said he was looking for sanctuary.'

Chapter 22

I put aside Fra Ezekiel's copy of *The Da Vinci Code* with a sigh. His annotations were quite interesting but reading about a psychopathic murderous monk, I decided, would not be the best way of guaranteeing a good night's sleep. The only other paperback I'd been able to find had been a dog-eared copy of *The Name of the Rose*, and I wasn't sure that would help much either.

That left the Bible.

Come on, Nathan, you're in a monastery where St Francis himself trod the earth eight hundred years ago. What would he do, eh? He'd read a few improving passages of scripture, that's what.

I picked it up. Someone had marked a page with a Post-it note and underlined a passage.

'And I looked, and behold a pale horse: and his name that sat on him was Death, and Hell followed with him. And power was given unto them over the fourth part of the earth, to kill with sword, and with hunger, and with death, and with the beasts of the earth.'

I sighed, put it down again, and lay back on my bed. Light bedtime reading, evidently, was thin on the ground. I'd have an early night. After all, I'd need to be in tip-top condition for Morning Prayer at six o'clock. And I'd had a busy day. I was sure I'd sleep well. I sent a brief text to Fede. *Not sure monastic life is really for me. Love you xx*

A few minutes later, my phone plinged. *Gramsci and I have successful non-aggression pact. Love you too xx*

I smiled, and turned the light out, letting my eyes adjust to the darkness that was broken only by a thin strip of light that streamed in from the window. Then I lay my head back on the pillow, and closed my eyes.

However tired you may be there is something that will always – always – wake you up. And that is the sound of a mosquito buzzing.

The insistent *bzzzzzt* raised me to a half-awake, half-asleep daze. When I'd first arrived in Italy, the slightest sound of any mosquito activity was enough to have me leaping out of bed to arm myself with a can of toxic spray in one hand and a rolled-up newspaper in the other.

But then Gramsci had come to stay, and small, flying, buzzing things were his own personal version of Disneyland. Admittedly, a large cat hurling himself with deadly force from the top of the wardrobe in the hope of trapping his tiny nemesis was not much of an improvement but I appreciated he was, in his own way, trying to help.

In his absence, however, I'd have to deal with the problem myself. Wearily, with my eyes still closed, I raised my hand above the sheets and waved it around in the general direction of the buzzing. Then I snapped it open and shut, multiple times, in the hope of squashing it, Venus flytrap-style.

It seemed to have worked.

I sighed, contentedly, lowered my hand and pulled the sheets around me.

Bzzzzzt.

Again, I raised my hand. Again, I snapped randomly at the air. And, again, the room fell silent. The mosquito had wandered off, presumably in a state of either confusion or pity. Again, I snuggled back into the sheets.

Bzzzzzzt.

Damnation.

I half-raised myself from bed, rubbing my eyes and trying to shake the sleepiness from my head. I should have asked Fra Vincenzo if they had a plug-in repellent device. Or perhaps a fan would have helped?

The mosquito buzzed once more and, again, I snatched randomly at the air. If I was going to get any sleep tonight, I needed to deal with my unwelcome guest. Wandering the ancient corridors of the monastery in search of a can of insect spray, however, seemed like hard work and there was always the risk of running into the brothers and being invited to join in a hitherto unknown session of late night/early morning prayer.

The Da Vinci Code or the Bible as weapon of choice, then? The complete Word of God was the heavier of the two, yet there seemed something a little disrespectful about that. No, Dan Brown and I would deal with the problem together. I picked up the paperback and hoped that Fra Ezekiel would forgive me.

The mosquito was clinging to the wall above my headboard, biding its time and waiting for me to go back to sleep. I weighed the book in my hand, and prepared to strike.

And then a blade of light shone under my door, as I heard footsteps outside in the corridor. The sudden shock made me drop the book, and I cursed as the mosquito buzzed and flew away.

The footsteps stopped, and the light disappeared.

I checked the time. Ten minutes past three. A strange time for one of the brothers – or was it one of the others – to be wandering the corridors, but then perhaps one of them was also in search of a can of mosquito spray. I reached once more for *The Da Vinci Code*, sat on the edge of my bed, and waited for the buzzing to begin again.

And then I heard it. The sound of a heavy metal lock turning. The creaking of a door opening. And then, silence, broken only by the sound of heavy, choking sobs.

I felt the hairs rise on the back of my neck.

Fra Vincenzo had told me that mine was the only occupied cell in this wing.

Calm down, Nathan. Calm down. So, you're in an ancient monastery in the middle of the lagoon, where a man fell to his death only a few days ago and now you're hearing footsteps and crying from a cell which you know is unoccupied? There is no need, no need at all, to overreact.

Should I go and have a look? Or would that be inviting disaster, like the scene in *Nosferatu* where Max Schreck appears at the end of the corridor and Gustav von Wangenheim realises that there is no lock on his door?

My eyes darted to the door of my cell, and I was reminded that there was no key. I took a deep breath. I was not unarmed. I had a heavy copy of *The Da Vinci Code* and so was prepared for pretty much every eventuality.

Should I open the door?

If one of the brothers wanted to go and cry in an unoccupied cell, in their own monastery, then what concern was it of mine?

I sighed and hefted the paperback in my hand. Come on then, Dan, let's get this over with.

I pulled the door open, ever so slowly, just enough to be able to peek through. The crying stopped, save for a muffled final sob, and then there was silence. I heard the sound of the door being pulled shut and a key turning in the lock. I could see little more than a shadowy figure in the darkness at the end of the passageway. Then a thin beam of light clicked on, either from a phone or a small torch.

The figure drew closer as it made its way along the corridor. It was one of the brothers, robed, but with the cowl raised so that the face was in shadow. Was there the hint of a beard? I couldn't be sure. I pushed the door closed, just an inch or two further, drawing a slight but audible squeak from the ancient hinges.

Oh shit.

The figure stopped moving and swung the torch from left to right. My door was barely ajar. Perhaps they wouldn't notice? I held my breath but then, satisfied that there was nothing of concern, they continued down the corridor, around the corner, and were lost from sight.

I breathed out, very slowly, and moved to the window. The figure was standing in the shadow of the *campanile*. It gazed for a moment in the direction of my window. Then, pausing only to give a gentle bow of the head in the direction of the bell tower, it strode away into the darkness.

I went back to the door, and wedged a chair under the handle. Then I lay down on the bed, breathing deeply.

Bzzzzzt.

The sound came from just above my ear, and in a single motion I picked up *The Da Vinci Code* and slammed it against the wall.

The buzzing stopped and, in spite of myself, I smiled.

Chapter 23

'You look tired,' said Lucarini. 'Slept badly?'

I yawned. 'You could say that.'

'Let me guess. The retreat has roused you to great thoughts about your own mortality and the need for God in an uncertain universe?'

'Worse,' I said, scratching at the back of my neck. 'Bloody mosquito.'

Fra Gregorio glanced across the refectory table, a look of admonishment in his eyes at my use of a mild profanity.

'Sorry,' I said.

Lucarini got to his feet. 'Well, I'm going to head into Burano for the morning. Pick up cigarettes, things like that. Anything I can get you?'

'I could probably do with some reading material. Any chance you could get me a copy of *Prog Italia*?'

'You what?'

'Ah, never mind. That's probably a bit specialist. Perhaps just a copy of *L'Espresso* then?'

'Sure. I can do that. He turned to the monks. 'Anything you'd like me to pick up on Burano, gentlemen?'

Ezekiel spoke. 'A copy of *Famiglia Cristiana* would be good.'

Jeremiah laughed. 'That's a terrible magazine, Zeke.'

'It's good for my Italian. And the crossword's good. That's the only reason I buy it.'

'Sure, just like you buy *Playboy* for the articles.'

Gregorio's coffee cup rattled ominously. Raffaele merely looked confused.

'He's joking,' said Ezekiel. 'You know he's joking, right?'

'I'm absolutely joking,' said Jeremiah.

Gregorio stared at him, his face like thunder.

'So,' said Lucarini, 'that's a *L'Espresso*, a *Famiglia Cristiana* and some cigarettes for myself. Anything else?'

'You know, I could do with some cigarettes as well,' said Ezekiel. He turned to Gregorio. 'I'm allowed cigarettes, right?'

'It's a weakness of the spirit, Fra Ezekiel.'

'That's a no, then?'

Gregorio waved a hand at him. 'Do what you must. Just don't let me see it.'

Lucarini turned to Pagan. 'Anything for you, Bruno?'

He shook his head. He looked tired and red-eyed.

'Okay. Well, it's a lovely day. I'll see you all later. *Ciao a tutti.*' He passed behind Pagan. '*Ciao,* Bruno.' Then he bent over and patted him on the shoulder. 'Remember what I said, eh?'

The other man merely scowled.

I waited until the refectory had cleared, before I approached Fra Gregorio.

'They seem like fun,' I said, gesturing after the retreating figures of Ezekiel and Jeremiah.

He grimaced. 'Too much fun, perhaps.'

'Well, they're quite young.'

'They're young, but they're not children. They're here to become closer to Christ. Not to waste time and money on cigarettes and magazines.' He smiled, thinly. 'Even if he does only buy them for the crosswords. So, Mr Sutherland, what are your plans for the day?'

'I honestly hadn't thought.' I yawned, again. 'I didn't sleep well last night, but I can't just fritter the day away snoozing in a cell.' Actually, I thought to myself, that was precisely the sort of thing I *could* do; but the sooner I could get all this sorted out to everyone's satisfaction, the sooner I could go home again.

'I'm sorry to hear that. Nothing troubling you, I hope.'

'No, not at all. Just a wretched mosquito, that's all. I could have done with St Francis. He could have told it to go away.'

Gregorio did not return my smile. St Francis, evidently, was not a subject for humour.

'And there was something else,' I continued. 'Sometime in the early hours. Someone went into the cell at the end of my corridor and, well, I could hear him crying. That was a little disturbing – well, a little upsetting – to say the least.'

Gregorio frowned. 'That sounds to me more like a bad dream than anything else, Mr Sutherland.'

'No, I was wide awake. I'd been trying to deal with the mosquito. I heard footsteps, and the door scraping open, and then the sound of someone crying. I opened my door and saw one of the brothers – or somebody – walking past. And then, when I went to the window, I could see them staring up at the *campanile*.'

He smiled. 'That sounds positively Gothic. Which makes me think, more than ever, that we're talking about a dream here. And that door, I've been told, is to remain under lock and key.'

'Oh, right?'

'It was Mr Vicari's room. The last occupant, who sadly died during his stay with us. Fra Vincenzo entrusted the keys to me and,' he smiled again, 'I can assure you that I was not pacing the corridors of the monastery last night. Neither have I been known to sleepwalk.' He got to his feet. 'I wish you a pleasant morning, Mr Sutherland. Try not to dwell on morbid thoughts.'

I returned to my cell and sat on the edge of the bed wondering what to do and how I was going to pass my morning.

It could all have been a dream. It had all the qualities of a quasi-nightmare brought on by reading too much about murderous monks, together with a side order from the Book of Revelation.

I walked to the end of the passageway and tested the door. Locked. That, at least, had not been a dream. Then I returned to the cloister and looked up at the *campanile*.

Not that high. Really not that high. But high enough.

I heard raised voices from behind me and turned to see Gregorio and Maria half-hidden from view in the cloister and in animated conversation. Gregorio, I could see, had hold of Maria's shoulder and the young woman twisted in his grasp. I heard her raise her voice and swear at him, and he released her. Then, before I could move, he slapped her hard across the face.

Maria said nothing, but merely turned on her heels and walked away. Gregorio looked over at me, aware of my presence for the first time. He was about to turn and walk away, but I called after him.

'Hey.'

He froze for a moment, and then continued along his way.

'Fra Gregorio. A moment, please.'

He turned around, with a smile on his face that was almost angelic.

'Mr Sutherland? Can I help you?'

'You can. Oh, you can. What did I just see there?'

'I'm sorry?'

'Maria. Just what the hell do you think you were doing there?'

The smile vanished, but only for a moment. 'Silly girl. I'm very disappointed in her behaviour.'

'You're disappointed in *her* behaviour?'

'Yes.' The smile vanished and, this time, did not reappear. 'It doesn't concern you, Mr Sutherland but—'

'You just grabbed a young woman and slapped her across the face. Oh, I think this does concern me.'

He raised a hand. 'If you'll allow me to finish? Maria's behaviour has been disappointing of late. We're doing her family something of a favour by allowing her to work here in the hope it will help to bring a measure of stability to a life that was in danger of becoming chaotic.'

'And physically hurting her is going to help how exactly?'

'No need to be so melodramatic, Mr Sutherland. It's discipline. Nothing more. Something that's been lacking here for some time.'

'And what do you think Fra Vincenzo would have to say to that?'

The smile returned. 'Fra Vincenzo – and this is quite important – is not here.'

'Oh, I see. Now your boss is away for a couple of days, you're going to see how well the position suits you, is that it? What are you going to do next, start measuring for curtains in his office?'

'We don't have offices, Mr Sutherland. And you're being melodramatic again. More to the point, please do try and remember that you are a guest here.'

'I've never been more aware of that.'

'Good.' He paused, and looked up at the *campanile*. 'Remember what I said about morbid thoughts, Mr Sutherland.' Then he turned and walked away.

Chapter 24

'He did *what*?'

'I swear to God, Fede, I just saw him grab her by the shoulder and slap her.'

'Bastard.'

'That was my thought as well.'

'What are you going to do?'

'I've decided that going for a long walk on a small island might help me to calm down. And if I don't, then I suspect I might have to punch a monk in the face.'

'No, *caro*. Don't do that.'

'No?'

'No. I want to do it myself.' She sighed. 'So what you're saying is that monastic life is not working out as you expected?'

'Oh, I don't know. A locked room, mysterious late night visitors, and abusive monks. It's all very Gothic.'

'It sounds like it. How much longer do you think you'll be there?'

'I'm hoping just another two nights. But it's not getting any less complicated, put it that way.'

'What are the others like?'

'The Filipino brothers seem quite fun. The old guy

– Raffaele – I haven't spoken to yet. One of the other guests has either taken a vow of near-silence or he's simply a right grumpy bastard. Oh, and then there's a guy called Carlo Lucarini who I think is okay. I just haven't quite figured him out yet.'

'So, what are your plans for the day?'

'Not sure. Just ask around a bit about Vicari, I suppose. Oh, and try and avoid Fra Raffaele showing me the treasury. I understand he can go on a bit.'

'Franciscans are mendicants. What are they doing with a treasury?'

'I guess over eight hundred years you just kind of build one up by accident.' I sighed. 'Anyway, cheer me up. What have you got planned?'

'Still no sign of that scaffolding being finished, so I'm going over to the Lido. *Mamma* is still a little nervous of travelling all the way to Venice so I'll go and meet her halfway, and we'll have lunch together.'

'Oh, that's nice. And Gramsci?'

'He's not joining us, no.'

'You know what I mean. Is he missing me?'

She paused. 'No. I don't think so.'

'Ungrateful cat.'

'Tell me about it. Well, I guess I'll have to be off then, *tesoro*. I suppose if *mamma* and I walked right up to the tip of the Lido we might be able to see you. Although I suppose Sant'Erasmo might get in the way. We could try waving?'

'Aw, that's sweet.'

'To be honest though, we almost certainly won't.'

'Don't spoil it!'

'Sorry. Anyway, I suppose I'd better be going.'

'Miss you. Love you.'

'You too. Try not to get into any trouble though. Don't punch any monks in the face.'

'I won't.'

'Actually, no, scratch that. He sounds like a bastard. Punch him if you want.'

A stroll through the trees helped to calm me down a little. Then I sat down in their shade, as Francis himself might once have done, and looked out across the lagoon towards Mazzorbo and Burano. In the distance beyond I could see the *campanile* of Santa Maria Assunta on Torcello, happily no longer disfigured by the scaffolding that had covered it for years.

No sound except birdsong and the lapping of waves. It must have been like that in his day. No wonder he decided to stay a while. Perhaps it really was good for the soul.

I started to make my way back to the monastery, and stopped when I heard the trilling of birdsong replaced with the clucking of chickens.

Fra Raffaele, a bowl of feed in his hand, waved at me as a gaggle of hens clustered excitedly around him. '*Buongiorno, signor* Nathan.'

It was the first time he'd spoken to me.

'*Buongiorno,* Fra Raffaele.'

'Are you coming to help me? I'd be very grateful. At my age, making sure my girls have enough to eat isn't as easy as it once was.'

'Of course. I have to warn you, I haven't done this before.'

'There's not much to it, I promise you. Could you just make sure they've all got sufficient water? There's a tap fixed to the coop over there if you need it. And if you give the ground a gentle hose down, they'll like that.'

'Sure.'

'And when you've done that, fill the plant mister up and give their feet a little spray. Then they'll be your friends for life.'

'Seriously?'

'Of course. They feel the heat as much as we do.' He bent to pour a measure of the feed into what looked like a length of plastic piping that had been cut in half. 'Do you know, they tell me that you can buy machines now for feeding chickens? Can you imagine such a thing?'

'I suppose it would make things easier.'

'Easier, yes, but would it make things better? Bit by bit, we're losing all our connections with the natural world.' He straightened up and gave a little groan. 'Although, I have to say my back would thank me for it. But my day wouldn't be complete without visiting my girls.'

I gave the ground a gentle spray with the hose, and picked up the plant mister. As soon as I did so, a chorus of clucking went up from the hens and they swarmed towards me. Pavlov's chickens, I thought.

'Ladies, please, no need to push.'

I gave one of them a little mist around her feet and she shivered with delight, as the cacophony of clucks built in crescendo.

'One at a time, please.'

They pressed upon me, wings flapping, as I frantically

tried to mist as many as possible. And then, inevitably, my legs went from under me as I slipped on the wet grass and fell backwards.

'Bad girls! Bad girls! Leave Mr Sutherland alone.' Fra Raffaele gently pushed my tormentors aside, until I was lying there with a plump, reddish-gold hen upon my chest.

'Are you all right, Mr Sutherland?'

'I'm fine. Just feeling like I'm in the world's worst remake of *The Birds.*'

He chuckled, and there was something warm and comforting and, indeed, hen-like about it. '*Gli Uccelli.* I remember that. I saw it in the cinema when it first came out. I was very young then, of course.' He looked down at the hen on my chest. 'Erminia, you naughty girl. Come on, get off him.'

Erminia gave a contented little cluck, and snuggled herself down even more.

Fra Raffaele sighed, bent down, and gave her a poke. Erminia squawked, ruffled her feathers, but did at least deign to get off my chest.

I got to my feet. 'Thanks.'

'I'm sorry, I should have warned you. The girls do get terribly excited.' He nodded at Erminia. 'And you've got to watch her. She's trouble. She managed to smuggle herself on the boat to Burano once. Lucky not to find herself in someone's pot for dinner. Weren't you, you bad girl?'

Erminia clucked, and stalked off.

'You talk to them?'

'Of course. That's what Francis would have done. Do you have pets, Nathan?'

'I have a cat. Of sorts.'

'And you talk to him, I imagine?'

'Sort of. Mainly along the lines of *No* and *Stop it.*'

He laughed. 'They seem cut from the same cloth, then.' Then he sighed. 'There'll come a day when my tired old bones won't be up to carrying me out here to see my girls. And the thought of that saddens me.'

'You're out here every day?'

'Come rain or shine. It never fails to make me happy. It reminds me why Francis preached to the birds. His heart was filled with such joy, that he wanted to share the Good News with everyone and everything.

'Now, could I leave a basket with you? You'll probably find that some of the girls will have left us a little present in their nest boxes. And then just take them over to Maria, once you're finished. I'd do it myself, but I promised *signor* Lucarini that I'd sit down and prepare a few more notes for him on the history of the treasury.'

'Er, yes. Of course.'

'Thank you. I'll see you at midday prayer.'

He turned and made his way, a little stiffly, back towards the monastery, leaving me with a basket and a flock of excited chickens.

Chapter 25

I walked back to the monastery with a basket of eggs under my arm, and a heart full of bucolic good humour. The sky was blue, the air smelled of warm, damp grass and maybe, I thought, there might just be something in the whole idea of monasticism.

My good mood lasted until I reached the kitchen, and saw Maria with a cheek still flushed red from where Gregorio had slapped her.

I tapped on the door. 'Can I come in?'

She scowled at me, but nodded. She looked at the basket. 'Put them over there. Next to the sink. They'll need to be wiped down.'

'Can I help?'

She shrugged, and I took that as a yes.

I dampened a cloth and, one at a time, gently wiped the eggs clean.

'Finished?'

'I think so.'

'Okay, then.'

'Look,' I said, 'it's none of my business, but are you all right?'

'I'm all right. And it's none of your business. And your fault.'

'I don't understand?'

'Fra Gregorio said there'd been a complaint about noises late at night. The corridor where you sleep. He said that someone had been into the locked room at the end.'

'First of all, I didn't complain. I just wanted to know what was going on. Come on, it's a bit weird, hearing someone crying behind a locked door late at night. Anyway, why would that be your fault?'

'The key to that cell. It wasn't in its usual place. Fra Gregorio accused me of taking it. Or of giving it to someone else.'

'Why would you do that? I mean, you don't even stay here overnight.'

'I think there are still some things in there. The Englishman's possessions. Perhaps money, maybe? He said I'd been stealing.' She scowled. 'Some bullshit like that.'

'Look, Maria, has this happened before?'

'Who the fuck are you?' The words echoed around the kitchen and I fervently hoped that Gregorio was nowhere in the vicinity. 'Seriously, who the *fuck* are you? My social worker?'

'I'm just trying to help.'

'My life is full of middle-aged men trying to help. My dad. Fra Vincenzo. Fra Gregorio. And now you.'

'Look—'

'No. You look. I don't know what you've been told about me—'

'Something about—'

'Something about *drugs*.' She drew out the word and

wiggled her hands as if to indicate just how scary that was. 'I sold a little weed around town. That's all. And Dad found out and now – because he can't actually send me to a nunnery – I'm spending the summer here cooking for a bunch of monks and,' she rubbed her cheek, 'getting slapped by that arsehole Gregorio for the privilege.'

'I'm sorry.'

'Yeah. Me too.'

'And I can't help at all?'

'You can help by backing the fuck off. And next time you think you hear noises in the night, don't go blabbing to Gregorio.'

Another *sorry*, I thought, would have been both redundant and unwelcome. I merely nodded, and left her to the cooking. It hadn't taken much for my good humour to melt away.

The chickens, I thought, would help. I'd go back and give their feet another misting and it would all be very jolly, and it would help me to clear my head.

They seemed pleased to see me. So much so that I wondered if I should introduce them to Gramsci, in the hope they'd set a good example. I even found a couple of extra eggs that had been laid in the meantime.

I thought about taking them back to Maria, but the idea of another difficult conversation did not appeal. I still had another hour or two before midday prayer. I'd go for a stroll around the island, maybe sit down under a tree, and have a proper think about just what I was going to do next. Or, more likely and given my lack of sleep, merely have a quick snooze in the shade.

The island was tiny, and didn't take long to circumnavigate, although one area was little more than a salt marsh, like many of the tiny semi-islands that rose out of the lagoon in this area.

I sat down on the edge of the shallow perimeter wall and, rather bravely I thought, swung my legs over the side. I perched there, shielding my eyes, and tried to triangulate. Straight ahead of me, beyond a tiny patch of salt marsh, lay Mazzorbo, and, to its left Burano.

Behind me lay Venice's orchard, the garden island of Sant'Erasmo which, from here at least, was hidden by the tree line. To my right, again beyond the salt marsh, lay the tiny private island of Forte Crevan, where the owner – an Italian politician – had lost his life in a helicopter accident some years previously. It was now for sale, with offers invited in the region of nine million euros. I tried to calculate how much translation work that would take, but then had to concede there probably weren't that many lawnmower manuals in the world.

To my left lay San Giacomo in Paludo, or, less romantically in English, *St James in the Marsh*. Or was I mistaken? The island looked a little too small, a little too irregular, to be that but, much as I racked my brains, I couldn't think what else it could be. A shame I hadn't thought to bring binoculars.

There are well over one hundred islands in the Venetian lagoon and I had to admit I would be hard pressed to locate the great majority of them on a map. *Zio* Giacomo, I knew, would be appalled by this. But there would be maps and charts at the monastery. I should make use of my time here to become at least slightly better informed on the city where I had spent well over a decade.

I swung my legs back over the wall. Midday prayers were fast approaching, which would be led by Fra Gregorio, who I had recently had a stand-up row with. This would be followed by lunch, prepared and served by Maria, with whom I had also had a stand-up row. Perhaps solitary monastic life would be better suited to me?

I had yet to speak with the fun-loving Filipino brothers. That was a project for this afternoon. And that only left Bruno Pagan, but he didn't seem to be the sort of person with whom one could enjoy an idle chat over lunch. Ah well, it would need to be done. Once I'd spoken to everyone, I could go back to Vanni and tell him – what? A tale of mysterious monks, and locked rooms? I shook my head. Whatever Gregorio had said, it had been no dream. I was sure of that. There was something here that was not quite right. My accidental pilgrimage would need to continue for a little while yet.

A clucking came from around my feet, and I looked down. 'Erminia?'

She gave her wings a little flap and puffed out her chest.

'Are you supposed to be here? You're a long way from your home.'

She clucked some more and then, her work seemingly done, wandered off in the diametrically opposite direction to the chicken run.

'Look, I'm really not sure you should be out?' Had I left it open? 'Oh, are you escaping again, is that what this is?' I bent down to pick her up, but she pecked at me and I drew my hand back. Then she turned around and trotted off.

I sighed. When Fra Raffaele turned up for duty tomorrow,

I really wanted him to find as many chickens as he'd left me with me. I set off in pursuit.

On the one hand, Erminia would almost certainly be fine. It was a small island with no natural predators. On the other hand, what if she tried smuggling herself on board the next boat to Burano again? Or could chickens actually swim? What if she tried to strike out for the mainland on her own?

Chickens, I was discovering, could run surprisingly fast. I pursued Erminia round the side of the monastery, nearly running into the Filipino brothers.

'Morning, Mr Sutherland.'

'Everything okay?'

I gave them a wave. 'Yes. Don't mind me. I'm just chasing a chicken.'

Small and agile is always going to best middle-aged and clumsy, and Erminia was capable of weaving through the cypress trees in a way that I wasn't. However, she finally ran out of island and had to stop when she reached the point of the patch of scrubland that faced on to the salt marshes, perhaps one hundred metres away. She put her head to one side, as if calculating if this was feasible swimming distance; then clucked, and turned to face me.

I wiped the sweat from my face. 'You're a big chicken, Erminia, but you're out of shape.'

She clucked again, as if to suggest that the same could be said about me.

'Come on. Let's get you back to the chicken run. Because otherwise I'm taking you back to Maria, who – I can tell you – is in a mean mood and might feel like varying the menu away from tomatoes.' I paused. 'Hey, look at me, I'm talking to a chicken. Francis would be proud of me.'

Erminia stepped to the left. And so I stepped to the right. She stepped to the right. And I stepped to the left.

I wondered if we'd be stuck in this particular version of the Time Warp for the rest of the day, but she seemed to have had enough of the game by now, and so ruffled her feathers and sat down.

'Good girl,' I said. I moved forward, ever so slowly, hands outstretched in a way that suggested *I am not going to attempt to grab you* whilst clearly meaning *I am going to attempt to grab you*; when something caught my eye, just on the edge of the waterline.

A chunky black object. I looked closer. A watch? No, a smartwatch?

There was a faded logo on the strap that I couldn't quite make out. The face was heavily scratched, but the LCD display was just about legible. The data onscreen was unintelligible to me, save for three words. *Bar. Depth. Nitrogen.*

Neither a watch nor a smartwatch, then, but a dive watch. And Marco on the police launch had told me he'd seen a diver in the water on the way back from the island. A part of the lagoon where diving was forbidden, for obvious safety reasons. Strange. I wiped it clean with a handkerchief and tucked it away in a pocket.

I picked up an uncomplaining Erminia, and stroked her feathers as I walked back towards the chicken run. It would soon be time for midday prayer. Questions were mounting up, and I wondered if the Almighty would be in the mood to answer them.

Chapter 26

'We're disappointed, Maria,' called Fra Ezekiel. 'We'd been expecting a chicken casserole.'

Maria looked confused. And then a little pissed off.

Jeremiah jabbed his brother in the ribs, then looked over at me and grinned. 'Too fast for you, Mr Sutherland?' He made a little scurrying motion with two fingers, until Gregorio glowered across the table at him.

'What was all that about?' said Lucarini.

'Oh, just chicken issues. You know what they're like. Successful morning?'

'More than yours, by the sound of it.' He patted his pockets. 'Should keep me going for a couple of days. And I picked up that religious magazine for one of the Filipino brothers. Was it Zeke or Jeremiah? Can't remember. Oh, and I've got your *L'Espresso* for you, I'll bring it along later. Something to read covertly at Evening Prayer.'

'I'm not sure I'd risk that. I'm not in Fra Gregorio's good books.'

'I'm not sure if anyone is. If we're playing good monk, bad monk I think we can see which sides Vincenzo and Gregorio are lining up on.'

He checked his watch and sighed. 'Right, time for my afternoon chat with Fra Raffaele. Mustn't disappoint him. He needs a regular afternoon nap, I understand.'

I nodded. 'Oh, just one thing before you go?'

'Yes?'

I took the watch from my pocket. 'It's a long shot I know. But I was hoping to reunite this with its owner. Not yours by any chance, is it?'

He gave it the most cursory of glances and shook his head. 'I don't even know what that is. Some kind of smartwatch?'

'It's a diving watch, at a guess.'

'Can't be. Not round here. Probably washed up years ago.'

'Maybe so. Maybe so.'

'I need to head off. As I said, I don't want Raffaele falling asleep on me.'

'Catch you later.' Lucky old Raffaele, I thought. He seemed to get the fun jobs, such as looking after the chickens, and he got a little sleep in the afternoon as well. So far, he was the only one really selling the idea of monasticism to me.

'Mind if I join you?' I gave a little start. 'Sorry, did I give you a fright?'

It was Fra Ezekiel, with a packet of cigarettes in one hand and a lighter in the other.

He grinned. 'Fra Gregorio hates me smoking. But if I'm out here talking to you, he won't feel he can really do anything about it.'

'He seems like a bit of a hard taskmaster,' I said.

'Oh, he's hard work. He's a very clever man. Very wise. But would it kill him to smile every so often? This is our vocation. This is supposed to be something joyful. And all it seems to do is make him grumpy. If you said to him, *"Have you heard the Good News, brother?"*, he'd probably say, *"What's good about it?"'* He looked over his shoulder, and then quickly glanced heavenward. 'Sorry, I know I shouldn't be talking like this. But back home, we had to think how do we get young people involved, you know? How do we stop them thinking about religious life being something old and dull and fuddy-duddy and not something that concerns them? We ran food banks in Manila. Okay, that's important but it doesn't get the kids in. So, we also ran a basketball camp. We ran a surf and snorkelling school for kids from the slums. But people like Gregorio, for him it's all about the study and the theology. And that's fine, too.' He dragged on his cigarette. 'But Jeremiah and me, we kind of like to go out and get our hands dirty. You know what I mean?'

'I understand.' Then a thought struck me. 'Hang on, you said you ran a snorkelling school?'

'Well, only one day a week. It wasn't like our main job.'

I pulled out the watch. 'Is this yours, then?'

He looked at it and laughed. 'No way is that mine, brother.'

'No?'

'That's a Garmin Dive Computer. That's top of the range. Hey, can I take a look?'

'Sure.'

He turned it over in his hands. 'The strap's broken but it's still working. You could get a thousand euros for that, easy.' He laughed. 'And this might come as a shock, but the average Franciscan is not going around with a watch like that on his wrist.'

'Sorry. Just when you mentioned snorkelling I put two and two together and made five.'

'No worries. Hey, where did you find this?'

'On the eastern point of the island. That sort of scrubland area, looking over towards the salt marshes.'

'Hang on, you found it here? On San Francesco del Deserto?'

'Sure. Whilst I was taking part in my new favourite sport of Chase the Chicken.'

'I don't understand. Nobody should be diving around here. I didn't think it was allowed.'

I shrugged. 'I guess it could have been washed here from anywhere.'

'Maybe so. Whatever the reason, somebody, somewhere is missing an expensive watch.'

'I'll hand it in to the police when I get back.'

'Or try some of the dive websites. If somebody's lost that, as I said, they're going to want it back.' He stubbed out his cigarette. 'Good talking to you.'

'Likewise. Oh, there's just one more thing, Ezekiel.'

'Call me Zeke, please.'

'Zeke, then. Dominic Vicari.'

'Uh-huh.'

'You ever talk to him?'

He shrugged. 'Sure. A bit.'

'About his brother?'

Zeke looked confused. 'He has a brother?'

'He never mentioned him?'

'No.'

'What about his mother?'

'Never mentioned her either.' He noticed the expression on my face. 'Something wrong?'

'No. Just surprised that's all. Could I ask what you talked about?'

'Sure. It was nothing private. I was spending some time cataloguing the archive. It's not that there's so much of it, but it's all in a bit of a mess. Anyway, Mr Vicari wanted to know if we had any charts or maps of the lagoon.'

'Do you?'

He laughed. 'Do we ever? He was a bit disappointed though. He wanted the most recent, highly detailed map that we had. Ideally from the nineteen eighties.'

'And you don't?'

'Nothing more recent than 1694. As I said, he seemed a little disappointed.' He patted me on the back. 'Right, I've got things to do. Monk things to do. I'll catch you later, yeah?'

I smiled in return and watched him retreat into the monastery. Then I shook my head. Whatever Vicari had been doing here, he didn't seem to have been in search of his brother.

Erminia fussed and fretted around my feet, as I turned the watch over in my hands. Expensive, Ezekiel had said. Very well, then, I'd hand it in to the *Questura* the next time I was in the *centro storico*.

I wondered when that would be. I wasn't sure my visit was adding much of worth. Perhaps there really was no more to it than a lonely man who'd chosen to travel halfway across Europe in the middle of a pandemic in order to find – what had Vincenzo said? – 'sanctuary'. Was that so surprising? His mother, we knew, had recently died. And, given the events of recent months, who would blame him for trying to get in touch with his spiritual side instead of sitting at home alone and doom-scrolling through the apocalyptic headlines.

Yes, there had been the sound of weeping in a locked cell late at night but maybe, with a bit of effort, I could convince myself that had merely been a dream. Perhaps I could even convince Vanni of the same. If, indeed, he really needed to know about it at all?

I checked my watch. I could call up Bepi the Boat and get him to take me back to Burano. Then another ninety minutes and I could be on the Street of the Assassins, drinking Negronis and eating things on sticks in the company of my lovely wife, instead of waiting to see what magic Maria could weave with tomatoes.

Erminia clucked again.

'Now then, Ermy. If I were to ask Gramsci what to do, he'd tell me to come home immediately. Purely for reasons of self-preservation, you understand? He feels more secure if he knows there are two people with access to the biscuit cupboard around. But what would you do, eh?'

She clucked and had an experimental peck at my shoes.

'You'd like me to stay and sort this out? Well, I can understand that but, you see, I think that both you and Gramsci are coming at this from the same angle. Namely, will our decision increase the chances of us being fed? And so, dear Erminia, I'm afraid I'm going to have to say *arrivederci*.'

Cluck. Cluckcluckcluckcluckcluck.

'Oh, don't look at me like that.'

Cluck.

'It won't work, you know. My cat's tried that and he's an expert at this sort of thing. So if that doesn't work on me, don't think for a moment that—'

Cluck.

'All right. All right. We'll give it one more day, okay? Just one. But I'm expecting a lot of eggs. Deal?'

Cluck. She waddled off, happy that her work was done.

I turned back to the dive watch, but then saw Fra Gregorio approaching and – for reasons I couldn't quite explain to myself – dropped it into my pocket.

'Mr Sutherland?'

'Fra Gregorio.'

'I'm worried that we seem to have got off on the wrong foot. I thought perhaps I should apologise.'

'Thank you. Although I'm not sure it's me you should be apologising to.'

He looked gratifyingly shame-faced. 'Of course. I've spoken with Maria. I offered her a day off. That's by way of an apology.' He saw the look in my eyes and rushed to continue. 'If she can find someone to cover for her, of course. And if not, who knows, perhaps it will do us good to manage by ourselves?'

'Maybe so. Although our bodies will presumably take some time to adjust to the lack of tomatoes.'

He smiled, as best as I suspected he could. 'And there is one thing I was hoping you might do. As a favour. It's nothing terribly arduous, I assure you.'

I shrugged. 'Sure. If I can.'

'We have a party of young Italians visiting this afternoon. Seminarians. Fra Vincenzo would normally show them around but in his absence Fra Jeremiah has kindly volunteered. Fra Raffaele is a little too old and, as for me – well, it's really not my sort of thing. I was wondering if you might like to help out?'

'Er. Okay. I suppose. But why me?'

'I think sharing your experiences as a pilgrim might be useful for them.'

'Well, sure. If you think it'll help. But why not—'

'*Signor* Lucarini and *signor* Pagan? They're not in the best of humour, it seems. I walked in on them in the chapel just now. They were having something that might be best described as somewhere between an animated conversation and a blazing row.'

'Oh. Well, okay then. It's the first time I've been asked to do anything like this, mind you.'

'I'm sure you'll be more than adequate. Thank you, Mr Sutherland. The boat will be here shortly. And in the event of any difficult questions – which is not my experience with seminarians, I have to say – Fra Jeremiah will be able to help out.'

He smiled again, and turned and made his way back to the monastery. A clucking came from around my feet. 'Well now, Erminia. I have to say I hadn't really seen Lucarini and Pagan as the sort of people to sneak in extra-curricular prayers. I wonder if that really is their spiritual side coming out?'

'Maria. Could I have a word?'

She leaned back against the stove and folded her arms. 'Okay.'

'Just to say, I'm sorry about earlier. I didn't mean to start a row.'

She rolled her eyes. 'Oh God. Are you going to go all social worker on me again?'

'Me? I can barely sort my own problems out, let alone other people's. Trust me, I'd be a terrible social worker. But I've got a problem with aggressive monks. That's just a personal thing, you know.'

'You're not going to have it out with Fra Gregorio, are you?'

'Not if you don't want me to.'

'He's a prick, but Fra Vincenzo's all right and he'll be back soon. I'll be in trouble with my dad if I lose my job and that, well, that never ends well.'

'I was just thinking. The key to that cell. The one that wasn't in the usual place.'

'Yes?'

'I was just wondering – where *is* the usual place?'

Maria put her head to one side. 'Well now. And just why would you want to know a thing like that?'

'Because I don't care what Gregorio says. There was somebody in there the other night. I know there was. And so I'd like to have a look in there as well.'

She frowned. 'You're not a cop. I can tell that. So, what are you doing here?'

'I'm trying to find someone who might be the last remaining relative of Dominic Vicari. So that I can get him home. Or at least try to. That's what I'm doing here.'

'Why?'

'It's kind of my job.'

'You need to pretend to be on a pilgrimage to do this?'

I sighed. 'It's a favour for a friend. Somebody who doesn't want policemen crawling all over the island in their anniversary year if there's any way of avoiding it.'

'That's weird.'

'I know it is. But anyway, did Dominic Vicari ever talk to you?'

She shook her head.

'He never mentioned a brother, relatives, anything like that?'

'I just said he never spoke to me, didn't I?'

'Maria. I need to take a look in that cell. Will you tell me where the key is?'

'I would. But it's not where it used to be. I think Fra Gregorio has it after what happened last night.' She shook her head. 'It's because Fra Vincenzo isn't here. He has to be seen as the Big Man on the Monastery.'

'Tell me about him.'

'Seems you want me to tell you a lot of things.' I sighed and reached for my wallet. She shook her head. 'I don't want your money. All I know about Gregorio is that he arrived from somewhere down south. Can't remember exactly where. But he's only been here since the middle of May. He couldn't travel before.'

'And you don't get on?'

'He doesn't really get on with anyone. But he's not the type of person to let that sort of thing worry him.'

'He told me he'd tried to apologise.'

'He tried. I wasn't in the mood to listen. But I'll take a day off. Although he wants me to find someone to cover for me though. That's not going to be easy.'

I smiled. 'Trust me. I don't think that's going to be a problem. What if your auntie covered for you?'

She frowned. 'I don't have an auntie.'

'No?' I paused. 'But you could have.'

And for the first time since we'd met, Maria smiled.

Chapter 27

'*Ciao, tesoro.*'

'*Ciao, carissima.*'

I could almost hear the frown. '*Carissima*, is it? What have you done?'

'Nothing at all. In many ways, I've had a most productive day since we spoke this morning. And I've discovered I'm good with chickens.'

'Oh. That's nice. Did you ring me up just to tell me that?'

'Not at all. I just thought that several hours had passed since I last told my lovely wife how much I loved her and so – I decided to call. And, well, I've got an idea and thought it might be good to run it past you.'

She sighed. 'Okay. I think I understand. Should I get a pen and paper?'

'That might be good.'

There was a short pause, followed by a deep sigh. 'Okay. Your cat is sitting on my notebook. And has swatted the pen under the sofa. Just tell me. I'll remember.'

'Okay. Well my idea is this …'

I was grateful we hadn't been on a video call, as it spared me the sight of her putting her head in her hands.

'That's it?' she said, finally.

'That's it. Brilliant, no?'

'It's – well, it's certainly *an* idea. Of sorts.'

'No, it's a *great* idea. Don't you think?'

'It's a terrible idea, Nathan. A terrible, terrible idea.'

I paused. I hadn't wanted to go nuclear so quickly, but it seemed there was no alternative. 'Fede,' I said, 'Two words. Infinity Pool.'

There was silence for a moment.

'Okay. I'll do it ...'

'Seminarians,' said Jeremiah. 'That means no girls.'

I nodded. 'I suppose not.' Then I realised just what he'd said. 'Are you quite sure you're a monk?'

'Hey, the chicks go crazy for a man in a habit.' He grinned. 'I am joking, you know?'

'You are? I wasn't quite sure.'

'I'm sorry. I do a lot of this stuff. Too much, probably. Zeke's always telling me I'm going to get myself in trouble one of these days.'

'I take it it's not just to wind-up Fra Gregorio.'

'No. Although it's partly about that. But mainly it's about when I was a kid, growing up in Manila. Priests, nuns, deacons, monks, friars – all of them – they might be people you respected. They might be people you hated.' He shook his head. 'And sometimes with good reason. They might be people you regarded as very wise, or sometimes very stupid. But you know what? As a kid, I never saw them as people who would ever have a good time. If you saw a priest smiling, you wondered what was going on.

'But I became a Franciscan because it made me happy. And it still makes me happy. Come on, look at all that out there.' He swept his arm from left to right, indicating the splendour of the city laid out before us. 'How can you not look out at all that, without your heart being filled with happiness?'

'Fra Gregorio seems to manage it.'

'He does. And maybe that's why I come out with things I probably shouldn't.' He grinned. 'We've got seminarians coming here today. The first ones of the year. I'd like them to go home thinking that there's something joyous about ministry, you know?'

'I understand. At least I think I do.'

We heard the gentle putter of the boat approaching, and Jeremiah clapped me on the shoulder. 'Come on, brother. We've got work to do.'

'And so, this is where Saint Francis himself came ashore, sat down, and preached the Good News to the animals. And, eight hundred years on we're still here. It's an inspiring place for me. A joyful place. I hope you'll find it inspiring and joyful as well.'

Three bored teenagers and a stern-faced priest stared back at him. Jeremiah had been trying his best but joy, it had to be said, was very thin on the ground.

The prospective Servants of the Lord had twice been told off for chewing, one of them had been glued to his phone, snapping off an endless series of photos that, he assured us, his Instagram followers would think was 'so cool'; and one of them had been given a withering look as he reached for a packet of cigarettes.

'Father,' the young man said to the Stern Priest. 'Jesus never said anything about smoking.'

'There might be a reason for that,' said Jeremiah. 'But, hey, post-ordination you can smoke away as much as you like.'

The Stern Priest glared at him. The three teens merely stared, as if aware that a joke might have been made but they certainly weren't going to give Jeremiah the satisfaction of actually laughing at it.

'Are they always like this?' I whispered.

'No. Sometimes they can be a bit uncommunicative.'

'Blimey.'

'Okay, then,' he said. 'I think you've maybe heard enough from me and enough about history. But the great thing about San Francesco is that we get visitors from all over the world who come here on retreat. And so, I'd like you to hear a few words from Nathan, who's on a pilgrimage with us.'

I stared at him. 'What are you doing?' I hissed in English.

'I'm sorry. I've done all I can. God bless you.' He smiled. 'Nathan, why don't you tell us a little about what brought you here?'

The three seminarians and the Stern Priest stared at me, waiting for enlightenment.

Start with a joke, Nathan. That always goes down well. 'Well,' I said, 'if I'm being literal I suppose I was brought here by Bepi the Boat.'

Silence, broken only by the distant clucking of Erminia, as if in sympathy with my hopeless task.

Okay. Never start with a joke.

'But as to why I'm here. Well, I'm' – *be honest with them Nathan* – 'I'm the same as you, I guess. I'm not quite sure what to believe any more. So I'm here to find the truth.'

Jeremiah smiled and wagged a finger at me. 'Ah, yes indeed. But as Pilate said, "What is truth?"'

I must have paused just a little bit too long. 'Pontius Pilate. Crucifixion guy. You know,' he hissed, in English.

'I know who he is! That was a pause for effect.' I switched back to Italian. 'Yes. Pontius Pilate, of course, God bless him. "What is truth?" Yes, indeed. I'm sure that's something we all wonder, isn't it?' I looked out at three blank faces. The Stern Priest looked as if he might actually be in pain. '"What is truth?", indeed. That's why I'm here. And that, I'm sure, is why we're all here.'

Another biblical quote came to mind. About there being silence in heaven, about the space of half an hour.

Jeremiah nodded. 'Well, I think that says it all, brothers. Now perhaps you'd like to see the chapel?'

'I think we would,' muttered the Stern Priest.

'Was that okay?' I whispered.

'Absolutely. You're a natural. It'll be ordination next,' grinned Jeremiah.

I felt a tug at my sleeve as we passed through the cloister. It was one of the young seminarians, but whether it was phone guy or smoking guy I couldn't be quite sure.

He pointed up at the *campanile*. 'This is where the murder happened, right?'

Jeremiah and I stopped dead in our tracks.

'I'm sorry?' I said.

'I saw it in the papers. This is where the murder was. There was some foreign guy pushed from the tower.'

'No, that's not quite right,' I said. 'It was a terrible accident. That's all.'

'Oh sure, that's what the papers are saying. But come on, dude travels across Europe in the middle of a plague, ends up falling from a bell tower. Sounds like murder to me.'

The Stern Priest, I thought, looked on the verge of tears. 'Come on, boys,' he said, 'we're wasting these good people's valuable time. There's the chapel to visit and, if we're very lucky, I'm told there's a splendid historic altar cloth to see.'

There was an outbreak of muttering and shuffling of feet, but it was fair to say that the lure of the altar cloth had not had the desired effect.

'Anyway,' I said, 'who'd be likely to commit a murder in a place like this? And what possible motive could there be?'

The youth stared back at me. 'I dunno. I expect they've got all sorts of expensive stuff hidden away here. There always is, right? I bet that altar cloth is worth a bit, now I think about it.'

'Ah,' I said. 'So one of us is a secret linen thief branching out into new areas. Is that what you think?'

'Sure. Why not? I mean, maybe not you.'

'You mean I don't look like a master criminal?'

'Nah. Maybe more like the next one to get murdered.'

'Oh, thanks. Terrific. At the hands of Fra Jeremiah here?'

'Sure, why not? Could easily be one of the monks. Spending all this time here alone, bound to drive you a bit crazy.'

Fra Jeremiah looked at me and held his hands up as if to indicate that the thought had never entered his head. 'I think time's running a little short,' he said. 'Perhaps we should move on to the chapel?'

'Quite so, quite so,' said the Stern Priest, who now bore

the aspect of a man wishing he had decided to pursue a secular vocation. 'Come on, boys. Be a shame to miss the altar cloth, wouldn't it?'

'This is hard work,' I said.

Jeremiah laughed. 'This is nothing. Trust me, these kids are some of the good ones.'

'Wow.'

'Fra Vincenzo explained it to me. Not everybody at seminary actually wants to be a priest. Sometimes it's down to the parents. Kids playing up at school? Grades not what they could be? Why not threaten them with seminary?'

'And does it work?'

'I think it does, for the most part. The kids either have the fear of the Good Lord put into them and start to apply themselves a bit more. Or they decide that, actually, seminary really is for them. Or—'

'Or?'

'Or they sort of finish up there by accident. Which is why we sometimes get really weird priests.'

The Stern Priest and his group of little acolytes emerged from the treasury. He smiled at us both. 'Well that was most refreshing. Fra Raffaele really is the most delightful man.'

'He is,' I said. 'I can see why his girls love him so much.' The boys burst out laughing. 'His chickens,' I added. 'He calls them his girls. Anyway, I hope the altar cloth was everything you'd hoped it would be.'

'Oh, it's exquisite. Simply exquisite.'

'How much do you reckon it's worth, *padre*?'

'Tommaso, I don't think that's an appropriate question.'

'Must be a packet, I reckon.' He tapped his nose. 'You ask me, that's probably what the murder was about. Burglary gone wrong. Happens all the time on television, it does.'

The Stern Priest sighed. 'Tommaso, once again, there has been no murder here. Just a terrible accident, that's all. Now come on, let's go and sign the visitors' book. And try and write some suitably godly thoughts. Serious ones this time. I don't want a repeat of what happened in Subiaco.'

Jeremiah led us to a tiny antechamber, just off the main entrance. A wooden key board was fastened to the rear wall, underneath yet another image of the Sacred Heart. In front of it was a desk and chair, with an ancient PC, positioned so as to face the entrance hall. I was finding the proliferation of Sacred Hearts ever more disturbing and if I had any reason to be working here for a prolonged period of time, I wouldn't care to have it smiling down on me constantly.

'Welcome to our IT hub,' smiled Jeremiah.

'Wow,' said Tommaso. 'That thing still work?'

'Better than you might expect. But we don't need it for much so there's no need to replace it. And it's not as old as all that. It's not as if it's dial-up or anything.'

Tommaso frowned. 'What's dial-up?'

The Stern Priest sighed. 'Come on, boys. Let's leave our thoughts and go.' They queued up to sign, most of them leaving little more than an illegible squiggle. Tommaso, however, took rather more time about it, scanning the previous entries.

'Lucarini, Giulio. Pagan, Bruno. Jeez, they've been here a long time. They must be going crazy by now. Sutherland, Nathan,' he looked up at me. 'That you?'

I nodded, and then his face broke into a grin. He jabbed a finger at me. 'It's you, isn't it?'

'What?'

'You're the murderer. *Padre* arrest this man.'

'Tommaso, please.'

'It's in the book, *padre*. He arrived the night of the murder. It's him!'

Tommaso's company, I decided, had delighted me enough. 'What are you talking about?' I said.

'It's there in the book. You arrived the night of the murder.'

I leaned over to look. There was no doubt about it. The name in the visitors' book was mine. The ID card number was mine. Even the signature was a passable copy. And the date was, as Tommaso had said, June 24th. The night before Dominic Vicari fell to his death.

'That's just a mistake. Somebody filled in my details and got them wrong.'

'That's your signature though, right?'

I shook my head. 'No.'

He wagged a finger at me. 'Ah, but you would say that, wouldn't you?'

I turned to Jeremiah. 'Could you tell young *signor* Poirot here exactly when I arrived.'

Jeremiah grinned. 'I'm sorry to disappoint you Tommaso, but Mr Sutherland here arrived only yesterday.'

'So you're in it together? Okay, it all makes sense now.' He looked down at the book. 'Tell you what, if I was *signor* Lucarini or *signor* Pagan I'd be making sure my room was well locked every night.'

'Tommaso,' sighed the priest. He looked at me. 'I'm sorry

about all this. Tommaso, just sign the book please, and then we can be gone. The boy sighed, scribbled away, and then turned back to me. 'It was nice meeting you. I hope you don't kill anyone else though.'

The Stern Priest rolled his eyes. 'I think that's quite enough for now. And I think it's high time we head back to town. I'd like to get there in time for Evening Prayer.' There was a chorus of boos. 'Which, I'd like to remind everybody, is not optional. Thank you for your time, Brother.' He nodded at me. 'And yours, Mr Sutherland.'

Jeremiah smiled. 'I hope it's been inspiring.'

'It most certainly has.'

'Lovely to meet you all,' I said. 'And Tommaso, I can certainly see why everyone thinks you're cut out for the priesthood.'

He was about to reply, but the Stern Priest ushered them out of the door and down the gravel path towards the waiting boatman before he could speak.

Jeremiah chuckled. 'Back in Manila, we'd call him a *tampalasan*. A ruffian, you know? But he was right about the book. That really is your name there.'

'Maria must have got it wrong. Although why she thought it necessary to write my name in, I don't know.'

'Ah, she was probably busy and didn't want to wander around looking for you. As far as she knew you were off chasing chickens.'

I grinned, but my smile vanished once I saw what he'd written in the book.

Tommaso had inked a large asterisk next to my name with the words IS THE MURDERER next to it.

Chapter 28

'Boys, eh?' said Jeremiah.

'I hope he enjoys a long and productive ministry,' I said.

He laughed. 'Oh, I was speaking to Fra Raffaele earlier. He was asking about you.'

'Oh yes? Is it chicken related?'

'No, but once he'd finished with the seminarians, he was going to go through some of the more interesting bits of the treasury with *signor* Lucarini. He thought you might like to join them.'

'And should I?'

'You into altar linen?'

'Absolutely I am!'

He grinned. 'Then there's no better place to be.'

The treasury at St Mark's Basilica glitters and shimmers with gold and silver, with precious gems and stones, and with the occasional bits of saints. The one at San Francesco del Deserto, as would seem appropriate, was altogether more modest; being little more than a glass-fronted cabinet of vestments, and a small library of books and scrolls.

'Mr Sutherland?'

'Fra Raffaele. *Signor* Lucarini.'

The elderly monk nodded and smiled at me. 'Tell me, Nathan, there was something I didn't quite understand at lunch. Something about a chicken casserole?'

'Oh that. The Filipino brothers noticed me chasing Erminia around the island.' He looked confused. 'She'd escaped. I was worried she might be halfway to the *centro storico* by now if I hadn't gone to bring her back.'

He chuckled. 'She might well have been. She's a little terror that one. Now, I was just taking *signor* Lucarini here through some of the more interesting parts of our collection.' He looked, perhaps, just a little bit embarrassed. 'It's nothing opulent of course, but not without interest. Would you care to join us?'

'I'd be delighted. Would that be okay, Carlo?'

He hesitated for a moment, but then smiled. 'Of course.'

Fra Raffaele took out a thick iron key, and opened the first display case. 'Let's make a little space first,' he murmured, and pushed the candlesticks to the far end of the table. 'Now we do need to be just a little careful here. Some of these are terribly fragile.'

He took out what had appeared to be a plain white bundle of folded linen and then, with infinite care, spread it out upon the table before us. Almost on cue, the sun streamed through the windows, revealing it to be the most beautifully embroidered lace.

Lucarini smiled. 'Fra Raffaele, I have to say, this is simply exquisite.'

'Wow.' I couldn't think of anything else I could productively add.

'An altar cloth, made for the church of the Holy Sepulchre in the Holy Land. The most perfect Venetian lace. At the end of the seventeenth century, there was no more precious textile in Europe. And none more precious than that from Burano.' He bowed his head. *'Ad majorem Dei gloriam.'*

'But what is it doing here?'

'This was to be a gift from Doge Francesco Morosini to the *Custodia Terra Sancta* in the Holy Land.'

I shook my head. 'You'll have to tell me more.'

'The Franciscans have had a presence in Jerusalem since the thirteenth century. Now, it was the custom of all the noble families in Europe to send gifts to the custodians of the holiest places in the city – the Holy Sepulchre, places like that. The Franciscans served as an intermediary. Hence they became known as the Custodians of the Holy Land.'

'Okay, so far I understand,' I said. 'But what's it doing here?'

'Well, now. Doge Morosini had other things on his mind in the latter part of the seventeenth century. Such as the Morean war. Otherwise known as the Sixth Ottoman–Venetian war. He was off fighting for the Republic. And, had it been known that a ship full of treasures was on its way to the Holy Land, it would have proved an irresistible target for the Turks. And so we,' he smiled, proudly, 'became temporary custodians. And it just stayed here, forgotten about over the centuries.'

'But what about Napoleon? And the Austrians? Why wasn't it just carted off to Paris or Vienna?'

'The brothers of the time could see what was to come. Even here, on our tiny island, they would have heard about the terrible storm approaching from France. They walled up the most precious of our treasures to hide them and the walls were plastered over. Napoleon couldn't have cared less about our little *convento* in the middle of a mosquito-infested lagoon. And when the Austrians turned it into a powder magazine, well, if they ever noticed that one part of the treasury was perhaps a little narrower than it should be, then no one ever commented on it. And so the treasure – for that is what it is, Mr Sutherland – remained here until the restoration of the monastery; the secret of its location passed down from brother to brother over the generations.'

'That's incredible.'

He nodded. 'It is. But, unfortunately, what Napoleon could not do, what the Austrians failed to do – time has done. It will have to leave us.'

'But why?'

'Look around you, Mr Sutherland. Only five of us are left. Brothers Ezekiel and Jeremiah won't be with us for ever.' He gave a dry little chuckle. 'Neither will I, for very different reasons.'

'Others will come.'

Raffaele looked straight into my eyes. 'Will they, though? Or is this where our story ends? Will we just live on as a museum, where boatloads of tourists will come just to see the spot where Francesco himself once sat down and preached to the birds?'

Lucarini gave a little cough. I'd forgotten he was there. 'And so what will happen to the altar cloth, Don Raffaele? This is the most valuable thing you own, I imagine?'

'Oh, invaluable I should say.'

'You must be worried about keeping it here.'

He smiled. 'We kept it safe from Napoleon and the Austrians. Now, Fra Vincenzo is in Assisi on pilgrimage. When that ends, he will announce that this lovely thing will be gifted to the Church of the Holy Sepulchre in Jerusalem. On the eight hundredth anniversary of our foundation, Morosini's gift will finally be where it was always meant to be.'

Lucarini tapped his fingers on the table. 'I imagine you must be more than a little conflicted about that, Fra Raffaele.'

'Oh, I am, of course. It will sadden me, not being able to look upon it. But we were fortunate enough to be custodians of it for over three hundred years. Time, now, for it to pass on to others.' He gave a little yawn. 'I think that's enough for today, gentlemen. It'll shortly be time for evening prayer, and then – perhaps – we may hope that Erminia continues to avoid the attentions of *signora* Maria.'

Chapter 29

I found myself at a bit of a loss after dinner. Lucarini seemed distracted and unhappy, and I left him on the jetty staring out at the lagoon and chainsmoking cigarette after cigarette. Conversation with Gregorio was polite but strained. The Filipino brothers seemed fun but they were, I reminded myself, still monks and probably not up for a few drinks and a game of *scopa*. Raffaele seemed happy to chat, but the old man was clearly tired and made his excuses early.

I went to say goodnight to the chickens, and then wondered just what was happening to my life. I texted Federica. *Everything sorted for tomorrow.*

The reply, *Yes.* Followed by, *This is never going to work.*

I tapped away. *It is going to work. I love you lots.*

A pause, then. *I love you lots too. But this is still a stupid idea.*

I smiled, and dropped my phone back in my pocket.

I made my way back to the *convento*. It was barely nine-thirty and yet everyone seemed to have retired for the night. I walked through the secondary cloister on the way to my wing, the scent of flowers everywhere in the warm evening air. The old *vera da pozzo* no longer served as a well but was instead overflowing with blooms of every description.

Something else, I thought, that would have delighted the heart of St Francis. Except that earth was scattered around the base at one point, where, upon looking more closely, I could see a bunch of flowers had been clumsily yanked from the ground. Maria, perhaps, fetching something to make the refectory look a little brighter over dinner.

The door to the *campanile* lay to my right, and I paused. Gregorio had told me it was locked and – given that a fatal accident had taken place there just a few days previously – there was good reason for that. I raised my eyes, and looked up at the bell tower. Then I clenched them shut, and opened them again.

There was someone up there. At least I thought there was. It was difficult to see in the late evening light. But there had been something, someone, I was sure, momentarily silhouetted in the belfry.

I laid my hand upon the door and pushed, just ever so gently. It swung open a few inches, and so I pushed again, bracing myself for the sound of wood against stone that would alert whoever was up there to my presence.

I looked upwards. I could see nothing, hear nothing. There was, barely, just about sufficient light for me to make out the staircase.

By *campanile* standards, this was relatively modest. Attempting to scale the one on Torcello even under my newer, fitter, non-smoking regime would probably have killed me or left me gasping for breath. This, by contrast, was manageable. It wouldn't take long to check out. In all likelihood I'd get to the top, see that nobody was there, and retreat to my cell armed with my copy of *The Da Vinci Code* against any unwelcome visitors.

I took the first flight of stairs, then paused and listened out. And then I continued upwards. After a few minutes of climbing I found myself at the bottom of the short flight of wooden steps that led up to the belfry. I placed my foot upon the bottom step, and then froze.

A voice, no, two voices, came from above.

'For Christ's sake, Bruno.' The voice was Lucarini's, exasperated and on the verge of desperation. 'Can't you rein it in a bit?'

Pagan laughed, mirthlessly. 'I don't know how you're so calm about this. Seriously. How can you be so calm?'

'Listen. I'm sorting things out, but I need you with me on this. I need you to sort yourself out.'

'No, you listen.' Bruno's voice was warm and blurry with booze. 'If Vicari finds out about this, we're fucked. Aren't we? Completely fucked.'

'He's not going to find out, Bruno. I'll make sure of that.'

'The Englishman. He's working for him, isn't he? I told you we couldn't trust him.'

'I don't think we can, either. Maria says he came over the day after the accident. With a cop.'

'Oh great. Oh well, that's just fucking great, isn't it?'

'As I said, Bruno. I'm on the case. I can sort this. I don't know if he's a cop or not, but he sure as hell isn't a translator of lawnmower manuals or whatever bullshit thing he made up. But Sutherland isn't the problem, he's part of the solution. As long as you rein it in, okay? I'm leaving tomorrow. Don't know how long for. Vicari's not telling me anything. But I need you to hold it together while I'm away. So just give me the bottle.'

'Piss off, Carlo.'

'Don't you say fucking say that to me, Bruno. Just give me that.'

'Fuck you.'

There was a sound of a brief struggle, and then the crash off glass against stone far below.

'Fuck.'

'You idiot.' I heard Lucarini take a deep breath. 'I'll sort it. Okay? But you – you just try not to kill yourself when you come down.'

I heard feet upon the staircase. There was a small recess in the wall behind, and I flattened myself into it as best I could. Lucarini thundered past me and, even in the near-darkness, I could see his body shaking with anger.

Should I follow him, I wondered? Perhaps not. After all, I hadn't managed to have a proper conversation with Bruno Pagan as yet, and there was no time like the present. I gave it five minutes before taking the remaining steps to the belfry.

'Carlo? You forget something?'

I smiled at him. 'Hello, Bruno.'

'You?'

'Nathan. Nathan Sutherland. We haven't really had a chance to chat.'

'What are you doing here?'

From below came a scraping of broken glass. 'I heard glass breaking. Hope everything's okay. Been a bit of an accident has there?'

'Yes.'

Bruno Pagan was becoming a veritable chatterbox.

I took a quick look over the edge and wished I hadn't, but

it was enough to be able to see a figure that might just have been Carlo Lucarini striding away into the darkness.

'I have to say, I didn't expect to see you here. Didn't expect to see anyone. I'm surprised anybody wants to come up here following the accident.'

Bruno said nothing.

'Then again, it's not like Britain, is it? None of all this "Health and Safety" business.' I made sure there was a good solid pillar behind me, and leaned back.

'What are you doing here?' he repeated.

I smiled at him.

'Salimmo sù, el primo e io secondo,
tanto ch'i' vidi de le cose belle
che porta 'l ciel, per un pertugio tondo.
E quindi uscimmo a riveder le stelle.

'Dante,' I said. 'The final canto of the *Inferno*.

'We mounted up, he first and I the second,
Till I beheld through a round aperture
Some of the beauteous things that Heaven doth bear;
Thence we came forth to see once more the stars.

'It was my project during lockdown, you see? I read the whole of the *Commedia*. One *canto* a day. And that one really made me think, so I memorised it. The stars, Bruno. Hanging there in the firmament. Our world has been so closed in these past few months. But now, we can look up and, as the poet says, *see once more the stars*. So that's what I'm doing up here, Bruno. Is that why you're here? Seeing stars?'

'No. I just needed to think that's all.'

'I understand. That's why we're all here I suppose.' I paused for a moment and then smiled at him again. 'It's just I noticed those. Around your neck. Binoculars, aren't they?'

He looked down as if noticing them for the first time.

'For the stars, of course,' I said. 'I mean, I don't know if the brothers have a telescope, but I don't think they're the sort of thing one brings on holiday. Whereas binoculars, you can just,' I mimed clicking a suitcase shut, 'in your luggage and you're good to go. Yes?'

He nodded, uncertain as to where this was going.

'I've got a set myself. Well, they're not really binoculars. They're really opera glasses. Built in the old Soviet Union. Last forever, they will. But they're not quite the thing for a night like this.'

'What are you on about?'

I ignored him, and looked upwards again. 'Thing is, it's all a bit cloudy isn't it? Not the best of nights for star gazing. A shame. There's so little light pollution here, it must be wonderful on a clear night. That's why Mr Vicari came up here, I imagine. To see the stars and then dawn breaking, and the sun coming up.' I paused again. 'Did you ever speak to him, Bruno?'

He shook his head. 'No.'

'There we go. Well, we should raise a glass to him anyway.' I looked around and then, ever so briefly, over the edge. 'Well, I guess that's not going to happen. Never mind, let's raise a virtual one.' I held my right hand in the air, holding an imaginary glass. 'Wherever you are, we salute you,' I paused, 'Danny Vicari.'

Bruno started.

'Sorry. *Dominic*, wasn't it? Dominic, wherever you are, we

salute you.' I spread my arms wide. 'It's tragic, of course, but think about it – that view over the lagoon would have been the very last thing he ever saw. In some ways there's something quite wonderful about that. Don't you think?'

He said nothing.

I stretched and yawned. 'Well, it's been lovely to chat at last, Bruno, but it's past all our bedtimes. I'll be off, I think.' I made my way to the top of the staircase, and then turned back for a moment. 'Oh, and don't worry, I won't lock the door. Wouldn't want you to spend the whole night in a bell tower. But be careful on those stairs, eh?'

I made my way – carefully – back down the steps. When I reached the bottom, I looked upwards to see Bruno gazing down at me. Then he turned and was lost in the shadows.

The paving was wet and there was the strong smell of booze. I crouched down and, carefully, traced my hand along the surface. I touched my fingers to my lips. Whisky. As I got to my feet, I felt something clink against my foot. A piece of glass, with a fragment of label attached.

...de of the Gle...

Pride of the Glens.

A brand that might best be described as 'cooking whisky'. And a brand that had, supposedly, been Dominic Vicari's tipple of choice.

I made my way back to my cell. It had been quite a productive evening. A seed had been planted and I wondered just what Carlo Lucarini and Bruno Pagan would have to talk about come the morning. Yes, a very productive evening indeed.

Nevertheless, I was careful to wedge a chair under the handle of my door.

Chapter 30

'Well, Mam, I've been in Naples for three days now and I've got to say I think you oversold Swansea Bay. Just a bit, mind.

It's crazy here, but in a good way. The streets are just full of people, you know? And not like back home, I mean this is crazy busy. Crossing the road here is the most frightened I've been since the days of the West Cross Boys.

So I went for a walk on my first night, and bought a gelato and ate it in the street. Got to say, Joe's ice cream parlour might have a bit of a rival. And then I found a bar, and sat outside with a cold pint watching the sun go down.

Wish you were here, Mam. You, me and Danny. Just sitting here, watching the sun go down.

Don't know why I'm writing to you, to be honest, Mam. I guess it just seems to help me a bit. Helps me get my thoughts in order, that sort of thing. Maybe I'll tear this all up later. But then again, maybe I won't. We'll see. And tomorrow, just maybe, I'll see Danny as well.'

It's a letter that I'm never going to send. I reread it and reread it and think about crumpling it up and throwing it away. As long as those words are there I can pretend that, maybe, I'm just on holiday. And tomorrow there'll be Danny and me, just like the old times, with drinks and laughs and nonsense. Except I don't think that's going to happen. I scrunch it up and push it into an overflowing waste bin.

I should have spent a bit more money on the hotel. I slept badly last night. Never thought about air conditioning, did I? And some bloody flying thing bit me during the night and now there's a bite on my ankle which is itching horribly. But then I go out and grab a double espresso and a sfogliatella frolla and start to feel better. I'm Italian, too, remember? And if I spent the night in a cheap and nasty hotel, well, I'm a private eye, aren't I? This is what we're supposed to do.

It took some work, but the last address that I could find for Danny is in the district of Vomero, high up above the city. I've heard it's possible to walk there. I've also heard that might kill you. In this heat I decide to take no chances and get the funicular railway.

I've only been on one of these once before, and that was on a day trip to Aberystwyth, back when Dad was still around. That looked like trains are supposed to look, whereas this one is shiny and modern, like a tube train. But that doesn't matter because the views are spectacular, and I forget for a moment about the heat and about the bloody mosquitoes or whatever the hell they are, and think just how bloody lucky Danny is to live here.

The address is on Via Scarlatti and my first thought is that Danny must be doing even better for himself than I thought, because this building is just gorgeous and I wish I knew about architecture and all that stuff so I could work out when it dates from.

His name isn't on the door. I take out my phone and check the address again, but this is definitely the place. I can feel my heart racing and my guts churning, and so I take a deep breath. Calm it down, Dom. This is something you might have expected, after all.

I run my finger down the list of names again, and there's definitely no Vicari. But one of them – I think it's a Rossi or a Russo but I don't really remember – has just been written on a piece of sticky tape. I look left, and then right, and then pick away with my nails as quickly as possible, easing it away.

And there it is. Vicari.

I smooth the tape back into place and take another deep breath. What to do? Do I ring the bell or not?

Stupid to come all this way just to turn back. I'm about to rest my finger on the buzzer when the choice is taken away from me, and the door opens inwards.

'Can I help you?' Like me, the speaker is a bald guy in middle age. Unlike me, he's dressed in T-shirt, shorts and sandals and, as a result, looks as if he feels more comfortable in the heat than I do.

'Maybe so. I'm looking for a Danny – Daniele – Vicari.'

'Nobody of that name here.'

'Not now, no, but this is the last address I have for him.' He shakes his head. 'Look, I just noticed on the panel here. There was a Vicari here, but his name's been covered over.'

He pushes me out of the way and runs his finger over the label reading Rossi or Russo. 'Hey now, you leave that alone.'

'I'm sorry, but he was here. I'm sure he was.'

'Mister, just who are you and why do you want to know?'

'I'm his brother, Domenico. And I've come all this way from South Wales to tell him that our mother's died and – and—'

The words choke in my throat, and I can feel the tears welling up inside me, and, right now, I have never felt less like Humphrey Bogart.

His expression softens. 'Hey now.' He lowers his voice. 'Look, okay, there was a guy called Vicari here but he moved out at the beginning of June.'

'So he was here. Do you have an address?'

He shakes his head. 'I didn't know him that well. Mister, I wouldn't go looking for him. The guy moved out overnight, nobody ever saw him again. I think he just doesn't want to be found.'

'Maybe he doesn't, but I can't leave it like this. Not after being so close. Is there anyone – anyone – who might know?'

It's his turn to look left and then right, as if afraid somebody might be listening. 'You could try at the Penny Black. It's an English pub not far from here. I know he used to drink there.'

'Thank you.' I tap the name into my phone. It's barely a couple of hundred metres away. 'Thank you,' I repeat.

He nods. 'Okay. Good luck. But like I said, maybe he doesn't want to be found.'

'You say you didn't really know him?'

He shakes his head. 'Not really. We'd say hello if we passed on the stairs. Not much more than that.'

'Did he ever talk about me? Or our mother?'

He nods, and suddenly there's so much sadness in his eyes. 'He said that – if you ever turned up here for whatever reason – you were just to go home. Stop trying to find him. Stop writing. And that he loves you very much.'

Then he turns and walks away, as I clutch the doorframe for support in order to stop the grief doubling me over.

***

A cardboard figure of a guardsman keeps watch over the interior of the Penny Black. To one side of him stands what appears to be an actual vintage red telephone box. On the other is a mural of the Beatles, in their Sergeant Pepper get-up.

My eyes dart around, looking for something that might be a bit Welsh, but there's nothing to be seen, not even a photo of Gareth Edwards or Tom Jones. Pinned to walls are photographs of celebrities who may, or may not, have dropped by for a drink. Rod Stewart, Roger Moore, that bloke from Simply Red, and someone I think might be the previous Archbishop of Canterbury. I nod to myself. Hang on, he was Welsh, wasn't he? That's nice, then. A group of five Brits in the corner are drinking and watching sport on the telly. It looks like they've settled in for the day.

This should be absurd. It's a little bit of a made-up UK in the heart of Naples. And yet it somehow works.

This is my country as well. I can speak the language. I could get a passport if I wanted. I could up and leave Swansea, and settle down here for the rest of my days just like I thought Danny was doing. And yet, there's something about that red phone box, the guardsman, the Beatles and even the bloody Archbishop of Canterbury that makes me terribly, terribly homesick.

'You okay, mister?' The voice of the barman snatches me back to reality.

'Yes, I'm sorry.' I rub my hand across my face, and it comes away damp with sweat.

'It's hot today. Need to be careful out there. Make sure you regularly rehydrate, that's what my doctor tells me.' He grins, and runs a hand across the row of pumps in front of him. 'So.

*What are you rehydrating with? Guinness, Tennants? Peroni, if
you want Italian. Plenty of others, as well.'*

'*I think a Guinness would be good.*'

He nods, and sets it pouring. 'Where are you from, my friend?'

'*South Wales.*'

'*Australia? You've come a long way for a Guinness.*'

'*No, the other one. South Wales. Wales Wales.' I switch to
Italian.* 'Galles meridionale.'

'*You speak Italian?*'

'*I am Italian. Well, Welsh-Italian.*'

*He frowns for a moment, and stares at me. Then he shakes his
head, and his face clears. 'Ah.* Galles. *Very good.*'

*He draws an acceptable shamrock on the head of my pint,
and passes it to me. He's about to turn away, but there's something about his expression that I latch onto.*

'*Have you had other Welsh-Italians in here?*'

*He shakes his head, but I'm already reaching for my photo of
Danny. 'Here. His name's Daniele Vicari. I'm told he used to
come in here.'*

He scowls. 'Who told you that? And no, I've never seen him.'

*He turns away and pretends to be doing something with the
optics, but I can see his reflection in the mirror and he's looking
back at me the whole time.*

*Danny's been in here, and this guy knows it, and he's lying
to me. I can see his eyes in the mirror, staring back at me, and
then – then – pinned above the bar I see a photo.*

*A man in a dark suit and tie, his fists clenched and arms held
in a boxing stance. He looks drop-dead cool, like someone who
might once have been in the running for James Bond.*

His name is Joe Calzaghe. And even at this distance I can see the words "To Danny. Keep strong. Cheers, Joe."

A photo that, for years, had stood on Danny's bedside table. 'He's been here,' I say. The barman's shoulders stiffen, but he continues with his work.

'Tell me about him. Please.' Desperation is creeping into my voice now because, if the guy just decides to clam up, I've no idea what I can do next. 'I'm his brother,' I add. 'I've come all the way across Europe because I think he's in trouble.'

He turns around. He looks uncomfortable, and he nods. 'He is.' He looks across the room to where the group of Brits are watching the football. He reaches for the TV remote control and turns the volume up a little. Not so much that they'll notice – even at this hour of the day it seems that they're beyond that – but enough to cover our conversation just a little more.

'His brother?'

I nod.

'He never spoke about a brother.'

'I haven't seen him in years and haven't heard from him in months. Our mother's dead and I don't think he even knows. I've got to find him. Please.'

'My friend, I don't think that's going to be so easy.'

'But he's alive?'

He shrugs. 'As far as I know. But, yes, he's in trouble.'

'Tell me.'

'I don't know much. I wish I had more to tell you.'

'He used to drink in here though? He gave you the photo?'

'That's right.' He glances around the room. 'He used to go on about Wales all the time, you see. He said he'd bring in a flag one day, and we could pin that to the ceiling.' He smiles for a moment. 'It's a really cool flag, you know? And then he brought *in that photo of the boxer. I didn't know who it was at first – thought maybe it was that actor who plays 007. Boxing's never been my sport. Anyway, he told me I could put it up behind the bar but I had to promise to look after it.'*

'Could I?' I stretch my hand out, but there's a suspicious look in his eyes. 'I'm his brother,' I remind him, and pat my head. 'Look, I know he's got more hair than me. But I really am his brother. And I'd like to give it back to him.'

He sighs, but then nods. He looks over to the TV, but the Brits are oblivious to us. Singing, I fear, might be imminent. The barman reaches up, eases the photograph off the wall, and passes it across the bar to me.

'Do you know what he was doing here? In Naples, I mean. I never figured it out. Something to do with our dad's business.'

'The Vicari family business yes.' He nods and starts to pour another pint of Guinness.

'I didn't ask for another.'

'This is on the house.'

'What do you mean by "the family business"? I sup at my Guinness, but the taste is sour in my mouth and, for a moment, I want to vomit.

Danny. What have you done?

'"The family business",' I repeat. 'What do you mean by that.' I screw my eyes shut because I'm silently praying please don't say Mafia. Please don't say Mafia.

'It's just business stuff, that's all I'm saying.' I open my eyes but he's waving a finger at me. 'Just business stuff that's gone wrong.'

'So, what, he's on the run from the police?'

'The police?' He stifles a laugh. 'Oh Gesù, no, not the police.'

'Then I still don't understand.'

'My friend, sometimes when business people fall out, they fall out very, very badly. Do you understand what I mean by that?'

I can only nod. 'I think I do. Which means I've got to find him. Do you know where he is?'

His eyes narrow and he looks suspicious. Then he looks at me, and then at Danny's photo and nods. 'Okay.' His voice drops, just a little more. 'He said he was leaving town for a bit, just until the air cleared. He said he thought he could sort everything out given time. He said he needed to get to Venice.'

'Venice. Great. Do you have an address?'

He shakes his head.

'Nothing at all? Just Venice.'

'That's all I know. I'm sorry.'

'Okay.' I drain my Guinness. 'That'll have to be enough. Thank you.' I slide ten euros across the bar. 'Keep the change.'

He nods. 'I hope you find him.'

I leave the bar, Joe Calzaghe's photograph in my bag. I'll give it back to Danny when I see him.

But just where the hell are you, Danny? And what have you done?

Chapter 31

I stood on the edge of the jetty and looked out across the lagoon, in the early morning sun. I yawned and stretched. I'd passed an undisturbed night, tooled up with mosquito repellent, a small fan and the comforting weight of *The Da Vinci Code*. Still, the morning routine of rising early for prayers was not getting any easier.

I heard the distant rumble of an outboard motor and shielded my eyes. Across the lagoon, I could see a boat heading towards the island. Bepi the Boat, I imagined, was not used to being up at such an early hour.

I gave him a cheery wave. Bepi grinned, and waved back. He pulled up to the jetty, tied up and jumped ashore.

'Everything okay, Bepi?'

He gave me a salute. 'Just fine, *capo*.'

He reached down into the boat, but his passenger ignored his hand and hauled herself on land.

'*Ciao, cara*,' I began, and then stopped.

It wasn't Federica.

Lucia Frigo put her hands on her hips.

'This isn't going to work, is it, Mr Consul?'

***

Lucia Frigo. Siouxsie Sioux lookalike. Guitarist with the finest – or, to be precise, only – black metal band in Venice. A young woman whose capacity for taking shit could not even be measured at a molecular level.

She was also someone who'd once helped me solve a murder.

'What are you doing here?'

'Same thing as you, Mr Consul. I'm investigating my spiritual side.'

'No, you're not. You're,' I fumbled for the words, and found the wrong one, 'interfering.'

'Oh, and that's not an accusation we could ever level against the great Nathan Sutherland is it?'

'You're not supposed to be here.'

Bepi frowned. 'Is there a problem?'

She smiled at him in a way that almost – but not quite – out-dazzled Federica. 'No problem.'

'So, as we agreed then?' he said. 'Early evening?'

'Early evening. Thanks, Bepi.'

She gave him a little salute, and he jumped into the boat and set off back to Burano, being careful all the while to avoid the crabs.

She lit a cigarette and leaned back against the mooring post. 'Lucia. Why are you doing this?'

'Oh, that's nice isn't it? No, *hello Lucia, how nice to see you again, how are you doing?* No, just a *why are you doing this?*'

'Hello Lucia, how nice to see you again. How are you doing?'

'I'm doing very well indeed, Mr Consul. How are you?'

'I'm fine.' I paused. 'Now what are you doing here?'

'Your wife called and told me you had this mad idea which involved her pretending to be the sister or cousin or whatever of this girl who cooks for the monks. But she asked me to remind you that she has a job that she needs to go to, thank you very much. Oh, and something about the scaffolding finally being up. So, she asked me. You know, you're very lucky to have her.'

'I know.'

'Punching above your weight, I'd say.'

'Oh, thanks for that. But, yes, I am. So, she's clued you in on everything?'

'You've got some British guy who fell to his death from a bell tower, and a mysterious locked room with somebody crying inside?'

'That's the gist of it.'

She grinned. 'Well, that's just really cool. Of course, I was going to help out when I heard that.'

'Great.'

'Oh, and there's some arsehole monk who slapped that young girl around yesterday.'

'Technically, he's a friar. But you're right about the arsehole bit.'

'Well, I'm looking forward to meeting him.' She twisted the skull ring on her right hand, lining it up with a knuckle.

'Yes, about that. I know how you feel, but could we start out with not hitting a monk? Please?'

'Or even a friar?'

'Even a friar. Sorry about that.'

She sighed. 'I'll do my best. But better hope he doesn't give me a reason.'

'It'll be fine. Well, it'll probably be fine. You remember the cover story? You're her aunt.'

'Am I old enough?'

'Aunts can work in mysterious ways. Cousin, then, if you prefer.' She nodded. 'Okay, I guess we'd better go in. Remember, we're not supposed to know each other.'

'So no "Mr Consul"?'

'Better not.'

'How about "Brother Nathan"?'

'Do you mind if you don't? Oh, by the way, what are you cooking us?'

'Cooking?'

'Yes.'

'Your wife told me that this Maria had left food for you all.'

'Yes. In kit form.'

'Christ.' She looked heavenwards. 'Sorry, wrong place for that I guess.' She turned back to me. 'I can do a pretty good chicken stew?'

'No. We're not going to do that. Something with tomatoes will be fine. We've got lots of tomatoes.' I smiled. 'Tell you what. I'll do it. I'll drop by the kitchen at some point and take over cooking. That'll give you more time to have a good look around. And remember, there'll be nobody around during prayers. I need you to get hold of the key to the locked door at the end of my corridor.'

'Okay. Any thoughts as to how I can do that?'

'You can walk around more easily than me. If I'm somewhere I'm not supposed to be, people will get suspicious. If you're there, all you have to do is say you're cleaning or something.'

'I can do that.'

'Excellent.' I smiled. 'It's been a while, hasn't it? Since last year, and the whole *acqua granda* thing.'

'And the murders, of course.'

'Those as well. You've been okay, I hope? These past few months. You and your dad.'

She nodded. 'Yeah. He's not the easiest person to have under your feet for three months. But then he'd say the same about me. We did okay.'

'I'm glad. Erm—'

'I'm hearing a "but" here, Mr Consul.'

'Did you have to wear a *Number of the Beast* T-shirt?'

'Greatest ever Iron Maiden album. And it seemed kind of religious so I thought, why not?'

'Yes. And no.'

'Look, Nicko McBrain – the drummer – he's a Christian, right?'

'He's not on *The Number of the Beast.*'

'He plays it live though. So, what's the problem?'

'Oh, no problem. No problem at all.'

The good brothers of San Francesco del Deserto would, I suspected, be learning rather a lot about the Gospel according to Nicko McBrain over the course of the day.

'I'm Lucia.'

Gregorio nodded.

'She's Maria's auntie—'

'Cousin,' said Lucia.

'Maria's auntie's cousin.'

Lucia put her hand on my arm and squeezed it, just slightly more tightly than was comfortable. 'Cousin. She calls me auntie. You know what it's like when you have an older cousin, right?'

Gregorio looked from Lucia to me and back again. 'Do you know each other?'

'Never met before,' I said.

'Just now, on the jetty,' smiled Lucia.

'I saw her getting off the boat, Fra Gregorio. She asked me to take her to the monks.'

'Friars,' sighed Gregorio.

'Yes, I explained the difference.'

'I see. Well, welcome, Lucia. I hope you enjoy your brief stay with us.'

'Cheers, father. Or is it brother? You know, Maria was upset about something. Said she wanted to make up for her behaviour. Don't know what all that's about, do you?' She stared at him, fixedly, and he pretended to be looking at something on the other side of the room. 'Anyway, here I am, just filling in.' She smiled and waved her hands, jazz-style.

'Can you cook, Lucia?'

'Can I cook? My dad says I'm a little demon in the kitchen.' She giggled. 'Sorry. Probably wrong thing to say here.'

Gregorio took a sharp intake of breath. 'Probably so.' He took a closer look at her T-shirt. 'And you can't possibly walk around like that. Find an apron or something.'

'But—'

'But nothing. Either that or get back on the next boat.'

Lucia shrugged. 'If you say so. So, what's it to be? Breakfast first and then a little cleaning?'

'A lot of cleaning would be even better. Maria's never exactly put her heart and soul into that.'

'Righto.'

'Lunch following midday prayers. Then I think we can give you the afternoon at leisure. Either go back to Burano, or you may spend your time here on the island if you wish. As long as you don't disturb the brothers. Then dinner will follow vespers—'

'Vespers?'

Gregorio sighed. 'Evening prayer. And then we can call for a boat to take you home.'

'And that's when I get paid?'

He shook his head. 'You'll have to arrange that with Maria. If she wants to make a goodwill gesture following her behaviour yesterday, well that's up to her.'

'I'll do that, then.' Then she frowned. 'What exactly did happen yesterday? She didn't seem to want to talk about it?'

'That doesn't concern you.'

'Whatever you want, Mr Monk. Now, let me find an apron.' And she went upon her way humming, perhaps over-enthusiastically, 'The Number of the Beast'.

Gregorio turned to me and scowled.

I shrugged. 'Young people, eh?' Then I turned and made my way through the cloister, on the way to Morning Prayer.

Chapter 32

'So how's it going?' said Fede.

'Great,' I said. 'They bought the whole thing.'

'And tomorrow morning, when actual Maria arrives, and everyone's all, "Oh hello Maria, you will be sure to thank your auntie won't you?", what happens then?'

'She's on my side now I've got her a day off. At least I think she is. Hopefully she'll cover for me. And if not, I'll be well away by mid-morning with the secret of the locked room and, hopefully, some proper information on what – if anything – happened to Dominic Vicari.'

Fede chuckled. 'Oh *caro*, you're going to be so disappointed if there's nothing in that room beyond a vacuum cleaner and some cleaning products, aren't you?'

'I'll be devastated. But it can't just be that. That wouldn't explain the crying.'

'I suppose that's true. How's Lucia?'

'I think she's having a good time. She's quite excited about the Mysterious Locked Room thing.' Clucking came from around my feet. 'Sorry, I think I'll have to go. Erminia's after my attention.'

'I'm starting to worry about you. The next thing I know, you'll be wanting to bring her home.'

'Would that be so bad? She could be a friend for Gramsci.'

'No, she couldn't. Not unless she was oven-ready.'

'Don't say that!' Erminia clucked around my feet and I wedged my phone under my chin whilst I picked her up and stroked her feathers. 'I think she might have heard that.'

Again, it was, perhaps, a good thing that we were on voice call only, and so I was unable to see Fede rolling her eyes. 'Well, I'll leave you two alone then. Give me a call later, eh? Just so I know what's going on.'

'I will. Love you.'

'You too.'

Erminia clucked. 'You hear that? She loves you too!'

There was a sigh, and then the phone went dead.

I put Erminia down. 'Right, come on then, ladies. Who hasn't had breakfast yet?'

'Okay, Mr Consul, how's the sleuthing been going?'

I hushed her. 'Mr Sutherland, remember?'

'Oh yes. As long as we're on a case.'

'And I'm not sleuthing. I'm exploring my spirituality. So what have you found?'

'Nothing yet. I've tried having a proper nosy around but monks keep turning up and getting in the way. And then I have to pretend to be cleaning.'

'Any sign of the key? It's almost certainly in Gregorio's cell. He took it out of the cabinet after the incident of the other night.'

'I've tried. He's been there all morning.'

'Wait until midday prayers. You'll have the run of the place then.'

'For how long?'

'Thirty minutes at most. I'll have to be there as well.' I looked at my watch. 'We've got about forty minutes before prayer. How long does it take you to prepare *panzanella*?'

She shrugged. 'Don't know. Never done it before.'

'Oh great. You and Federica. Two non-cooking Italians. In that case, I'll get it all prepared before I join the brothers in the chapel. That frees you up to have a poke around. Just make sure you get back here two minutes before the end of midday prayers, plate it up, and serve us our delicious lunch shortly after.'

'Right you are, Brother Nathan.'

Tomatoes, many. Check. Onions. Check. Garlic, lots of. Check. Basil. Check. Cucumber. Check, fortunately. Oil, Vinegar, Salt, Pepper. All Check.

Bread. Check. Already going stale? Check, even better.

It suddenly struck me that I'd never made *panzanella* for more than two people before. How many of us were there? Five monks. Three pilgrims. Or only two? Lucarini had told Pagan he was leaving today. And Lucia, of course.

Scaling that up meant multiplying everything by four and a half. That was okay. The recipe wasn't an exact one anyway.

However, my cooking method would have to change. No Hawkwind on the stereo, no Spritz Nathan near to hand. And an actual deadline.

I supposed I could save a bit of time by not peeling the tomatoes. But the very thought of that brought to mind the eyes of all my Italian friends gazing at me in disappointment. Hawkwind or no Hawkwind, spritz or no spritz, it needed to be done.

I finished with about five minutes grace, washed my hands and nodded in satisfaction at the great bowl of bread salad that I had prepared.

'Mr Sutherland?'

I yelped and jumped.

'I'm sorry, did I startle you?'

'Just a bit.'

Fra Gregorio gave a hint of a smile. 'I'm sorry.' He looked around the kitchen. 'Where's,' he put a hand to his forehead, 'I'm sorry, I can't remember her name.'

'Lucia? She's off cleaning somewhere, I understand. Or maybe she's with the chickens.'

'I hope she's not taking advantage of you?'

'Not at all. I enjoy cooking.'

He nodded. 'Well, perhaps one day we'll be needing to employ you?'

I smiled. 'I'm not very good at mass catering. And this, for me, is mass catering.'

Gregorio looked at my handiwork and nodded, I thought, approvingly. 'Simple, healthy food. Excellent. You'll be joining us for midday prayers, then.' It wasn't a question.

'Of course.' I thought about saying, 'I'll see you there', but Gregorio, it seemed, was intent on escorting me.

'No bad dreams last night, I trust?'

He was testing me. For a moment, I thought about lying and inventing a suitably dark Gothic tale, but the truth seemed simpler. 'None at all. I slept like a log.'

He smiled, this time I thought with some genuine warmth. '*I slept like a log.* I like that. We Italians would say *I slept like a rock.* Or perhaps even like a dormouse.'

'Well, we're British. We're very fond of our trees. In the same way that Italians are fond of their dormice.'

Lucia walked towards us, a broad smile on her face.

'Not joining us for prayers?' I smiled back.

'No time, brothers, no time. I've got work to do.'

'It seems Mr Sutherland has already done most of it for you,' said Gregorio.

'Well, not all of it. Just let it all macerate in the oil and vinegar for another twenty minutes. Tear some basil in. And then, by the time we're finished it'll be—' I made a chef's kiss motion.

'Blimey. That good, eh? Okay brother, I won't forget.'

Gregorio shot her an irritated glance. 'Come on, Mr Sutherland, I think we'd better leave her to it.'

Lucia shot me a wink which I fervently hoped Gregorio missed, and we continued on our way.

'So, how was it?'

'Even though I say so myself, it was something of a triumph.'

'Yeah, but how would it have been if I hadn't torn the basil in at the end?'

'Oh, Lucia, it would have been nothing without the basil. So, tell me, how did you get on?'

She grinned and fished a bunch of keys out of her back pocket. 'Here we go.'

'You genius.' I paused. 'These are for the cell, right?'

She shrugged. 'Who knows? But they're the only ones I could find.'

'Okay. Well, in that case I think your work is done. I can cook dinner, and you can get back to Venice if you like.'

'Are you serious?'

'How do you mean?'

'You've got a mysterious hidden chamber to investigate, and you want me to go home?' She folded her arms and shook her head. 'Yeah, like that's going to happen.'

'Well, I was going to leave it until later tonight.'

'And what if Fra whatsisname discoverers the keys have gone in the meantime?'

'Hmm. Fair point.'

'Now, then?'

'Okay. Let's do it.'

'Oh, one other thing. The Italian guy. Grumpy. Looks hungover. Who's that?'

'Bruno Pagan.'

'That's the one. Anyway, I was cleaning his cell and guess what I found?'

'A bottle of cheap whisky called *Pride of the Glens*?'

'That's one of the things, yes. I tell you what, I think he can't half put it away. But more than that. I found his wallet.'

I narrowed my eyes. 'And?'

'Well, I figured if I'm supposed to be here sleuthing I might as well – you know?'

'Lucia, all I wanted you to do was find the keys. Not do actual thievery.'

'Don't get grumpy. I just had a look, that's all.'

'And?'

'Oh, so you do want to know then?'

'Given that it's done now, yes.'

'Okay. Well, there wasn't much apart from a few bank-notes and an ID. And something else, as well. I took a photo so I'd remember. Take a look at this.'

She passed her phone to me. I struggled to see the image on screen and expanded it as much as I could. It was a simple business card.

'Facility Zorvic,' I read. I gave her the phone back. 'What the hell is that?'

'I don't know, Brother Nathan. But it sounds scary doesn't it?'

'It could be anything. It could be a home for lost kittens as far as we know. Or else—'

'Or else?'

'It means something scary and Bruno Pagan really does have some questions to answer.' I sighed. 'Come on then. Let's go and break into a cell.'

Chapter 33

I laid my hand upon the door and turned to Lucia. 'Okay, let's make this as quick as possible. In we go, quick look around, and then we just wait for Bepi the Boat to come and pick you up.'

'Now there's a plan I can sign up to. Trust me, I wasn't intending to stay the night here.' She paused. 'What if they start asking Maria about me, though? You know, questions that she can't answer about her imaginary auntie. I don't want that Gregorio giving her a hard time again.'

'Then I'll just say that I met you off the boat and you told me you were here to cover. One of those strange women who gatecrashes monasteries. I'm sure it happens all the time.' I clicked the door open. 'Okay. Just don't touch anything.'

'All right, Brother Nathan, I watch *CSI* as well.'

The air inside the cell was warm, damp and stale. There was a hint of sweetness in the air, yet with a touch of decay about it.

The room was bare, as I remembered it, yet with a spray of faded flowers that lay upon the bed. A black and white photograph had been propped against the pillow.

'I don't understand,' said Lucia.

I shook my head. 'Me neither.'

I wrapped a handkerchief around my hand and pulled the door of the wardrobe open. Nothing. Then the bedside table. Nothing, again, save for the obligatory Bible.

'What is this?' said Lucia, pointing at the photo.

I bent closer. The picture was crumpled and creased, but there was no mistaking the image. That iconic figure in trench coat and fedora, a cigarette dangling from his right hand.

'It's Humphrey Bogart,' I said. 'Playing Philip Marlowe in *The Big Sleep*. He was—'

'I know who Humphrey Bogart was.'

'Sorry.'

'What's he doing here?'

'I've no idea. And more to the point, he wasn't here when I came here five days ago with Vanni.'

'So now what?'

'I don't know. I'd been hoping for something more.'

'Such as?'

'I don't know. Just something rather more than some flowers and a photo of Humphrey Bogart. That's too cryptic to be useful and yet not normal enough to indicate "Oh he just fell off the tower." Worst of both worlds, in other words.' I sighed. 'As to what we do next, I guess we need to put the keys back in Gregorio's cell before he notices they're gone.'

We scurried down the passageway and back through the cloister.

Lucia stuck her head around the corner of Gregorio's cell.

'Clear?'

She nodded.

'Okay, quick as we can.'

She pulled open a drawer in the writing desk. She frowned, looking confused, then she closed it and pulled the drawer below.

'What's the problem?'

'You know, I can't really remember which one it was.'

'You're kidding?'

'No.'

'Do you remember what was in them?'

'There was a Bible in one, I remember.'

'Great.'

'But there was one in the other as well.'

'The same?'

'No. But they're both Bibles. Sorry, I didn't realise this sort of thing was going to be important.'

I clutched my hair. 'Shit. Just choose one. Any one.'

'Okay. I think it was probably the top one.' She pulled it open again. 'Probably.'

'It'll have to do.' I stuck my head out into the corridor and looked left and then right. 'Clear. Come on, let's head to the kitchen.'

'Sure. Why?'

'Dinner to prepare.'

'*Pappa al pomodoro*,' I sighed, slinging my tea towel over my shoulder in what I hoped was a suitably cheffy way. 'And now I never want to see another tomato again as long as I live.' I checked my watch. 'Okay, Bepi the Boat will be here in ten minutes. And then I think your work is done.'

She grinned. 'No, I don't think so. You're getting on that boat with me as well.'

'I am?'

'You are. Call it a surprise, if you like.'

'But I'm supposed to be staying one more night.'

'Bepi will give you a lift back later. Don't worry, I wouldn't want you to miss the religious life too much.'

'And who's going to serve dinner if neither of us is here?'

She rolled her eyes. 'How long has this place been here, again?'

'Eight hundred years.'

'Right. Eight hundred years, and you think the whole place will collapse if you're not here to serve the monks their tomatoes. Bloody hell. Find a monk to do it, Brother Nathan.'

I sighed. 'Okay. So let's go find a monk. Any chance you're going to tell me what this is all about?'

She grinned once more and shook her head. 'Not a chance.'

Chapter 34

There are a number of trains heading for Venice. But there's something I need to sort out first.

Someone's been following me since I left Vomero. Maybe from Danny's apartment, maybe the Penny Black. Somebody – presumably one of his ex-business colleagues – wants to find Danny just as much as I do. And they've been waiting and watching in the hope that he'd return. Or that someone like me would blunder into it.

The thing is, though, that a private investigator gets very used to noticing things like this. And it doesn't matter if you're a jealous husband or an actual mobster. I'm very, very good at spotting you.

I take a wander through Spaccanapoli, stopping occasionally to look in a restaurant window or to admire one of the many shrines to Diego Maradona, all the while checking reflections in windows.

I pause at the entrance to a side street. Long, narrow, possibly a dead end. Stinking piles of rubbish in plastic bags are sweltering in the early evening heat.

Perfect.

I take my phone out and pretend to be making a call. My

shadow is on the opposite side of the street. I check his reflection in the mirror of a scooter as I set off down the alley. I'm still pretending to be talking on the phone. The footsteps behind me are getting ever nearer.

We're a good distance from the main drag by now. Far enough, I think. I turn around.

'Excuse me, I'm a bit lost. Can you help me?'

My shadow stops, confused for a moment. Perhaps he's genuinely made a mistake. Then he reaches into his jacket.

'Where is Vicari?'

There's a butterfly knife in his hand. That makes it a bit more difficult. Irate ex-husbands in Swansea tend not to carry butterfly knives.

I hold my hands up. See, I'm cooperating. No reason to do anything stupid.

'I'm sorry, I don't know who you mean.'

'Where is Vicari?' he repeats. He swooshes the knife through the air, perhaps six inches from my face. He's not trying to hurt me so much as scare me. At the moment, anyway.

But Danny taught me a few things, and what worked with the West Cross Boys will work just as well with some bruiser in the back streets of Naples.

'Danny Vicari?' I say. 'I'm looking for him as well.'

That's enough. He looks confused for a moment, just a moment, but it's enough. Three jabs to the face, two rights and a left. I feel my knuckles crunching, and pain shoots up my arm, but it hurts him a hell of a lot more than it hurts me.

He's on the ground now, and probably out of the game, but why take chances? I kick him in the face, and his body goes limp. Something else Danny taught me. You can dance around like Ali *as much as you like, but – if you're in trouble – the direct route is always best.*

I'm breathing deeply now, and wipe the sweat from my face. The knuckles of my right hand are grazed, but otherwise I'm fine.

I drag my new acquaintance to the side of the road, hidden behind a pile of rubbish bags. He's going to have one hell of a headache when he wakes up, but he'll be okay.

I reach into his jacket, feeling around for his wallet. I've got no gloves, but that can't be helped. This is going to have to be quick.

Banknotes, driving licence, identity card.

I flick through it. Luigi Esposito. Neapolitan address. Occupation recorded as Primary School Teacher. I shake my head. Presumably he has a robust approach to classroom management.

There are a stack of business cards, mainly for bars and pizzerias. One of them appears to be for a strip club in Naples, with a phone number scrawled on the back. And there are three crumpled photographs. I recognise Danny immediately. The others are strangers to me. I turn them over. Their names are scrawled on the back. Bruno Pagan. Carlo Lucarini. And all of them have the same two words underneath.

Facility Zorvic.

What the hell is that?

My new friend groans, and I check the time. Then I look at my reflection in my phone. Looking good-ish. Knuckles aside, it's not too obvious that I've been in a fight.

I keep the photographs, and drop the wallet onto his body.

'You wouldn't last five minutes in West Cross, sunshine,' I call over my shoulder as I make my way back to the main street. Bogart, I think, would have been proud of me.

I make my way back up through Spaccanapoli and along to the Stazione Centrale. No time, sadly, for a final pizza and beer. And no time for a final look at the Bay of Naples. As I expected, crossing the road to the station is infinitely more terrifying than a man with a knife.

Ninety minutes later, I'm in Rome. And thirty minutes after that, I'm on a sleeper heading for Venice. I have no idea where Danny is, but I have names now. And a reference to something called Facility Zorvic.

Chapter 35

'Leaving us so soon, Mr Sutherland?' There was genuine sadness in Fra Raffaele's eyes.

'Only for the evening. I have to get back to,' I managed to bite back the word *civilisation,* 'Venice. Work reasons. I'll be back later, and here tomorrow morning as well.'

'Oh good. I was rather afraid I might not have had time to show you more of the collection.'

'I wouldn't miss it for the world, Raffaele.'

He turned to Lucia. 'I'm sorry we never had the chance to talk properly, *signorina*. But thank you for our splendid lunch.'

'It was a pleasure.'

'I can't work out what that image is on your shirt?'

'Oh,' she blushed and crossed her arms over the demonic figure beneath the Iron Maiden logo, 'it's nothing, really.'

'Hey, *capo*?' It was Bepi, calling from the boat. 'Ready when you are.'

'Well goodbye, Raffaele. See you all later.'

'Goodbye, Mr Sutherland. Goodbye, Lucia.'

We settled into the boat, and Bepi steered us back towards Burano.

'He was nice,' said Lucia. 'Raffaele, I mean. Reminded me of my *nonno*. That Gregorio guy is a dick, though.'

'I can't really find it in my heart to disagree.'

'What's going on then? You dragged me out here to help me break into a room and find – what – a photo of Humphrey Bogart and a bunch of flowers? So what do we do now?'

I shrugged. 'I don't know. I'll go to Vanni at the *Questura* and tell him a story about strange monks crying in locked cells.' I swatted away a mosquito. 'There might be something else as well. Fra Raffaele showed me an embroidered altar cloth from Burano. It's the most precious thing they possess. They've kept it safe for three hundred years. And now, in celebration of the eight hundredth anniversary of the monastery, it's going to be gifted to a church in Holy Land. Where it was always meant to be.'

'And?'

'And Carlo Lucarini was showing quite a lot of interest in it.'

'What, you think he was after stealing it or something?'

'It's a possibility. But he left this morning. Maybe I got that wrong.'

She shook her head. 'Come on, Brother Nathan. Who steals altar cloths?'

I had to concede that was a fair point.

The mosquitoes were rising thick and fast now in the damp, warm evening air, and I swatted at them uselessly. But as I thrashed around, I became aware of a weight in my jacket pocket and I remembered the diving watch.

'You ever go diving, Bepi?'

'In the Bahamas, a few years ago. Like I said, I used to

work on a lot of yachts.'

'How about round here?'

'Not so much. Here, I'd rather be on top of the water than under it. And diving's illegal, in this part of the lagoon anyway. Too dangerous. Sure, it's quiet now, but you should be here in a normal summer. There's boat traffic all the time. Also, what is there to see around here? All the good stuff is above the water if you ask me. Why so?'

'It's just I thought I saw someone in the lagoon the other day.'

'Probably a dolphin. Everyone's seeing them now, you know?'

I shook my head. 'I don't think so.'

He laughed. 'You're going full 007 on me tonight, *capo*.' He throttled back on the engine, and the boat slowed as he pulled up to the jetty. I noticed a figure standing there and looking down on us. The light was fading, but I recognised her at once.

'Fede?'

'You took your time, *caro mio*.'

'Sorry. I've been busy. Being a monk.'

In a perfect world, I would have leapt out of the boat like Errol Flynn and taken her in my arms as if she was Olivia de Havilland. In the imperfect reality, however, I slipped and set the boat rocking. Bepi swore under his breath as he grabbed my arm, and helped me ashore. Lucia tried, and failed, to stifle a laugh.

'Ciao, *caro*.'

'Ciao, *cara*.'

I gave her an awkward hug and a kiss, aware that Lucia

and Bepi were pointedly pretending to stare at things in the opposite direction.

Lucia cleared her throat. 'Is it okay to turn around now?'

'It is,' said Fede.

'I mean, it must have been – what – all of forty-eight hours now?'

'So,' I said, 'and what brings my lovely wife out to Burano on a warm summer's evening?'

'Well, mainly to see you of course.'

'Gosh. Really?'

'Yes, of course. I think you owe us all dinner.'

'I do?'

'Yes. Lucia's given up her time to help you out with this little problem of yours. The least we can do is stand her dinner.'

Chapter 36

'Sardines, again?' said Fede.

'Of course. It's wasting an opportunity otherwise.' I looked at the waiter. 'Can you remind me, does the salad come with tomatoes?'

He nodded. 'It does, sir.'

'Right, well in that case can you hold the tomatoes?'

'Of course, sir, I'll tell them in the kitchen.'

'It's not that I've got an allergy or anything. It's just that I've been living on them for two days now. I think we need a break from each other.'

Lucia looked around the restaurant, and smiled. 'I've not been here since I was a little girl.'

'Oh right?'

'Mum and Dad used to come here a lot. They weren't Buranese, but this is where Dad proposed to her. Stuck the ring in an oyster, he says. So they used to come back every year, on the day. Until the year when Mum left and so – well, we didn't come back any more.'

Fede took her hand. 'Sorry. I never even thought about something like that.'

Lucia smiled again. 'No problems. I might pass on the

oysters though.'

I nodded. 'All those memories, eh?'

'No. They just make me throw up.'

'Coffee and *grappa*, sir?'

'Oh, I think so!'

Lucia nodded. 'If you are then I will. I'll swap *grappa* for *limoncello* though. I can't do proper spirits.'

Fede shook her head. 'Not for me, thanks. I'll never get to sleep.'

'That's what the *grappa*'s for. To balance out the coffee.'

'Is that proper medical advice?'

'It is. Possibly.'

She turned to the waiter. 'Do you have *sgroppino*?' He nodded. 'I'll have one of those then.'

'Of course.'

I frowned, and wondered for a moment if I'd made a bad call. *Sgroppino* — a lemon sorbet mixed up with Prosecco and vodka – was, in many ways, the perfect end to a meal. Perhaps – after a couple of days of near total abstinence – I'd be allowed one of those as well? Then I saw the warning look in Federica's eyes, and I decided not to push it.

She folded her fingers together. 'Well now. You've got a British citizen soaked in booze, who fell from the *campanile* whilst he was up there looking at the stars or whatever else you do late at night whilst staying in a monastery?'

'Pretty much that.'

'And somebody left a photograph of Humphrey Bogart and a bunch of flowers in his cell?'

'Yes.'

'And someone called Carlo Lucarini seems to be taking something of an interest in the most precious artifact in the monastery's collection, just before it disappears forever?'

'Yes.'

'And someone else called Bruno Pagan likes spending his evenings watching the lagoon from the bell tower, and knocking back the same cheap blend of supermarket whisky that Mr Vicari favoured?'

'And, again, yes.'

She nodded. 'Hmmm.'

'What are you thinking?'

'I'm thinking I'd love to be there when you try and explain all this to Vanni.'

I rubbed my forehead. 'Oh God.' I caught the waiter's eye and made the 'signing a cheque' sign to call for the bill. 'I guess I'll need to be getting back then. Bepi will be waiting for me. The last night of the pilgrimage awaits.' I turned to Fede. 'You'll explain to Gramsci that I'll be back tomorrow, yes?'

'I'll do my best not to break his heart.'

'I've got to say, Brother Nathan, you're a lot better at this sort of thing than I am. I've only done one day and it was doing my head in. How you've done nearly a week, God only knows.'

Fede raised an eyebrow. 'A week?'

'Ah, it just feels like a week, that's all. Being without my lovely wife.'

'Blimey,' said Lucia, 'I've just remembered it's not just oysters that make me throw up.'

'Anyway, it's not been a week. Somebody – and I suspect

it was Maria – wrote down the night of Vicari's death as the date I arrived. And had a go at writing my signature as well.'

'How would they do that?'

'It's on my ID card. Fra Vincenzo said he'd pass it on to Maria to record all the details. You know, just like when you check into a hotel.'

Fede frowned. 'Why do that, though?'

'Trying to frame him for the murder?' said Lucia. 'Don't worry, Brother Nathan, we'll come and visit you in prison.'

'We can go back to *Englishman* or *Mr Consul* if you like. I'm off duty now. And as far as we know there's not even been a murder. Anyway, it'd be pointless, I was fast asleep in the Street of the Assassins at the time, and Federica is my alibi.'

'*Probably* your alibi,' said Fede.

'What?'

'Well, first we might need a discussion about how many hours in the day can be spent playing your horrible record collection. But, seriously, a plan like that wouldn't work. Would it?'

I shook my head. 'It seems pointless to me. But there was something I heard Lucarini say last night. *Sutherland's not the problem. He's part of the solution.*' I sighed. 'I suppose there's no chance of an extra *grappa*?'

Fede shook her head. 'Not a chance.'

'Oh very well. Do you think you'll ever get married, Lucia?'

'I dunno. Never thought about it. Can't imagine it really. Why?'

'Oh, it's just that – in some respects at least – married life is surprisingly good preparation for the monastic life.'

'Cheek.' Federica flicked a napkin at me.

I got to my feet. 'Right then. Back to the pilgrimage. A final night in the cell awaits.' I kissed Fede on the cheek. 'I shall see you tomorrow, *cara*. And Lucia—'

'Yes, Brother?'

'Iron Maiden or no Iron Maiden, you were a wonderful housekeeper.'

Chapter 37

Sutherland's not the problem. He's part of the solution.

There would be a conversation to be had in the morning with Maria, but there was little to be done now. In the meantime, another night awaited in the company of Dan Brown, Umberto Eco and the Book of Revelation. It had been tempting, so tempting, just to head back to the Street of the Assassins with Fede, to where Ed would greet me with Negronis and Gramsci with all the enthusiasm of a cat who hadn't been fed in at least three hours.

But I'd arranged to stay for three nights and I was going to do three nights. I was not going to be the sort of person who'd take a pilgrimage lightly.

Besides, there was Dominic Vicari to think on. The quiet man, who kept himself to himself, who carried sadness with him, who'd come to San Francesco del Deserto in search of sanctuary. Who wanted nothing more than to look at the stars with his heart and soul warmed by whisky.

Except that Dominic Vicari had also been a man stargazing on a cloudy night, and a man with more whisky on his shirt than in his bloodstream. A man over whom somebody had wept, and left a bunch of flowers and a photo of

Humphrey Bogart by way of tribute.

Was this something I could realistically take to Vanni? Again, perhaps. That was something to think on come the morning after a good night's sleep.

I'd attempted *The Name of the Rose* on a number of occasions, without success. Perhaps another attempt would help me get to sleep. I turned, yet again, to the preface, and wished that William of Baskerville could be here to help me unravel the case of Dominic Vicari.

I awoke with a start as I dropped the book onto my face and cursed as I wished I had chosen some lighter reading material. I supposed it could have been worse. The hardback Bible might have crushed me in my sleep.

I tossed and turned, feeling cramped and sweaty in the single bed, my feet tangling in the sheets as the tiny fan hummed away to little effect. I turned the pillow over, and then over again, in the hope of finding a cool spot. And then, just as I was about to drop off once more, I heard the damned buzzing of a mosquito. I reached for the can of repellent, shook it and waved it around. A feeble little *pfft* came from the nozzle. Empty. I sipped from the glass on my bedside table, and found the water stale and warm.

To hell with it. I'd go for a walk. The air outside would be cooler, and less stale than that within the thick stone walls of the monastery. And then maybe I'd get a glass of water from the kitchen and try and find another can of insect repellent prior to hunting the little bastard down. And tomorrow I'd be tucked up in my own bed with nothing to worry about except what time Gramsci would decide he'd need feeding; and dinner would be something other than tomato-based.

I pulled on some clothes, and opened the cell door. The passageway was dimly lit, and my eyes flickered for a moment to the door of Vicari's room. A room where a stranger had wept over his bed and left a cryptic tribute. I thought again on how I was the only living person in this wing of the monastery, and that made me a little uncomfortable.

I padded down to Vicari's cell, and laid my hand upon it. There was nothing to be heard from within. Whoever had been there, perhaps, now considered his – or her – work to be done. I tried the handle. Locked, as it had been since Lucia and I had left it earlier.

Silly, of course. What had I been expecting to find? And yet, as I padded down the corridor, I stopped and looked back, just to reassure myself that the door was indeed still closed.

The night air was warm and muggy, a sign that the height of summer was now almost upon us, a period stretching until early September when it would prove near-impossible to keep cool at night, and leaving the house during daylight would leave one bathed in sweat within minutes. Add to that the press of huge numbers of visitors – this year excepted – and one soon realised exactly why so many Venetians headed for the mountains or for the beaches of Croatia. I smiled to myself. In just a few weeks – days perhaps – Fede and I would up in the mountains, enjoying the clear fresh air and the infinity pool with a view of the Dolomites.

I passed through the cloister, and looked up at the *campanile*. No sign of anyone. Pagan had evidently tired of his night watchman ritual.

I filled myself a jug of water in the kitchen. A search of the cupboards under the sink revealed a couple of citronella candles and a single can of mosquito spray. I wondered what the consequences would be of burning one of the candles in my room. Perhaps if I left the window ajar? I gave the can a good shake, and nodded. There was enough there, I was sure, to deal with my unwanted lodger.

I considered making myself a sandwich – tomato, of course – but transporting my haul back to my cell was going to be difficult enough as it was. There were fresh eggs in the fridge, and a little cheese. Perhaps I should make myself a cheese omelette? There was also a jug of white wine, perhaps half full. A veritable feast! Well, why not? It had been hours since dinner on Burano, it was my last night here, and I was pretty sure I'd sleep better with a full stomach and a glass or two of wine inside me.

I found a suitable-looking frying pan, and a bottle of olive oil, when I heard voices. My immediate reaction was to try and cover up any evidence of my illicit cooking activities, but I realised that was useless. Besides, the voices were not coming any closer.

One was low, calm, controlled; the other higher pitched and increasingly desperate but, try as I might, I could not make out the words.

And then, as soon as they'd begun, they stopped. I strained to listen, and there was a thud, as of a heavy object falling. And then, seconds later, the breaking of glass.

I ran back through the kitchen, and into the refectory where the apostles stared down from their Last Supper in the dim light. There were footsteps now, running footsteps, and the sound of feet upon gravel.

I realised I'd brought the can of mosquito repellent with

me. Well, it wasn't the obvious choice of defensive weapon, but it would have to do. It was at least solid and metal and whatever the effects might be of spraying the contents into somebody's face, I was pretty sure they wouldn't be good.

The door to the chapel lay open in front of me and, within, I could see a figure stretched out upon the floor.

Bruno Pagan lay sprawled at the foot of the altar. Even in the dim light, I could make out that his face was purple and his eyes red, his tongue protruding grotesquely through blackened, bloody lips. I pressed my ear against his chest. No movement, no heartbeat. Then I held my hand above his nose and mouth. He wasn't breathing.

Footsteps, and then more footsteps. I felt a hand upon my shoulder and looked up at Fra Gregorio, his face stern yet not unkind. I let him move me aside, as he knelt down by Pagan's side. He took his hand, bent further and whispered something into his ear. Then he shook his head, crossed himself, and laid a hand upon Pagan's head.

'*May holy Mary, the angels and all the saints come to meet you as you go forth.*

May Christ welcome you into his garden of paradise.'

Other voices joined in. Jeremiah, Ezekiel and Raffaele.

'*May Christ the true shepherd welcome you as one of his sheep and acknowledge you as one of his flock.*

May He forgive all your sins and set you among those he has chosen.

Amen.'

A Franciscan prayer for the dead.

He got to his feet. 'Mr Sutherland. The police will need to be called.'

'Of course.'

I took out my mobile and was about to dial when he stretched out his hand. 'I'll call. If I may.' I nodded, and brought up Vanni's personal number before passing it to him.

Gregorio frowned. 'Who is this?'

'A friend. From the *Questura*. He'll try and be as discreet as possible.'

'Mr Sutherland, a man is dead. I don't care about trying to be discreet.' He dialled the emergency number instead.

I shrugged and looked around the chapel. Ezekiel, Jeremiah and Raffaele knelt in front of the altar, praying softly. The door to the sanctuary, I noticed, was ajar and I stepped through.

The cabinet that held the altar cloth had been smashed open. Broken glass lay on the floor, and fragments were scattered over the precious relic. Yet nothing, as far as I could see, had been taken. From the other room I could hear the sounds of the brothers praying, and Gregorio talking on the phone. And, from far away across the lagoon, I thought perhaps I could hear the sounds of an outboard motor.

Chapter 38

'Well, Nathan,' said Vanni as he sighed and folded his newspaper away. 'It seems we've gone full Monastery of Death now.'

'Sorry.'

'Well, how was I to know that asking the British Honorary Consul to spend a couple of days there, just being inconspicuous, would work out this way?'

'Again, sorry.'

He tapped the newspaper in front of him. 'I see they've kept your name out of it?'

'I'm not sure for how long. I guess Roberto Bergamin at the *Gazzettino* owes me a favour.'

'I wish he owed me a favour. Lots of people are going to be very unhappy with me.'

'Look, if my name comes out the Ambassador isn't going to be happy with me either. The British press love a good "Honorary Consul in the Monastery of Murder" story.'

'Is that a thing?'

'They'll make it one.' I sighed. 'So, what happened to Bruno Pagan?'

'Strangled, they tell me. Garrotted, to be precise. Three

deep bruises,' he tapped his neck, 'about here. Oh, and whoever he was, his name wasn't Bruno Pagan.'

'I don't understand.'

'False ID. Whoever he is, he's not the person on the card.'

'Can you be sure?'

'Given the original possessor is dead, yes.'

'Oh. Nobody at the monastery noticed?'

'Nathan, there are upwards of one hundred thousand
fake identity cards in this country. Some of them remark-
ably sophisticated. It was good enough to fool a monk who,
more than likely, is not trained in the latest police techniques.
More than that, they were Venice ID cards.' He reached into
his jacket and brought out his own. 'Yours is like this, yes?
Laminated, like a credit card?'

I nodded.

'We were still using paper cards until a few years ago,
remember? Venice was the last place in Italy to change. Now
they're biometric, they're much harder to forge. But there are
still plenty of these old ones in circulation.'

'I see. Okay then, Vanni. What do we do now?'

'You, nothing. Your work is done. As for me,' he sighed,
'we'll have a better idea once we've managed to identify *signor*
Pagan here.'

'And Lucarini?'

'That's the other thing, Nathan. There is no Lucarini
either.'

'What?'

'Another false ID.'

'Two people, on a retreat on a remote island. Both with
false ID. Are there any actual pilgrims there at all?'

'No. Given the third one was you.'

'So either two people with false IDs coincidentally arrived on the same retreat. Or they knew each other, and they were there for some other purpose. The altar cloth.'

He nodded. 'Seems reasonable, doesn't it?'

'So,' I rubbed my temples, 'they were going to lift it a few nights before. Only something happened with Dominic. Maybe he interrupted them, who knows? And he ended up taking a short walk off a high tower.'

'Perhaps so.'

'They wait for a few days. I turn up and, for some reason they suspect I'm not who I say I am. Maybe they think I'm an undercover cop or something? And they change the date in the guest book so it looks as if I arrived the night before Vicari's murder. As if they're trying to give themselves an alibi.'

Vanni tapped his pen on the desk. 'And how do you think they went about that?'

'I don't know. But Maria – the young woman who basically fetches and cleans for them – deals with all that. Maybe they slipped her some money to put the wrong date down.'

'Uh-huh. But how was this supposed to work? The friars would have confirmed that you weren't there in the event of an investigation.'

'Maybe it was just to buy them some time? A false lead, no matter how weak. Anything to gain them a little time.'

'Well, we'll be wanting to talk to *signora* Maria when she turns up for work, of course.'

'I don't think she's a bad sort, Vanni.'

'Maybe not. Although she was selling drugs on Burano, I hear.'

I was about to protest but Vanni was, I reminded myself, still a cop and still needed to think like one. 'So going back to the problem. Vicari is dead, maybe murder, maybe accident. Whatever it is, Pagan is working himself up into a right old state. He's drinking too much. Lucarini makes out that he's leaving the island, and then comes back with theft on his mind. Then last night, he slips back and the two of them have some sort of falling out. Bruno ends up dead. Lucarini doesn't have time to grab the altar cloth, and makes a run for it.'

'A classic falling out amongst thieves. It all fits together quite nicely, doesn't it?'

'It does. But what's with all that business in Vicari's cell?'

'What about it?'

'The first night I was there. I heard somebody crying in Vicari's cell.'

'Maybe they were praying. They're a religious order, Nathan. That's the sort of thing they do.'

'Okay, okay. But what about the flowers? And the picture of Humphrey Bogart?'

'One of the brothers left some flowers as a tribute. You saw yourself, the old *vera da pozzo* was overflowing with them.'

'And Bogie?'

'One of the things we missed when we were clearing the cell. It was probably under the bed like that bottle of whisky you found.'

'So your guys missed not one but two things? How likely is that, Vanni? Really?'

'You're over-thinking this, Nathan. Means, motive, opportunity. We've got all of those. Humphrey Bogart and his flowers don't have to come into it.'

I sighed. 'Okay. Okay, you're probably right. So, what's going to happen now? With Fra Vincenzo, I mean?'

'I spoke to him this morning. He wanted to cut short his pilgrimage, but I persuaded him not to. It means a lot to him, I know.' He shook his head. 'Poor Enzo. Two deaths in less than a week. Which statistically makes the monastery of San Francesco del Deserto one of the most dangerous places in Italy.' He got to his feet. 'Okay, Nathan, I think that's everything. Thanks for coming in. And, for what it's worth, I know it wasn't your fault.'

'Thanks, Vanni.' A thought struck me. 'We are still okay with the whole apartment in Cortina thing, though, aren't we?'

'Don't push it.'

'A deal's a deal, Vanni.' My phone rang. I looked at the number and my heart sank.

'Aren't you going to answer that?'

I shook my head. 'No. Not just yet. I think I need to be at home with a good stiff Spritz Nathan for this one.'

'Bad news?'

'It's the Ambassador. I'm hoping it's just about rearranging dates for the next Honorary Consuls Virtual Pub Quiz.'

'And if it isn't?'

'Then I suspect "Honorary Consul in the Monastery of Murder" is about to hit the shelves.' I shook my head. 'Oh God.'

Vanni grinned. 'Welcome to my world, Nathan. Welcome to my world.'

Chapter 39

'So where does that leave you?' said Fede.

'With my ears burning. Maxwell's not a happy bunny. Which I can kind of understand.'

'That's not fair. You were only trying to get that poor man home.'

'I know. And if I'd managed it, I'd be a shoo-in for Consul of the Month award. As it is though,' I shook my head, 'he's saying the same as Vanni. Do nothing. Leave it to the police. Which I'd have been happy to do had Vanni not involved me in the first place.'

'And so?'

I grinned. 'Well, quite obviously I'm going to ignore everything he said. Which means starting with this.' I placed the watch upon the table.

Fede picked it up, and turned it over in her hands. 'So, what is this?'

'Fra Ezekiel says it's a dive watch. Expensive, he reckons.'

'Okay. So why didn't you hand this in to the police?'

I shrugged. 'It's a bit of flotsam and jetsam I found on the beach. That's all. As a piece of hard evidence, it's right up there with photographs of Humphrey Bogart. Except I started thinking about that Facebook message for Vicari. The one from Deep Dive. Now, I thought that meant conspiracy theory stuff, the sort of craziness that might get thrown up along the way whilst investigating a missing person. *Aliens took your brother*, that kind of thing. But what if it was literal? Maybe they actually are a deep diver?'

Fede put the watch down. Gramsci knocked it to the floor, scrabbled around with it in his paws, and knocked it under the sofa.

'Expensive, you said?'

Frantic mewing came from under the sofa, followed by the sound of the watch skittering across the floor. I sighed and bent to retrieve it. 'Well, it *was* an expensive dive watch. Now it's a rival to the fifty cent foam rubber ball as Gramsci's favourite plaything.' I snatched it away from him, just as his paws scythed through the air. 'I thought you'd established a non-violence pact?'

'We had. It's because you're back. He can't deal with all the excitement.'

As if aware of her words, Gramsci flopped down upon the sofa, threw a paw across his eyes, and promptly went to sleep.

'So, what are we going to do with it?'

'We use this to try and find Deep Dive.'

'Sure, but why should this belong to them?'

'No reason at all. But it's a coincidence, and I don't like coincidences.' I held it up to the light. 'You see, there's some sort of identifying mark on this. I don't think it's the brand, either.'

'Okay. Let me have a look.' She brought the strap closer to her face. 'And my glasses, please. They're on the table.

For some reason, Gramsci doesn't find them as much fun as yours.'

I passed them to her, and she slid them to the end of her nose. She smiled. 'You're right. There is something here. It's faded but you can still make it out.' She frowned. 'God knows what it is, though.'

'Let me see.'

'Here. Halfway down the strap.'

I held it up to my face. Then further away. Then further away still.

'Arms not long enough, *caro*?'

'Why are people printing everything so much smaller these days?' I patted my pockets, and then scanned the desk. 'Where are my glasses?'

'Somewhere under the sofa, I think.'

'What?'

'Well, where else would they be? I told you, Gramsci prefers yours. You should feel flattered.' She passed me hers, smiling. 'Will these do?'

'They will.' I kissed the tip of her nose.

'Thank you. What brought that on?'

'It's just that your nose wrinkles when you smile. I've never noticed that before.'

'It does not!'

'It does. It's kind of cute.'

'"Cute" and "wrinkles" in the same sentence. Ah, Mr Sutherland, what you give with one hand you take with the other.'

'Aww. I mean it.'

She smiled and touched my cheek. 'Come on, we can leave

my nose for another day. What can you see?'

Fede's glasses weren't quite right for me but, given I was unlikely to see my pair ever again, they would have to do. I closed one eye, held the watch away from me, and tried to make sense of the shape that swam into view.

'Bloody hell!'

'What?'

'Do you know what this is?'

'No idea. Looks a bit like an octopus, maybe?'

'No, not an octopus.' I paused and looked again at the strap. There was no doubting it. An octopus, perhaps, but one with bat wings. 'It's Great Cthulhu.'

My words didn't seem to have the expected impact.

'Okay. I was with you up until the word *Great*.'

'Great Cthulhu,' I repeated. 'One of H. P. Lovecraft's Great Old Ones.'

Fede blinked.

'Great Cthulhu, who sleeps in the the sunken city of R'lyeh, waiting for the moment when the stars will align and he shall emerge once more to bring chaos to the world.'

Fede rubbed her eyes. 'Do you know, I think I'm getting a migraine?'

'But this is so exciting!'

'What, because Great Cthulhu, or whatever his name is, is on a watch strap? Tell me you're not going to want one for Christmas?'

'No. Well, yes, I am. But don't you see? This makes it easier to track the owner down.'

'It does?'

'Of course. It's an expensive watch, or dive computer, or

whatever we're calling it. That narrows it down. That strap narrows it down even more.'

'Oh, I see. You know, that's a good point.' She flipped open the cover of her laptop. 'Come on, let's have a look. There can't be that many dive schools in Venice.' She tapped away. 'Just three as far as I can see. *Dive Venezia. Subacquea Venezia. Venezia Subacquea.* What an imagination these people have.'

'I suppose there's only so many variations on a theme.'

She frowned, and tapped the screen. 'Only thing is, none of them seem to have that logo of Great – what was his name again?'

'Cthulhu. Great Cthulhu.'

'Cthulhu. Thank you. Am I saying it right?'

'Well, Lovecraft himself said the name was merely an approximation of non-human speech and so—'

'I had to ask. Anyway, there's nothing like that image on any of these sites.'

'Hmm. That's a shame. Can I take a look?'

She swivelled the laptop around to face me, and I clicked through the three sites.

'*Venezia Subacquea.* No. Doesn't look like it's them. *Subacquea Venezia* doesn't look any more promising. *Dive Venezia.*' I shook my head. 'No. Damn.'

'Is it really the sort of image they'd use to advertise their business, though?'

'I imagine it might attract a certain type of customer.'

'You mean people like you?'

'Well, yes. Only without my innate cowardice.' Something caught my eye on the screen. 'Hang on, though.' A smile broke across my face. 'Here we go. Take a look at this.'

I turned the screen to her. '"Be one of the Deep Ones",' she read. 'What does that mean?'

'Lovecraft again. The Deep Ones are a monstrous humanoid aquatic race from the city of Y'hanethlei.'

'R'lyeh. Cthulhu. Y'hanethlei. Did he just have a typewriter with a broken keyboard or something?'

'Maybe so. But don't you see? Deep Ones. What better tag line for a diving school?'

She nodded. 'Okay. I guess that if you view it through a particular – very particular – lens, it does make sense.'

'The owner, then – or at least one of them – is something of a Lovecraft fan boy. Or fan girl.'

'Do such people exist?'

'Trust me, they do.' I clicked away at the *Dive Venezia* site. 'The address is in Treporti.' I clicked further. 'There are four of them. Eleonora. Cristiano. Giovanni. Arturo.' I snapped my fingers. 'And that's him. Arturo.'

Fede peered over my shoulder at the photo of a young man, perhaps in his late twenties, grinning at the camera. With his long blonde hair he resembled a young Rick Wakeman, minus cape but plus wetsuit.

'He's rocking that hairstyle, I'd have to say. But how do you know it's him?'

I raised my right hand, mimicking Arturo's on-screen gesture. 'Because he's making the Voorish Sign.'

Fede rubbed her temples. 'Do I need to know?'

'No.'

'Are you going to tell me anyway?'

'Well, it's from "The Case of Charles Dexter Ward" and—'

'Okay. I think that's enough information.' Then she

smiled. 'But I guess you're right. That's him. So what now?'

'Well, I guess tomorrow I'll head over to Treporti and have a word with him.'

'You could always just phone him?'

'I suppose I could,' I said, unenthusiastically.

She gently punched my arm. 'Or are you hoping to have a good old chat with him about H. P. Lovecraft?'

'Well. Yes. Yes, I am.'

She smiled and kissed me on the cheek. 'Oh *caro*, don't ever change. Now, is it the Negroni hour?'

'Oh, I think it is.'

'Come on then. Down to Eduardo's. Maybe he'll have little octopuses on sticks. You can pretend they're Great what's-his-name.'

'Cthulhu.'

'Great Cthulhu. There we go. Come on!'

Chapter 40

I never had much occasion to go out to Treporti. It wasn't somewhere that British tourists tended to go, despite its fifteen kilometres of sandy beaches. The Lido was closer to the *centro storico* after all and somehow felt just, well, more *Venetian*. So, complaints from distressed tourists whose wallets had gone walkabout were mercifully thin on the ground.

It wasn't even part of Venice any more, having declared independence from the *comune* of Venezia a decade before I arrived in the city; a decision, I thought, that many residents of Venice might be wishing they could take themselves when it came to their larger neighbours on *terraferma*. But it offered one thing that the Lido didn't. You could dive, properly dive, in the Adriatic.

The two guys outside *Dive Venezia* were tanned in a way that could only come from a life lived in the open, and weather-beaten in a way that made them both look older than they probably were. They were playing cards and cheerfully smoking away, dropping the ashes into what I hoped was an empty beer can. They looked up as I approached.

'Cristiano? Giovanni?'

One of them, distinguished from his friend by a goatee

beard and a man bun that I thought would struggle to keep its shape under water, tapped his chest with his thumb.

'I'm Gio. And this here,' he patted his companion on the shoulder, 'is my baldy buddy, Cristiano.'

Cristiano rubbed his bald pate. 'Mate, if it's a choice between your hairstyle and no hair at all, I'd be reaching for the clippers every time.'

They both laughed. Gio smiled at me. 'What can we do for you, *capo*? Lessons, boat hire, gear?'

'Er, none of that, I'm afraid.'

Cristiano shook his head. 'Pity. We could do with the business.' He looked around. 'As you can see.'

'I'm sorry. But I'm looking for Arturo.'

Gio rolled his eyes. 'Aren't we all, *capo*?'

'He's not here, then?'

'Not seen him in a week.' He craned his head around to the front door of the shop. 'Elly? You got a moment?'

A young woman appeared, pressing a bottle of water to her forehead. 'Sure. Anything to get out of the heat. Seriously guys, it's a sauna in there.' She turned to me. 'We're trying not to run the air con too much. Just to save on the electricity.'

'Elly, it's about not using the air con until we need it. Not some sort of endurance test to see how long we can physically stand it.'

She nodded, and drained the bottle of its water.

'Look,' said Cristiano, 'I'll mind the office this afternoon. The break will do me good. You stay out here and let Gio win all your money at *scopa*. I'm nearly flat broke.' He pointed a finger at me. 'Our new buddy here wants to know if we've heard anything from Arty.'

'Arturo? No. Not for a few days. And why should I know?'

Gio grinned. 'Well. You did have a bit of a thing.'

'We did not have a thing!'

'Oh, you *so* did.'

'Once. When we were drunk. That does not make it a thing. No, I don't know where he is.' Her eyes narrowed, either with suspicion or alarm. 'Why?'

I sighed. 'I don't really know myself. Probably no reason. But you remember reading about the British citizen who fell from the *campanile* on San Francesco del Deserto a few days ago?'

Three blank faces stared back at me.

'You remember reading about this, right?'

Gio scratched his head. 'Uh. Maybe.'

'I think Arturo had been in touch with him just a couple of days before. I'm trying to find out why.'

Gio frowned, suspicion in his eyes. 'Can I ask why?'

'I'm the British Honorary Consul. I've got a dead British citizen to repatriate who seems to have no living relatives. So, anything I can find out about him is potentially useful. Please.'

He nodded. 'Okay. But it was probably just about lessons.'

I shook my head. 'Travel is difficult at the moment. Do you have any other foreigners making their way across Europe for diving lessons?'

'Okay. Fair point. But it'll be something diving related. Arty didn't do much else.'

Elly spoke. 'Arturo has form for this sort of thing, Mr?'

'Sutherland. Nathan Sutherland.'

She nodded. 'He's done this any number of times before. He'll just go off and do things. That's what Arty does. He sees himself as a bit of an eco-warrior. He's always off saving the world somewhere. We lost him for three months once. Next thing we knew, we got a video from him on his dive log. From the Great Barrier Reef. He was out there on some sort of project involving coral bleaching.'

'And he didn't tell you?'

Cristiano laughed. 'It's the way his mind works.' He made a little twirly motion with his finger next to his temple. 'He gets a call from a pal in Australia – somebody he's never met in real life – who says, hey you want to come and work on this project on the Reef? And he says sure, no problem, just let me get packed. And then he's on a flight to Australia, and he's flying somewhere over the Middle East and thinks, shit, maybe I should have told the guys?'

'You let him keep his job, though?'

He shrugged. 'He's good at what he does. And we get on. Have a laugh. That's enough.'

'So, what's he been working on recently?'

'Same as the rest of us. Just about nothing.'

Gio tapped more ash into the beer can, shaking his head. 'Not quite. He'd spent a few weeks working with ISMAR.'

I shook my head. 'You've lost me.'

'*Istituto di Scienze Marine*. They're based over in Castello, at the Arsenale.'

'And what do they do?'

'Scientific research. Marine geology. Archaeology. They needed a short-term contract diver.'

'For what?'

'Marine archaeology in the Treporti Channel. Arty was kinda tight-lipped about exactly what it was. Think about it, though. There's barely been any marine traffic for months. This is the clearest the lagoon has ever been. There couldn't be a better time for an archaeological project down there.'

'And then he just disappeared?'

'Sure. But as we said, he does this sort of thing. The guy's been going stir-crazy for months. We all have. He's probably at the other end of the country, just so he can travel a little bit.'

'Okay. Maybe so. You mentioned his dive log earlier? Is there anything on there that might tell us where he is?'

'You really are keen to find him, aren't you?'

'Like I said, there's a British citizen who's died over here. I want to get him home, if I can. Anything that can help me track down family, friends – anyone like that – would be useful.'

Elly nodded. 'Okay. Give me a minute, I'll grab a laptop.'

Gio lit up another pair of cigarettes, and passed one to Cristiano. Then he gathered the cards together, and shuffled them.

'You play *scopa*?'

'Badly.'

He grinned. 'My kind of player.'

Cristiano looked at me and shrugged, apologetically. 'I know what you're thinking, *capo*. What are this pair of wasters doing drinking and smoking their lives away and playing cards? And the truth is, there isn't much else to do. Business is piss-poor. Sure, the locals are happy to be back in the sea, but the tourists aren't coming. Not this year, anyway. So that's why we're smoking and playing cards.'

'I understand.'

'So this job of yours – Honorary Consul – that keeps you busy?'

'Busy enough. People trying to get home. Trying to contact relatives if somebody's ill. Or worse, if they've died. Irate holidaymakers. People wondering if I can go round and check up on their second homes, "just to make sure everything's okay". Zoom calls with the Ambassador.' I sighed. 'It's been non-stop this past six months.'

'I hope you're getting overtime, my friend.'

I laughed. 'Thing is, Cristiano – I don't actually get paid at all. Just expenses. Not much more than that.'

'Seriously?'

'Yes. The "Honorary" in Honorary Consul is actually spelled P-E-N-N-I-L-E-S-S.'

'Wow. Why do you do it?'

'Job satisfaction, I suppose.' Then I frowned, and scratched my head. 'Well, most of the time. When the Ambassador's not shouting at me or people are trying to kill me.'

'That happens?'

'More than you'd think. It's not in the job description. I think I must just be unlucky.'

'Wow. Well, I guess I'm glad you're busy, *capo*.' He raised the beer can, remembered that it was full of cigarette butts, and sat it down again.

'Here we go.' Elly returned with a laptop that she set down before me. 'From three weeks ago. He took two tourists out.'

I looked at the photo on screen, and was unable to prevent myself from starting backwards.

'What the hell is that?'

She looked offended. 'That's Topolino. He's a basking

shark. Arty is just scratching him under the chin.'

I had not known that it was advisable to scratch basking sharks under the chin. For that matter, I had not even known that they had chins. Elly must have seen the doubt in my eyes. 'Scratch him there and he'll be your friend for life. He might look scary but he's an absolute pussycat.'

'I have an actual pussycat, and if I did that to him he'd have my fingers off.'

She wasn't sure if I was joking. 'Anyway,' she said, 'there they are. Arty and Topolino.'

I nodded. A Rick Wakeman lookalike eco-warrior who'd just headed off somewhere to right wrongs that needed righting. Maybe there was nothing more to it than this.

'When and where was this, Elly?'

'Three weeks ago. In the Adriatic, not far out from Chioggia.' Then she frowned, and shook her head. 'But this is strange.'

'It is?'

'Yes. He updates his web log constantly. That's the one thing he's efficient at. Half the time that's the only way we know where he is. But now we've got a three-week gap.'

'That's never happened before?'

'No. He's a bit of a tart when it comes to the socials. Says it's all about building his brand, giving his readers material, that sort of thing.' She shook her head. 'What's going on here?'

I turned to Gio. 'You said he was working on some sort of short-term project for – who was it?'

'ISMAR.'

'So why aren't there any photos from them?'

'Maybe they didn't allow it.'

I scratched my head. 'Okay. Now there might be nothing in this. I hope there isn't. But do you recognise this?' I took out the watch. 'Is this his?'

Gio and Cristiano shrugged, but Elly reached over to pick it up. She turned it over and over, running her fingers along it. Then she put her hand to her mouth and nodded. '*Dio.*'

'It is?'

She passed it to the others. Gio looked at Cristiano, and nodded. 'Yeah, that's his. Nobody else we know uses a logo like that. And this is a serious bit of kit. He spent a lot of money on it.'

'Where did you find this?' said Elly.

'On the shores of San Francesco del Deserto.'

She frowned. 'What was he doing there?'

'I'm not sure.'

Gio shrugged. 'It's not far from the Treporti Channel. Where he was working with ISMAR. If he'd lost it, the current could have carried it there.'

Elly turned the watch over and over in her hands, her face troubled. 'This is probably the most expensive thing he owns. I don't understand. What's happened?'

'Elly, this is ISMAR. This isn't some cowboy diving outfit. If anything had happened to him, we'd know it. Trust me, he's probably down in Calabria, diving the wreck of the *Pasubio* at the moment.'

'Then why isn't there anything on his dive log?'

'Because he's lost his watch? Seriously, you know what Arty's like. He does this sort of thing all the time.'

Elly didn't look convinced. 'I hope so.'

I tapped the watch. 'Is there likely to be any data on this?'

Gio nodded. 'Sure.'

'And can you extract it?'

He shrugged. 'Maybe. Depends if he's set a password. Or if it's encrypted.'

'Why would you do that with a diving watch?'

'Arty's an eco-warrior, remember. Sometimes he goes diving places where you're not supposed to be.'

I slid the watch across the table.

'Can you take a look at this for me? And let me know if you find anything. Anything at all, pictures of basking sharks, whatever.'

Gio looked doubtful but took it from me. 'Can't promise anything. But I'll do what I can.'

I reached for my wallet and took out a business card. 'Look, here are my details. Hopefully, there'll be soon be something on the socials with a photo of him diving a wreck in the south, and a selfie with a large beer afterwards. And then you can call me and tell me what a silly old Englishman I've been.'

There was silence for a moment. Gio lit a fresh cigarette from the remains of the old, and exhaled the smoke slowly.

'And if there isn't anything like that?'

'Then call me anyway. The sooner the better.'

I turned and made my way back to the *vaporetto* pontoon leaving Elly, Gio and Cristiano to a game of *scopa* that was, in all likelihood, never going to be finished. It was late in the day now, too late to consider trying to find someone at ISMAR who'd talk to me. It was definitely the spritz hour and, by the time I got home, it would be the dinner hour as well. I wondered what there was in the fridge, and hoped fervently it wasn't tomatoes.

Chapter 41

I put the phone down and smiled. 'Okay. I've found somebody at ISMAR who's willing to talk to me. They were a bit
cagey about it at first, mind.'

'Why's that?'

'I'm not quite sure, but it sounds like they're going to
make some sort of big announcement in the next couple of
weeks. I think they worried I was a journalist sniffing around
in hope of a scoop. So, there we go. That's my little project for
tomorrow morning.'

Fede looked at me from over the cover of the enormous
coffee-table art book she was reading. 'Well done, *caro*. I've
had a productive afternoon myself.'

'Oh yes?'

'Yes. I think I might have solved it.'

'You're kidding?'

'No. Serious.'

I jumped to my feet. 'Well, come on then.'

She shook her head. 'No no. Spritz first. And then I'll tell
you how brilliant I've been. But you'll have to do a bit of work
as well.'

'Hence the spritz?'

'Exactly.'

I rushed to the kitchen and threw together two hastily-assembled Spritz Nathans. Gramsci mewled up at me, and I tossed some kitty biscuits into his bowl, without bothering to measure them. I must have erred on the over-generous side as he looked up at me and miaowed with something that might even have been gratitude.

'That was just me being in a hurry, okay? Don't go thinking we've established a precedent here.' He turned back to his food, evidently pretending not to have heard me.

'So go on then,' I said, pressing a spritz into Fede's hand. 'What have you found?'

'It's not so much what I've found. It's just that something got me thinking.' She sipped at her drink. 'Bit heavy on the Campari, this one?'

'Sorry. I was in a hurry. It wasn't a precision job. Go on. Please.'

'I just got to thinking about St Francis.'

'As you do?'

'As all good Catholic girls do, of course. And I started thinking about representations of him in art. Now, fortunately, I've got this lovely book here.' She tapped the volume on her knee. 'Now, take a look at this.' She flicked back towards the beginning of the volume. 'What do you see?'

'Erm, St Francis?'

'No. Not good enough. And also wrong.'

'I am?'

'This is a fresco from Subiaco. And he wasn't St Francis at the time. Just simple Brother Francis, in the Benedictine Abbey there. Hence, no stigmata. But tell me more. Come on, what does he look like?'

'Okay, well he's quite young, I'd say. Quite good looking, I suppose, if you're into the whole monk-ey thing. Tonsured. Nearly trimmed beard. The eyes are striking. In short, if there was a medieval equivalent of those "Foxy Priests" calendars that the newspaper stands sell, I guess he'd have been in with a shout.'

'That's good. Very good.' She patted my cheek. 'Now, moving on. Take a look at this one. Giotto. About seventy years after the death of Francis.'

'Uh-huh. Okay, so this is Francis preaching to the birds, I guess. On the left of the painting, there's a surprised-looking monk. Which, I guess, is unsurprising given what's going on. And then we've got the birds, who seem to be taking it all in. And then in the middle of them, we have the man himself.'

'How does he look?'

'Happy enough for a man preaching to the birds, I suppose.'

'I mean describe him, silly!'

'Oh. Okay, well in this one he's obviously a bit older. Grey haired, a bit more ruddy of cheek.' I paused. 'I'm not sure I can really say any more than that.'

'No, that's okay. That'll do. Moving on again.' She flicked through the book. 'Here we are. Lodovico Cardi. Sometimes known as *Cigoli*. Late sixteenth century. Again, tell me what you see.'

The painting showed the monk, his head bowed in prayer in front of a copy of the Scriptures atop what might have been a crude altar of stone, against a background of a hilltop village and stormy skies.

'Okay, well he's quite young again in this one. Darker of hair and beard. He looks kind of sad, I'd guess. Or perhaps tired. He's a little red-eyed.'

'Or perhaps just thoughtful. I'm never quite sure if he's got quite the requisite number of fingers in this one. Maybe that's why he's pensive? Anyway, on we go. Last one, I promise.

'This is Franciso de Zurbarán. *St Francis in Meditation*. Maybe about 1635. What do you see here?'

I looked at the picture, and smiled. 'Wow.'

She smiled back at me. 'Wow?'

'Wow. I mean, this is a bit special. And given this is a list that includes Giotto, that means very special indeed.'

I looked back at the painting. The penitent Francis, on his knees, his hands folded in prayer, clutches a skull to his chest as he gazes – questioningly, I couldn't be sure – towards heaven.

'Okay, so this I imagine is Francis meditating on death – maybe his own death – given the skull. We can see that he's a poor man, or at least a humble man, given the wear-and-tear we can see on his robes. He might be quite young, it's difficult to tell.'

Fede smiled at me. 'Now, what makes you say that?'

'Well, you can't really see his face. Much of it is in shadow.'

'Exactly. You know, I first saw this painting in London. I think I must have been in my early teens. I was with *mamma* and *papa* you know, just before things went wrong. And I just remember sitting there in front of it, and looking up at Francis and trying to get a look at the face under the hood. I think at one point, *papa* almost had to haul me to my feet because I was literally kneeling in front of it, looking upwards, hoping to make something out. And, of course, you can't. That's just one of the things that give it so much power. And so,' she paused, 'what does this make you think?'

I shrugged, and sipped at my spritz. 'I don't know. I mean, they're all good in their own way.'

'Not all of them. Zurbarán in particular. What makes it special?'

'Erm, the extraordinarily powerful sense of a man in awe in face of the infinite?'

'Not that. Try again.'

'The existential dread of confronting ourselves with the question "What if there is no God?"'

'I'm starting to wonder that myself, right now. You're over-thinking it. What makes it different?'

'Oh. Oh, I see. It's just the fact you can't see his face. Well, not properly.'

'Exactly. And so?'

'And so—' And then light dawned and I kissed her full on the lips, as I twitched her spritz out of her hand in order to stop it going flying. 'And so – you can't see his face. That's the thing. Stick a robe on, pull the hood up, and you could be any old monk under there.'

'Any old monk or?'

I smiled. 'Any monk at all. But more than that. You could be anyone at all. If you want to prowl around a monastery late at night, what better disguise? You could be Pagan. Or Lucarini. You could even be Maria.'

'Or you could be the man who wept over his dead brother's bedside, late at night.'

I nodded. 'Vicari. Danny Vicari. But why?'

'Oh, when I said I'd solved it, I didn't mean I'd completely solved it. Perhaps they'd arranged to meet there and whatever happened to Dominic happened before Danny arrived.'

'Perhaps.'

'None of which explains why the two of them wanted to meet in a remote monastery in the first place, though.'

'Do you think he's really a monk? Danny, I mean.'

'Again, it's possible. It would go a long way towards explaining why he'd lost touch with his brother for so long.' She tapped the book. 'And there's one more thing. These pictures even give us the murder weapon.'

'I don't understand?'

'Come on. This one is easy. What are they all wearing?'

'Erm robes, sandals,' then I smiled. 'Cincture?'

'Exactly. The *cintura bianca* with three knots.'

'That made the three impressions on Pagan's neck. My goodness me, you really have done it. The only thing is – if it was Danny, it doesn't tell us why on earth he'd kill Pagan. Or where he is now.'

Fede sighed, and closed the book. 'Sadly, *caro*, there are some things that are beyond art history.'

Chapter 42

On a warm July morning the Arsenale would normally be overrun by visitors to either the Art or Architecture Biennale. Residents in the area of the Riva degli Schiavone and the Riva Ca'di Dio had become used to their view of the lagoon being interrupted by maxi-yachts owned by men (for they were always men) whose good taste was outweighed by the size of their wallet.

But this year, there would be no Biennale, and the men with maxi-yachts had found other places to go. That is, if there *were* other places to go. The unconvincing lions that had kept guard over the Arsenale for centuries would be able to rest easy this year.

ISMAR was headquartered in the northern part of the Arsenale, near the *Bacini vaporetto* stop, a lonely place at the best of times. I was the only passenger to get off, and nobody was waiting to get on. Because, really, where was there to go? The warehouses that had been converted into art spaces stood empty. Lorenzo Quinn's sculpture *Building Bridges*, a series of gigantic hands linking across the waters of the Arsenale, now served as a melancholy reminder of the days when it was safe to hold hands. The rugby ground, unused in months, was now overgrown and silence and sadness hung in the air.

ISMAR's office was situated in between a bar which looked as if it might be fun if it were open, and something called the Arsenale Carnival Experience, which didn't.

I checked the name I'd been given, rang the bell and waited.

'Mr Sutherland? I'm *dottoressa* Zenardi.'

'*Piacere, dottoressa.* Thanks for agreeing to meet me.'

We made to shake hands, and remembered in time to change it into a bump of elbows. She rolled her eyes. 'God, nearly six months on and it still feels strange. I swear when this is all over I'm going to start kissing random strangers in the street.'

'How do you think I feel? I'm a British man who can no longer exchange a good solid handshake between stout fellows. It's like amputating a limb.'

'My sympathies.' She smiled. 'What can I help you with, Mr Sutherland?'

'Nathan, please. It's about the project you had running in the Treporti Channel. I wonder if you could tell me a little more about it?'

She shrugged. 'Yes, of course. Most of it will be in the papers in due time. We might even go international on this one, I understand. And there'll be a properly academic paper on it within the year but I'm afraid that might be unintelligible to the lay person. No offence.'

'None taken.'

'What do we think about when we think about the birth of

Venice? A lagoon city founded on nothing more than deserted marshlands. A city slowly dug out of swampland, built upon a petrified forest, that rises to be one of the great civilisations of the age. A civilisation begun by the first Venetian, the first to swing his axe and decide that this was where they were going to settle. It's our creation myth.

'The actual story is a little more complicated than that. The Romans were here before us. That's beyond a doubt. We've found amphorae in the lagoon, and traces of what could only be a Roman road were discovered as far back as the 1980s. The trouble is, it was so damned difficult to investigate further. Funding wasn't easy back then, and even less so now.

'Then, in late March, we started to realise what an extraordinary opportunity we had. The lagoon was almost completely untrafficked, and clearer than at any point in decades. We knew we had a golden moment, perhaps just a couple of weeks, between the end of lockdown and the traffic opening up properly on the lagoon again. We needed qualified people, and we needed them quickly.'

'Including divers?'

She nodded. 'Normally we get volunteers from the police but, as you might imagine, the project wasn't seen as high priority for them.'

'So you went to Dive Venezia?'

'Where we found Arturo Franceschini. Who was super-enthusiastic about working with us.'

'Marine archaeology was his thing?'

She shook her head. 'I don't think it was. Not really. It may be that he was just stir crazy after all those months of lockdown, but there was something that seemed to enthuse him. He'd have stayed with us longer, had it been up to him.'

'What do you mean, "had it been up to him"?'

'I had to tell him we were letting him go. It was only ever going to be a short-term project given the amount of money we had and the limited timeframe.'

'And he was pissed off?'

She shook her head. 'Oh no. I can't imagine him getting pissed off about anything. He's not that sort of person.'

'What sort of person is he?'

She grinned. 'Honest or tactful?'

'Honest.'

'I thought he was a bit of an idiot. A likeable one, sure, but absolutely incapable of following the most basic instructions.'

'Such as?'

'He kept wandering off from the main dive site. The first time he just said he got disorientated. Okay, he's an experienced diver, but I can still imagine that happening. But then it happened again. And again. And he wouldn't tell us why. And I started to think that his interest in the project wasn't anything to do with Roman roads at all, and the fact that he wouldn't tell us what it was started to piss me off. I think he just wanted the opportunity to dive in that part of the lagoon. Something he wouldn't normally be able to do.'

'Look, this is a long shot, but did he ever speak to you about a man called Dominic Vicari?'

She shook her head. 'No. But that name sounds familiar from somewhere.'

'The British citizen who died on San Francesco del Deserto recently.'

'Oh yes. The poor man. But what would he have to do with Arturo?'

'I don't know. But there's a connection there. And it might be important. I'm trying to track down any family that Vicari might have left behind.'

'I see. Is that part of your job?'

'It is.'

'My goodness. That doesn't sound like much fun. But I'm afraid I can't help you with that. I have the strong impression that Arturo is something of an unreconstructed alpha male. Sharing information with the little woman wasn't really one of his things.'

I drummed my fingers on the table. 'Okay. Have you got a large-sized map of the lagoon by any chance?'

She laughed. 'This is ISMAR. Yes, we do have maps of the lagoon. Do you go into *Toletta* and ask if they have any books?'

'Sorry.'

'Just teasing. Now what do you need to look at?'

'I'm not sure yet. I'm going to need you to help me make sense of it.'

'Okay then. Let's just make some space here.' She swept the papers on her desk to the side. 'That'll do. Now let me see what I can find.' She went to the shelves. 'Here we go. A lovely, large-scale map. From *Mare di Carta*. Do you know it?' I shook my head. 'Lovely bookshop up in Santa Croce. I sometimes think they have a better selection of materials about the lagoon than we do.'

She spread it out upon the table. 'Now then,' she smiled, 'where are we going to go today?'

'Well, why don't we start with that Roman road of yours?'

'The *Canale di Treporti*. Or, if you prefer, the Treporti Channel. Which, as you can see, is bounded on one side by Sant'Erasmo, and on the other by Punta Sabbioni and Treporti itself.'

'Okay. This I understand. So, if this is where the road is, where was Arturo?'

She moved her finger round in a circle. 'Just here. Near San Francesco del Deserto. He went over there three times. If the project had been continuing, I'm not sure we'd have kept on using him. It would just have been a waste of money.'

'What was he doing there?'

She shrugged. 'I think he thought he was on the trail of buried treasure.'

'Is it possible he might have been?'

'Possible but unlikely. There's little evidence of Roman remains over there. And that part of the lagoon was heavily dredged back in the 1970s.'

'Why so?'

'There was talk about disposing of factory waste there. From Marghera, you know? The environmental damage would have been enormous. There was a public outcry and the project was cancelled. But if there ever was anything of archaeological significance there, it's almost certainly been lost or destroyed.'

'Aren't you curious?'

'Of course we are. But we have limited time and even more limited money.'

'That path again. The Roman road. Tell me about it.'

'We started to find evidence of it back in the 1980s. There

had been a Roman road in that part of the lagoon almost two thousand years ago. The sea level would have been at least two metres lower then, and the theory is that the road would have formed part of a network linking Clodia to Altinum. Or, as we would say today, Chioggia to Altino.'

I pointed to the map. 'But what about this area here? Where Arturo was. Roundabout San Francesco and Crevan?'

'As I said. There's no convincing evidence on which to base a serious investigation of the area. These places wouldn't have existed back then.'

'No. But they do now. And that might be what's important.' I smiled. 'Thank you, *dottoressa*. You've given me a lot to think about.'

Chapter 43

'Fede? Cristiano?'

The two of them were seated outside the Magical Brazilians.

'Ciao, *caro*. We've been waiting for you.'

'And I'm Gio. Not Cristiano. But he'll be pleased when I tell him he was mistaken for a man with hair.'

I sat down next to them. 'Treporti's an awfully long way to come for a drink.'

'It's not just for that. There's stuff we need to talk about.'

'Sure. Do you want to come up to the flat?'

He shook his head. 'No. Your cat seemed to find my hair a source of entertainment.'

'Ah. Sorry about that.'

'I had to bribe him to get off with kitty biscuits,' said Fede.

'No long-term damage, I hope?'

Gio ran his hands through his hair, adjusting his bun. 'I don't think so. But I was starting to wish I'd sent Cristiano or Elly instead.'

'Okay. Well let us – well, I say us, I mean Nathan – at least buy you a drink. What's everyone having?' said Fede.

'Spritz Campari for me,' I said.

'A beer would be good,' said Gio.

'Things on sticks?'

'What?'

'Mixed *cicchetti*. Which may or may not be on sticks. Small octopus. That sort of thing.'

'Oh, right. No, just a *toast* for me. I'm sorry. It's just I see a lot of octopuses in my line of work. I'm – well, I'm not very good with eating them.'

'No problems. How about you, Nathan?'

'Octopus on a,' I paused, 'you know what. Maybe I'll have a *toast* as well.'

Gio looked concerned. 'You don't have to, you know? Just because of me, I mean.'

'No, it's no problem.'

'It's just that they're very intelligent creatures. You know the Beatles song? Well, they really do make little gardens.'

'Right.'

'Very high emotional intelligence as well.'

'Maybe they could make some sort of vegetarian alternative. They could call it a *mocktopus* or something?'

Gio grinned. 'I'm sure the technology must be there. It just depends if there's the will, that's all.'

Ed arrived with a round of *toasts* and, as I bit into mine I reflected that Ringo Starr had ruined the small octopus on a stick for me, perhaps forever.

'So, Gio,' I said, 'you've come a long way from Treporti in order to not eat a small octopus.'

'I was thinking about what Elly said. About Arty not having updated his dive log in weeks. That's something he always did. Even if he was just taking beginners down a few metres. He never missed one. And then, all of a sudden we have this three-week gap when we know he was working on a project for ISMAR.'

He pulled Arturo's dive watch out of his pocket. 'Do you know how these things work?'

I shook my head. Fede, likewise.

'A lot of people would look at this and just call it a dive watch. That's not what it is. It's way more sophisticated than that. It gives you decompression times, max depth for your mixture, pressure readings for your gas. Everything.'

'And this is something you need in Treporti?' said Fede.

'Not at the depths we take people to. But Arty had been everywhere, the Great Barrier Reef, all over. Remember what I told you about the whole eco-warrior thing?'

I nodded.

'The really clever thing is this,' he continued. 'You can bluetooth this device to your camera and then link it to your dive log, website, blog, whatever.'

'Does that work underwater?'

He shook his head. 'No. But you can either set it to update automatically when you surface, or do it manually. So, I figured I'd have a play with the watch and see what I could get out of it.'

'And you found something?'

'I did. He'd changed the settings. It wasn't linked to his public dive log any more but to a private page. But with the info on the dive watch I was able to get access to it.' He took a tablet out of his bag. 'And look what I found.'

The picture showed an image of the sea bed, a few rocks and rusting beer cans, and some bored-looking fish.

'Doesn't look like much, does it? But, trust me, that's as

clear as the lagoon has ever looked at that depth. It would normally be silted up from all the traffic. Now take a look at the next one.' He swiped right on the tablet.

I peered more closely. 'What the hell are those?'

'Barrels.'

'I can see that. But of what?'

He tapped away. 'Let's zoom in.'

Fede craned over my shoulder. '*Gesù!*'

'What?' I said.

'That logo. Those barrels contain PCBs.'

Gio nodded. 'Polychlorinated biphenyls. This shit is highly toxic.'

'Where is this?'

'About one hundred metres from the Treporti Channel. The part of the lagoon that stretches from Crevan, and past San Francesco del Deserto.'

'Where I found the watch. And where ISMAR told me that Arturo had been exploring. Despite being way off the Roman road.'

'I don't understand,' said Fede. 'PCBs have been banned for years. Decades, even.'

I shrugged. 'Maybe they were dumped back in the eighties or the nineties? Before disposing of this crap was properly regulated.'

Gio shook his head and pointed at the tablet. 'No. Look at the state of them. No barnacles, no corrosion.' He looked up at us both. 'This is recent. Toxic waste. In the lagoon.'

'They call it legacy pollution,' he continued. 'PCBs were banned decades ago, sure. But there are abandoned factories in Marghera that still need clearing out, even after all these years.'

'So how do you dispose of this stuff?'

'That's the thing. It's not easy. You can't just pour it down the drain or into the soil. You need proper, specialist incinerators. You need professionally trained staff in proper protective gear. It's expensive. Very expensive.'

'So, what, this stuff was just floated out into the lagoon and dumped overboard?'

'I don't know. It seems hard to believe people could be so stupid. But there's the evidence.'

Fede shook her head. 'I don't get it. The lagoon in that area isn't deep enough, surely?'

'Wait a minute,' I said. 'There was something they told me at ISMAR. The lagoon was dredged in that area, back in the seventies, with the intention of disposing of waste. The plans never went through, but now there's a channel there deep enough to ensure this stuff never came to light. And if Arturo hadn't been exploring down there, it wouldn't have.'

'So, is this anything you can go to the cops with?'

'I don't know. Gio, is there anything more on there?'

'I think there is. A lot more. But we'll need to link it to his camera, wherever that is.'

'And you said that webpage is a private one?'

He nodded. 'The app on the watch gives you an option to publish. To make it public. He hasn't done that yet. I think he was waiting to gather more info. To release it all in one go.'

I shook my head. 'So, we've just got one photo. That's all. We need more. And I think maybe we'll need the help of the Fourth Estate.'

'You know someone?'

'Maybe. A guy at the *Gazzettino*. Name of Roberto Bergamin. We've kind of helped each other out before.'

Fede raised an eyebrow. 'Is he really the right man for something like this?'

'He'll sell his grandmother for a good story. That makes him the perfect man for something like this. And Gio, could you and your buddies try and get some better photos down there?'

He shook his head and then sighed. 'No. I'm sorry.'

'I don't understand?'

'I would – we all would – but it's like this. Arty built up a number of enemies over the years. He was hospitalised after a Greenpeace demo in Rome. Beaten up by cops. He got death threats after his photos on coral bleaching went viral. And now he's removed his public webpage and all his social media accounts. He was frightened of something, genuinely frightened. That's not like Arty. And so,' he shook his head again, 'I don't want to get involved. None of us do. I'm sorry.'

'Gio, people are dumping all sorts of toxic crap in the lagoon. You must want to help with this, surely?'

'I do. But there's a connection between Arty and a man who might have been murdered. You worked that connection out. That means somebody else could do the same. And get back to me, and my buddies. I do want to help. But I don't want to put them at risk.'

He pushed the watch towards me. 'I'm going to leave you this. And I'll send you the image.' He scribbled on the back of a business card. 'And this is Arty's address and telephone number. Just in case he answers. But that's it. I'm sorry. If I were you, I'd just go to the police, okay?' He pushed his chair back. 'I'll pay for my own lunch.'

As soon as Gio had gone, Federica decided that it was safe enough to treat herself to a small octopus on a stick. I wasn't quite sure I was ready for that or, indeed, if I ever would be again. It would have to be *baccala mantecato*.

I dialled and redialled Arturo's number, again and again. There was no answer. I hadn't expected there to be. Eventually I gave up and put my phone away with a sigh.

'So, where does that leave us now, *caro*?' She rubbed my arm. 'Look. Maybe there isn't much more you can do. Why don't you go to Vanni?'

'Vanni's happy to leave the whole thing as an argument between thieves. And I can understand why. Also, I don't think what we have is enough. We need more evidence than a single image.' I tapped the business card that Gio had left us. 'We've got Arturo's address now. Maybe there's a computer there. Or a camera. Or something we can use.'

'Maybe so. But how are you going to get hold of them?'

'You remember a few months ago? When I needed to get into a locked briefcase?' I smiled. 'Once again, I think I need the services of the best thrash metal guitarist in Venice.'

Chapter 44

'You know, Brother Nathan, I should be offended by this,' said Lucia.

'Look, you're the first person I thought of.'

'And that's why I should be offended. You thought, *Oh Lucia knows how to open a locked briefcase, therefore she can definitely break into a house*, right?'

'Right. Well, not quite so right. I thought you might know how to do it. Not that you were a career criminal or anything.' I paused. 'But you do know how to do it, yes?'

It was her turn to pause. 'Yes, I do.'

'Right. Good.'

'And no, I'm not a criminal.'

'Good.'

'I'm just really shit at hanging on to keys and things, that's all.'

'Uh-huh.'

'Federica didn't want to come then?'

'No. She said that if she had a few hours to herself she could probably solve the whole thing by the time I get home to cook dinner.'

'She did? That's really cool.'

'She also said she didn't want to get arrested.'

'Worries way too much. We're not going to get arrested. Mind you, I've only done this sort of thing breaking into my dad's house, so I guess it's not really the same.'

'Right. Okay. You probably didn't need to tell me that, but never mind.' I changed the subject. 'How well do you know Treporti?'

'I've been there once. With my band. At one of the camping villages.'

'Right. How did it go?'

'Like I said, I've been there once.'

'Oh.'

The walk through Treporti was hot and sticky and I was deeply regretting not having taken an air-conditioned bus, but Lucia assured me it wasn't far. Mauro the keyboard player, she said, had transported all his gear for their single gig out here in a shopping trolley and so I had little reason to complain.

'You could always take your jacket off, you know? If you're getting hot.'

'I don't feel properly dressed without a jacket. So I stick it out as long as physically possible.'

'Fair enough, Englishman. Up to you.'

'Anyway, you can talk, person who always wears black. How far is it now?'

'Just five minutes more of bickering and we should be there.'

'Oh good.'

Arturo's apartment lay just a few minutes away from the Camping Village dei Fiori and, with a little bit of effort, I thought I could just about hear the sound of the sea over the traffic. Pretty wooden white houses, all in a row, in a tree-lined avenue.

I nodded. 'Nice,' I said.

'Uh-huh. I think there's a bar down the road that we went to before we played.'

'Any good?'

'It played Italian summer party music.'

I winced. 'Ouch.'

She looked left and then right. There were no pedestrians to be seen, the heat of the noonday sun keeping them indoors. However, cars did seem to be passing with some regularity.

'Okay, we'll have to make this quick. And hope his door works in the same way as my dad's. Otherwise—'

'Otherwise?'

'You'll have to kick it down, Mr Consul.'

'Wait a minute, wait a minute. That's your plan? Kick the door down is your plan?'

'Look, you asked me if I knew how to open a locked door. I said yes, if it's like my dad's. I'm sorry if you thought you were hiring that bloke from *Mission: Impossible*.'

I shook my head. 'Oh, come on then. Let's get it over with.'

We walked up the path that led to Arturo's door, the garden scrubby and untidy. Perhaps Arty needed an octopus to really sort it out.

Lucia crouched down. 'Okay. Letterbox. That's good.' She turned her head. 'Give us your belt then.'

'What?'

'Your belt.'

'That's going to look really weird if somebody walks past.'

'And it'll look even weirder if I'm removing the wire from my bra. Come on.'

An elderly lady with a shopping trolley chose that moment to walk past. She stopped and eyed us with suspicion. I took out my phone and smiled and nodded at her as I pretended to be talking away. Eventually, she turned and made her way down the road. When she reached the corner, she turned around and looked back at us. Once more, I took out my phone and made big operatic gestures as if to indicate both the importance of the call and my right to be where I was.

'What was that?' said Lucia, once our elderly friend had finally given up.

'It's a disguise. Pretend to be talking loudly on the phone and people will assume you have a right to be where you are.'

She shook her head. 'Come on. Belt. Quickly.'

'Christ. All right.' She made a crude loop out of it and passed it through the letterbox.

'Now, if this is like my dad's, the handle should be about here.' She smiled. 'And it is. And as long as he hasn't double locked the door, just a little pull and,' the door clicked open, 'we're in.'

She passed me my belt.

'That was brilliant.'

'Easy. Only works with a certain type of door though so that's why I decided a life of crime wasn't for me. Come on then.'

We closed the door behind us. Arturo's apartment seemed to consist of little more than a single living room with a tiny stove, and a sofa bed.

I looked up at the poster on the wall. A strikingly beautiful woman, in a long black dress, a white fur coat dangling from one hand and a cigarette in the other.

'Who's that?' said Lucia.

'Rita Hayworth. From a movie called *Gilda*.' I smiled. 'Boy, they really knew how to smoke in those days.'

Lucia looked around the room, hands on hips. 'There's a whole load of crap in here.' I nodded. There was, indeed, a whole load of crap. 'What are we looking for?'

'Anything that might be connected to the dumping of PCBs in the lagoon. Which means photos, maps, charts, that sort of thing.'

'You know how to read those?'

'Not really. Do you?' She shook her head.

'A computer would be good.'

'I'm not so sure. He seems to have deleted almost everything. His social media presence seems to have gone altogether.'

'Why would he do that?'

'I can only assume he was scared. But it also means he probably kept a hard copy of everything. Just as insurance.'

She nodded. 'Okay. Let's get to it.'

And so we did. We went through his wardrobe. We checked the inside of the tiny fridge. I went through every book on the shelves and had to admit that Arturo really knew his stuff when it came to H. P. Lovecraft. I took the lid off the cistern in the bathroom. We shook out his wetsuits. We unfolded the sofa bed. Nothing.

Lucia shook her head. 'This has been a waste of time, Mr Consul.'

'You might be right.'

'If he was that scared of – whatever – maybe he just destroyed everything. Didn't want to leave a trail that could lead back to him.'

I rubbed my forehead. 'No. What do we know about Arturo? Eco-warrior, environmental campaigner, passionate about green issues. A guy who'd fly to Australia at the drop of a hat just to protest about something. I don't care how scared he might have been, if he'd found evidence of toxic waste in the lagoon he'd have kept a record of it.'

'If you say so. But think about what we haven't found.' She ticked them off on her fingers. 'No wallet. No bank cards. No phone. No driving licence. No ID card. He's out there, somewhere. And maybe he's got all the useful stuff with him.'

I nodded. It was a fair point. I scanned the room once again, looking for something, anything, that we might have overlooked. Then I shrugged and looked at Lucia. 'I guess you're right. This has been a waste of time. Sorry.'

'Ah, don't feel so bad, Mr Consul. It's been an adventure. And it's good to be reminded as to how the belt trick works. For the next time I forget my keys, you know?'

I smiled at her, and then froze as I heard the doorbell ring.

'Oh shit,' said Lucia.

I waved at her to keep quiet.

'What do we do?' she whispered.

'We ignore it. Whoever it is will go away in a bit.'

The doorbell rang once more. And then once more, this time continuously.

Finally it stopped, and I breathed deeply.

'Think they've gone?'

I nodded. 'Let's just give it a couple of minutes.'

The bell rang again and then someone started to hammer furiously on the door.

'Shit.' Lucia looked at me. 'You'll have to let them in. They'll have the whole street round making a racket like that.'

'Christ.' I half-walked, half-ran to the door, and yanked it open. The momentum of the hammering from the very large man on the doorstep carried him over the threshold and into my arms.

He shook his head in confusion, then grabbed me by the lapels and threw me up against the wall.

'Where's my bloody money?' he said.

Chapter 45

'There seems to have been some kind of misunderstanding?' I said, hopefully.

'I'll show you a right good misunderstanding, mate, if I don't get my bloody money.'

'What money? I don't know who the hell you are or what you're doing here?'

'I'm a very angry man who's a lot bigger than you. That's who I am. And I've told you why I'm here. And that's for my bloody money.'

'I don't have your money. Why would I have your money? Money for what?' He was pushing me harder and harder against the wall, his face red with anger and moist from his exertions. His nose, unpleasantly sweaty, was now touching mine.

'Where's Franceschini?'

'I don't know.'

'Who are you? His dad or something?' Then he paused, and relaxed his grip, mercifully pulling his nose back. He frowned. 'You're not Venetian?'

'You noticed? Sorry, the accent's imperfect even after all these years.'

He stepped back. 'What are you doing here?'

'I could ask you the same thing.'

'I told you I'm—'

'After your money. Sorry, slipped my mind.' I rubbed my forehead. 'It's been a bit of a long day.'

'And who's this?' My new acquaintance pointed at Lucia.

'Tell you what. Let's just close the door, eh?' I said, pushing it shut. 'Wouldn't want the neighbours to think there's a bit of a scene going on.'

'So why are you here then? He seemed to be working himself up again, but at least he was only pointing a finger at me now, and the threat of nasal contact seemed to have receded.

'Same reason as you,' I said, and nodded at Lucia. 'Isn't that right?'

'That's right, Mr Con— Er, I mean that's right.'

'We're here for the money as well.'

He looked at the two of us, suspicion in his eyes. 'I don't understand?'

'Diving lessons,' I said. 'We've both paid for private diving lessons.' I rubbed my fingers together. 'Proper money, you know? And this Franceschini guy just never turned up. Never returns calls.'

'Diving lessons?' he repeated. He looked at Lucia. And then at me. Just a little bit too long, I thought.

'Hey, you're never too old, you know?'

'Sorry.'

'So, we thought we'd come over here and ring on his bell. Just like you did.'

He grinned. 'Ah, so that's what old *signora* Rossi was on about. She said she'd seen two people hanging around outside his house. What's the matter, you get tired of waiting?'

'Something like that.'

'Any sign of him?'

'Nothing at all. But his gear's still here. Tell me then. What's your beef with him?'

'Same as you, basically. Guy called me beginning of June, told me he wanted his boat servicing. Clean the hull. Give the engine a look over. Usual things.

'And I tell him, sure, I can do that. Only he'll have to wait a bit, see, because all of a sudden all the world and their brother has realised that, just maybe, they're going to be having a proper summer after all and, most likely, they're going to be spending it here in the lagoon. Suddenly I've got a ton of work coming in from people who want their boats all fixed up nice, and – and this is the problem, I tell him – they're all in the queue ahead of you.

'So he offers me twice as much money if I'll do his first. And, of course, I say yes. I know this guy, he works at the dive school, he seems honest. And so I fix his boat up – and I do it properly mind you, no cutting corners here – and I'm aware that I've got regulars who I'm pissing off but still, this guy is going to pay me double,' he coughed, 'in cash, and so I think it's worth it.'

'And, what, you let him have the boat back without getting the money?'

'What can I say? I thought I knew the guy. Then, all of a sudden it's *I'll pay you next week* and then – *I'll pay you by the end of the month* and then,' he shrugged, 'he stopped answering his phone.'

I gave an exasperated little sigh and roll of the eyes. 'Just like us, eh, Lucia?'

She scowled, and I realised I shouldn't have used her real name. Then she brightened and smiled at our new friend. 'Just like us.'

He shook his head. 'Blimey, we've been played for right mugs haven't we?'

'Seems we have.'

'Sorry about earlier, you know.' He reached over and brushed some imaginary dirt from my jacket. 'Just a misunderstanding.'

'Ah well. Can happen to anyone. No hard feelings.'

'So, do you know where the guy's gone?'

'Not a clue.'

'And no chance that you found, well, you know—'

'Any money. No.'

'Damn. That'd have been good. D'you mind if I have a quick look around. Just in case.'

'Go ahead,' said Lucia. 'Another pair of eyes might be good.'

And so the two of us stood there and watched our new friend – Angelo, he said his name was, although we were pretty sure that wasn't his real name – go through everything that we had thirty minutes previously, and with a similar lack of success.

I gave him a hand to open out the sofa bed and, suddenly, his eyes brightened. 'Ah-hah!'

'You've found something?'

He tapped his nose. 'Always down the back of the sofa, isn't it?'

'What have you got?'

He stretched down and rooted around, and then straightened up. He opened his hand. 'Here we go. I make that seven euros fifty cents.' He frowned. 'Mind, I suppose I should give you half of that?'

I looked at Lucia. 'No, it's okay. I think we can let this one go.'

She nodded. 'Yeah, you go ahead. You can stand us a drink sometime.'

'Well, that's very kind of you.' He put his hands on his hips and nodded with satisfaction. 'It's a start, isn't it? Hopefully we'll track him down and get the rest back.'

'Ah well. You never know.'

'Suppose I'd better be going then.'

I sighed. 'I suppose we ought to as well.' I turned to Lucia. 'Sorry. Not been the most productive of days, has it?' She shook her head.

'Right then.' He made to shake my hand and then drew it back. 'Sorry. Forget we're not doing that sort of thing any more. Nice to meet you both.' Then he turned to the poster of Rita Hayworth. 'Lovely to see you as well.' He smiled. 'I love that film, you know?'

'*Gilda*?'

'No, the other one. *Shawshank* wotsit.'

I looked at him and blinked. 'Oh yes. That one,' I said, trying to keep my voice calm.

'Well now. We all going to head off together, or what? I'd stand you a drink but you don't get a round for three people out of seven-fifty, even round here.'

I shook my head. 'Tell you what. Why don't you head off first and we'll follow in about five minutes. It might look suspicious if we all head off together.'

'It will?'

'It absolutely will.'

As if by magic, Lucia had already opened the door, and held it open for him.

'Nice to meet you.'

'You too, *signorina*. Have a good day both.'

She clicked the door shut.

I smiled, and looked up at the poster of Rita Hayworth. Of course.

'*Shawshank*,' I said.

'I don't understand?'

'Watch the film.'

I eased the adhesive away from the wall as best I could, not wishing to damage Rita any more than necessary.

Lucia grinned at me. 'Don't tell me you're taking that home, Mr Consul?'

'I don't think my lovely wife would let me have this in the house, Lucia. But no. Our friend Arturo obviously had excellent taste in cinema. Which makes me think that, if I gently pull this away, there'll be—'

I stopped, and smiled. A manilla envelope was taped to the wall, about halfway up the length of the poster. 'I'm sorry Rita, excuse me a moment.' I slid my hand between poster and wall and tugged the envelope away.

'Now what have we got here?' I looked around, searching for a clear space on which to empty out the contents, and decided the back of the sofa would have to do.

If I'd been expecting a smoking gun, I'd have been disappointed. There were no further underwater images of barrels of toxic waste. What we had was a photograph, taken at night, of a barge.

'Where is that?' said Lucia.

'I'm not sure but – if we look to the left – that's got to be the *campanile* on Burano. Nothing else leans quite like that. Which means the other tower we can see in the distance must be on San Francesco.'

'So where was it taken from?'

'Must be one of the small islands round there. Any ideas?'

She shook her head. 'One of the small deserted ones, I guess. But there's so many I couldn't put a name to it. What's this boat, then?'

'I'll have a guess as to what it's doing. But as to the name,' I shrugged, 'Can't read it. Arturo had a good camera, but not good enough to make out the name of a boat at night. Wherever it is, he must have been there trying to gather evidence. Okay, what else have we got?'

Photographs, stuck together with a paperclip. Two of them, I recognised at once.

'Bruno Pagan. Carlo Lucarini. From the island.'

'Who's the other guy?'

The figure that smiled out at me from the photograph looked relaxed and happy as if he were posing for a cover shoot for *GQ*, albeit with a haircut that he was really too old for. I turned it over and whistled when I saw the name scrawled on the back.

'Daniele Vicari.'

'That's who we're looking for, right?'

'It is.'

Three photographs remained. One, a long distance shot of an industrial cooling tower. Lucia looked at me. 'Somewhere in Marghera, I'd guess.'

'Chances are.'

The other two photos were closer range. A man in a dark suit with a briefcase exiting a door at the base of the tower.

I tapped the photo. 'You recognise him?'

She shook her head. 'No idea.'

'Me neither. But even at this range I can tell it's a good suit.'

Lucia had the final photograph in her hands. 'He's in this one as well. With some other guy.' She frowned. 'Wait a minute, I think I recognise him.'

'Let's have a look.' I took it from her and almost dropped it. 'Jesus!'

'You know him?'

'You could say that. The last time we met was at Harry's Bar. Back in January. Just before the mayoral election.'

'He's a mate, then?'

'Not exactly. We had a Martini and exchanged mutual threats.'

'Brother Nathan, you're losing me here.'

'This is a man called Giuseppe Meneghini. Businessman. Very probably a corrupt businessman. And if it hadn't been for me he might very well have become Mayor of Venice.'

Chapter 46

Fede tapped away furiously at her computer. Then she looked up at me and held out her empty glass. 'Definitely a two-spritz problem, *tesoro*.'

I made my way to the kitchen, and returned with a brace of Spritz Nathans, trying to ignore Gramsci's accusing gaze. 'Don't give me that look, okay? I've just dropped some pretty heavy news on secondary care-giver. I don't give you a hard time when you need extra biscuits, do I? Well, okay, I do. But that's not the point.'

I sat down next to Fede, and sighed. Giuseppe Meneghini, standing in front of a cooling tower, stared out at me from the screen. 'I was hoping I'd not have to see him again,' I said.

'Given you punched him in the face on one occasion, *caro*, I imagine he feels the same way about you.'

'So where is this place?'

'In Marghera. It's called the Venezia Heritage Tower.'

'And what is it?'

'What it looks like. It's a converted cooling tower. Now it's a museum of Marghera's industrial heritage.'

'Wow. I hadn't even heard of it.'

She smiled. 'Hey, it's not all Titian and Tintoretto in my job, you know?'

'So what's he doing there?'

'It's office space as well. Oh, and I'm told the restaurant's very good. Wonderful views, apparently. The perfect space for the businessman who, shall we say, might be *compensating* for something.'

'He's got a business there?'

She nodded at her laptop. 'I had a quick look. Didn't take long to find out. They're called Rifugio. And they're in the waste disposal business.'

'Oh really? And would that be the *toxic* waste disposal business?'

'Right first time, *caro mio. Il Gazzettino* ran a story on them recently. They won a contract for waste disposal in the city. The spin put on it was how this is a creditable attempt by an honest company to take back control of waste disposal from criminal organisations.'

I shook my head. 'I mean, I knew he had to get his money from somewhere. I just didn't realise it was anything like this.'

'Oh, it's not just that. He's got all sorts of schemes running in Mestre and Marghera. Urban regeneration, that sort of thing.'

'Waste disposal, though?'

'Parts of Marghera have been a toxic swamp for years. Respiratory illnesses, chronic lung disease – worse things – all uncommonly high amongst the population. I imagine telling people that they'll safely dispose of all the crap that's blighting their lives goes down very well. Tell them their kids will be able to grow up breathing clean air in a safe, non-poisonous atmosphere and I imagine that will go down even better.'

'So, what, do you think he fancies another crack at being mayor?'

'I doubt it. And the next election is years away unless the current one does something stupid in the meantime. Which, given our history, isn't impossible. I think it's more likely that people will give you public money if they think it's for a cause their voters will like. Think about it. The recent events will have concentrated people's minds. That the very air you breathe in could be a danger to you.'

'And who's the other guy? The one in the good suit.'

She shook her head. 'I don't know.'

'Okay. Let's get these photos scanned and I'll send them to Roberto Bergamin. Maybe he can find out. In the meantime, what's Meneghini's address?'

'You know where he lives. That's where you punched him in the face, remember?'

'Not his personal one. Probably wise if I don't go there again. Where's Rifugio?'

'Marghera. As I said. It's a big cooling tower. You can't really miss it.' She frowned. 'What are you thinking of doing?'

'Well tomorrow I think I might go and have a little chat with *signor* Meneghini about what's turning up in the lagoon.'

'Are you sure that's a good idea?'

'No. I think it's more likely to be a very stupid idea. But I'm not going to hit him in the face.'

'You promise?'

'I do.' Then I frowned, as a thought struck me. 'The name of his company. Rifugio.'

'Yes?'

'The translation in English would be *refuge*. Or *shelter* or *haven*.' I paused. 'Or *sanctuary*. And that's what Dominic Vicari was looking for.'

Chapter 47

Few visitors, I imagine, ever came to Venice to see one of the finest examples of twentieth-century hyperboloid cooling towers still in existence. Some, perhaps, may have seen it simply by passing through Porto Marghera, either by accident or on purpose. Others, perhaps students of industrial archaeology, might have made a mini-pilgrimage to see a structure that, although unlikely ever to feature alongside St Mark's or the Doge's Palace as one of the city's unmissable sights, was nevertheless a not-unimportant part of Venice's history.

The Venezia Heritage Tower was the sole survivor of the three great cooling towers that had been erected in Marghera's industrial zone in the late 1930s. And then, like so many other industrial structures at the turn of the century, it fell into disuse. It stood there, its exterior filthy and blackened with pollution, a memorial to the poisons belched out daily for over seventy years.

Yet there was an unwillingness to see it demolished. Like it or loathe it, the tower was part of Venice's history. And so, when a consortium of local and national businesses acquired it, with the intention of turning it into both office space and a museum of Porto Marghera's industrial heritage, there were few objections. It would, after all, be cheaper than merely knocking it down.

It stood in the triangle formed by Via dell'Idrogeno and Via dell'Azoto. Or, if you prefer, Hydrogen Street and Nitrogen Street. The town planners of Porto Marghera had been nothing if not literal.

Dario and I climbed out of the Fiat Panda and, immediately, the heat hit us, the sun beating down out of a mercilessly clear sky, and the streets pitilessly clear of shadow.

'You pick the best places to visit, *vecio*.'

'No kidding. San Francesco del Deserto's probably only about ten kilometres away as the crow flies but it feels like another world.'

'You getting nostalgic for the monastery?'

'I think I might be.'

'You think Meneghini will see you?'

'Oh yes.'

'You think he's going to be trouble?'

'He already is. But I don't think he's actually going to be violent, if that's what you mean.'

'He did shoot somebody, remember?'

'Self-defence. Though there's only so many times he can try that one before people start getting a bit, you know, suspicious.'

Dario shook his head. 'I don't like it. I'm coming up with you.'

'It's okay, Dario, I know this guy.'

'No. You pissed off this guy. That's why I'm not letting you do this alone.'

'What do you think he's going to do? Throw me off the

top of a cooling tower?' Then I looked upwards at the great hyperboloid sweep of the tower, and wished I hadn't said – or thought – that.

'Who knows? Anyway, can we argue about this somewhere air conditioned and in the shade?'

The Venezia Heritage Tower was, by some distance, the nicest cooling tower I'd ever been inside. The lobby was mercifully, blissfully cool; a modernist symphony in gold and steel and glass.

'Can I help you?' The receptionist was an impossibly handsome young man, elegantly dressed despite the blistering heat outside, who looked like he might have been designed by the consortium to match his surroundings.

'Yes, I'd like to see *signor* Meneghini please. Of Rifugio.'

'Of course.' He waited for me to say something more and, when nothing was forthcoming, manage to frown and yet smile at the same time. 'You have an appointment?'

'I'm afraid not.'

The smile didn't even flicker. 'I'm sorry sir, but it's most unlikely *signor* Meneghini will see you without an appointment.'

'Oh, he'll see me. Trust me.'

The smile vanished, and the young man's eyes flicked over to two burly men, in blue security uniforms, both of them carrying guns.

'We know each other. I'm just passing through and thought it would be nice to drop by.'

'Just passing through Porto Marghera?'

'Absolutely. Now why not just give him a call, eh? Tell him

my name is Nathan Sutherland.'

His eyes flicked from me, to Dario, to the two security guards and back again; but he made the call.

'*Signor* Meneghini. There's an Englishman here to see you. A *signor* Nathan Sutherland.' He paused for a moment, then pointed to a small camera fixed to the desk. 'Can you stand in front of that, please? And your friend?'

I smiled at the camera and gave a little wave. The receptionist whispered something into the phone, and then hung up. He was no longer pretending to smile. He pointed to the lift.

'Okay, you can go up.' Then he pointed to Dario. 'Not your friend.'

Dario looked at me. 'You okay with that?'

'Sure. Don't worry.'

'Can I get a coffee around here?'

The receptionist nodded. 'There's a bar on the other side of the industrial exhibit.'

'Okay. I'll do the museum first and grab a coffee.' He took out his phone. 'But you'll give me a call if you need me, right?'

I smiled. 'Don't worry, Dario. Enjoy the exhibit.'

The elevator was glass-sided and with a glass floor, as if specifically designed to torment me. It rose at a deliberate pace through the centre of the cooling tower, giving me plenty of time to wonder about the possibilities of something going wrong, and, in the event of the cable breaking, if doing a little jump before the moment of impact would be enough to save me.

I looked up, that seeming preferable to down, but the sight of the polished grey concrete sliding past gave me the impression of being fired out of the barrel of a gun, and so I closed my eyes until I felt the jolt of the lift arriving.

The doors slid open, and Giuseppe Meneghini was there to greet me, hand extended.

'Good afternoon, Nathan,' he said.

Chapter 48

'You're looking well.'

'Thank you,' I said.

'Although you've put on a little weight since we last met.'

'I'd like to say it was too much gracious living, Giuseppe. But it was more enforced lack of exercise.'

'Should have bought a dog, Nathan. That's what I did. Best exercised Bichon Frisé in Venice.'

'It's a thought. My cat would have had strong opinions on the subject.'

He shook his head. 'Never been a cat person. Or better to say, they don't really seem to like me very much. You want to talk, I understand?'

'That would be good.' I smiled. 'Thank you for giving up your time.'

He checked his watch. 'I can't give you long, I'm afraid. It's always better to make an appointment.'

The corridor, again of smooth, polished concrete, curved away in both directions, windows set into it at regular intervals looking down upon Porto Marghera.

'This isn't all ours, you know?'

'It isn't?'

'We're doing well. But not quite that well. We share the space with a number of businesses, and there's a restaurant as well. They, of course, have the side that looks over to Venice.' He led me along the corridor, pausing to nod at the restaurant as we passed it. 'It's good, I understand.'

'Never eaten there?'

'It would feel a bit strange. At the end of a day's work, going to the restaurant next door. Next thing would be bringing a sleeping bag into the office. Oh, I forgot to say, there are no hard feelings about the last election and all that unpleasantness. At least on my part.'

'Really?'

'Of course. It turned out it was a good election to lose.' He smiled. 'Because of the virus. Imagine having to deal with all that. I'd never have had the stamina for it. Anyway, here we are.'

He held the door open for me.

I hesitated, and he smiled. 'Oh, come on. Do you think the floor is suddenly going to open and you'll be dropped into a tank full of sharks?'

'I wasn't thinking that. But now I'm thinking that.'

He shook his head. 'Allow me.' He stepped through, turned to face me, and jumped up and down a couple of times. 'See. Perfectly safe. Come in, Nathan.'

The office, save for a polished oak desk the size of a tennis court supporting the largest computer monitor I'd ever seen, and a pair of designer office chairs in leather and chrome, was almost completely bare. It was a space for being seen in, rather than working in; an office for the front cover of the glossies.

'Nice,' I nodded.

'To be honest, it's a little impractical. The rent isn't cheap, and it's not always a pleasure to schlep out here in the mornings. But it is, you have to admit, one hell of a view.'

I could only agree. If the view of the warehouses and factories of Porto Marghera was less than lovely, the sight of the Dolomites on the horizon was spectacular.

'I'm told in the past that there'd even be snow on the peaks at this time of year. Less and less of that, sadly. Environmental changes. Pollution.' The irony of his words seemed lost on him.

'You know what strikes me as incredible?' He beckoned to me. 'Come and take a look at this.' I approached the window, a little nervously. 'Come on now, what do you think I'm going to do? Push you out?' He tapped the glass. 'That would have to involved somebody a lot stronger than me.' I walked over to stand next to him, and he clapped me on the shoulder. Try as I might, I couldn't hold back a shudder. 'You get used to the height, trust me. Now take a look down there.'

I followed his gaze down – far down – to a dilapidated, heavily graffitied block of buildings next to an anonymous block of grey warehouses.

'Not much to look at, is it? Care to guess what it is?'

I shrugged. 'I'm guessing storage of some kind.'

'And you'd be right. That's the scenery depot for La Fenice. Think about it. When a production calls for something, they can stick it on a boat on the Western Industrial Canal and carry it all the way across the lagoon, down the Grand Canal, through that spidery little network of canals and bring it to the water gate at the opera house.'

'Going past your house, practically.'

'Indeed. And you know what the brilliance of it is? You have the Fenice, this perfect symbol of historical Venice co-existing perfectly with what we have here out on the mainland.' He chuckled. 'Now, if I say Mestre and Marghera are the future, you'll think I'm a monster. But really, it's nothing more than being practical. How much land, how much space would those warehouses tie up in Venice? Land that could be used for affordable housing.'

It was my turn to laugh. 'Except, it's never affordable housing, is it? It's unaffordable housing. Or just another hotel.'

'That's unfortunate, but that's the market. And after all these years in business, I've learned that's the one thing you can't beat.'

'That's what they keep telling us, at any rate.'

'Because it's true. No matter how much you might like to wish it away.' He checked his watch again. 'So. What would you like to talk about?'

'You work in waste disposal. I didn't know about that.'

'Waste disposal covers a multitude of professions, from the *Veritas* barge that takes your garbage away in the morning to a hitman from the Mala del Brenta. But, yes, this is one of the things that I do. Rifugio deals with the safe removal and disposal of PCBs, heavy metals, industrial slurry, all kinds of unpleasant material.' He tapped on the glass. 'Look down there. At the lagoon. People arrive from all over the world and they think, my goodness, a city with no road traffic. This must be the cleanest air in Europe. Perhaps they even kid themselves that it is. But the reality is that people are breathing in poisons, day in, day out, and living in a city built on a toxic soup. And if it wasn't for me, and people like me, it would be a whole lot worse.'

'You make it sound like a public service.'

'In many ways it is. One that Rifugio gets handsomely remunerated for, of course, but that doesn't seem iniquitous.' He grinned. 'I'm sorry if that doesn't fit the narrative. I know you don't particularly like me.'

'Well, I did punch you in the face once.'

He rubbed his chin. 'Yes. You did, didn't you?'

'It's a difficult job, I imagine. All this.'

'Like you wouldn't believe. The regulations are incredibly tight. That's why I envy you British. Not so constrained by EU red tape any more.'

'But that red tape's there for a reason, right? For the whole "avoiding poisoning people" thing.'

He shook his head. 'Little thought experiment, Nathan. How much do you think should be spent on cleanly disposing of this stuff?'

I shrugged. 'Whatever it takes.'

'That's what everybody says. How much more, then, would you be prepared to pay in tax for this to happen?'

'Again, whatever it takes. We're talking about people getting cancer here.'

'And, once more, that's what everybody says. "Bury it a hundred metres deep and concrete it over." Of course. That's the only human response.

'But then you show people the cold, hard figures. And they start to wonder if perhaps fifty metres might be just as good. If it was slightly more economical. Or perhaps twenty-five metres. Or perhaps—'

I waved a hand. 'Okay, okay. I get the point.'

'And so that's what Rifugio does. We find the best balance between safe, efficient disposal of toxic waste, the amount of public money that needs to be spent and a satisfactory profit for the company.' He put his fingers together in a triangle. 'Like this. Our challenge is to keep everyone happy.'

'And you do?'

'I'm pleased to say we do.'

'Okay. I'll get to the point. There's a photograph I'd like to show you. May I?' I didn't wait for him to reply.

'These are canisters marked with a PCB warning somewhere near the Treporti Channel. Now, normally they'd have lain there undisturbed, quietly corroding away. But here's the thing – the lagoon is clearer than it's ever been at the moment, because of the lack of traffic. And so, when a group of researchers from ISMAR went to investigate the possible site of an old Roman road, this is what one of them came across.'

Meneghini shook his head. 'That's impossible. Dumping of PCBs at sea is against the law.'

'I know it is. Nevertheless, this seems to have happened.'

'And what's that to do with Rifugio?'

'I'm sure it's just coincidence that your company was recently awarded a contract to dispose of legacy pollution, and barrels of toxic waste are turning up in the lagoon, that's all.'

'Yes, that's exactly what this is. A coincidence, that's all. That crap could have been down there for decades. If that photo is even real to begin with. I mean, look at it.' He picked up one of the photos, and shook his head. Then, staring me straight in the eyes, he crumpled it in his fist. 'I believe the word is Deep Fake.'

'Technically, that's two words.'

'Shut up. And listen to me. What do we have here? A shitty, blurred photograph that any wannabe eco-warrior could have knocked up in his bedroom. That's all. And what exactly is your interest in this, anyway?'

'You need to ask that, Giuseppe? You don't need to be an eco-warrior to think that introducing cancer-causing chemicals into the food chain is fundamentally a bad thing.' Now it was my turn to put my fingers together. 'Even if it does keep the triangle intact.'

He slapped at my fingers, breathing deeply.

'What are you doing here, Sutherland?'

'Oh, I'm just wondering what your totally legitimate business – a business so profitable that it allows you to rent an office in a building who's shape seriously makes me think you must be compensating for something – has to do with the death of a British citizen and the disappearance of a young Venetian diver.'

Meneghini sat down behind his desk, and rubbed his face. 'Okay, Sutherland. Let me just repeat this. I don't know anything about a dead Englishman. I don't know anything about a missing diver. I don't know anything about toxic waste dumping because I am running a clean business here. But I'll tell you what I do know: I know that if you repeat a single word of what you've just said to me outside of this office, I'll bury you deeper than those canisters.'

'It's the fact that they're not buried deep that's the problem, Giuseppe.'

He slammed his hand down on the desk with such force that the sudden shock made me jump backwards. He rested an elbow on the table, and waved a finger at me. I could see his palm was already reddening from the impact. 'That was instead of punching you.'

'Well, thank you.'

'Now listen to me, and listen good. If you repeat any of this – if I even so much as think that you've repeated any of this – I will bury you. I will impoverish you. I will sue you so hard your ancestors will feel the pain. Because I tell you this, you can come in here and you can make fun of me, and you can make these utterly scurrilous allegations, but I have a very, very good team of lawyers on my side and there is no way – no way in hell – that you'll be able to beat them.'

'Oh, I understand, Giuseppe. I understand very clearly.' I walked over to the window and stared out. 'It's one hell of a view, it really is. But is it worth it?' He said nothing. 'I'll see myself out.' I laid my hand upon the door, and then turned back to him. 'There's just one thing more, Giuseppe. You might have an army of lawyers on your side. But I've got an art restorer, a thrash metal guitarist, and the biggest Genesis fan in the Veneto on mine. And we're not just going to beat you. We're going to kick your arse.'

'How was the exhibit?'

'Pretty good. I could have done with a little more time. I never knew the history of a cooling tower could be so interesting.'

'Well, we haven't got to go just yet. If you want to have more of a wander around that is?'

'No, it's okay. Let's get back to town, ditch the car and then maybe go for a beer, eh? Or do you want to grab one in the bar upstairs?'

'I'm not so sure that's a great idea. I suspect *signor* Meneghini is sitting there now with a strong drink in his hand and plotting something terrible.'

'Oh. It went like that, did it?'

I grinned. 'It most certainly did.'

'Mr Sutherland?' I felt a hand on my shoulder, and had to restrain myself from jumping.

I turned around. I recognised him at once, from the photograph in Arturo's apartment. One of those Italian men of a certain age who manage to look good in a three-piece suit even in early summer. Jet-black curly hair, with just a touch too much oil, and a neatly trimmed beard, he was pretty much the definition of the term 'handsome bastard'.

'Erm, good afternoon,' I said.

'I wonder if we could have a quick chat.' He looked around the reception area. 'Not here, of course. I'd suggest the restaurant but,' he looked at his watch, 'I really don't have time for lunch.'

'We could take a look around the museum together. My friend here tells me it's very good. Or perhaps we could all just have a drink at the bar?'

Handsome Bastard shook his head. 'Just the two of us, if you don't mind.'

Dario smiled at him. 'I think I do mind.'

Handsome Bastard ignored him. 'Just a stroll along the canal for a few minutes. It won't take much of your time. And then you and your friend can get back to town.'

Dario shook his head. 'No chance.'

'Dario, it's okay.'

'Nat?'

'Seriously. It's broad daylight, people – lots of people – are out and about enjoying the sunshine and me and my new friend here are just going to go for a delightful stroll together.'

'Are you sure?'

'Absolutely. Don't worry. I won't be long.' I patted his shoulder, and then took Handsome Bastard by the arm. 'Let's go.'

'This is what I wanted to show you.'

We looked across the expanse of the Western Industrial Canal to where a crane was loading pallets onto a gigantic barge.

'Flour. Ready to be shipped all over Italy. And the world. As Venetian as glass, yet nobody ever thinks of it as such. It's not the loveliest view in Venice, I know. But it's part of our heritage as well. Because this – Mestre, Marghera – this is Venice as well. It has no gondolas, no opera house, no carnival. But it's still Venice.'

I nodded. 'I understand that. I don't imagine many of the tourists ever come out here to look at a barge and a flour mill though.'

'And that's a shame. The tower back there. The Industrial Museum. More people should come out here to visit somewhere like that. Because, as I said, this is part of our heritage as well. Now then. There's something else I want to show you. Right there. On the main deck, just below the bridge.'

The words 'No Smoking' were painted in red, metre-high letters, so as to be visible from every part of the deck.

'It's flammable,' Handsome Bastard said. 'Flour, that is.

More explosive than gunpowder. It seems strange, doesn't it, but it's true. A stray cigarette end, a spark from a lighter and – BOOF. So, this is a reminder to everyone that they have to be very careful.'

He patted me on the back. 'You'll be careful. Won't you? Not just you. I'm also thinking of the young people at the diving school. The nice young woman you went out to Treporti with. And your friend back there. You're all going to be careful.' He mimed the action of flicking a cigarette lighter. 'Because sometimes all we need is a spark. A silly little mistake. And bad things happen. Nobody wants that.'

I was about to speak but he put a finger to his lips. Then, once again, he flicked his imaginary lighter. 'Boom,' he whispered.

'So,' said Dario. 'Want to tell me all about it?'

'Oh, I think you can guess how it went.'

'Outwardly pleasant, but with nameless threats hanging in the air?'

'That was it. Did you recognise the guy.'

Dario shook his head. 'No. But he's kind of a "type" isn't he?'

'The "Handsome Bastard" type?'

'Yeah.' He looked at me. 'You sure you're okay?'

'I think so. It's not as if I've not been threatened before. And it usually means we're onto something.'

'Okay. Let's get back to town. And think about what we're going to do next.'

I shook my head. 'That's the problem, Dario. There is no *we*. Not this time.'

He shook his head. 'I don't get it, *vecio*. What do you mean?'

'I mean this is something I need to sort out on my own.'

'You're losing me.'

'There's just things he said, you know? He knows I've been out to Treporti with Lucia Frigo. He knows about the dive school.'

'How?'

'I don't know. But he must be looking for Vicari as well. And now, of course, he knows about you. He could find out who you are through Meneghini. And I can't have that. Not you. Not Vally. Not Emily.'

'Nat, I'm not going to leave you alone on this. That's not how it works.'

'It's the way it's going to have to work this time, Dario. I'm sorry.' He shook his head. 'You're going to have to trust me on this, okay? I promise I'll be careful.'

'You better be.' He shook his head. 'You better be,' he repeated. He switched on the car stereo, then shook his head and clicked it off again.

'Something wrong?'

'Nothing wrong, Nat.'

'Come on. Let's have a little bit of Black Sabbath to cheer ourselves up.'

Again, he shook his head. 'Do you mind if we don't? I'm not really in the mood right now.'

We drove back to Venice in silence and, whenever I looked over at him, I could see the hurt in his eyes.

Chapter 49

Roberto Bergamin grinned as we sat down outside the Magical Brazilians.

We bumped elbows. 'Mr Sutherland. It's been a while.'

'Must be nearly six months now, Roberto.'

'And what a six months they've been. I'm one of the lucky ones, mind you. Journalist is an essential job now, it seems. Otherwise how would the good people of this fine city know that one of their neighbours was fined for taking their dog for a three hundred-and-fifty-metre walk instead of three hundred?'

'Your public service does you proud, Roberto.'

'Mind you, you're a cat person, aren't you? What was that like? Did you ever manage to take him for a walk?'

'From the sofa to his bowl. Multiple times a day. I guess that counts.'

Eduardo appeared, clutching a pad. 'Hello, Nat. Drinks for you and your pal?'

'Spritz Campari for me, Ed. Bit early in the day for a Negroni, and I've got a hunch there'll be work to do.'

'Spritz Campari,' he scribbled away. 'How about you, my friend?'

'*Bionda media*,' said Roberto.

'Uh-huh. Anything to eat?'

'Just a *toast*.'

'Nathan?'

'Just a couple of *polpetti*, please Ed. One meat, one tuna.'

He frowned. 'They're not on sticks.'

'That's not a deal-breaker. Really.'

'Okay. As long as you're sure.'

Roberto adjusted his shades, and smiled. '*Una bionda media*. How would you say that in English?'

'Pint of lager would be the equivalent, I suppose. But, literally, a medium-sized blonde.'

He grinned, stretching his legs out and folding his arms behind his head. 'A medium-sized blonde. Blimey, we could all do with one of those on a hot day, couldn't we?'

I gave him a weak smile in exchange. Bergamin's company had grown on me, but every so often he reminded me that he was a man of unreconstructed views on certain things.

'So is this place doubling as your office, these days?'

'I suppose it is. It ticks most of the boxes. We can meet outside, just in case anybody's nervous about being in a confined space. Free wifi. Drinks and snacks when we need them. I'm thinking about making Ed a formal offer for a long-term rent on this table.'

He checked his watch. 'Okay, now I need to make this a quick lunch. I'm supposed to be on the Lido, taking photos of social distancing on the beaches in about an hour. Not much of a story, I know, photographing people not sitting together. But what you've found sounds a little more exciting.'

'Our old friend, Giuseppe Meneghini.'

'Failed mayoral candidate, friend of football hooligans

and far-right historians?'

'The very same. And just possibly a man responsible for dumping toxic waste into the lagoon. So, go on Roberto, tell me what you've found.'

'Well, sorry to disappoint you on this but – for a company involved in waste disposal – Rifugio appears to be clean. Tax returns filed on time, no evidence of mismanagement of any sort. In fact, they're so clean that's kind of suspicious in itself.'

'Damn. That's not what I was expecting. I was hoping for a smoking gun.'

'And that's exactly what we're not going to get from Rifugio. But the other guy, Good Suit Guy – now that's another matter.

'His name's Pietro Zorzi, and he co-owns a company called Facility Zorvic. They're registered as a waste management company in Naples. Again, they seem to be relatively clean. There's not much about them on the internet. But I've got a mate who works for *Il Mattino*, one of the big newspapers down in that part of the country. See, most of their archive isn't online yet, but he was able to tell me all about them.'

Facility Zorvic. The name on the business card that Lucia had found on San Francesco.

'What do you know about them? Beyond the scary name, that is. They sound like the sort of organisation James Bond would be fighting.'

'The name's the least scary thing about them. That just comes from the owners. Pietro Zorzi and,' he paused, 'a man you just might be interested in. Daniele Vicari.'

'Seriously?'

'Absolutely. Zorzi. Vicari. *Zor Vic*, get it?'

I frowned. 'Zorzi. That's not really a Neapolitan name.'

'You're right. But there is a Venetian connection. There's an area in Campania, just northeast of Naples. Three *comuni* – Acera, Nola and Marigliano. It's the largest illegal waste dump in Europe. And they call it the *Triangolo della morte*. The Triangle of Death. Half a million people live there. And the cancer rate is higher than anywhere else in Italy. Heavy metals, toxic waste, you name it – it's been burned, or shovelled into landfills or just sprayed over the countryside.

'And here's the thing. Industrial waste from Marghera was found to have been used as compost on agricultural land. Some of the most toxic material on earth. Going straight into the food chain.'

'Zorvic?'

'They were investigated. Several times. Nothing ever got as far as a prosecution.' He rubbed his thumb and two fingers together. 'I think we can guess why.'

'And Meneghini's working with these people?'

'That's where it gets complicated. There's been some sort of power struggle within Zorvic. See, the company was formed after the Second World War by the Vicari and Zorzi families. Working in reconstruction, that sort of thing. Then they moved into waste disposal. Some people call it *ecomafia*. Danny Vicari arrived years ago, taking his share of the business. Then this guy, Pietro Zorzi – like Vicari, he's a descendant of the original owners – seems to have moved in round about the time that all this shit was being dumped in the Triangle of Death. It sounds like it was some sort of genuine collaboration at first, but the organisation seems to be slowly breaking in two. Zorzi is the face of the company now. My source at *Il Mattino* says that Vicari hasn't been seen in Naples since the beginning of June. When we could all start moving around again.'

'So there's been a power grab by Zorzi, sidelining Vicari and making some sort of deal with Meneghini's Rifugio.'

'That's what it looks like, doesn't it?' He grinned, and looked at the photographs in front of him. 'Nathan mate, this story is going to be dynamite. Absolute dynamite.'

'I thought you'd be pleased.'

'Oh, I am. This makes shit like going out to the Lido to photograph people sitting a long way apart from each other worthwhile. We're going to blow those bastards at *Il Mattino* out of the water with this.'

'I thought this guy was a mate of yours.'

'He is. He's still a bastard though.' He paused for a moment. 'Only thing is, we're going to need more than this.'

'I don't understand.'

'You know what Meneghini's like. Mr Litigation. If I go to my editor with these and seriously suggest sticking them on the front page, I'll be back reporting on pickpockets on the *vaporetti* before he's slammed the door on me.'

'What's wrong with them?'

'To me, nothing. But they're not enough. We've got a photo of a guy standing outside a cooling tower, and an underwater picture of some barrels.'

'Barrels with skulls and crossbones, and words saying *Polychlorinated Biphenyls* in multiple languages.'

'Sure. It's not me you have to convince though.' He smiled. 'Can you get me some more photos?'

I sighed. 'I was afraid you were going to ask me that.'

Chapter 50

Mare di Carta did indeed have a splendid range of books and maps, and I spread my new purchases out upon the table, together with the night-time photograph taken by Arturo Franceschini.

Two *campanili* were visible. One, the crazily leaning tower on Burano. The other, I figured, would have to be that of San Francesco. There were any number of tiny uninhabited islands in that area, little more than patches of scrubland rising out of the lagoon, but if Arty had needed to remain hidden, there was only one place he could have chosen. The island of Madonna del Monte.

I turned to my other new purchase, a history of the abandoned islands of the lagoon. If I was going to head out there – or, more likely, if I was going to ask Bepi to take me – it would be good to know as much as possible in advance.

Strictly speaking, Madonna del Monte was two islands, although it was once linked by a thin strip of a land and a paling long since lost to flooding. Four Benedictine nuns arrived there in the fourteenth century, nearly a hundred years after Francis had settled down just a few hundred metres away, and dedicated a convent to Saint Nicholas.

It seems to have been an unlucky place, that never quite settled down over the centuries. The Bishop of Torcello closed it down, following the death of the last nun, in 1432. In the seventeenth century a group of hermits tried, and failed, to establish a community dedicated to St Paul of Thebes. In 1712, a certain Pietro Tabacco dedicated a new church to Our Lady of the Rosary. And so it was that the island of San Nicolò della Cavana became Madonna del Monte. The period of stability lasted less than a century, until the arrival of Napoleon.

The church was burned to the ground in the middle of the nineteenth century, and, once more, the island was abandoned until the construction of yet another gunpowder warehouse that endured until the end of the Second World War. Since then it had lain empty, increasingly overgrown, and every year just a little bit more of it slid into the lagoon.

I put the book away. Okay, so the island was abandoned but unlike, say, Sant'Ariano, it didn't seem to be actually physically dangerous to go there. Neither, encouragingly, were there reports of rats or snakes.

I was about to give Bepi a call when the doorbell rang. Bad timing, but hopefully it wouldn't take long.

'Hello?'

'Mr Sutherland?' The voice was muffled as if the speaker had a heavy cold. 'I need your help.'

Damn. Still, never turn away potential business. 'Come on up,' I said, and buzzed him in. I heard footsteps upon the stairs, and opened the door to let my visitor in.

Carlo Lucarini was already on my doorstep. 'I need your help,' he repeated.

***

'I knew you were lying with that lawnmower manual crap.'

'I wasn't lying. That's my job. Not just lawnmowers of course. Fridges, microwave ovens. All sorts of white goods and beyond.'

'So what's that sign on the door outside all about? And why does everybody I've spoken to call you the English consul?'

'That's my other job. My other unpaid job. And it's an honorary position only, I'm not a diplomat or anything. So, what can I do for you, Carlo? Do you mind if I keeping calling you Carlo? I know it's not your real name but it seems easiest.'

'Call me what you like. And I meant it when I said I needed help. I know you have the dive watch. I need you to give it to me.' He paused. 'Please.'

I shrugged. 'I offered it to you on San Francesco. You said it wasn't yours. Why?'

'I panicked because I knew what it meant. I didn't want to be linked with it.'

'You mean linked with Arturo Franceschini?' He nodded. 'He's dead then?'

'I don't know. I honestly don't know. Only Danny can give us an answer to that one.'

'Tell me more.' Lucarini said nothing. 'Look Carlo, if you want me to help you, you need to tell me everything. I'll save you some time. I know about Zorvic and Rifugio. I know you didn't kill Bruno Pagan. And I know you were watching the lagoon, waiting for the boats to arrive and drop their poison. To give you some sort of hold over Giuseppe Meneghini and Pietro Zorzi. Am I right?'

Again, Lucarini said nothing. 'Am I right?' I repeated.

He sighed. 'Pretty much. The idea was Danny could force Zorzi and Meneghini to give us lots of money to go away and say nothing.'

'So how did Arturo come into this?'

'We saw someone diving in the lagoon. Then we read about the ISMAR project and found they'd been employing someone from a local dive school. The Franceschini boy had been scouting out that area of the canal for weeks. The more we checked him out, the more we realised what he was doing. He was looking for evidence that Rifugio were dumping crap in the lagoon.'

'The same as you. So what was the problem?'

'Because the kid wasn't in it for the money. He would just have put the evidence out there for free, doing his bit to save the environment. And we couldn't have that. If he already had information, we had to make sure that we had it as well. Danny was on the mainland keeping an eye on Zorzi, and said he'd deal with it. In the meantime we were to keep watching the lagoon.'

'And that was the problem, wasn't it? Danny wasn't on the island. If he had been, none of this would have happened. So, you were watching the lagoon by night and pretending to be pilgrims by day. And then Dominic Vicari arrived. You recognised him, of course?'

'Not at first. He was just introduced to us as "Dominic". But we could tell he recognised us. And he was spending hours in the bell tower. Looking at the stars, he said. But we could tell he wasn't. He was looking at the lagoon. And if he wasn't looking at the lagoon, he was looking at us.

'And then we got thinking, hey this guy doesn't have as much hair as the boss but there's still a hell of a resemblance. The next day we check the guest book and there it is: Dominic Vicari. But he's never mentioned Danny at all, hasn't even mentioned his name. I'm all for phoning the boss and asking him what's going on but Bruno is beyond paranoid by now. This guy, he tells me, is obviously spying on us. Is he an undercover cop? Or, worse, what if he's working with Danny and they're preparing to sell us both out?

'That last night I was up in the tower, trying to keep an eye on both Bruno and the lagoon at the same time. We normally worked it in shifts, you know, only by then I didn't like leaving Bruno alone up there with a bottle of cheap booze. Vicari was there as well, just to look at the stars, as always. Except there were no stars that night. And then Bruno snapped. He told Vicari we knew who he was, and he grabbed him, and shook him, and started shouting for him to tell us just who the hell he was working for. All the time I was trying to shut him up, but Vicari was a strong guy, trying to shake him off. And then Bruno pushed him back, further and further, right to the edge and suddenly – Vicari was over the side and lying at the base of the tower.'

I nodded. 'And then you persuaded Pagan to hand over his supermarket whisky and doused Vicari's body in booze. Then you both ran like hell before Fra Gregorio arrived and found the body. Vicari's cell door was unlocked, of course, and so you rolled the bottle under the bed for the police to discover. The trouble is, Vicari hadn't really drunk that much. Not enough for it to be written off as a drunken accident. You've killed Danny's brother. And you wonder just what the hell he's going to do to you when he finds out.'

Lucarini shook his head, and looked so tired. 'It wasn't me. But I didn't think Danny would care about that. The next day the police came. They took statements. Bruno held it together enough for that, at least. And then you arrived, along with a plain-clothes guy. Two days later, I noticed Maria was making up one of the cells. I asked her what was happening and she said that some British guy who'd been out here with the police was coming to stay for a while.'

'So you came up with – forgive me – an even more half-arsed scheme which involved forging my name in the visitor's book in the hope that Danny would blame it all on me. A scheme that was never going to work. It was just to buy you a little bit of time in the hope that something better would turn up. And it did. With the dive watch.

'In the meantime Danny worked out that it was nothing to do with me. So he knew you'd been lying to him. But he let you sweat for a couple of days. After all, you might still have been useful. He sent you off one morning. Told you, I don't know, go and spy on Zorzi for a few days. Something like that.

'He took a boat out to San Francesco late that night. Bruno, I imagine, was keeping watch and getting happily drunk. Danny needed to get him downstairs in order for his plan to work. He needed to be near the treasury. Bruno was half-cut, I don't imagine he took much persuading. Maybe Danny suggested to him they could split the money two ways instead of three. We'll never know. And then he strangled him with a cincture. Hence the three bruises on his neck.

'He broke the glass in the treasury to make it look like an argument amongst thieves. Within an hour, the cops were there and they were all looking for the missing Carlo Lucarini.

'Thing is, though, I heard most of what was going on. He first throttled Pagan and then he broke the glass in the cabinet. But he didn't even bother taking the altar cloth. That didn't make any sense. For that matter, what's the market like in stolen altar cloths? I don't imagine there's an oligarch in Russia inviting his mates round to admire his collection. No, it felt like a stitch-up from the beginning.' I smiled. 'Am I right?'

'In all the important bits, yes. You're very clever for a lawn-mower translator.'

'Now the big question for you must be – how do you get back into Vicari's good books? What can you possibly do that'd be big enough to make up for accidentally killing his brother?'

'It wasn't me. It was Bruno.'

'It's not me that you have to persuade, Carlo.'

'The dive watch. That's what I need.'

'Because you can use it to find Arturo's camera. Once the two are linked you can threaten to upload everything he found to a public website. Unless Zorzi gives Danny what he wants. A perfect demonstration of your loyalty.'

I looked down at the map on my desk. Gramsci promptly went and sat on it, until I shooed him away. 'Bad cat. You're okay with cats, I hope, Carlo?' An idea was beginning to form in the back of my mind. I smiled at Lucarini. 'Okay, you can have it. Because someone's either going to get killed or hurt because of this and, with respect, rather you than me.'

I made my way over to the safe, rested my hand upon the dial, and paused.

'What's wrong?'

'Nothing, I'm just a bit stressed that's all. I keep getting the passcode wrong, you see.' I scratched my head. 'Now, the number is Gramsci's birthday. Not his real one of course, I don't know that. But just taking it from when he moved in.'

'Your passcode is your cat's birthday?'

I grinned. 'Ridiculous, isn't it? And, of course, my wife had plenty to say about that when she found out. Didn't she, Grams?'

Gramsci miaowed at the sound of his name.

'So, remind me again. When did you turn up, Grams? Was it 2013 or 2014? I can't quite remember.'

He miaowed again.

I smiled and turned to Lucarini. 'He says it's 2014, but I think he's taking a year off his age again. He does that, you know?'

'Are you insane? Just open the damn safe.'

'Okay. Okay. *Tranquillo*. Here we go.' I counted out the digits. '2-click-0-click-1-click-3-click ... plus the date ...' I heard the chambers rolling back. 'There we go.'

I reached inside and took out the dive watch. Lucarini's fingers twitched for a moment, but I shook my head and dropped it into my pocket.

He smiled. 'How did you know I wouldn't just take it and kill you?'

'Well, whatever else you may be, I'm prepared to believe that you're not a killer. Also, it's broad daylight and there are people in the bar downstairs. My wife will be back in a few minutes, as well.' I looked down at the sofa. 'And there's him of course.'

Gramsci chose that moment to throw a paw across his eyes

and go to sleep. 'Oh, don't be fooled by that. Between the two of them they've taken out better people than you.'

I heard the rattle of keys in the door.

'*Ciao, caro.*'

'*Ciao, cara.*'

Federica stared at the two of us.

'Is now a bad time?' she said.

'Not at all,' I smiled. 'In fact, we were just talking about you.'

She sighed. 'Okay. I think you need to get me up to date.'

Chapter 51

'And so,' I said, 'Lucarini here needs the dive watch to inter-
face with Arturo's camera – if it's anywhere to be found, that
is, and not just at the bottom of the lagoon. And the most
likely place, going by Lucarini's evidence and the photos we
have, is Madonna del Monte. Question is, then, what's in it
for us? Why don't we just call the police, Carlo?'

'How about because I haven't done anything wrong?'

'I believe you. At least in the context of killing Bruno. But
the cops wouldn't. You're a very nice, convenient solution to
a problem.' I looked down at the map, and traced my fingers
around Madonna del Monte. 'Thing is, though, those photographs might be useful to us as well.'

Fede frowned. 'What are you thinking?'

'I'm thinking they could help us nail Meneghini. I don't
want him standing as mayor again. Not even in five years. I
don't want him dumping waste into the lagoon. And I don't
trust him to be involved in any other scheme that's allegedly
good for the city. So if this will bring him down, I say let's
do it.'

Lucarini looked at me. 'Okay then. Give me the watch
and I'll get you everything you need.'

I laughed. 'No deal, Carlo. If it's on that island then we'll find it together.'

He stared at me, hoping I'd blink first. And then he nodded. 'Okay then. Both of us.'

'Good. Let me just make a call.' I dialled Bepi's number. '007?'

'That's me, Bepi. I need your help.'

'Sure, *capo*. Are we going out to the monastery again?'

'Not this time. I need you to take me out to Madonna del Monte.'

I could hear the puzzlement in his voice. 'Madonna del Monte? Why do you want to go out there? Place has been deserted since the war.'

'I'll explain on the way. But trust me, it's important.'

'Okay, *capo*. Does this mean we're fighting crime?'

'It certainly does, Bepi. It certainly does.'

I hung up. 'Right, let's get going.' I pulled on my jacket and patted my pocket to reassure myself that the watch was where I'd left it.

Fede cleared her throat. 'You're sure you can trust this guy?'

'I'm not so sure I can. But there'll be me and Bepi. One of him and two of us.'

'You mean three of us. Of course?'

I looked at her and read the expression on her face.

'Of course,' I said. And she smiled, just ever so slightly.

Chapter 52

He doesn't look like I expected. I'd always thought that conspiracy theorists, or free thinkers, or whatever the hell you want to call them, were sad middle-aged men living in bedsits or in their mam's spare room. Although, come to think of it, that could describe me.

But the Deep Dive bloke is different. He looks like he's walked in from a cover shoot for Men's Health *or* GQ. *Great hair and a tan that sure as hell wasn't picked up in West Cross.*

His apartment is near a camping village somewhere called Treporti, which is a long haul out of Venice on a bakingly hot boat. There's a small fridge, a two-ring hob, and what I assume is a sofa bed. There are wetsuits, flippers, masks and stuff that I don't even recognise taking up much of the floorspace. And Rita Hayworth is on the wall. Rita Hayworth in Gilda, *all gorgeous and looking as if she's about to burst into 'Put the blame on Mame'.*

'Dominic?'

I nod.

'I'm Deep Dive.'

'Should I call you Deep or signor Dive?'

He shakes his head. 'I'm not joking. I've got to be careful. Just in case.'

So far, perhaps, so predictable. Mr Dive knows The Truth and so dark forces are conspiring against him. I hold back a sigh. Surfer boy here might be a fantasist but, so far, he's all I've got.

'I'm sorry, my English isn't so good.'

'That's okay. We can use Italian.' He looks confused. 'My name's not Dominic. It's Domenico. And back home they'd call me one of the Bracchi.'

'What?'

'Over a hundred years ago, Giacomo Bracchi rocked up in the Rhondda Valley and opened a cafe. I don't know if he came for the weather. At the time, it probably wasn't for the food.' I tap my chest. 'And so, today, we're all Bracchi back home.' He nods, but I can tell he isn't taking it in. 'Okay, so let's get down to cases. You know something about my brother. Danny – or Daniele – Vicari.'

He nods. 'I think your brother's in loads of shit.'

I take a deep breath. 'Okay. Tell me more.'

'What do you know about him? Really know, I mean? About what he's been doing these past few years.'

'I don't know. This is the thing. I don't know. He never telephoned, never wrote. All I had from him was an address in Naples. I've been down there. People just say he was some sort of businessman. And his neighbour had a message for me. Telling us how much he loved us. And that I was never to attempt to get in touch with him again.'

Deep Dive nods. 'Smart guy.' He opens a small fridge, takes out a can of beer, and cracks it open. 'You having one?' I shake my head. 'So you don't know what your brother was doing in Naples?' he asks.

I'm starting to get angry now. He's only asking me this so that he can show how clever he is. I suspect he doesn't really want that beer either. It's similarly part of the act. Any minute now, I think, he'll light up a cigarette to go with it.

'No. I don't know what he was doing there. When my parents split up, Dad went back home to Naples to take over Granddad's business. Whatever that was. He only ever told us that he was "a businessman". Even at that age, we thought we shouldn't ask about it.

'And then one day, he wrote to me and Danny, and told us he needed help with the business. But we knew somebody would have to stay with Mam. And, well, I was the obvious one. So Danny left one day, with a rucksack over his shoulder. And things were never quite the same again.'

'So he was a "businessman"?' Deep Dive makes little quotation marks with his fingers, and I feel the anger rising within me again. 'That's what he told you?' He reaches into his shirt pocket and takes out a packet of cigarettes. He sparks one up and inhales deeply, nodding all the while.

'Okay, Arturo Franceschini,' I say, and I linger over his name, enjoying the expression in his eyes. 'Why don't we skip the bullshit, and you tell me all about it? There's a good boy.'

'You know my name?'

'I'm a private investigator and this stuff isn't difficult to find out. In fact, it's childishly easy. So if you're worried about other people finding out whatever it is you know, you'd better hope they're not as good at their job as I am at mine.'

He looks at me. 'You've been in a fight.'

I rub my knuckles. 'Yeah.'

'Want to tell me about it?'

'Is it important?'

'Might be.'

'I was looking for Danny. In Naples. Someone followed me from his apartment, his local bar – I can't be sure where – and tried to stick a knife in me before I could get on the next train to Venice.'

He takes a deep breath. 'Okay. That makes sense.' He drinks from his can. 'Peace, eh? You sure you don't want one?'

I smile as best I can. 'Okay. Thanks.'

He opens the fridge, takes out a can and tosses one to me. It's cold and fizzy and, on a hot day, it's enough to hit the spot.

'Naples, eh?' he continues. 'Here's the deal.' He takes a deep breath. 'Your brother works, or at least he worked, for a company called Zorvic. You heard of them?'

I shake my head.

'No reason you should have. They're based down south. And just recently they started working for a company called Rifugio, based out in Porto Marghera. And they also got awarded a nice fat government contract for disposing of what's called "legacy pollution". By which I mean all the crap, all the filth that somehow has to be cleaned out of disused factories before they can use the ground again.'

'Okay. So what's that got to do with Danny?'

He takes a deep breath. 'All right. You're not going to like this and so I'm just going to come out and say it. Your brother was working in what we might call "waste management" down in Naples. Stuff gets shifted down there from all over Italy, and gets disposed of in the cheapest way they can think of. There are farmers' fields in Campania covered in toxic slurry from Marghera. Ecomafia, they call it.' He pauses, and stares straight into my eyes. 'That's what your brother does.'

I shake my head. 'Danny wouldn't do that,' I say.

'I said you wouldn't like it. Can I go on?'

'I don't like it because it's bullshit.'

He shrugs. 'You want me to continue?'

I dig my nails into my palms, but nod. 'Go on.'

He lays a photograph upon the table. Two men, shaking hands, in front of what looks like the base of a cooling tower.

'The man on the left here is Pietro Zorzi. One of the partners in Zorvic. Zorzi. Vicari. You get it?' I nod. 'The other guy is Giuseppe Meneghini. A few months ago he almost became Mayor of Venice. And he's the owner of Rifugio. And Rifugio are telling anyone who'll listen how all this toxic crap, all this legacy pollution, will be disposed of in a nice, clean and – above all – safe way. Whereas, what they're actually happy to do is get your brother's company to ship if off to some dodgy business in Campania who then get rid of it in a very quick, very dirty and very unsafe way.'

He pauses again. 'The trouble is, Zorvic are greedy sons-of-bitches.' His eyes flick across at mine. 'They start thinking that maybe – instead of transporting all this crap halfway around Italy – they can do it on the cheap and bury it in an abandoned trench off Madonna del Monte. More profit, see?'

I get to my feet, breathing deeply. 'You're telling me that my brother is basically in the cancer business? And I'm telling you that he wouldn't do that.'

'He wouldn't? Maybe you don't know him very well at all.'

'I don't know what he's involved in, but he wouldn't do shit like this.'

'But he is. Listen, man, I don't want to piss you off or anything, but you asked me to tell you the truth. Your brother's *company is disposing of chemicals that cause cancer in the lagoon. He's sprayed carcinogens all over fields in Campania. He's—'*

And he has to shut up at this point because I've hauled him to his feet and my fist is balled and I'm about to punch him in the face to shut his stupid mouth up.

'Is this going to make you feel better? Is it?'

And I think, for a moment, yes. It is. Then I look down at him and I realise that he's basically just a kid. A well-meaning kid who's bummed around the world trying to make it better and has stumbled on something that's too big for him.

'I'm sorry,' I say. The kid – because that's how I'm thinking of him now – slumps back onto the sofa.

'I'm sorry too,' he says.

'So what do we do now? And where's Danny?'

'Okay, for the last couple of nights I've been camping out on Madonna del Monte. Trying to get photos of the barges that are running that route. Trying to catch them in the act. I've done one dive in the area and I've got photos of barrels of PCBs down there. I've got a photo of one of the heads of Zorvic meeting the head of Rifugio. It's nearly complete. I just need a few more photos. And then I'll upload it to my website, press the Publish button and blow the whole thing open.'

'And what happens to my brother?'

'If he's involved in this then,' he shrugs, 'I'm sorry, but he gets taken down as well. You must understand that. Surely?'

I take a deep breath. 'I understand. But give me a couple of days. Please. Just to find Danny, just to talk to him.' He looks uncertain. 'Arturo, I am ready to get down on my knees and beg. Just give me a couple of days.'

He nods. 'Okay. But no more.'

'Do you know where he might be?'

'Maybe. See, when I've been heading off to Madonna del Monte, I pass by the island of San Francesco del Deserto. It's a monastery, you know? And if you go up the bell tower there, you'd have a perfect view of the whole of the lagoon. And I've seen people up there, watching.'

'What, signalling?'

'I don't know. But I've seen it several times now. Late at night. Camera flashes, things like that. It's not a coincidence. There are people there watching that area of the lagoon.'

'Monks? Why would they be doing that?'

'Not the brothers. People go there on retreat. On pilgrimages, that sort of thing. But if you wanted to go and spy on that area of the lagoon, there's no better spot.'

It's not much to go on. But Arturo's only going to give me a couple of days' grace, and it'll have to be enough. I take out the photos I took from the guy in Naples. 'This is my brother. These two others – Pagan and Lucarini – I don't know who they are. But you hang onto these. If you see them, then you call me. I'll give you my number.

'And a word of advice. You stay off the socials. You take all those accounts down. You keep quiet about this. You don't do anything that can identify yourself. Because if I can find you, then other people can. You understand?'

He nods. 'It's okay. I've done this stuff before. I can look after myself.' We shake hands. 'And I hope you find your brother. Really I do.'

I rub my face. My eyes are gritty and I'm tired, so tired, that I feel I've got sand in my veins. 'People go on retreat to this island, you say?' He nods. 'Okay. Then that's where I'll start.'

I turn to leave and then I remember the words of the man in Naples, the one outside Danny's apartment block. He said he loved you very much. *And I think that, yes, he really did. All these years, of no contact at all. He was trying to keep us safe.*

I keep thinking I should know more about St Francis than I actually do. Mam, I know, would be disappointed. But all I can think about on the boat from Burano is what the hell is going on over on Madonna del Monte, and trying not to think that Danny might have anything to do with it.

The boatman chatters away the whole time. He's picked up that I speak Italian. Trouble is he doesn't realise I've got no handle at all on Veneziano, or whatever it's called and so much of it is going over my head. He wants me to go and buy Murano glass from his pal, and Burano lace from his mother – or is it the other way round – and seems disappointed when I keep insisting no. I also think he says something about glass crabs in the lagoon, but I must have got that bit wrong.

And then we're there, and he holds out an arm to steady me and help me on to the jetty. I give him a smile and a thumbs-up, but he seems disappointed.

One of the brothers is there to meet me. He introduces himself as Fra Vincenzo. It'll be good to have me with them, he says. Pilgrims have, of course, been thin on the ground this year. He hopes that I find whatever I might be in need of and that my retreat will be fulfilling. It could sound like any New Age bollocks but there's something about this guy that reads as sincere.

'It's good to have you here with us,' he repeats. 'I'll introduce you to the fratelli *later. And Bruno and Carlo – they're the other*

pilgrims.' He pauses. 'I hope we help you find what you're looking for. Whatever that might be.'

I smile back at him. 'I suppose you could say I'm looking for sanctuary.'

Chapter 53

'Who are these two?' said Bepi.

'I'm Carlo.' Lucarini stretched out his hand, but Bepi did not take it.

'Are you a 007 as well?'

'He's a – well – let's call him a *colleague*,' I said.

He nodded and turned to Federica. 'I guess that makes you the Bond girl,' he said.

I winced, but she restrained herself to a look that could have curdled yoghurt.

He shrugged. 'Just a little joke. Come on, everyone.'

The journey to Madonna del Monte took little more time than the trip to San Francesco. There were a number of flat areas of scrubland to navigate around, inhabited only by birds, but, as Bepi explained, they were easier to see than the giant underwater crabs.

There was no jetty, nor any proper place to moor to speak of. Bepi took the boat in as close as he could, tied it up to some blocks of fallen masonry, and the four of us squelched through the muddy incline that led up to the remains of the gunpowder warehouse, half-hidden behind a thicket of acacia trees.

'So where do we start?' said Lucarini.

I took the watch out and strapped it to my wrist. 'I guess I'll just walk around for a bit.'

'Just in the hope of seeing something? Yeah, that'll work.'

'Look. The watch will be trying to connect to the camera as soon as it's in bluetooth range. Once it is, there should be some sort of audible signal.'

'And you know this – how?'

'I don't. It's an educated guess, that's all. But you're welcome to get down on your hands and knees and search through the mud if you like?'

'*Capo*, you need to be careful around here,' said Bepi. 'I don't know how safe these buildings are.'

'I'll be careful. Come on, Fede. Let's take a stroll.'

Fede took my hand as the two of us stumbled over the rocks and threaded our ways through the trees that choked the interior of the warehouse.

She leant her head into mine. 'You know you can't trust this guy, of course?'

I nodded. 'Sure. But there's only one of him, and there's three of us. We'll be fine.'

She tapped my wrist. 'What's the range of this thing?'

'No idea.'

'Terrific.'

We reached the westernmost point and looked across to the smaller island, separated from us by a thin strip of shallow water. It would, I supposed, be possible to ford it but there was little there, save for a broken-down building in an even worse state of dilapidation than the warehouse.

'What's that?'

'Remains of a guardhouse from the war I think.'

'D'you think it's worth a look?'

'In these shoes? Besides, if Arturo was out here night after night, why would he go there? There's hardly any cover. Here he could have got a clear view of the lagoon without worrying about being noticed.'

'I guess you're right. Oh well, I wasn't really in the mood for wading over there. Let's do another sweep and then – well, maybe Lucarini really can get down on his hands and knees.' I noticed something out of the corner of my eye.

'Oh shit.'

'What? What's the matter?'

'There's something down there in the water.' I took her hand and the two of us half slid down the bank to the edge of the shore. 'There.'

The water at this point might have been a metre deep at its shallowest point before shelving away and, as the waves gently ebbed and flowed, they revealed the prow of a small white boat just beneath the surface. Stencilled on the side was the image of a great bat-winged octopus-like creature.

Fede squeezed my hand. 'The same as the watch strap.'

I nodded. 'Arturo's boat.'

'And so, where's Arturo?'

I looked down at the waves lapping against the shore and shook my head. 'Somewhere near.' I shivered, despite the heat. 'Come on. Let's get back.'

'We should call the police. Seriously. The guy's been missing for days now and we've found the wreck of his boat. He's not diving wrecks in the *mezzogiorno*. He's down there in the lagoon. Or somewhere—'

The watch buzzed.

I looked down at the screen. 'It's found it. Look, it's connecting. Uploading photos.' A message flashed up on screen. *Publish to site Y/N*. 'It must be round here somewhere.'

Lucarini patted me on the back. 'Nicely done, Nathan. Nicely done.' He grabbed for my wrist. 'Now, I'll take that if I may?'

I punched him in the face and sent him staggering back. 'I don't think so, Carlo. I'll look after this if you don't mind?'

'Nathan. One moment, *capo*.'

I turned to see Bepi. A camera dangled from a strap around his left hand. In the right, he held a gun.

He smiled. 'Be a pal, and let us have the watch, eh?'

Chapter 54

I shook my head. 'Bepi, if this is some sort of joke, then it's not funny.'

'I know it's not funny, *capo*. I'm sorry.'

'Arturo's down there, isn't he? In the boat.'

He nodded. 'He's been there since the night after my brother died. Lucarini here spotted lights from the island, three nights in a row. I came out here to watch him. I saw him photographing the same boat from Marghera each time. A boat registered to Zorvic, dumping barrels of toxic waste into the lagoon.

'And we couldn't have that. I'm sorry, but we just couldn't. If he had information that we could use, then so much the better. But he wouldn't have done that. He'd just have put it out there for the public and the ecowarriors to see. Whereas we've got something else we need to use it for. So I waited out here for him one night. He put up a good fight, fair play to him. But that's how the dive watch ended up in the lagoon. And then I found that, without that, I couldn't unlock the camera.'

Again, he stretched out his hand. I shrugged and passed the watch to him. He strapped it to his wrist and swiped a finger across the face.

He smiled. 'Okay. It's all there. Shots of the boat. Shots of the barrels. Meneghini and Zorzi shaking hands. It's all there. Everything we need. Press a button, and this stuff goes out to the socials, to his website, everywhere.'

'Unless?'

'Zorzi gives me what I want. Money, basically. To go away.'

'One last big job, that sort of thing?'

'Exactly. They'll never see me again and Zorzi and Meneghini can do whatever the hell they like.'

'Including dumping waste into the lagoon? Spreading radioactive slurry over the fields of Campania?'

He shrugged. 'If they don't do it, then somebody else will. It's the way the world works now.'

'Then I can't let you do that.'

Lucarini laughed, but Bepi – Danny – glared at him.

'And all this? The whole "affable boatman" thing?'

He grinned. 'Come on, that was clever, admit it? Maria just let it slip to Lucarini that there was another pilgrim turning up at the monastery. Only this one she'd seen a couple of days before. With a cop.

'So we needed to keep an eye on you. I bought a cheap boat from a guy on Burano who was desperate for the cash. And I sat there and waited for you. Nobody else was ever going to take you to the island, I was going to be damn sure about that. And while you thought that you were asking me the questions – I was getting all the information I needed from you.'

'You really thought I was a cop?'

'Maybe Europol. Or private. At any rate, there was a possibility you'd killed my brother. Now, I could have taken you out to a deserted island in the middle of the lagoon on that first day and shot you in the back of the head. But there was something about Carlo's story that didn't quite ring true. The whole business about you arriving the night before his death. I needed to find out more.'

Lucarini leapt in quickly. 'It was Bruno who killed Dominic, Daniele. He was going to pieces. I knew we couldn't trust him. It was his idea.'

Danny nodded. 'Bruno's idea. As you say.'

'So, you guys are just going to let bygones be bygones?'

Again, Lucarini was the first to speak. 'I explained how we could still work it all out as long as we stuck together. We watched the lagoon for night after night. And then it turned out that Arturo was doing all the hard work for us. With the information on his dive watch and camera, we've got Meneghini by the balls. And what's more, we've got Zorvic by the balls. We get their money, go our separate ways and never see each other again.'

I turned to Danny. 'I don't understand. If you already had the camera, then why bring us all the way out here?'

Danny shook his head and raised the gun. 'Because it's a long way from anywhere. And it's been good to talk. Just to clear the air. But this is it, I'm afraid.'

'Oh Christ.' I grabbed Fede's hand. 'Jesus, Danny, just wait a minute. Your brother wouldn't want this.'

'My brother's dead, Nathan, so what he does or doesn't want is kind of irrelevant, no?'

'Danny, just wait. Please.'

'Shut up, Nathan.' He smiled. 'I'm not talking to you.' And then he turned to Lucarini and shot him through the chest.

The shot echoed around the crumbling buildings as he dropped to the ground. He moaned, clutching at his chest; but then Danny stood over him, shot him once more, and Lucarini stopped moving.

'Danny. Jesus.'

Vicari raised the gun again and moved it from me, to Federica, and then back again. Then he nodded to himself and put the gun away.

Chapter 55

'If you're wondering why you're still alive, Nathan, it's very easy. You told me when we first met that you were trying to get Dom back home. That buys a lot.'

He looked back towards the lagoon, and to where the boat was moored. 'And now I've got work to do. Things to settle with Meneghini and Zorzi.'

'Bepi – Danny – I know Meneghini. Trust me, he's not going to give in so easily.'

'And in that case, things will get messy.' He held out his hand. 'Phones, please.'

I shrugged, reached into my pocket, and passed it to him. Federica did the same.

'Thanks.' He tossed them into the lagoon.

'What are you going to do?'

'Finish my unfinished business. And you're not part of that.' He turned his back on us and trudged back through the crumbling warehouse to where his boat was moored. Then he pushed it out into the shallow waters and climbed aboard.

'Hey, wait a minute. What the hell are we supposed to do?'

'Mazzorbo's less than a kilometre. And you could probably

wade quite a lot of it. Good luck.' Then he started the engine, and we watched as the boat pulled away.

I turned to Federica. 'So. What now?'

She shrugged. 'As he said. We wade and we swim, or we wait for a boat to come past.'

I shook my head. 'That'll take too long. Way, way too long.'

'Any better ideas?'

'None that I can think of. I don't suppose your phone's waterproof?'

'I don't think so.'

'There must be something round here. Something to signal with.'

'You could try rubbing two sticks together?'

'Tried that in the Scouts. Never got it to work.' I snapped my fingers. 'Hang on a minute. Arturo's boat.'

'You'll need a crane to get that righted.'

'No, that's not what I'm thinking. There might be something on board we can use.'

I ran back through the warehouse and to the shore. Arturo's boat was less than ten metres away. The water couldn't be that deep. If I could just get to the cabin. Or maybe there'd be a locker.

'What are you thinking?'

'I'm thinking you were right, *cara*. It's not jackets weather.' Before she could say anything, I'd removed it and started to wade out towards the boat.

The water came up only to my waist, but the mud and sand beneath me clung to me and sucked at my feet. Wading a kilometre through this was not an option. There'd have to be something useful on board.

I reached the prow of the boat and clung to the side. The cabin was submerged. Not too deep, but deep enough if I got into trouble or found myself trapped. I took a deep breath and plunged my head underwater.

My eyes stung, and I struggled to keep them open. But there was something there, a bright orange bag resting beneath the wheel of the boat. I reached for it but the motion of my hand must have disturbed something as I sensed something behind me.

I turned to see Arturo Franceschini's dead eyes staring back at me from behind his mask. His hand stretched out towards me, his cold fingers brushing mine.

I tried to scream but sucked in the brackish water. I yanked myself upwards and vomited it up as I clung, shaking, to the prow.

'*Caro*, what's the matter? Are you all right?'

'It's Arturo. He's down there.' I vomited again.

'Come back. This is stupid.'

'I know.'

I braced myself and plunged my head back under the surface, trying to focus only on the orange bag. I stretched down for it and felt, yet again, something move across my back. My fingers scrabbled at the bag, and then it was in my grasp. I closed my eyes, tried to ignore the movement around me, and pulled myself back to the surface.

I splashed my way back to the shore, clutching the bag to my chest.

'*Caro*, you look like hell.'

'I feel like hell.'

'You're shaking.'

'It's not the cold. Arturo's down there. He's been down there for days. I saw him.'

'Would a hug be good?'

'I look disgusting.'

'I know.' She hugged me anyway, and I clung to her as I waited for my heartbeat to return to normal.

I opened the bag. A Mars bar, a packet of cigarettes and a lighter. And a bright orange flare pistol with a pack of cartridges.

'Are they wet?'

'Only a little. It must be a hell of a good bag. But as to whether they'll still work—' I fumbled with a cartridge, and slotted it into the gun before turning to Fede. 'You realise I have absolutely no idea what I'm doing here? I don't even know if this is the right way up.'

She smiled. 'Point it upwards. I think that's the main thing.'

'Okay. Cover your ears. Or maybe eyes. Both if you can.' I raised the pistol, turned my head away, and squeezed the trigger.

It was the first time I'd fired a weapon of any kind in my life. I felt the recoil in my hand and the flare streaked into the air before falling back to earth, trailing red smoke behind it.

'Wow,' I said.

Fede squeezed my arm. 'Well done, *caro*. It would have been a bit of a long walk. And now, I guess, we just wait.'

Chapter 56

'Mister, what the hell are you doing out here?' The boatman looked around. 'How did you even get out here?'

'Long story. Long, long story.'

'You've been swimming as well. That's a really stupid thing to do.'

'I know.'

'And now you've got stuck and I've had to waste my time coming to save your arses.' He muttered the words *maledetti turisti* under his breath.

'We're not tourists. We live here.'

'You live here? Even more stupid, then. You should have known better.'

'Sorry.'

'You know what I should do? I should turn this boat around and leave your miserable arses here. Teach you a lesson. Saw the flare and thought somebody was in big trouble. Not some idiot deciding to go for a paddle.'

As far as rescues went, I'd been hoping for something more. A police launch would have been nice. A helicopter even more so. But a rescue was a rescue and if it had to be the angriest fisherman on Burano, well, that would have to do.

'Sorry,' I repeated.

He shook his head. 'Come on then. And hurry up. I've got better things to do.'

We waded out to the boat and clambered in.

'And watch where you sit. You look like shit, you know that?'

Federica squeezed my hand and tried not to laugh.

'And I don't know what's so funny. Your boyfriend's an idiot, you know that?'

'Husband.'

'Husband? Even worse.' He revved the engine. 'Okay, I'll take you back to Mazzorbo. Where you go after that is up to you.'

'How about Marghera?'

'Marghera?' He spat over the side of the boat. 'Boat to Piazzale Roma, then you get a bus. That's how you get there.'

'No, no. That'll take far too long. I want you to take us out there now.'

'You want *me* to take *you* to *Marghera*?'

'Yes. Right now. Please.'

'How shall I put this?' He scratched his chin. 'No.'

'It's important.'

'No.'

I sighed. 'I am prepared to throw large quantities of money at you, if that'll help?'

'Really?' He frowned. 'Let's see it.'

I took out my wallet, and flicked through the handful of notes inside. I looked at Federica. 'Well, you see, I haven't been to the bank for a few days and so I—'

She sighed and reached for her handbag. 'Well, this day

keeps getting better and better doesn't it?' She passed me the contents of her purse.

'Will this do?' I said.

'Nobody ever paid me to take them to Marghera before. Plenty of people paid me *not* to take them to Marghera.' He took the money from me. 'You want the scenic route?'

'There's a scenic route to Marghera? No, we don't. As direct as you can possibly find.'

He shrugged. 'Okay. Let's go. Where exactly?'

'The Venezia Heritage Tower.'

'And where's that?'

'Near the storage warehouse for La Fenice.'

'Mister, I'm a fisherman. Where the hell is that?'

'Never mind. I'll guide you. And can I borrow your phone?'

'What for?'

'Because I need to call the police.'

His eyes narrowed, but he passed me it anyway. I was about to dial, but then stopped and looked at Fede.

'Do you know Vanni's number?'

She shook her head. 'No idea. Don't you?'

'No. I don't need to know it because I just bring up his name or say "Call Vanni". I've no idea what his number is.' I looked over the side of the boat. 'And our phones are at the bottom of the bloody lagoon.'

'Okay. Call 113.'

'I will. Trouble is, it's going to take a lot of explaining.'

I tried not to think about how much of a head start Danny Vicari had on us as I did my best to explain to the operator exactly what sort of crime might be being committed at that moment.

The boatman took us round the top of Murano, under the Ponte della Libertà, and then up the Western Industrial Canal until he pulled up and moored outside the La Fenice warehouse.

'Thank you very much. Thank you for rescuing us. And for the lift.'

He shrugged. 'Pleasure.' He held his hand out. 'The phone?'

I looked at the handset. On the other end of the line, the operator was still trying to understand the nature of my emergency.

'I'm sorry,' I said, 'I'm going to have to pass you over to somebody else.'

I handed it back to the boatman. 'What am I supposed to do?' he said.

'Just tell them that I think somebody is going to be murdered at the Venezia Heritage Tower. Hopefully it won't be either of us.' And with that, I grabbed Federica's hand and we ran.

Chapter 57

The receptionist glared at us as we ran in. 'We normally require our guests to wear smart casual for lunch, I'm afraid.'

'We're not here for the restaurant. We need to see *signor* Meneghini now.'

'Of course, sir.' He picked up the phone. 'Who shall I say is visiting?'

'My name's Nathan Sutherland. I was here the other day.' I ran my hands through my hair. 'You probably don't remember me. I looked a bit smarter then. Anyway, he knows who I am.'

'Nathan—' His hand paused in the act of dialling. 'Mr Sutherland.' He gave me a sickly smile. 'I'm afraid *signor* Meneghini has given strict instructions for you not to be admitted.'

'Christ.'

Federica gently moved me out of the way. 'And how about me?'

'Your name, *signora*?'

'Federica Ravagnan.'

'And your business with him is?'

She looked across at me. 'Stopping him getting murdered, is that right?'

I nodded. 'That's right.'

'I don't understand.'

'Someone called Daniele Vicari is in with him now, yes?'

'*Signor* Vicari,' he tapped at his computer screen, 'is in a meeting with him now, yes.'

'Right. So just about now he should be attempting to either kill or blackmail your boss. Can we go up, please?'

He looked over at the security guard. 'Sergio?'

'Yes, come on Sergio, be a chap, you've got a gun and everything, why don't you come up with us?'

The guard shook his head, with the look of a man who, despite having both a badge and a gun, really didn't get paid enough for this. 'I'll call the police.'

'Brilliant. Thanks, Sergio, you're a star. Come on Fede.' I ran to the lift, my thumb hammering away at the call button as, far above us, we heard the elevator whir into life.

'*Signori*, what are you going to do?'

'Stop any murdering, hopefully.'

'Are you with the police?'

'She's an art historian. I'm a translator. I guess that's the best you've got right now.' I stood there, thumbing away at the button again and again in the hope that it would speed things up.

'Have you really thought this through?' said Fede, as the doors opened.

'Not really.'

'He's got a gun, remember?'

'And he's got no reason to hurt us. And if Meneghini is prepared to be reasonable, then he's got no reason to hurt him either.'

'And if he isn't reasonable?'

There was no time to answer. We heard the screaming begin as soon as the lift doors hissed open.

I had seen Giuseppe Meneghini face down a man with a gun. Whatever else he might have been, he was not someone who would scare easily.

There hadn't been a lot to disturb in his office, but Danny Vicari had done his best with the little he had to work with. The expensive monitor lay smashed on the floor, and the heavy oak desk now lay on its side, with Meneghini's right leg pinned underneath it.

Vicari had Handsome Bastard by the scruff of the neck, and turned to face me as we entered.

'Nathan? Didn't expect to see you here.' He looked me up and down. 'You look like shit, mind.'

'Thanks. So people keep telling me.'

'*Signor* Zorzi here was just about to transfer over a great deal of money to me. Weren't you?' He released his grip and stepped back.

Handsome Bastard patted himself down. He smiled at me and gave Federica a little bow. '*Signor. Signora.*' He turned back to Vicari. 'Daniele, *carissimo*. Let's talk about this as friends should.'

'We're not friends, Zorzi. We never were.'

A groan came from behind me. Meneghini was trying, and failing, to lift the heavy desk off his leg. Vicari walked over and looked down at him, smiling. He raised his leg, ready to stamp down, and Meneghini whimpered, throwing his arm across his face as if that would somehow help to cushion the impact. Then Vicari paused and shook his head. He waved the gun at the two of us. 'You two. Lift the desk off him. And do it slowly.' He smiled. 'Be careful not to drop it. It's going to hurt him an awful lot if you do.'

Meneghini whimpered again.

We bent down, grabbed an edge of the desk each, and, bracing ourselves, managed to haul it up enough for Meneghini to drag himself free.

Vicari kicked him with the toe of his boot. 'Okay. You. On your feet.'

Meneghini dragged himself onto his hands and knees, attempted to raise himself, and then slumped back to the floor. 'Can't,' was all he said, as the tears flowed down his face.

'Yes you can.' Vicari cocked his gun. 'I'll count to three.'

Meneghini grabbed the edge of the desk, and hauled himself upright, grimacing with the pain.

'Good. That's better.'

Federica cast me a glance, and I shook my head. If we tried anything, one of us was going to end up being shot. The police – unless they'd decided to take the stairs – surely couldn't be far away. All we could do was keep Vicari talking.

'Daniele, don't do this. Your brother wouldn't want this.'

'The fuck you know what Dominic would want? He's not here to tell anyone, is he? Since he was pushed out of a bell tower.'

'That wasn't me,' Meneghini sobbed. 'I swear to God that was nothing to do with me. I didn't know about dumping the waste in the lagoon. I swear to you I didn't know about that.'

Vicari nodded. 'I believe you. Zorzi double-crossed you. As he does with everyone. But if your company hadn't hired him, my brother wouldn't have been on that island. And so you're going to pay me every last penny that Rifugio was paid for that contract.'

'Blood money for Dominic?' I said.

'If you like.'

Meneghini nodded. 'You can have it. You can take it all.'

Vicari turned back to Zorzi. 'And, as I was saying, you're going to pay me the money that Zorvic received from Rifugio. Every last cent.'

Zorzi smiled and shook his head. 'And I'm not going to do that, Daniele. It's my money. I negotiated the contract. I earned it.'

'Zorvic is half my company, Zorzi.'

He shook his head. 'Not any more. It's mine now. And it was never really yours in the first place. What did you have to do with it anyway? Just helping out your grandfather and father. Driving trucks full of waste out into the countryside. That's all you ever were. A courier. The idea of you running the company once your father had died,' he shook his head again, and smiled. 'I'm sorry.'

Vicari tapped the dive watch strapped to his wrist. 'Then you know what I'll do. I touch this and everything about you will go round the world in seconds. Everybody will know what you've done in the lagoon.'

Zorzi shrugged. 'But as you keep telling me, Zorvic is your company as well. You'll be in just as much shit as me.'

'I'll take that chance.' He took out his gun and levelled it at Zorzi. 'You're going to give me everything you owe me, Pietro.'

'Danny,' I said, 'just leave him. Everybody is going to find out what he's done. He's going to go to jail for a long time.'

Vicari just laughed. 'Go to jail, you say? How long have you been in Italy, Mr Consul? People like me go to jail. People like him don't.'

Zorzi spread his hands apologetically. 'He's right, Mr Sutherland. Prison isn't for people like me.' He checked his watch. 'All this noise must have been heard. I imagine the police will be here soon. If you're going to press that magic button of yours, then do it now. But do you really want to risk ending up in prison? Italian prisons are dreadful, I understand. And what would your brother have thought of that?'

Vicari closed his eyes and took a deep breath. 'You know, everyone's keen on telling me exactly what my brother would have thought. And I'm tired of having to repeat myself. It doesn't matter what Dominic would have thought because Dominic is dead. Dead because he came looking for me in Venice. And he's fucking dead because of you and that piece of shit over there.'

Meneghini whimpered, as if anticipating another beating.

Vicari's eyes snapped open, and he grabbed Zorzi by the lapels.

'You want to know something about Dominic? He was one of the good guys. He was smarter than me. He was nicer than me. A lot nicer. Because he would never, ever have thought of doing something like this.'

'Jesus, Danny, *no!*'

Vicari shook his head. Then he spun Zorzi round and, with all his strength, pushed him through the angled glass window.

He barely had time to scream.

I dropped to my knees, trying to wipe the image from my

mind, my heart beating painfully within my chest. I looked over at Fede, whose face was white, and then at Meneghini, curled up on the floor and whimpering.

'Oh Jesus, Danny,' I said.

Vicari looked at the two of us, and then down at Meneghini. There was silence for a moment, and then screams came from the piazza below, followed by the sound of footsteps and shouting as two cops burst into the room.

Danny half-raised his gun, but heard the click of weapons from the two, and thought better of it. It seemed, perhaps, as if his heart wasn't really in it. For all that he'd spoken about money, perhaps what he'd really wanted was to see Zorzi falling, as Dominic had fallen.

He dropped his gun to the floor and smiled at the cops.

'Guess we ought to be going then, eh boys?'

Then he tapped the device on his wrist, and the dive watch plinged as everything Dominic Vicari and Arturo Franceschini had found was uploaded to the internet.

Chapter 58

'Vicari. Pagan. Lucarini. Zorzi. Franceschini. Five dead,' said Vanni. 'Five dead and a lagoon full of poison.'

'A lagoon *almost* full of poison, Vanni. We avoided that at least. So, what's going to happen to it all?'

'It'll have to be removed. Public opinion wouldn't stand for just leaving it all there. Imagine the newspaper headlines. Not just here, but around the world. But it's a big job. There's hundreds of barrels down there. It's not just a case of sending down a frogman to haul them to the surface one at a time. It's going to be expensive.'

'Oh, the mayor will just love that.'

'I don't imagine he's very happy about any of this. Fortunately, we have an unexpected benefactor.'

'We do?'

'A certain *signor* Giuseppe Meneghini.'

'You're kidding me.'

'Yes, it seems he's going to have an expensive time of it. That office of his is going to need a lick of paint. And he really should get some proper safety glass put in. But more than that, he wants to make a proper contribution to the city, by paying for the waste to be safely removed. As a gesture of gratitude. *Putting something back*, he says.'

'Putting something back? Not putting it there in the first place would have been better.'

'He says he was genuinely deceived and acted in good faith in trusting Zorvic as a third-party contractor. His lawyers,' Vanni rolled his eyes, 'can show us contracts to the effect that Zorvic had been employed to safely dispose of the waste in an environmentally sound manner.'

'Vanni, these are people with a record of spraying radio-active slurry on farmland.'

He wagged a finger at me. 'I've read those stories as well, Nathan. And there have been investigations, yes, but no prosecutions. Zorvic, technically, is a clean company.' He chuckled. 'Not many of those around.'

'So, he waves money at the problem until it goes away. Is that it?'

'I think that's exactly it.'

'Be honest with me, Vanni. Do you think he knew?'

He sighed. 'Nathan, I have no idea. I think it might just be possible that he didn't. Not because he's a particularly admirable man, but because I think he just didn't care. Have you heard of a guy called Fabio Trincardi?' I shook my head. 'He's director at the National Reseach Council, or something clever like that. I was reading a paper by him this morning. About the state of the lagoon. He described it as the result of "Malice and Unawareness". That's what this is. An unlovely mixture of Malice and Unawareness.'

'So, he's going to get away with it?'

'Oh, I imagine a few fines will be handed out. But I'm afraid I don't see it going beyond that. But it's not a totally lost cause. Vicari has decided he wants to turn *pentito*. Which means we'll find out exactly what Zorvic has been up to over all these years and hopefully get some further inside information on *ecomafia* as well. Dominic Vicari and Arturo Franceschini. They're the heroes in this.'

I nodded. 'It's nice to think that.'

'Thanks, Nathan. It's a messy business but, like the lagoon, we'll clear it up.' He shuffled the papers on his desk together. 'Drink?'

'I think so. And then I'll need to get packing.' I smiled. 'I hear the weather in the mountains is wonderful at this time of year.'

Chapter 59

'So here we are again, Giuseppe.'

Meneghini nodded, smiled, and raised his glass. 'We are indeed. Cheers, Nathan. How long has it been?'

'Barely six months. It seems a lifetime ago now. Different times.'

Harry's Bar in June. In normal times, we would have had to fight our way through the crowds to get to a table. But times were very much not normal, the interior was half-empty and the baristas masked.

'Strange days, Nathan. Strange days.'

'They are.' I sipped at my Martini. 'How's the leg?'

'Hurts like hell. But my doctor says there's no permanent damage.'

'Glad to hear it. So, what do we do now, Giuseppe?'

'We make conversation. We enjoy our drinks. I ask you – politely – to kindly leave me alone in future. And then we'll never have to see each other again.'

'You must realise I can't do that, Giuseppe.'

'No?'

'No. These Martinis are just too damn good.'

'Do you ever think that running your life according to the

qualities of Negronis or Martinis might not be the healthiest way to live?'

I sipped again at my drink, closing my eyes with pleasure at the hit of icy alcohol. 'It's served me well so far. But, seriously, no I can't.'

'Why not?'

I shrugged. 'Dead British citizen, Giuseppe. I can't let that one go.'

'And I'm sorry about that. Really.'

'You are? But you are kind of respo—'

He cut me off with a wave of his finger. 'Now now, Nathan. There are other people here who might be listening. Defamation can carry up to three years in prison, you know?' He grinned. 'Articles 594 and 595, I believe.'

'You seem very well informed.'

'I did a Masters in Jurisprudence. In Padua. It's served me well.'

'I can imagine.'

'As I said, I'm sorry about Dominic Vicari. I'm sorry for the actions of Zorvic. And I admit my mistake was to trust them with far too much responsibility. Perhaps I should have vetted Zorzi more closely.' He shrugged. 'There's nothing to be done now, unfortunately. I'd make some sort of donation but, of course, Mr Vicari has no family.'

'Not quite. There's still Danny.'

'Yes, but I don't imagine he's going to have much use for money where he's going.'

'Don't bet on it, Giuseppe. Especially if Danny really does turn *pentito*.'

Giuseppe nodded. 'He might. These things can take ever

such a long time to reach trial, of course. And anything might happen in the meantime. There are, I imagine, any number of *ecomafia* businesses that might be more than a little nervous at the prospect of what *signor* Vicari might have to say. Let's just hope the authorities take proper care of him.'

'And there's still the little matter of hundreds of barrels of PCBs at the bottom of the lagoon.'

'As I said. I'm sorry for the actions of my employee. I'll be paying for them to be retrieved and safely stored elsewhere of course.'

'Of course.'

'There'll be a fine, I imagine. But again, these things take so much time to get to court. And all documentation clearly shows that Zorzi was acting by himself and under his own responsibility.'

I smiled. 'You know Giuseppe, waste disposal really did turn out to be your sort of game. You're extremely good at cleaning up a mess.'

'I am, Nathan. I am. But can I ask you a question?'

'Fire away.' I smiled. 'Not literally. For the avoidance of doubt.'

'My question is, Nathan, where would you like all this to go?'

'I don't understand.'

'The rubbish. This toxic filth you're so concerned about. You don't want it in the lagoon. So. Where would you like it to actually go?'

'I don't know. Somewhere safe.'

'Well, now. Would the bottom of the Mariana Trench be acceptable? The trouble is I suspect that's going to cost a lot more than most people – even you – are prepared to pay. But that's a possibility. Bit harsh for the primitive lifeforms down there but,' he chuckled, 'the primitive lifeforms up here won't have to worry about it, so that's okay.'

'That's a ridiculous argument, and you know it.'

'Very well, then. Maybe somewhere in the Third World?' He frowned. 'I'm sorry, I know we're not supposed to call it that any more. How about Dandora in Kenya. One of the biggest dumps in the world. Provides employment for local children, I understand, sorting through other people's plastics. There is the unfortunate side effect of cholera, of course but at least,' he jabbed a finger at me, 'we wouldn't have to look at it. Would we?

'Or how about Malagrotta, in Rome. Used to be Europe's largest landfill, I understand. Something for Italy to be proud of. Still used. Air quality's not all that it could be, but – again – it wouldn't be your precious lagoon that's being poisoned, so presumably that would meet with your approval?'

I sipped at my Martini. 'I see the way this is going, Giuseppe. You give me a number of absurd situations as an alternative, and I agree and say, fair point, your solution was no worse.'

'But these situations aren't absurd, Nathan. They're very real.'

'Don't give me this crap, Giuseppe. This entire scheme was set up by you to build up a whole "saviour of the city" narrative. Whereas we all know you went for the cheapest possible solution and turned a blind eye to the possible consequences.'

He shook his head. 'It's not like that at all. Hard as it may be for you to understand, Nathan, I genuinely didn't know what was happening. And if it's any consolation, I imagine it's going to cost me a great deal of money.'

'I didn't think you worried about such things.'

'I always worry about money, especially if it's my own. So, yes, I imagine there'll be a heavy fine. And I'll need to be seen to be making a big gesture. As I said, I'll personally pay for the recovery and safe disposal of the PCBs myself.'

'Safe disposal, where?'

He sipped at his Martini and set the glass down. 'Don't worry, Nathan. I'll make sure it's somewhere where neither you nor anybody else in Venice will have to think about it.

'And I need to thank you. You might just have saved my life. Maybe I'll get to do the same for you one of these days.' He smiled and reached across the table to grasp me by the shoulder. Just a little too hard. He leaned towards me. 'But as much as I enjoy our little meetings, I think this is probably the last Martini we should share together. This is getting expensive.'

'I guess it is. There are cheaper places, though.'

'I'm not talking about the cocktails, Nathan. I don't want to be having one of these conversations again.'

'That suits me fine, Giuseppe. I mean, it shouldn't be difficult. Just try and be a nicer human being and we'll never have to see each other again.'

We clinked glasses and, for some reason I couldn't quite put my finger on, I found myself smiling.

'Cheers, Giuseppe.'

'Cheers, Nathan.'

Chapter 60

'You came to see me?'

Danny Vicari stared back at me through a thick layer of bulletproof glass.

'Least I could do, Danny. For Dominic, you know?'

He nodded at the guards. 'They let you in then?'

'It wasn't easy. Three sets of documentation to compile. Two scanners to walk through, and then one of the guys gives you a final check with a magic wand. Everything that could conceivably be used as a weapon is taken off you.'

Danny tapped the glass, and one of the guards hissed at him. He threw up his hands. 'Sorry.'

The guard shook his head. 'Back from the glass.'

Danny nodded. 'Sure. Sure.' He turned his attention back to me. 'I guess they're thinking two things. Either you've come to kill me and you're going to try and stab me or something. Or you're going to try and slip me a weapon. But either way I think you'd have a hell of a job trying to get through the safety glass.'

'Well, you're a VIP now, Danny, a Very Important Prisoner. They're not going to take any risks.'

'You know what happens next, then?'

I nodded. 'It'll take a while. These things always do. But I think you're going to be kept quite busy. It can't take more than six months, however. Those are the rules for turning *pentito*. And then, at some point, you'll be taken to the *aula bunker* in Mestre, to testify.'

He frowned. 'The *aula bunker*?'

'It's what they call the Court of Appeal. They built it in the late seventies. It's one of the most secure facilities in Italy. For *mafiosi*, Mala del Brenta, Brigate Rosse. Those sorts of people.'

'And people like me?'

'*Ecomafia* is big, big business Danny. As you know better than I do. So, are you sure turning *pentito* is what you want to do?'

'There doesn't seem to be much of an alternative.'

'There are some. Your lawyer explained them all to you, I hope?'

'Oh, she did. Normally, I'd expect twenty-one years. I think I could do that.' He sighed. 'The trouble is, if they decide to be bastards about it, I could face a Mafia-style sentence. No parole. Not going home again, ever. And if they decide to go further, if they decide to be *absolute* bastards, then I might be facing *41 bis*. You know what that means?'

'Solitary confinement?'

'It's *absolute* solitary confinement. It cuts you off completely from the outside world. It seems specifically designed to drive you mad. So, no, I don't fancy that. But if I tell them everything I know about what went on down in Naples, about what went on up here in Venice – there might just be a way out.'

'Danny, you'll be looking over your shoulder for the rest of your life.'

'I know. Still sounds better than staring at the ceiling in a prison cell for the rest of my natural, though. So, I'm decided.'

'Five minutes,' called the guard.

I nodded. 'Okay, Danny. Is there anything I can do?'

He grinned. 'I suppose you could bring me a cake with a file in it?'

'I'd have trouble sliding that under the glass. Anything else? I mean, do you want to see a priest or anything?'

'Bloody hell, Nathan, you make it sound as if I'm going to the chair.' He looked sad for a moment. 'Reminds me of one of those films Dom always used to be watching. *Angels with Dirty Faces*, something like that.' He rubbed his eyes. 'I hadn't written to him in years. Hadn't spoken in years. Mam, neither. I think if they knew what I'd been doing – what Dad had been doing – it would have broken their hearts. But here's the thing. It just started as a job. As a bit of a laugh, almost. Just trucking barrels of stuff around the countryside, getting paid in cash, having more money than I'd ever imagined. And I found I could just kind of tune out the bad stuff, turn a blind eye to it.

'And then Dad passes away, and it's half my business now together with Pietro Zorzi. And it's no longer trucking stuff around Campania. It's meeting with men in expensive suits in expensive offices and I realise that it's not fun any more but there's no getting out now.'

I couldn't think of anything to say, and just nodded.

'Like I said, it would have broken their hearts. But that's not why I never got in touch. It was to try and keep them safe, that's why. To keep them as far away from all this as possible. And I got that wrong.'

I reached, slowly, into my pocket. 'I've brought something for you. I'll have to leave it with the guard, of course. Hopefully he'll be a good guy about it.'

He raised an eyebrow. 'Oh, yes?'

I held the crumpled photograph up to the glass. Humphrey Bogart as Philip Marlowe.

He smiled. 'You know, I found that at the bottom of my rucksack when I arrived in Naples. Dom must have slipped it into my rucksack. Maybe he thought I needed someone to watch over me. A guardian angel, or something. And Dom was such a fan, I thought maybe he should have it back.' He shook his head. 'So, what happens to him now?'

I sighed. 'That's the problem. Your brother had no travel insurance. There are, as far as I know, no living relatives apart from you. And as all your accounts are frozen, there's no way for you to pay for his repatriation.'

'Which means?'

'He'll be cremated here.'

'And that's it?'

'I'm afraid so.'

'And his ashes?'

'They'll be placed in a common grave.'

He shook his head. 'No. Not going to happen. Nathan, I need you to do something for me.'

'There really isn't much I can do, Danny. If you're going to ask me to take him back to Swansea, or something like that, I really can't. I'm sorry.'

'I understand. What about San Francesco, though?'

'Seriously?'

'Absolutely.'

I nodded. 'I don't know. I honestly don't know. But I could talk with Fra Vincenzo. I reckon he'd be okay with it.'

'Okay. Settled then. You'll do that?'

'If it's at all possible.'

'Thanks.' He grinned. 'I'd shake your hand, but that really *isn't* possible. Take him out to San Francesco, Nathan. It was the last place he saw, after all. And he was doing some proper sleuthing. For one time in his life, he got to be Humphrey Bogart.'

Chapter 61

'Erminia will miss you,' said Fra Vincenzo, as we walked through the cypress trees. 'We all will.'

I raised an eyebrow. 'All of you?'

'Well, perhaps not Gregorio. Just between the two of us, I suspect he thinks you've been a disruptive influence.'

'Me? I'm the disruptive influence? Not the people who've been, you know, doing actual murdering and things?' Vincenzo winced. 'Sorry. I know I shouldn't joke about such things with you.'

'Four human souls, Nathan. Four human souls. That's what they were. That's what they are. It's no matter now the sorts of people they might have been in life.'

'And Gregorio,' I said, changing the subject, 'is he pleased to see you back?'

'Oh, I think so. Don't be fooled by that gruff exterior. It hides—'

'A gruff interior?' We both laughed. 'I thought it was him at one point, you know? A beardie man in a tunic and cowl sneaking into Dominic's room.'

'Seriously?'

'I thought he fitted the part.'

'Well, a few years here will help rub the sharp edges off him.'

'Are you sure about that?'

'Of course,' said Vincenzo. Then he shook his head. 'At least, I hope so. Ezekiel and Jeremiah, I suspect, will not be with us for long. Not now that people can travel again.'

'That's a shame,' I said. 'I liked them both. They seem fun.'

'They are. But that's why they'd be happier on the streets of Mestre working with underprivileged kids or the homeless. As our Saviour would have done. They're what we call "social gospel" people.'

'And Gregorio is more anti-social gospel, is that what you mean?'

He began to laugh but turned it into a tut. 'Don't be so cynical, Nathan. God, I think, needs the thinkers as well as the doers. And that's what Gregorio is. He wants to be cloistered away, thinking godly thoughts and writing godly things. We need those people as well.

'And, as I said, a few years here will do him the power of good. Think of Francis, preaching to the birds because there was so much joy in his heart he just had to get it out. That's what we are. We're a joyous order, a joyous people at heart. That'll come to Gregorio one day.' He smiled. 'It's even come to you. I can see that.'

'You can?'

'Of course. Everyone tells me how you've been talking to Erminia.'

'That's not the same!'

'Don't be so certain. Who knows, perhaps in a hundred years, visitors will come here and be told of the strange

Englishman who spoke to the chickens in a language only they could understand.' His expression changed and became serious. 'The altar cloth will be leaving us tomorrow. In a few days it'll be in the Holy Land. Where it should have been for the past three hundred years.'

'I called that one completely wrong at first. I genuinely thought Pagan and Lucarini were here to steal it. But what I thought was a studied, professional detachment was just extreme boredom.'

Vincenzo chuckled. 'I suspect that, even for the aficionado, Fra Raffaele's enthusiasm runs away with him.' He paused for a moment. 'We're having a special service before dinner this evening, Nathan. Just to speed it on its way. Would you like to join us for prayer?'

I looked at my watch. 'I really should be heading back,' I said.

'I understand. But will you, anyway?'

'I don't think I've learned very much about praying,' I said. 'I'm sorry. I'm not sure I've been the best of students.'

'I think you know more than you think. The whole world's been on an extended retreat these past few months, Nathan, with nothing to do except think about what's most important to them.'

'And Netflix,' I said.

'And that. But my point still stands. People have been thinking, really thinking, about what matters in their lives. And they came to the conclusion, almost as one, that what matters, surprisingly, is other people. So, if you don't want to call it "prayer" you can call it anything you want. But I think it would be nice if you joined us.'

I smiled. 'Okay. I can do that.'

'Good man.'

'I just need to say goodbye to Erminia first.'

'Of course.' He patted me on the shoulder. 'Francis would have understood. I'll see you in the chapel.'

I watched him as he walked away, his sandals crunching on the gravel path. Erminia fussed and clucked around my ankles. I picked her up and stroked her feathers.

'Well, Ermy. It's like this. I need to head back to Venice proper now. I imagine my wife's probably had enough of me living on retreat. And my cat will be pleased to see me. Actually, I'm not so sure about that, but that's another story. Anyway, I just want to say – you're a very good chicken.' She cooed, and tried to snuggle into my arms, but I placed her gently down upon the path. 'You're a very good chicken,' I repeated.

There were still hours of daylight left, but it wouldn't be too long until the shadows started to lengthen along the tree-lined paths. Back in Venice proper, people would nervously be taking their seats with friends and family in bars and restaurants, taking a few more baby steps along the road back to normality. But here, the silence was everything, as it had been for centuries and perhaps always would. Nothing but the lapping of waves against the shore, the clucking of chickens and the sounds of a far-off boat.

'Mr Sutherland?'

Maria's voice broke in on my thoughts.

'Mr Sutherland, I think Fra Vincenzo and the others are waiting for you.'

'Of course. Thank you, Maria. I'll be right there.'

'And there's one other thing.'

'Oh yes.'

'I just want to say sorry. About forging your name in the visitor's book. *Signor* Lucarini offered me some money and said it wasn't anything for me to worry about.'

'And I don't think it is. And for my part, I'm sorry too. If I acted like your dad. Or your social worker.'

She smiled at me and then looked down at Erminia as if, perhaps, weighing up the possibility of a dinner that was not completely tomato based.

'Don't even think about it,' I said. Then I looked down at Erminia. 'And you – don't take any nonsense from her, okay?'

Then I smiled at them both and made my way along the path to the chapel, where evening prayer was about to begin.

Chapter 62

'So, it's safe for you to hang out with us now, Brother Nathan. Is that what you're saying?'

'Can we stop with the Brother Nathan thing, finally? I'm officially retired now.'

'You mean excommunicated or something?' said Dario.

'I don't even know if there's a word for it. But I'm not a monk any more. Or a friar. Or even a humble pilgrim.'

'And cheers to that,' said Fede, and the four of us clinked glasses.

'I'll be paying for these, by the way. I think it's the least I can do in exchange for everyone's help.'

'That's okay, Mr Consul. I got to pretend to be a cook. And break into a house. It was all kind of cool.'

'And I got to drive you to Marghera,' said Dario. 'I get all the glamorous jobs.' He punched my arm, drawing an *ow* from me. 'Just don't do anything like this again, ever, all right? No cutting me out next time. Handsome Bastards or no Handsome Bastards.'

'I promise, okay, I promise.'

'What do you think he was like?' said Fede. 'Dominic Vicari, I mean.'

I shook my head. 'Face it, we know next to nothing about him. And now we never will. But he loved his brother so much that he travelled halfway around Europe in the middle of a pandemic to try and find him. That must mean something.'

'Maybe it's as well he never found him.'

I nodded. 'Danny said it would have broken his heart.'

'I have to say, I'm not sure I'd have travelled halfway around Europe in order to find someone like Daniele Vicari.'

'I don't think he was always like this. I think the job – if you can call it a job – turned him into someone else. Into *something* else. It was toxic in itself and it corrupted him. *If you gaze into the abyss, the abyss gazes also into you.*'

'Blimey, it's a right old laugh hanging around with you,' said Lucia. She turned to Fede. 'Is he like this at home?'

'No. Sometimes he can be quite serious.'

Dario smiled. 'Well, it's time I was heading back. I'm cooking tonight. Emily's decided she prefers my pizza to restaurant ones.'

'Wow. This could be the start of a whole new career.'

'It might just be, *vecio*.' He patted my shoulder. 'We'll see each other around, eh?'

'And I'll be off as well,' said Lucia. 'Cooking for my dad. As usual.'

'Tomatoes?'

'Maybe not tonight. Or ever again. Bye-bye Fede. See you around, Brother Nathan.'

Fede linked her arm in mine, as we walked through the streets.

'Where are we heading?'

'Nowhere, really. It's just nice to walk. Nice to see somewhere other than the inside of the apartment or the interior of a monastery.'

'And what about tomorrow? What shall we do then?'

'Anything normal sounds good to me.'

'We could go to the beach?'

'Seriously?'

'We probably won't. But we could if we wanted to. And that's a nice thing.' She paused. 'We could even go and visit *mamma*.'

'We could.'

'We could even stop off for lunch on the way, at Pellestrina.'

'We could do that, as well.'

'So yes,' she paused for a moment, 'we *could* do all those things tomorrow. Or the day after. But for now, it's just nice to walk.'

'I think so, too.' I looked around. 'Do you know, I've got no idea where the hell we are?'

'Santa Croce, somewhere.'

'Santa Croce Somewhere? Are you sure?'

'As sure as I can be bothered.' She unlinked her arm, and yawned and stretched. 'Oh, this is nice. Just walking without thinking. Without having to worry if we've broken any rules.'

'Santa Croce Somewhere,' I repeated. 'You know, I'm sure there's a decent bar around here.' I clicked my fingers. 'Or, you know what? We could go for an ice cream. I think I could find my way to the Gelateria Alaska from here. Or maybe we could find a *bacaro* for snacks. Or—'

Fede linked her arm in mine, again. 'Or maybe we could just keep walking. And eventually, I suppose, we'll end up back at the Brazilians. Spritz before dinner. Negroni if we're feeling brave. And then, if you can be bothered, you can cook us something fabulous. And if you can't, there's always pizza.' She smiled "'Always pizza." That's funny. Because for three months, there was no pizza.'

'I did have a go. It's just—'

'Yes, I know. *How can I be expected to work without a proper pizza oven?* We've had this conversation. And the answer is still no.'

'So just drinks and dinner at home then?'

'I think so. Whenever we get there.'

'And tomorrow?'

'Who knows? But just normal stuff. That'd be nice.'

'I know,' I sighed.

'What's wrong.'

'The "N" word. Normal. That's what we've got at the moment, I suppose. Everything just normal enough. But for how long?'

Fede shrugged. 'Who knows? That's tomorrow's problem. And so—'

'And so?'

'And so we just keep walking. That's enough, I think?'

I smiled at her, and then kissed her. 'It certainly is.'

And then, linking arms again, we walked off through the streets of Santa Croce in search of a path that, at some point, would lead us back to the Magical Brazilians and the Street of the Assassins.

I looked up at the sky. And it was so blue.

Epilogue

There was no infinity pool.

Glossary

41 *bis*	Article 41 *bis* (41 plus), also known as *carcere duro*, is a punitive form of incarceration in which almost total isolation is imposed upon a prisoner.
ACTV	The company responsible for public transport in Venice.
acqua bassa	The opposite of *acqua alta*, the phenomenon of low water in the lagoon
Bacaro	A bar, typically one serving *cicchetti*
Baccalà mantecato	Traditional Venetian appetiser made by whipping together stockfish and olive oil.
Campanile	Bell tower
Carrello	A shopping trolley
Centro storico	The 'historic centre' of Venice
Che cazzo	Expletive, along the lines of "what the fuck?"
Cicchetti	Traditional Venetian snacks
Chioscho/Chioschetto	Kiosk – in Venice this might been a stand selling snacks or drinks
Convento	Convent or Monastery

L'Espresso	Centre-left weekly news magazine
Famiglia Cristiana	Weekly Catholic news magazine
Fondamenta	Typically the street alongside a canal
Fritto misto	Small fish, shrimps, prawns and calamari; all battered and fried.
Gesù	Jesus
Insalata Caprese	A salad of fresh tomatoes, mozzarella and basil, dressed with olive oil
Lovecraft, Howard Phillips	American author of horror, science fiction and fantasy stories, perhaps most famous for his creation of the so-called Cthulhu Mythos
Marinaio	Sailor – here, the 'conductor' of a *vaporetto* or water bus
Maledetti turisti	Damn tourists!
Panzanella	Salad of stale bread, tomatoes and onions, dressed with olive oil and vinegar and much more exciting than it sounds!
Pappa al pomodoro	A thick Tuscan soup of bread and tomatoes. Also much more exciting than it sounds.
Pasta alla genovese	Pasta with an onion and meat sauce, typically associated with the Campania region
Pentito	Literally 'repentant', but in this context it means something more akin to 'supergrass'
Piacere	A pleasure, pleased to meet you
Plateatico	That area reserved for chairs and tables

	outside a bar or restaurant (which were allowed to expand to allow better social distancing as an emergency COVID measure)
Questura	Police station
Ragazzi	Lads, boys
Sarde fritte	Fried sardines
scuola elementare	Elementary school (the equivalent in English would be Infant school)
sfogliatella	A sweet flaky pastry in the shape of a shell, typical of the Campania region
sfogliatella frolla	Similar to the above, except the pastry is more akin to a sweet piecrust instead of the thin, flaky layers of a regular *sfogliatella*
SMB	Submersible Marker Buoy
Un soldino per i tuoi pensieri	a penny for your thoughts
Straniero	Foreigner, stranger
sugo di pomodoro crudo	A simple cold pasta sauce made from fresh tomatoes
Toast	A toasted cheese and ham sandwich, a welcome snack that can be found in almost every bar
Vafancul	Fuck off (variation of *vaffanculo*)
Vaporetto	The style of boat used in the public transport system in Venice
Vecio	Mate, pal, buddy
Vera da pozzo	a well

Notes and Acknowledgements

Don't write a COVID novel. That's what everyone told me. And, at first, I thought that was good advice. Who would possibly want to read a novel that might bring back memories of those terrible months and years? And yet the experience of living in Venice during that extraordinary period when the city was briefly returned to the Venetians was, I thought, worth sharing. Quite simply, I thought this was a book that needed to be written.

The locations in this book exist and are as described, with the exception of the deep trench in the canal that links Madonna del Monte with the Treporti Channel. The issues of pollution in the lagoon, sadly, are still current and very real. For a more detailed examination of this and of the history of Marghera, I can recommend Gianfranco Bettin's wonderful novel *Cracking*.

My thanks to all of you who take time to write, and to those of you who've taken time out whilst on holiday to visit some of the locations in the books. I know the owners of the Magical Brazilians are very grateful.

I finish, as ever, with my thanks to my agent John Beaton; to Colin Murray; to Krystyna, Peter, Lucy and everyone at

Constable; and, of course, to Caroline, without whom I really would be lost!

Philip Gwynne Jones, Venezia 2023
www.philipgwynnejones.com